'I was hooked from the first page by this deftly written, emotionally charged domestic drama. Captivating and at times crushing, this story will stay with you.'
Alice Hunter, *The Serial Killer's Wife*

'Unsettling, intriguing and with beautifully written characters that are by turns sinister and tender, this is a psychological thriller of the first rank.'
Alex Lake, *Seven Days*

'You will not see the twist(s)
I didn't see the twist(s)
Twistier than a twisty thing doing the twist.'
Tina Baker, *Call Me Mummy*

'A compelling and intriguing tale with a twist that will take your breath away.'
Sarah Linley, *The Wedding Murders*

'Uniquely illustrated with a compelling, domestic cat and mouse vibe, Arrietty is bursting at the seams with suspense!'
Paula Johnston, *The Lies She Told*

'*Arrietty* is a compulsive psychological thriller with a jaw-dropping, heart-breaking twist which is sure to satisfy Abby Davies's many fans.'
Carolyn Kirby, *The Conviction of Cora Burns*

By Abby Davies

Mother Loves Me

The Cult

Arrietty

ARRIETTY

Abby Davies

Apple Loft Press

ARRIETTY

For my little piece of magic, Heidi

Part 1

Chapter 1

Sunlight blasted through the glass panels, stinging my eyes. I wiped the worktop, checked the copper clock. Looked away. Checked again. Fought the urge to re-check. The hairs on my neck prickled. A shift: from tickling panic to the scraping, scratching kind. I glanced at Eddie. My little brother and I were alone in the glass-walled kitchen. Alone and worried. Putting on our brave faces.

Not scared, not quite.

Not yet.

I scanned the flowerless garden, trailed my gaze up to the cliff edge, out to the panoramic view of the Mendip Hills that lay in the distance. Paradise, Dad called it.

In the middle of bloody nowhere, I called it. Under my breath, of course.

Legend told that those hills had been carved by the devil.

Eddie wiggled on his knees, desperate for me to get out what he called – because it made me laugh – his play poo. I massaged the homemade dough to warm it up and tore it into four lumps. Concerns rocked my gut like choppy waves as I helped my brother roll out the first piece. I contained a sigh, the help of eager four-year-old fingers making hard work of a simple task. While we worked, clouds gobbled the sun and the sky turned grey, the hills two shades darker.

'What do you want to be when you grow up?' Eddie said, peering up at me through his floppy fringe, button nose wrinkled.

1

I watched as he pushed his tawny hair out of his eyes with a careless swipe, grabbed his Paw Patrol beaker and slurped warm milk.

My heart twinged. *God, could he be any cuter?*

'I *used* to want to be an artist,' I said quietly.

'Like Mummy?'

I nodded.

'I want you to be an artist. You can be,' he said, stabbing the dough with a plastic knife.

'Maybe. It's just...I'm not well at the moment, remember?'

'Chron-ic fat-igue,' he said, grinning, proud of himself.

'Yes.'

'Is Mummy poorly too?'

I hesitated. 'No. I don't think so.'

Eddie threw his arms around my waist. 'I love you.'

I stroked the baby-soft hairs on the back of his neck and kissed his head. 'Love you too, little man.'

He pulled away and puppy-eyed me, grabbed the lump he'd stabbed and said, 'Can we make a dinosaur now? Pleeeeease.'

'Of course.'

I rolled out another piece of dough, grabbed the T-rex cutter and pressed the red plastic into the doughy slab. Eddie peeled the edges away and held it up triumphantly.

'Eyes next,' he said, rolling two large balls and squashing them onto the dinosaur's face.

'Teeth?' I said, beginning to cut two long triangles.

'No – I want to do it,' he said, snatching the knife.

'Hey. Don't snatch.'

He stared at me, little forehead pinched. To my surprise, his chin wobbled. 'I'm sorry.'

'It's all right. It's not nice to snatch, that's all. You know that.'

His shoulders slumped. Two fat tears rolled down his cheeks.

'Eddie? What's wrong?'

'I want Mummy,' he said, lower lip quivering.

My tummy churned a little faster. I pulled him onto my lap and held him until he stopped crying. He smelt so good, like Johnson's baby shampoo. There was also a faint scent of the chocolate cereal he'd eaten for breakfast, the remnants of which circled his mouth in an adorable, milky ring.

Settling him back on his stool, I said, 'Hey, I know, why don't we make fairy cakes!'

It was one of his favourite things to do. Though his eyes still watered, a smile brought out his one dimple. I tried to smile as he lowered himself clumsily off the stool favouring his good leg.

'Arrietty,' he said, 'you're so cool.'

'Oh, I know.'

I pulled his step over to the counter and grabbed our aprons. Mine was pink with white hearts, his green and covered in cartoon dinosaurs.

Eddie wiggled like a puppy, clapped his hands and limped the short distance to the ivory cabinets. 'Can we make green icing?'

'Let me see if we've got food colouring.'

I crouched down and opened the baking cupboard. The back door slammed, and I looked up. Dad trudged into the kitchen with weighty steps, one hand rubbing the back of his neck. Two deep grooves scored the space between his dark eyebrows and his skin was waxy. He smelled like he hadn't showered, and he hadn't shaved. He was usually clean-cut, well-kempt. This scruffy look jarred with the Dad I knew. Seeing him like this made me queasy.

Without speaking, he flicked on the kettle and leaned his broad back against the counter. Popped his knuckles one by one. I watched his calloused thumb press each joint and tried not to cringe. Mum hated it when he did that.

Eddie grabbed my arm for balance, got off his step and

squealed, 'I need a wee!'

He limped out of the room as quickly as possible. We watched him go.

I glanced at Dad. 'Anything?'

Dad shook his head and massaged his neck. I tried to catch his eye, but he wouldn't look at me. A long red scratch ran down his forearm. I stared, wondering how he got it. He caught me looking and lowered his arm.

'You've tried calling again?'

He sighed, turned away and poured water into his mug. 'Want one?'

'No thanks.'

He puffed out a heavy sigh, sipped his coffee and winced. He always drank it black, no sugar. The mug said, 'No. 1 Dad.' A Father's Day present from me five years ago. His thumb smoothed the white porcelain over and over again.

'Why is there Play Doh out?' he said sharply.

'I haven't put it away yet. Sorry.'

I hurried over to the island and tidied away the cutters, dough and mat. All the while, I felt him watching me, his pupils boring into my back. A prickle of unease caught at my neck. I turned around and faked a smile. 'I'm sure she'll come back soon. She's probably on her period. Just needs a break from everything.'

One day when she was in her early twenties and I was little, Mum had lost the plot and stormed out of the house then driven around not caring or knowing where she was for a few hours before finally calming down and heading home. A mixture of terrible twos, hormones, Dad having a near-miss on his motorbike and him tactlessly commenting on the state of the house had driven her to the brink. Thankfully, she'd come to her senses and gone back to Dad and me, apologising for running off. As far as I knew, she'd never done it again.

Until, perhaps, now.

I glanced at the clock. It was four in the afternoon. I'd been woken by the door slamming at midnight, but I hadn't gone to investigate. If only I could rewind time, things might be different.

There was no note. No message. No explanation. No upturned furniture or smashed glass. Nothing.

Mum had been gone for sixteen hours and she'd not even bothered to text or say goodbye.

Chapter 2

TWO YEARS AGO

ARRIETTY

The new art teacher was tall and muscular, hot for an old guy. Like most of the girls in the class, I gawped shamelessly at his butt when he turned to point at the whiteboard. As a rule, I didn't have time for boys, but this...this was a *man*.

Beside me, Isla sighed and cupped her chin, a lazy smile on her face. Her ice-blonde fringe skimmed her eyelashes, and I wondered for the millionth time how it didn't annoy her. I mimicked her pose and let my eyes trail up to Mr Broughton's broad shoulders. In a slim-fit navy shirt and grey suit trousers, he looked young and trendy, and I liked his Clark Kent-style glasses. He turned and his eyes met mine. Behind the glass, his irises were the colour of granny apples. They popped against his tanned skin, looking almost edible. I wanted to draw them.

He was still looking at me. Blood rushed to my cheeks. I glanced down quickly and picked at my nails.

'You can begin your portrait now, ladies,' Mr Broughton said.

Chairs scraped against sticky laminate as the class rose and everyone moved to stand at their easel.

Sunlight screamed into the room prompting Rosie to tweak the blinds. I tilted my head and contemplated my drawing. Someone sneezed. The muffled chorus of laughter sounded from next door. Perfume and the waxy scent of oil pastels clung to the muggy air. Mr Broughton scratched his neck, clasped his hands behind his back and began to roam the room inspecting other students' work. I bit my lip and tried to focus but butterflies erupted in my belly. Isla nudged me and nodded in his direction, mouthed the words 'Hot or what?' and mimed smooching the space between her hands.

Giggles burst out of my mouth. Heads swivelled and Mr Broughton strode across the art studio, a slight smile tugging at his mouth, one dark eyebrow raised. 'Is everything all right, Arrietty?'

'You know my name,' I said stupidly, earning a snort from Isla.

'I know everyone's names,' he said, smiling.

I swallowed and hoped my cheeks weren't as red as they felt. I tightened my ponytail, glad I'd washed my hair this morning.

He moved to stand – or rather, to tower – next to me, close enough that I could smell his aftershave, which was nice but a bit too strong.

I looked at my portrait, tried to see it through an art teacher's critical eyes. It wasn't my best work, but it was pretty good. I'd drawn a pencil sketch of my little brother Eddie. He was only two years old with adorable chubby cheeks and tons of floppy hair that constantly fell into his eyes.

'I see you share your mother's talent,' he whispered, patting my shoulder. 'Good work. Keep it up, Miss Black-Hawkins.'

He drifted away, taking my butterflies with him.

Isla murmured, 'He knows your mum?'

I frowned. The fact that he knew Mum made him less exciting. 'It's news to me.'

Chapter 3

NOW

That night the rain surged down battering the hell out of the glass walls. Eddie clambered out of the bath, and I wrapped him in his towel. Save for the rain, the house was quiet. Dad was shut away in his office. I hoped he was emailing or ringing people about Mum. I was sure he would be. He wouldn't just do nothing. Sitting it out and waiting for her to come back wasn't his style. At least, I didn't think it was. It was hard to know, because this was the first time something like this had happened since I was a toddler, and I didn't know how he'd reacted then.

I chewed my lip, watched Eddie bend over the side of the bath to play with leftover bubbles. Earlier, stress had flowed out of Dad like invisible magma. Beneath the worry I'd sensed anger. Was he angry at Mum? I hoped not. I needed to trust that he was doing all he could to contact her and find out where she'd gone, and why.

I squeezed toothpaste onto Eddie's brush and handed it to him then gazed blindly at the shower curtain, seeing through its geometric pattern to my frenzied thoughts. Rain slashed the house, drilling into my brain like gunfire. What would I do if I was him? Was it too soon to call the police? I tried to think about all the missing people programmes I'd watched. I knew they investigated quickly if a child went missing, but feared they waited longer when it was an adult. Maybe Dad knew that and thought there was no point in phoning the police. Maybe he'd already called them. Maybe he thought Mum would come home soon with her tail between her legs like the first time. If she did that, I didn't know how I'd react. Part of me would be mad at her for worrying us so much. The rest of me would be weak with relief.

As I towelled Eddie – whose fidgeting was driving me crazy – I tried to think back to yesterday and how Mum had seemed, but tiredness fuzzed my mind. Try as I might, only a general sensation that she'd seemed OK pierced the fug in my brain. My condition was clearly playing up. I'd had a tiring day looking after my little brother. I probably needed to go to bed and stop worrying. Worrying achieved nothing. Mum loved us. Things would be OK soon. They had to be.

With a squeal, Eddie twisted away and sprinted out of the bathroom. I watched his tiny bottom and smiled at how small and cute he was. He seemed happier now. Baking cakes had worked wonders. We'd heaped tons of green butter cream on top of the sponge. I'd eaten three and made myself feel sick. Comfort eating no doubt. When I'd offered one to Dad, he'd said no, and he hadn't eaten any dinner. I'd got two microwave meals out, but his had gone untouched. We'd barely spoken. His expression had been so bleak that I'd not known what to say.

Dragging my hands down my face, I left the bathroom and entered Eddie's bedroom. He was bouncing on his bed howling like a wolf. A wicked grin brightened his face, and he grabbed his pillow and threw it at me. I ducked and it sailed over my head and hit the dinosaur print wallpaper.

'Hey!' I lunged forward and tickled his sides.

He shrieked with laughter, and I let him go.

'Look at me, look at me,' he cried, jumping as high as he could.

Worried he was going to break the bed, I told him to stop, but he ignored me.

Outside, as if compelled by an irate Greek God, the downpour escalated. A chill crawled under my skin. I wished it would stop but the torrent grew in strength, pounding mercilessly at the glass like vengeful hornets. Feeling jittery, I lunged across the room and yanked the curtains across the windows to try and keep the weather at bay.

'Eddie. I mean it. Stop that now.'

He jumped again, intending to fall on his back, and his head whacked the shelf. He went still. Terrifyingly limp.

I dashed forward and pulled him onto my lap. 'Eddie? Are you OK? Is it your head?'

He wasn't crying or moving.

'Eddie! Speak to me.'

I felt the back of his head and my fingertips came away wet with blood.

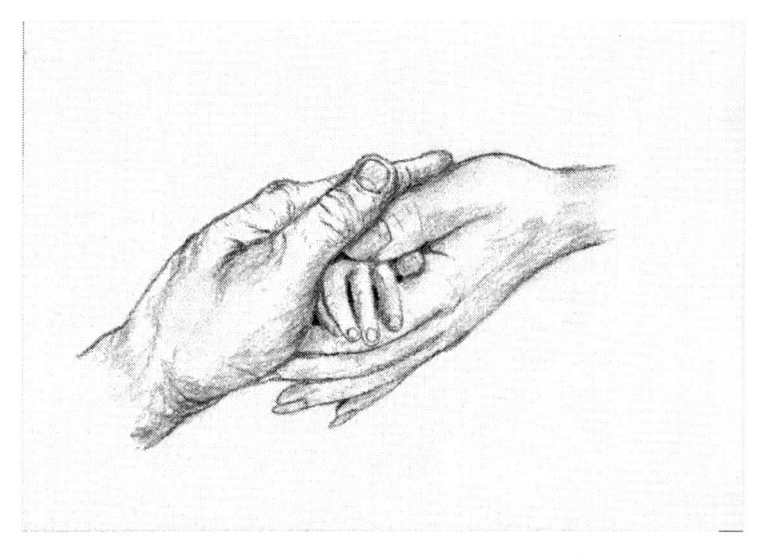

Chapter 4

TWO YEARS AGO

SOFIA

I arrived at the gallery an hour before the event. Arrietty was at Isla's house revising so Alec had stayed at home to look after Eddie. I'd wanted Alec to come but he'd emphasised how important it was that our daughter prioritise her revision. End of year exams were on the horizon. She was predicted As and Bs but wasn't one of those genius types (like my husband) who could ace exams with little prep and a hangover in tow; Arrietty was more like me – bright but cursed with a shoddy memory and an unhealthy dose of self-doubt.

Nerves fizzed in my stomach. My first solo exhibition. This was a big deal. I exhaled, told myself what would be would be, and headed for Patricia's office. As I walked the sharp click of my stilettos bounced off the floorboards into the vaulted space between the high white walls, making me wish I'd worn lower heels that didn't draw so much attention. At present, the gallery contained ten pieces of my work and three viewing benches, but soon – fingers crossed – it would be buzzing with potential customers with fat wallets.

My favourite piece caught my eye and I moved to stand in front of it.

'Extraordinary.'

I jumped at the voice in my ear and turned to Patricia's smiling face. 'It's not too…dramatic?'

Her soft, wrinkled cheeks shook as she laughed. 'It's

brilliant. My favourite yet. I love the way you've interwoven Arrietty's, Alec's and Eddie's fingers. So casual yet poignant. The interplay of negative space and shadow makes it feel intimate and somehow relatable. It's special. It'll get snapped up tonight within the first half hour, mark my words.'

'I hope so.' I smiled, remembering how I'd needed to draw extra fast due to Eddie's inability to stay still and Arrietty's unconcealed longing to check her phone.

I eyed the price tag. 'Hands' was priced at £2500. My most expensive piece ever. We didn't need the money, but I wanted to contribute towards our finances. Alec was a successful architect and earned a lot, so we could have survived on his salary alone, but I'd always wanted to earn my own keep. I also wanted Arrietty to know that if you worked hard enough at something you could reap the rewards financially as well as emotionally. Art had been a lifejacket for me when I was growing up and it still was in many ways now. With an emotionally distant mother, an absent father and no siblings for company, I'd often felt lonely as a child, but painting and drawing had given me a life beyond the confines of my home, an escape of sorts.

Patricia hurried away to put out the nibbly bits. I called after her offering to help, but she waved me off, saying I ought to relax. I cleared my throat and straightened my too-tight red dress. Was it that obvious I was nervous?

I felt a presence behind me and turned. A man in a cream leather jacket with striking white hair stood in the doorway. He strode over and shot out a hand. 'Such a talent and beautiful to boot! Hugo Grimes. Huge fan of your work.'

'Oh, thank you.' I shook his hand, shocked at the tightness of his grip – some people didn't seem to be able to get the right pressure; floppy and limp as a dead fish or vice-hard. Alec's handshake was always too firm. I often joked that he was doing it to be macho. This man however, had a wonderful smile and bright, shiny eyes which made me think he had no idea that he'd almost crushed my hand to death.

I smiled back, and watched as he gazed around the room appreciatively.

His gaze landed on 'Hands' and his eyes darted to the price tag on the wall beside the canvas. He gave a sharp intake of breath. I blushed and began to splutter that it was probably overpriced, but he laughed and beamed at me, 'I'll take it.'

I glanced at my watch – it was 7.30 – the event started at 8pm and I'd already sold a piece!

'Really?'

He nodded and rubbed his hands together. 'It'll go in pride of place above the mantlepiece in the great hall.'

'The great hall?'

He winked and linked arms with me. 'Let's go get this deal done, shall we Sofia?'

I felt uncomfortable at his familiarity but his exuberance and my excitement at the sale pushed any awkwardness beneath my sharp heels and I walked with him towards Patricia's office. She emerged carrying two plates of nibbles, eyes brightening at the two of us.

'You look happy,' she said, placing the plates on the long table at the side of the room.

'Mr Grimes wants to have 'Hands',' I said.

He unlinked his arm from mine, turned and said, 'Please, call me Hugo.'

Swivelling to Patricia, he said, 'I do indeed. But I'm not done yet. I want to take my time, see if anything else catches my eye.'

'Of course. Take all the time you need. I'll mark that it's already sold. Back in a jiffy.' She winked at me then speed-walked to her office.

Hugo thanked me for creating such wonderful work – his words, not mine – then excused himself to peruse the rest of my pieces.

I rushed after Patricia and squealed.

She hugged me and whispered in my ear, 'Told you so.'

After she let go, I grabbed my phone out of my handbag. I wanted to ring Alec and tell him straight away. He'd be so pleased for me, and so so proud.

Chapter 5

NOW

'Oh God.'

White-hot panic reared as I carried Eddie to the bathroom. In the brightly lit room, I laid him on the bathmat on his side and fumbled in the medicine cabinet for cotton pads. I wet the pads and cleaned his head. He groaned but didn't struggle away. I looked up sharply as the rain stopped with uncanny suddenness. The house was once again silent. Beads of water speckled the glass behind Eddie. They looked like droplets of wet tar. *Or ink. Or blood spatter.*

'Good boy. That's it. I'm just cleaning the cut so I can see how bad it is,' I said, aware there was a tremor in my voice.

I dabbed and dabbed, and the cut stopped bleeding. Parting his hair, I leaned in for a closer look. It wasn't too bad. I didn't think it would need stitches. Relieved beyond measure, I found a bandage and wrapped it around his head. Eddie vivified, sat up and darted to the sink.

'I want to see,' he said, standing on tiptoe.

'OK.' I lifted him up, marvelling at his ability to bounce back so quickly.

He stared in wonder and delight at the bandage.

'I look like a mummy!' he said with a giggle.

'Does it still hurt?'

He shook his head then looked at me excitedly, 'Can you wrap me all up so I look like a proper mummy? Pleeease.'

'No, buddy. Not now. It's time for your story then

bed.'

He frowned and pouted. A split second later, a smile broke out. 'Can we have *The Smeds and The Smoos?*'

'Definitely.'

A wave of exhaustion attacked as I followed him back into the room.

I read him the story as quickly as I could then tucked him into his dinosaur-shaped bed and switched off his light, making sure to leave his door ajar and the landing light on the way he liked. He was much later to bed than normal, so I hoped he'd wake up late in the morning so I could have a lie in. Dad seemed content to leave me to look after Eddie now that Mum wasn't around, but I was happy to do it because it kept me busy.

As I headed for the stairs, I heard a little voice call, 'Arri.'

I hesitated.

'I want Mummy,' he said.

I went back inside and perched on his bed. Stroking his hair, I whispered, 'I've got an idea. Why don't we make a wish?'

'A wish about Mummy?'

'Yes. Come on.' I picked him up and carried him to the window. 'Can you see that big star?'

'That one?'

'Yeah. It's called Venus. It's actually a planet. Shall we make a wish on it?'

He nodded eagerly. 'Yes, please.'

'Okay. When I say, shout your wish as loud as you can. Ready?'

'Yep!'

'One, two, three – go.'

He squeezed his eyes shut and shouted, 'I wish Mummy to come home right now!'

He looked at me, breathless with excitement. 'Is she here yet?'

I bit my lip, wishing I'd explained a bit better. 'Not yet, but your wish will travel to her. She'll hear your voice and try to come back as soon as she can.'

Disappointment rounded his shoulders. I held him tight and carried him back to bed. Smoothing back his fringe, I murmured, 'Don't worry. She'll be back soon.'

I tucked him in with Eric and stroked his soft cheek until he fell asleep, hoping I was right. Mum loved us. There was no way she'd abandon her family. When she was ready, she'd come back and explain everything. She had to. And besides, Dad was on the case.

Bed was calling me, so I went downstairs to say goodnight to Dad.

*

Opposite the foot of the staircase the night was completely black. Anyone could be out there looking in. Unless they held a light, I wouldn't see them. The automatic lights were sensor-driven and only came on when triggered by a presence, which offered some comfort. Unless, of course, the sensor wasn't working. Why I was thinking about this I didn't know.

The rain was back, angrier than ever. I hoped wherever Mum was she was somewhere dry and comfortable. Somewhere safe.

Shivers plucked my spine and trailed along my vertebrae with the lightest touch. *Cervical, thoracic, lumbar, sacral and caudal.* How I knew them I didn't know. Couldn't remember. The answer dangled on the edge of my mind, hanging by frayed rope. I felt rattled. Unsure. I wanted Mum back where she belonged. With us. Safe and sound. This topsy-turvy reality was wrong. Alice in Wonderland wrong. Any moment the white rabbit would jump out and say he was late, or the Queen of Hearts would threaten to chop off my head.

Frowning, I turned left and followed the long white walkway that divided the front of the house from the back. Open plan so that every space branched off from this central path.

I reached the end of the house and knocked on the office door, trying not to hope too hard that Dad had good news about Mum.

He didn't answer but I heard the low grumble of his voice. Crossing my fingers behind my back, I inched open the door, wrinkled my nose. The room smelt off. Like stale coffee and sweat. Only the desk lamp was on.

Feeling nervous, I poked my head inside - saw his wide back pressed against the wood of his chair. He held his phone to his ear, speaking softly, tone hushed to little more than a whisper.

The door creaked and he frowned around at me and hung up without saying anything to the person on the other end of the line.

'Who was that?' I said, keeping my tone light.

'Oh, no one.'

'Have you found out anything about -'

'No.'

'Sorry, I just -'

'No need to apologise. You off to bed? You look exhausted.'

'Uh, yeah. You?'

He nodded. Raked a hand through his hair. Grey streaked the black. He seemed to have aged years since yesterday. I wanted to ask him for a hug, but he moved away and sat down at his desk. Without looking up, he said, 'Night.'

I opened my mouth. Closed it. The desire to ask for my mobile hovered on the tip of my tongue. I didn't want to cause him any more stress, but I needed it now more than ever. I hadn't had it for ages, and it was unbearable, especially now Mum had gone. But he peered up and gave me a strange look. In the half-light he was a sepia version of himself, older and more unreachable than ever. 'What?'

'Are you going to kiss Eddie goodnight?'

His eyes narrowed as if he was annoyed at me for telling him what to do, but after a few seconds he stood and trudged out of the room.

I sighed. Dad was struggling. I couldn't make things worse for him. I would wait to ask for my phone when Mum came home, and things were back to normal.

Chapter 6

TWO YEARS AGO

SOFIA

Three missed calls. I frowned and left a voicemail telling Alec I had some exciting news and would he call me back ASAP. But half an hour later he still hadn't called, and a steady stream of people were trickling into the gallery. I sipped at my glass of Cava and watched from beside the nibbles table, delighted to catch snippets of conversation praising my work. Everything seemed to be flowing smoothly. Patricia was doing the rounds telling people about me and my background, nodding in my direction every now and then. I smiled back but kept my distance; talking up my own work wasn't my cup of tea.

Every now and then I felt like I was being watched. Once I glanced across the gallery to see Hugo Grimes looking at me. He raised his glass, and I raised mine back with a smile. He'd been here for ages now. I doubted he'd buy anything else. He'd already spent a lot. He was probably hanging around to make the most of the free nibbles and Cava.

A strong wave of aftershave hit me, and I looked to my left to see a vaguely familiar face smiling at mine. For a second I couldn't place him and then...bingo!

'James? James Broughton?'

'Hello Sofia,' he said, clinking his glass against mine. 'Long time no see, hey?'

'Gosh. What is it...eighteen years since we last saw each other?'

'Must be.'

'You haven't changed a bit…well, except for getting hairier.'

James laughed and drank half of his Cava in one swallow. 'Thanks?'

'And taller,' I said with a grin. Alcohol swirled behind my eyes, and I silently admonished myself for flirting. It was impossible to deny though that the boy I used to babysit had grown into a very attractive man.

'So, what are you doing with your life now that you're no longer – I hope – obsessed with Spiderman and Lego?'

'I'm an art teacher. In fact, I teach at your daughter's school.'

'What? Seriously? But I thought your family moved to the other side of the country?'

'We did, but I decided to move back a few months ago.'

'Amazing. And are you – do you teach Arrietty?'

He nodded. 'Yep. And she's following in your footsteps. Spitting image of you too.'

'Thank you. Is she being well-behaved for you?'

He grinned. 'Absolutely. She's such a lovely young lady. Kudos to you for doing such a great job with her. Do you have any other children?'

'Yes. A two-year-old. Eddie.'

'Oh wow – congratulations.'

I glanced at his ring finger. There was no ring. 'And you?'

A slight frown dipped his forehead. 'No. Not yet. Still a lonely bachelor looking for love.' He laughed weakly and scratched his throat.

I sensed sadness there and rubbed his arm. 'You're only – what? Twenty-nine. You've got years to meet someone.'

He cleared his throat and looked past me.

I dropped my hand and followed his gaze to see Alec

standing a couple of metres away watching us. I waved him over. He hesitated then joined.

'James, this is my husband, Alec. Alec, this is James Broughton, the boy I used to babysit when I was eighteen. Oh, and Arrietty's new art teacher!'

They shook hands. James smiled warmly but Alec didn't return his smile. While I didn't have a jealous bone in my body, my husband was the opposite.

I shifted my weight awkwardly and blurted, 'Anyway, it was so lovely to see you again James.'

'Yes, you too. I'll see you at Arrietty's parents' evening.' James wandered away humming to himself. I hoped he hadn't noticed Alec's rudeness.

I turned to my husband and smiled, 'You came.'

'I did.' He grinned, and I felt my shoulders drop an inch. 'And I see you've already sold 'Hands'. Congratulations darling. That's fantastic.'

I grinned as he tucked a wayward strand of dark hair behind my ear.

'Who bought it?' he said, glancing around the room.

'A man called Hugo Grimes. Quite a character. Let me see if I can spot him…there he is. The one with the white hair chatting to that tall woman.'

I looked back at Alec. He nodded at me, but his mind was elsewhere.

'Is Arrietty with Eddie?' I said.

'Uh, yes. She and Isla offered to revise at ours so I could come.'

'That's sweet of them.'

'Yeah.'

'Is Isla sleeping round?'

'No. I'll take her back when we get home.'

'You're staying for the whole thing?' I said, pleased.

He met my eye and pulled me close. His familiar smell entered my breathing space and I sighed, happy he was present and in a good mood.

Lowering his voice, he put his lips to my ear and said, 'I wouldn't miss it for the world.'

Chapter 7

NOW

I woke up feeling groggy and sick. For most of the night sleep evaded me and I chased after it like a dog after its tail, round and round, tossing and turning, groaning, sweaty and frustrated, my mind speeding a mile a minute as I tried to reassure myself that things would return to normal the next day, that this was a blip on the radar, a glitch that would resolve itself come morning. It was only when I visualised Mum coming home, wrapping her arms around all of us in one of her infamous family cuddles and saying how sorry she was that I managed to nod off. But today was a new day and I knew she wasn't back. I could feel her absence. It hung in the house like the whisper of a bad dream.

Despite everything, when I opened my eyes and looked around, my room gave me a hug. The shabby chic furniture - the bookcase bursting with books - the plush cream carpet that kissed my feet - it was all there and a warm cuddle to my fraught mind.

Hauling myself out of bed, I pulled on my red silk kimono – a gift from my parents on my sixteenth birthday – and left the room.

Outside my bedroom, I hovered on the oak floorboards and eyed the new painting. Dad had hung it there a few days ago. It was a watercolour of a white vase containing red tulips. There was nothing disturbing about it, nothing terror-inspiring like Munch's 'The Scream', nothing at all, and yet looking at those scarlet petals sent spiders' legs crawling down my spine and an icy clamminess creeping through my skin. I leaned a little closer, chest tight. It wasn't Mum's work, and there was no signature. I wondered where Dad had found it. Why he'd put it in this specific place, right outside my room - why it made me feel so weird.

Stroking my throat, I hurried past the painting into the bathroom, brushed my teeth and avoided my reflection, knowing I'd look like death. In the gleaming white tiles, I saw Mum smiling, laughing, plucking her eyebrows and wincing. She was everywhere and nowhere. The not-knowing was gnawing at my bones. Squinching my brain.

Names flashed into my mind like red warning lights –
Shane
James
Hugo
Alec
Could any of them have had anything to do with Mum's 'vanishing'?

No. No way. That was history. All of it. And Dad was…well, he was Dad.

Dad wouldn't hurt a fly.

Are you sure about that?

I scowled, shook my head to erase such stupid thoughts.

I sniffed my armpits. I didn't smell and a shower would require too much energy, so I splashed hot water on my face and nothing more. It wasn't as if I'd be going anywhere today. I probably wouldn't venture off our land for weeks. Mum and Dad didn't want me to risk catching a virus that could set back my recovery.

Eddie wasn't in his bedroom. I was surprised he hadn't slept for longer given he'd gone to bed so late, and even more surprised he hadn't burst into my room, jumped on the bed and woken me up. Staring at his rumpled cover, I wondered how he was feeling today. Hoped he wasn't too upset about Mum. Knew he would be worrying even if he didn't say anything. He was a sensitive little chap. Bright too.

As I headed downstairs, I prepped myself for any questions he might have. Knowing I'd need to hide my concern and lie to his face, my heart squeezed. I hated lying to him – to anyone – and I was rubbish at it, but sometimes white lies were necessary to protect those you loved.

At the end of the hallway, I steeled myself and stretched my lips into a grin. Smiley, happy Arrietty was what Eddie needed to see, not worried, sour-faced Arrietty.

In the kitchen, I was pleased to see him on the floor with his colouring book and wax crayons engrossed in his artwork. The light was off, so he lay in a puddle of shadows. Colouring in such bad light didn't seem to bother him, but I worried about it straining his eyes, so flicked on the light.

'Where's Dad?' I said, ruffling his hair.

'I don't know.'

'You OK, buddy?' I watched him attack a teddy bear's face with a sludge-green crayon.

He didn't answer. Sometimes he was so busy concentrating he didn't hear me. Dad was similar.

'Choco Crackles for breakfast?' I said.

'I'm bored of Choco Crackles.'

'Peanut butter on toast then?'

He looked up, eyes bright, 'Yey!'

I popped two slices of bread in the toaster and peered outside. Despite the previous day's torrent, the sky remained overcast. More rain to come.

I scanned the grass. Apart from the odd rebel daisy, the 200-foot garden was free of flowers. Neither Mum nor Dad was green-fingered, which meant the grass behind the house spread out to the cliff edge like a rippling green sea. Mum's art studio stood at the very back right of the garden, not far from the precipice. It was a cedar clad garden room with a curved roof and a black finish. At seven years old, bombarded by all forms of weather, the rich reddish-brown wood had mellowed to a silvery grey. Mum adored the building, called it her Zone. Eddie and I weren't supposed to go inside unless supervised. I hadn't been in there for ages, but it didn't bother me. Mum's work was precious, and everything was in its special place, in 'organised chaos' she called it. Dad used to joke that she had OCD when it came to her Zone. Even he wasn't allowed to go in uninvited.

A lump entered my throat and a wave of homesickness washed over me. The urge to break the rule exploded; I wanted to be close to her, look at her work.

I stared at the copper clock, unable to squash my worries. Mum should be back by now. Surely two nights away from us was enough time for her to get over whatever it was that had made her need a break. I looked at Dad's office. I didn't want to make him more stressed or worried, but I couldn't stand around hoping she'd come back. I had to do something.

Leaving Eddie with his toast, I crossed the long kitchen into the hallway and knocked on the office door. There was no answer. The back door opened, and I glanced to my right, surprised to see Dad entering the house.

I raised my eyebrows in question.

'I was going to mow the lawn, but it's too wet.'

'You were going to mow the lawn?' I said, unable to hide my disbelief. Mowing the lawn now, really?

'Yes. It needs it,' he said, wiping his hands on his jeans.

I bit my lip and fought a flash of annoyance. 'Toast?'

He smiled and yawned. 'Yes. That'd be good.'

He disappeared into his office.

I told Eddie to go upstairs and play in his room while Dad and I had an important chat. To my relief, he went without argument, leaving me alone to mull over the gentlest way to question Dad about Mum.

Dad trudged to the kitchen bench and sat down with his head in his hands. That pose almost stopped me, but I had a right to ask, a right to know. My mum was missing. Dad would probably tell me not to worry, that I should trust him, let him sort it out, yet that wasn't possible, not for me - not now that she'd been gone another whole night.

I slid his plate of toast in front of him and he tore into it like a starved dog. I watched him eat, half-disgusted, half-mesmerised. His complexion was pasty, eyelids as bruised as the sky.

He sat back and sighed. A little colour had returned to his face. 'That was good. Thanks.'

'Want another piece?'

He shook his head and made to stand, but I moved closer to the bench. 'Dad, I know this is hard, but can we talk about it please?'

'What do you want me to say?'

'I don't know. That you think you know where she is, maybe. Or that you've called around, asked people if they know.'

'I'm doing everything I can. I'm sorry. I'm clearly not doing a good job.'

I frowned. 'No, you're doing great. It's just...I'm worried about her. Do you really have absolutely no idea where she is?'

He swallowed, stared out at the back garden. 'I don't know what to do any more.'

'Well, have you called the police?'

He laughed. I frowned, annoyed by his reaction.

'I think you should call them. She's been missing for over twenty-four hours now. Surely, they have to investigate.'

'The police can't do anything to help us,' he

murmured, rubbing his face.

'Then what are you going to do?'

'Believe me, I've done everything possible. There's nothing more I can do. We just need to wait, and hope.' He stared at me when he said this, and I shifted my weight and glanced at my hands. It was almost as if he was suggesting this was my fault.

I swallowed thickly. 'So, you think we should just wait until she comes back?'

Dad dropped his gaze. It was answer enough.

I hesitated, worried about upsetting him, but too desperate to bite my tongue. 'Can I have my mobile – just for five minutes or so? I can call her. She might answer if she knows it's me. Maybe -'

Dad stood abruptly, violently, knocking the stool over. It crashed to the floor making me jump. His voice was hard. 'No. The light could make you worse.'

'But it's only five minutes. Surely -'

'No. You know that light exposure can trigger your fatigue. The doctor said you're sensitive to light so any exposure to blue light wavelengths or fluorescents can worsen your symptoms, from increasing headaches and fatigue to reducing your cognitive ability and interrupting your sleep and affecting your memory. Cutting out devices is an easy way to make you feel better. It'll stop you feeling so exhausted all the time. I know it's not easy, but you don't have a choice.'

I fought the desire to eyeroll and snap that he sounded like he was reading from a script.

'But isn't that a bit extreme? Can't I just this one time? I don't mind if it makes me a bit tired. I've been feeling really good today. Please. I'm so worried. I can help. I -'

He slammed his palm down on the kitchen bench so hard I flinched. His eyes bulged. Two lurid spots of colour flushed his cheeks. 'No. And don't ask again.'

I folded my arms and blinked back tears.

His face softened a touch and he said, 'It's not good for you. I'm doing this because I care.'

Before I could speak, he strode away and locked himself in his office.

I waited for my pulse to die down. His reaction unnerved me, but the anger in him spoke volumes. It suggested three things: he was angry at *me*, because I'd done something to upset Mum; he was mad at *himself* for upsetting Mum; or he was angry at *Mum*. Or, maybe, it was a case of all three.

Despite the mugginess, I shivered.

Looking out at the tortured sky, I told myself the stress was getting to him, but a warning burrowed into my mind. Upsetting Dad would be a stupid thing to do.

Chapter 8

ARRIETTY

I poked Mum's back. 'Surprise!'

'Arrietty – what are you doing here? Where's your brother?'

Dad laughed and wrapped his arm around Mum's waist. 'Isla's mum volunteered to stay at ours for a couple of hours so the girls could join us.'

'That's so kind of her,' Mum said.

'We've been hiding in Mr B-H's car,' Isla said with a giggle.

Mum jabbed Dad's small potbelly then lunged forward and tickled me. 'Cheeky!'

I eyed the nibbles table and did begging hands, 'Can we have a glass of Cava? Please.' I made puppy dog eyes and Isla copied. 'Please Mr and Mrs B-H?'

'Pleeease,' I said.

Mum sighed and Dad rolled his eyes. They exchanged bemused looks and then Mum said, 'Half. You can each have half a glass. No more. Got it?'

'Thank you!' I grabbed Isla's hand and pulled her towards a long table smothered with edible goodies. A silver bucket full of ice and Cava sat in the middle of the display. I seized a handful of crisps and shovelled them into my mouth.

Isla poured us half a glass each and handed me one. We clinked and turned to survey the huge white room. Pride exploded in my heart as I watched a ton of strangers

33

roaming around loving my mum's art. People were smiling and pointing and chatting and laughing, having a great time. I hoped everything would sell. It would make Mum's year.

'OMG! Arri, is that who I think it is?'

I followed the direction of Isla's gaze and stared open-mouthed at Mr Broughton who was talking to a bald man whose sinewy arms were blitzed with tattoos. Butterflies whizzed into my belly. My art teacher was looking super-cool in grey chinos and a white T-shirt that hugged his big muscles like a Care Bear.

'This must be how he knows my mum. He's met her before at one of these shows.'

'Shall we say hi?' Isla said, wiggling her eyebrows suggestively.

'Let's down our drinks first. He might not approve of underage drinking. I don't want Mum and Dad to get in trouble.'

She nodded eagerly, and we finished our Cava, found a side table and deposited our empty glasses.

I grabbed her hand and pulled her through the crowd. The place was really buzzing now. I couldn't believe all of these people were here to see my mum's stuff. At the same time, I got it; Mum's charcoal pieces were special. I hoped I would be half as good as her one day.

To my horror, Isla tapped Mr Broughton on the back. Actually touched our teacher. Both men turned and stared down at us. Tattoo dude was even taller than Mr Broughton but there was something hard in his pale blue eyes, a coldness that prickled my neck. He also smelled of weed, which was just plain wrong for an old guy.

'Isla, Arrietty! What a pleasure to see you here,' Mr Broughton said, 'Shane, this is the artist's daughter. I teach this fantastic duo.'

Shane smiled revealing stained teeth. 'Nice to meet you, young ladies.' He elbowed Mr Broughton and said,

'Are all the girls you teach this beautiful, Jay?'

Mr Broughton laughed and swept his arm towards the canvas on the wall. It was 'Cliff', Mum's interpretation of the view from the bottom of our garden. 'Now this, this is what I call beautiful.'

He proceeded to describe in detail what he admired about my mum's work. Isla zoned out and wandered off to the nibbles table, and Shane turned his attention to his phone. I watched Mr Broughton's eyes light up as he talked about the drawing and felt even prouder.

'Do you think I could ever be this good?' I said.

He looked straight in my eyes and nodded. 'Definitely. From what I've seen so far, you've got it too. Just keep practicing, develop your own slant. Be you and the magic will happen.'

I giggled. 'That's really cheesy Mr Broughton.'

He dragged his hand through his hair. 'It is, isn't it? God, I'm getting old.'

I felt eyes on me and looked up to see Shane staring.

Mr Broughton cleared his throat and said he really ought to get going, what with work tomorrow and all. 'Fancy grabbing a quick drink, mate?'

Shane shook his head. 'Thanks mate, but I'm going to stick around for a bit. Hey, Arrietty, fancy giving me a tour?'

Luckily Isla grabbed my elbow and said, 'Some old lady's just brought out cake! Come on, quick, before it all goes.'

I gave him an apologetic glance and hurried off with Isla, glad to have an excuse to get away. There was something weird about that tattooed guy. Something I didn't like.

Chapter 9

NOW

The weather was as bad as my mood. Outside, in the drizzly dusk, a blackbird stabbed the ground. My fingers itched as the desire to draw came. I hadn't drawn since Mum left and the urge was mounting, the need to release all pent-up emotion through sketching an impulse I wouldn't be able to suppress for much longer. But I couldn't go to my room now, not when we were all together for once – me, Eddie and Dad, that was.

Eddie and I sat on the sofa in the living area playing Broken Telephone and eating popcorn. Dad sat in his black leather armchair flicking through his phone. I stared at his mobile, almost salivating with the need to hold it. I wanted to text my friends, post on Instagram, do something to alleviate the crushing boredom of my existence. I needed to feel normal again, re-enter society, catch up on the real world. Most of all, I needed to contact Mum and make sure she was OK. She'd been gone for four whole days. Eddie wasn't his usual bubbly self. He kept crying at things he normally wouldn't cry at and arguing about petty stuff. I was tearing my hair out. Several times I'd thought about stealing Dad's phone, but I didn't know his passcode, so it would be pointless. I'd even tried watching while he tapped it in. No luck yet. Sometimes it seemed as if he knew what I was trying to do and was shielding his mobile with his body to block my view. He'd also pulled away from us, shutting himself in his office for longer and longer periods of time. He was trying to avoid us, I felt sure of it. For the life of me, I couldn't work out why, but there was a blockish aura around him, and I felt edgy in his presence. Eddie did too. He kept trying to get Dad's attention by doing silly dances and asking stupid questions, and Dad barely reacted. Normally, he'd play with Eddie, wrestle and throw him in the air, tickle him until my brother screamed, but it seemed Dad only had the energy to fret about Mum.

I wanted to strive for normality amid the weirdness, but I was failing. Mum leaving was too much for all of us and the lack of explanation was driving everyone crazy. We reacted in our own ways. Eddie cried and argued, Dad retreated to his cave and snapped when provoked, and I worried and wondered and hoped and feared. Ultimately, I did nothing of any real use. There was nothing I could do to help Mum. It was excruciating.

Right now, Dad staying in the living space with us was golden. A rarity. I got the feeling he wanted peace and quiet, so Broken Telephone was the perfect game – until Eddie burst out laughing.

Dad's head whipped around. He stared at us and raised an eyebrow, 'What's so funny?'

'Nothing,' I said quickly.

Outside, the blackbird yanked a worm out of the ground and turned its eyes on me. I wondered if it was afraid. I looked away and eyed Dad's mobile hungrily.

'No, go on. Tell me. I could do with a laugh.' He put his phone on his leg.

I peeled my eyes away from the screen. 'All right. Eddie thought I said, 'I want to go to the poo' rather than 'I want to go to the loo'.' I smiled.

Dad looked from Eddie to me and sighed as if disappointed. 'Right. I see.'

Eddie patted my arm with sticky fingers to signal he'd finished his popcorn. Smiling sweetly, he said, 'More?'

Knowing he'd eaten all of his dinner, I nodded. 'Back in a sec.'

He did a nutty dance as I left the room. Because of his bad leg he danced in a slightly jerky way that was utterly adorable. Of course the time would come when he got older and dancing like that would no longer be cute. I tried not to think about the accident, but as always guilt stung like a wasp, vicious and precise, aiming for my gut.

Halfway along the hallway, I heard steps and turned back. Dad was following me. He approached looking uncertain.

'There's something that might help you feel a bit better about…everything,' he said.

Hope snared my heart. 'What is it? Have you found her?'

'No, not exactly, but I have an address. You can write letters to her and I'll, uh, post them.'

'What do you mean? Is she living at this place or not?'

'It's more complicated than that,' he said, looking away.

'How did you get this address?' I said.

'I — uh — sorry. I shouldn't have said anything. I thought it would help, but it's clearly upsetting you.'

He turned and I grabbed his arm. 'No. Wait. Let me get this straight. You don't know where she is, but you know she'll get my letters if you send them to this address?'

He nodded, glanced away.

'Can I have the address?'

His teeth snagged his lower lip. The flesh turned yellow as he bit into it. He seemed to be thinking, trying to work out the right course of action. Finally, he laid a heavy hand on my shoulder and said, 'No. Not yet. She needs time. But you can write. Get all your thoughts and feelings down. It'll be good for you.'

I nodded and turned away, unsure what to make of him. Again, names darted into my head — *Hugo, James, Shane.*

'This has got nothing to do with them,' Dad snapped.

Did I say that out loud?

I looked up at Dad.

'Don't even go there,' he said, more gently this time.

I swallowed uneasily. He couldn't make eye contact. He looked shifty too.

Or did he? Was it just my imagination making something out of nothing?

Movement caught my eye. The blackbird had moved. It was outside the dining area now, looking in through the glass, almost one with the papery darkness.

Chapter 10

TWO YEARS AGO

SOFIA

People were starting to trickle out of the gallery. Arrietty and Isla were absorbed in conversation near the food table, most of which they'd devoured all by themselves. I looked across the room to see Alec talking to a tall woman in a fifties style dress. I couldn't see her face. I didn't recognise her and wondered if Alec knew the woman or if they'd struck up conversation tonight. She looked to be about his age, a few years older than me at least.

Outside, night had fallen. The few remaining people's reflections hovered like ghostly shadows in the large glass wall that fronted the gallery. A jolt of surprise struck me as I recognised the reflection of our cleaner, Maggie. I turned around to see the live version of the sweet woman waving at me, her soft grey curls skimming her jawline, one of her handmade necklaces – a pretty affair made of painted shells – around her neck. We walked towards each other and hugged. She looked lovely in a turquoise gypsy skirt and white blouse – a striking difference to her usual black leggings and baggy grey top.

'Maggie, it's so wonderful to see you here. I wasn't sure you'd make it.'

A tall, tattooed man with a skinhead appeared at Maggie's side. She introduced him as her son Shane. I'd never met him but had seen photographs of him as a young boy. He'd changed immensely, growing from a scrawny little kid to a giant of a man. I wondered how

Maggie felt about his tattoos. The one of a rose circling his neck was especially eye-catching.

'Shane, it's so lovely to meet you at last. How were your travels?' Maggie had told me he'd been traveling through Southeast Asia for the past year.

Confusion flickered in his eyes, and he glanced at his mother, then gave me a warm smile. 'Good thanks. Rejuvenating you could say. But let's not talk about me. This is your big day, and I have to say your work has totally blown me away. It's incredible. If I could afford to, I'd buy the lot.'

I flushed, embarrassed by the price of my work – was it overvalued? Did he mean anything by his comment or was he being nice?

Maggie laughed and asked him to grab her a piece of cake before Arrietty and Isla ate it all. We grinned and Maggie touched my arm. Her eyes turned serious. In a hushed voice, she said, 'Could we have a quick word? In private?' She seemed nervous and kept glancing towards her son, who seemed to be taking a long time choosing a slice of cake. Arrietty and Isla stood next to him immersed in their phones.

'Of course. Let's go in the office. Is everything okay?'

'Yes, well, no, not really.' She was wringing her hands.

'Here, sit down.' I pulled Patricia's swivel chair out from behind her desk and shut the door.

Maggie sat down and I perched on the edge of a blue tub chair.

'What is it? You're not quitting on me, are you?' I said half-jokingly. Maggie had been our cleaner for years. I didn't have many friends, but I counted Maggie as one of them.

'Oh no, definitely not. It's not about me. It's about Shane.' Tears welled in her eyes. She pulled a tissue out of her sleeve and dabbed at the moisture.

I waited for her to carry on, gave an encouraging smile.

She sniffed and said, 'I lied to you. To everyone. I'm so sorry.'

'Lied about what?'

'About Shane. He wasn't travelling. He was in prison.'

I nodded, trying to process what she was saying while telling her not to worry about the fact that she lied. 'What did he do?'

'He, um, he was arrested for GBH. He was in a drunken brawl, hit a teenager and broke his jaw. He was released three months ago but can't get any work. No-one will hire him, and I'm not in a great place right now money-wise, so I hoped that maybe, well…'

'Absolutely,' I said, thinking Alec might not agree but not caring enough to stop the words, 'I'm sure we can find some work for him around the house. Oh – is he any good at gardening?'

Maggie's face lit up. 'Yes. It's actually his dream to be a landscape gardener. You should see what he's done with my front garden since he's been out.'

'Well that's perfect. Problem solved. I'd love to turn our boring back garden into a proper one with beds and everything. How does twenty pounds an hour sound?'

'Really? Oh Sofia, that sounds amazing. But…don't you need to discuss this with Alec first?'

I crinkled my nose and shook my head. 'No, it'll be fine. He hates gardening as much as me and is sick to death of hearing me complain about our lifeless garden. Trust me. It'll be fine. Can Shane start next week?'

'Absolutely. Thank you so much. You're a lifesaver.'

Maggie rushed out from behind the desk and threw her arms around me. Her sweet, familiar perfume rushed my senses, and I hugged her back, glad I was able to help.

Chapter 11

NOW

With sluggish arms, I hung up my clothes. They weren't ironed but they were clean. Ironing was my nemesis. The boredom it inspired was enough to give me the shakes.

Mum had been gone a whole week. I'd written her a letter, which Dad said he'd post for me. In the kitchen I'd hovered behind him trying to steal a peek at the address, but he'd retreated to his office, locking the door and shutting me out. Why didn't he want me to see the address? I wondered if it was because he feared I'd try to leave and go there to find her, but I was housebound. I couldn't drive and I didn't have a phone to call a taxi. Besides, I wasn't supposed to go anywhere until my symptoms subsided. My immune system was low. If I caught a virus now, it could knock me back months. And I was dying to go back to school. See Isla again. And Mr B. I knew he was right. I had to be sensible and play it safe or I could scupper my chances. Still, when I was feeling really down, I considered lying and telling him I didn't feel exhausted all the time, but I knew he would see through it. I was a terrible liar. Always had been, always would be. I wore my heart on my sleeve. I often wished I didn't.

For the last two days, he'd gone out in the afternoon at around the same time. He hadn't said where to. He was out again this afternoon for the third day in a row.

The desire to sneak into his office and try to find out the address tickled my feet, but I couldn't do that. He was suffering. I needed to support him, not go behind his back.

Eddie was content playing in his room, so I went

downstairs to cook Dad's favourite meal: sausage and mash with Dijon mustard gravy. Mum had taught me to cook, and I enjoyed it. Dad's culinary skills extended to fried chicken with curry sauce from a jar. We used to wind him up about it. My tummy twinged at the memory and I released a long-held sigh.

With conscious effort, I tuned out of the past and let my gaze drift beyond the confines of the house.

It was a perfect June afternoon. Outside, the long, wide stretch of grass that made up our back garden glimmered bright green, making it look edible. The garden ended at the cliff, exposing the hills and an expanse of sweet blue that made me want to whiz into the air like a hummingbird. Sunny with clear skies. Not a cloud in sight. It was dreamy on the surface. But clouds were always on the way, lurking just out of sight, gathering force.

The thought of hot sun caressing my skin reeled me in. I ditched the idea of cooking the meal, ran upstairs and fetched *Little Women* off my pillow. A good book could erase my worries and plunge me into a much-needed dreamscape where I inhabited other characters' lives and ventured into worlds entirely different to my own. It could dispel this skulking dread and take my mind off my problems.

Clutching the book, I hesitated opposite the tulip painting. Excitement at reading in the sun died a sudden death, and ice-cold guilt slithered into my belly. I darted away from the red petals and lingered on the stairs. Sunbathing when Mum was missing was a shameful thing to do, but the Vitamin D would help my mood. Lying in the sun reading was so relaxing, and I needed to relax and recharge my batteries. Mum would want that. She knew I was unwell and would want me to do everything I could to help myself get better.

I looked down at my book. *Little Women* was one of Mum's favourite classics. Reading it made me feel closer to her. It also brought a sharp pain. I sat down on the step. Put my head in my hands.

What if Mum didn't leave voluntarily?

No. That's not possible. Dad knows an address to send her letters to. He knows she's OK.

So why hasn't she got in touch? Why doesn't she want to see us?

My head banged. It didn't add up. The only explanation I could think of was that she was having a nervous breakdown or that she was too angry with me and Dad to come home, but I couldn't think of anything I'd done to annoy her and there was nothing that stressful going on in her life that I knew of. Her art was selling well, she was healthy. I'd thought she was happy too, until now.

In a daze, I walked through the house, went out into the back garden and lay down on the sunbed. The blackbird was back, and it had brought a friend, a larger one with a crooked foot.

Wanting to be alone, I hid behind my book. The words bled into each other. I couldn't focus. Everything was so confusing, so out of touch with normality. I was Alice again in a world of strangeness. But this was a bad dream from which I couldn't wake. I felt my chest tightening. I was beginning to panic. To distract myself, I focused on the warmth of the sun. Tried to pretend life wasn't spiralling out of control.

It was impossible. I scratched my arm. The sun was a demon burning my skin. A poisoned yolk. The sky suddenly seemed too blue.

I pushed myself off the sunbed and the blackbirds' heads snapped up. They eyed me boldly, eyes glinting like black pearls. I gave them an evil then went inside to hunt for the sun cream, pausing on the landing as a horrid retching pierced the silence.

'Eddie? You OK?' I dashed into his bedroom, but he wasn't there.

The sound stopped and a weak voice groaned, 'Arri?'

The bathroom. I hurried inside the large, porcelain room. Eddie was kneeling by the bath. Vomit trailed down the side of the tub, pooling in a puddle on the base. The air was fetid and close.

'Poor little thing,' I said, smoothing back his sweaty hair.

He was burning up.

'Do you think you need to throw up again?'

He shook his head, face a ghastly shade.

I cleaned his lips, peeled off his top and carried him into his bedroom. Leaving him with his cuddly T-Rex, Eric, I hurried back into the bathroom, grabbed the thermometer and Calpol and returned to his room.

'Have you got a headache?' I said, filling the Calpol syringe.

He nodded.

'Tummy ache?'

He nodded again.

'I think you've got a nasty bug.'

I fed him the medicine then slipped the thermometer into his mouth. When it beeped, I took it out. 39°C. *Shit.*

I made sure he was comfortable, cleaned the tub and ran him a cool bath.

He winced when I put him in. He was quite floppy. More than ever, I wished Mum was here. This wasn't my job. Eddie wasn't my son. I didn't know if I was doing everything the right way. What if I made a mistake?

As if reading my mind, Eddie said, 'I want Mummy.'

'I know, buddy. I know.'

I couldn't think of anything else to say. Anger at Mum threatened, and I pushed it away. She'd never cheated on Dad. I was sure of it.

She wouldn't leave us without good cause.

So why did she leave?

I nibbled my nails to the quick. Looked out at the pair of blackbirds. There had to be a reasonable explanation.

Chapter 12

TWO YEARS AGO

SOFIA

Alec had driven Arrietty and Isla home. Everyone else had gone. I'd offered to tidy the last bits and lock up so that Patricia could go. She'd looked pale and exhausted. Brown shadows had circled her eyes. I wondered if her Crohn's was playing up again. When I'd told her to go home and said I'd drop off the keys on Monday, she'd looked faint with relief.

Not for the first time in recent years, I thought how lucky we all were to be so fit and healthy. In a small, dark corner of my mind, I worried how long it would be until our good luck died.

The empty gallery felt strange now, void of people and colour. Five out of ten pieces had sold. Their buyers had taken them home, leaving negative space on the crisp white walls. I smiled and gave myself an imaginary pat on the back. Tonight, five people had loved my work so much that they'd wanted it in their homes. The icing on the cake was that I'd earned just under £6000. Enough to contribute towards our unending energy bills and buy some presents. Arrietty was desperate for the new iPhone and Eddie would love a scooter. Alec needed new golf clubs. As for me, I'd have to think about it. There wasn't anything I wanted really. I felt complete.

With a happy sigh, I shouldered my bag and switched off the main light. The gallery turned black and the abrupt cut from light to dark made me feel blind. Feeling a little vulnerable, I hurried out of the building, turned and locked the door. A crescent moon gave scant light, so I turned on my key laser and aimed it ahead. My heels echoed across the car park out towards the bordering woods. An animal scurried across the tarmac and disappeared into the trees, making me jump.

To my surprise, there was another car in the car park in the space next to mine. The interior light was on, and I could make out the silhouette of a man sitting behind the wheel. Panic thickened my throat, and my heart began to pound. I slowed, slid my hand into my bag and pulled out my mobile. A bat whizzed past, and I flinched and dropped the phone. I scrambled to pick it up and froze at the unmistakable sound of a car door opening.

I grabbed my keys off the ground, stumbled backwards and pointed the key laser at the approaching man. He was tall and well-built with long, determined strides. I took another step back and scanned the car park, hoping someone was close by in case something bad happened.

The man stopped a few feet away with his hands raised in surrender. He looked down at the red laser aimed at his chest. 'You got me.'

Relief exploded in my heart: I recognised his voice straight away. It was just James Broughton, the boy I used to babysit. I laughed and put a hand to my chest. 'Thank God it's only you. I thought for a moment -'

'Oh crap – really? I'm so sorry. Didn't mean to scare you.'

We laughed. Fear and tension whooshed out of me like air out of a balloon, and I almost hugged him.

'I was waiting here for you. Bit stalkerish I know, but I thought you might like to grab a celebratory drink? Catch up after so many years?'

The idea was appealing, but then I thought about Alec. I really ought to go home and celebrate with him. 'I'd love to, I really would, but can we have a rain check? I'm tired and, well, Alec will be expecting me home soon…'

'You sure? I'd love to talk art with you. I'm working on this project, sort of hoped I could pick your brain a bit. You're such an inspiration to me, but – no - I get it. You'd better go. Play it safe.'

I heard the disappointment in his voice. I was flattered by his request and keen to know what he'd been up to these last eighteen years.

A burst of excitement at tonight's success flicked away any concerns and I said, 'All right. Yes. Just one drink though. I'm driving and I've already had a bit of Cava tonight.'

He whooped and grinned. 'Excellent. Hey – don't tell Arrietty I just did that.'

I laughed. 'Trying to be the cool teacher, are you?'

He weaved a hand through his thick dark hair and said in an Elvis Presley voice, 'You betcha sweetheart.'

A girly giggle came out of me. Our eyes met in the darkness, just for a second, and there was a spark there; a connection borne of knowing each other from our youth that felt sort of wonderful. 'Where shall we go?'

'The Red Lion?'

'Great. See you there in five.'

He flashed me a grin. 'Great! Can't wait.'

I watched him jog to his car, excited for our chat, but a little worried about Alec's reaction to my choice. In the car, I sent Alec a quick text telling him I was going for a drink with a friend but that I'd be home by 10.45pm. I waited for a response – he usually messaged back really quickly – but there was nothing. I stared at my phone for another minute, hoping to hear it ping or see him typing but again, zilch. Setting my jaw, I slipped my mobile back in my bag and told myself everything would be fine. Alec would understand. After all, it was only one drink with an old friend.

Chapter 13

NOW

Once Eddie was clean, I lifted him out of the tub and swaddled him in his towel then carried him into my room. I tucked my brother in bed, cuddled him close and read *Fantastic Mr Fox* until he fell asleep. A moment later, I heard footsteps on the landing.

Dad knocked on the door. 'Can I come in?'

'Yes, but be quiet,' I whispered.

The door creaked open and Dad nodded. 'Good. You're resting.'

'Eddie's not well,' I said, 'he threw up and he's got a fever.'

'Oh.' He shifted his weight. 'How are you feeling?'

'It doesn't matter how I'm feeling. I'm worried about Eddie.'

He nodded and scratched his scalp. He looked as though he was about to speak then changed his mind. Light flamed behind Eddie's navy curtains, making the fabric look as though it was on fire. The room felt like a furnace. I sat up, and absently stroked Eddie's hot forehead.

'Where were you?' I said.

He looked at his feet. 'Just out. Getting a few bits we need.'

There was something off about the way he spoke. I didn't know what, but he looked so drained and miserable, I decided not to push it.

'Don't worry. I'll take care of him,' I said, smoothing back Eddie's fringe.

Dad's eyes darted from me to Eddie. He gave me a long, hard look, jaw clenched. After a tense silence, he left without a word.

I stared after him, unable to believe his lack of concern for Eddie. He was getting more and more distant. He was different. I could feel it. I thought about how he'd slammed his hand on the kitchen bench, and a chill cut across my shoulders. Tears came and I let them fall. Blurry-eyed, I left my brother sleeping in my bed and sat down at my desk to write Mum another letter. Maybe if she knew Eddie was poorly, she'd come home.

*

Six more days passed. Six more days of worrying and questioning and fearing. Six more days of struggling to jolly Eddie along and calm his understandable fears. Six more days of battling the desire to pull the covers up over my head and sink into despair.

Mum was still gone, and Dad was being weird. Straying into his path was like walking into a black void. He never smiled and barely acknowledged mine and Eddie's existence. A heavy frown was tattooed onto his forehead. Like me, worry was a constant for him, but we were different. I hadn't allowed my distress to change me.

No matter how odd he was being, I had to do something. Mum had been gone too long and the need to know was killing me, dragging me down into a dark, frightening place.

I sat in bed and listened. There was a quietness in the house that prickled my nerves. Eddie was having a nap in his bedroom, door closed, curtains drawn over the windows like lids over eyes. I pictured him lying there, arms above his head, eyelids twitching as he dreamt of prehistoric beasts roaming moss-smothered forests. In contrast, my dreams were dark. I often woke crying, feeling confused and disoriented, unable to breathe.

This morning, I'd thought I was blind. Tears and sleep glued my eyelashes together. A vulture tore at my chest. It had taken a long time for the panic to subside.

I felt calmer now but no less worried, especially as I'd decided to bring up the subject of Mum with Dad.

I placed my beautiful Wordsworth Collector's edition of *Emma* on the dresser and swung my feet off the bed into my slippers. My fingers shook as I picked up my letter, sprayed perfume on the envelope and kissed it for good luck.

Wiping my mouth with the back of my hand, I crossed the carpet, opened the door and stepped out onto the landing. The tulip painting tried to catch my eye. A cold shudder vibrated in the base of my neck as I walked past.

I tried to descend the stairs with soundless steps, but the slap-slap rhythm sailed up the glass walls and echoed through the house. Open plan was too open; houses ought to have doors, not endless paths that made you vulnerable. Walls ought to be opaque so no one could see inside.

I looked down; the envelope in my hand felt so thin and meaningless, but the words it contained meant everything.

My toe touched the bottom step. I paused and listened. Heard footsteps heading my way.

The lights were off, the air gloomy. I peered up the walkway; it appeared empty, but I could hear him coming. I looked back at the living space. Even the crystal chandelier lacked life. I tried to recall happier times in this room and failed. Without Mum, the house felt empty and cold. Quiet smothered the building like a weighted blanket. It was suffocating.

I glanced back up the stairs, heart thudding. This was what I needed, but the urge to race back to my room was almost overwhelming.

Fast footsteps pulled my gaze. He was hurrying

towards me, head down, strides jerky. There was no chance to change my mind.

At the double-sided fireplace our eyes locked. I licked my lips and tried to stand tall on the step. He lowered his gaze and strode into the room, keeping to the left side, as far from me as possible.

I watched him settle himself into the black armchair. The seat faced the sea of grass that stretched behind the house and ended at the cliff. Beneath a gloomy sky the countryside was dull and static; beyond the glass walls nothing stirred.

I shifted my weight, chewed my lower lip, tried to think of the best way to phrase my question. Mum had become a barred subject. Mentioning her would make him angry, but I had to try.

Dad stared out at the drab sky with a face like stone, his body as motionless and hard as a rock. More alien than ever.

A beat of anger thwacked my ribs, but I stayed where I was on the bottom step of the staircase and racked my brain for the right words.

'Say what you need to say,' he said.

I stared at the back of his head. His body was rigid, knuckles tapping a random beat on the armrests; pretending to be relaxed.

I sucked hot air. His tapping stopped.

Now was the time. I couldn't put it off any longer.

I snatched another breath. 'Where is she?'

His head twitched. He didn't look around.

'Please tell me.'

'There's nothing I can say -'

'Why won't she write back? What's wrong with her? Is she angry with us? With me?' My voice was whiny, desperate. I looked at the envelope in my hand. My heart throbbed.

Dad dragged his fingers through his hair and cracked

his knuckles.

'Please -' I said.

'That's enough. It's not doing you any good. Rest.'

My head burned. Every part of me ached with longing and worry. I stepped off the stairs and took two steps towards him. 'Nothing else matters to me except this. I want to see her. I need to know she's OK. I want -'

'You need to trust me. Keep writing your letters. Now go and have a rest.'

'I don't need to rest. I'm fine. I want to go out again. Go back to school. I want to see Mum.'

He was quiet a long time.

I waited.

In a harsh tone, he said, 'Just trust me. Can't you do that?'

'I want Mum back. I need to know she's OK. Eddie's starting to ask questions. He needs to know she's OK too.'

'Enough.'

I glanced up, fearful he'd woken Eddie.

He stood quickly. I flinched as he strode over and stopped a foot away, chest rising and falling faster than it should, eyes unblinking. I jerked back as he raised his hands. He stared hard at me, then dropped his arms, rubbed his jaw and stormed away.

I watched him go, heart pounding.

I sat down on the stairs and stared out at the garden, not really seeing the physical world. Instead, I saw Dad's face and his simmering rage. Did he blame me? I didn't think I'd done anything wrong. Tears choked my throat. I swallowed them down and pinched my eye ducts, exhaling the toxicity of his words. With a shaky sigh, I placed my letter on the coffee table. He'd see it there, write on the address, add a stamp and post it for me tomorrow. It would have been so much easier to write an email, but he still wouldn't give me access to my phone or laptop, not even for two minutes, and I was too afraid to ask for them.

Chapter 14

SOFIA

At 11.10pm I parked around the side of our large glass house and hurried through the gloom towards the back door. The automatic light came on bathing me in gold, making me feel like a thief caught red-handed. I tried the back door to find it locked. Disappointment slipped under my skin. I wanted to have a nightcap with Alec, talk all about the evening, my sales and so on, but the door being locked meant he'd gone to bed.

In the kitchen I slipped off my heels, poured myself a glass of water and made my way through the long central walkway as quietly as I could. The house was dark and silent, fresh with the scent of furniture polish.

I stopped at the living room, surprised to see lamplight coming from the coffee table next to the armchair that looked out towards the cliff. I reached down to switch it off and a hand grabbed mine. I cried out, lurched back and spilled water over my arm.

'Alec, don't do that. You scared me,' I said, walking around to stand in front of him.

He was still in the clothes he'd worn to the event, jeans and a T-shirt. In his hand he held a can of lager. He raised his drink and said, 'Congratulations, darling.'

There was something off in his voice and he wouldn't meet my eye. He downed the rest of the can and burped.

'Alec, are you drunk?' I said.

He shrugged, grabbed a second lager and opened it.

I hesitated as he gulped the can down. He was clearly upset. Anger came swift and sharp; how dare he ruin this moment for me? But I didn't want an argument. He was notoriously difficult after too many drinks. If I didn't go now things might take a nasty turn.

'Well, enjoy your drink. I'm tired. I'm going to bed.'

His lip curled and he said, 'Like you enjoyed your drink?'

I sighed and yanked my hair out of its bun. 'I did enjoy my drink with Arrietty's *teacher*, yes, thanks for asking.'

He barked out a humourless laugh and opened another can. The fizz bit at my nerves.

'So that's who your date was? Lucky man.'

I snorted and turned away. 'I'm not having this conversation with you now. And besides it's not even a conversation worth having. Our meeting was completely innocent. When he was 11 and I was 18 I babysat him a handful of times. We met tonight and wanted to catch up. And that's all there is to it.' That wasn't completely all there was to it, but I wasn't going to tell him that.

I headed for the stairs, head throbbing with disappointment and anger. I'd never given him any reason to doubt my loyalty. Men had come on to me before, but I'd never reciprocated their interest. Maybe I was flirty after a drink, but that was where it ended.

I whirled around halfway up the stairs. He was standing on the bottom step frowning heavily.

'You know what Alec? It's time you grow up and stop with this absurd jealousy. If anything, I'm the one who ought to be worried, not you.' I left it hanging, the memory of his almost-betrayal heavy in the gloom, tainting the air between us.

He bowed his head, swayed, leaned against the banister, mumbled something I couldn't make out then stumbled back to his chair. He was drunker than I realised.

Rage and resentment resurfaced, thick and bitter as

bile. I stormed down the stairs into the living room. 'And who was that woman you were talking to for so long?'

He shrugged and dragged a hand wearily down his face.

'Answer me,' I said, worried I was onto something.

'No one. I don't know what's wrong with me.'

'Jealousy's what's wrong with you.'

He nodded glumly. 'Sorry.'

'Sorry's not good enough. Not this time.'

I waited a beat, gave him time to stand up and pull me into an apologetic cuddle, but he just sat there staring at his lap, feeling sorry for himself. I was so angry I could have slapped him.

'You embarrassed me tonight. You were rude to James. If it happens again...' I left the threat dangling. Tears blurred my vision as I spun around and stomped upstairs to bed.

On the landing I stopped and called, 'You can sleep in the spare room tonight.'

Chapter 15

NOW

Sometimes I envied Eddie. He was so young and innocent, so full of hopes and dreams. Despite Mum's disappearance, the world remained a magical, exciting place brimming with adventure, while for me it was the opposite.

My brother's bedroom lay at the far end of the landing. I paused outside his room and put my ear to the wood to see if I could hear him. Silence pulsed in my ear, but I knew he was a quiet sleeper. Eddie didn't toss and turn like me. He slept like the dead.

After another second of silence, I pushed open the door and slipped into the room. A little heap lay beneath the dinosaur duvet. Eric lay on the pillow, yellow eyes bulging. Above the bed hung Eddie's stegosaurus lamp. Glow-in-the-dark stickers danced a zig zag pattern down the wall behind his bedframe. His rubbers were out on his little blue desk ordered in size from smallest to largest.

I watched him sleep for a while and wondered how on earth Mum could bring herself to miss this. She hadn't seen her little boy for ages now. As far as I was aware, she hadn't even rung Dad to check on him. I suppose she had my letters. I'd given her regular updates. Maybe she was too upset to speak to Dad. Maybe she felt too guilty to write back to me. But something chewed a hole in these explanations. They didn't hold up. Not really. If Mum was OK, *surely* she'd have made the effort to speak to me and Eddie by now.

I rubbed my tummy and perched on the edge of the

bed. Dipping my head to the pillow, I tried to inhale Eddie's smell. For a horrible moment, it evaded me. I sniffed my way across the pillow and…there – I found it: his lush little boy smell. Faint, but undeniable. I smiled and raised the cover to peek underneath, but he wasn't there.

I jerked as if I'd been slapped and ripped back the cover. Someone had stuffed a pillow underneath to create a child-sized lump.

A giggle came from under the bed. Shaking my head, I knelt and darted my hand into the gap. My fingers made contact with a warm arm and I said, 'Found you!'

Eddie crawled out from his hiding place and threw his arms around my neck. He grinned and licked my nose like a puppy. 'Tricked you, Arrietty!'

'Ew. Don't. That's gross,' I said, letting him twist out of my arms.

He ran over to his desk and started rearranging his dinosaur rubbers into colour groups. I poked his shoulder and handed him his jeans and T-shirt, 'Get dressed. We're going out to play.'

He grinned and tried to pull on his clothes as fast as he could.

I could tell the jeans were about to go on backwards, so I helped him then let him lead the way out of the room. His little feet pounded the landing, and I called out to him to slow down and be quieter, and he did. Halfway down the stairs, he looked back over his shoulder with a grin that would melt the hardest heart, and held out his hand to me. I slipped my hand into his and we went downstairs together singing Baby Shark in our quiet voices.

When we reached the lounge, I put my finger to my lips and said, 'Shoosh now. Dad's working, remember?'

Eddie nodded and we tiptoed through the lounge into the dining room past Dad's office through the vast marble-top kitchen out into the back garden.

The sky was dirt-grey and plump raindrops started to

fall making the grass slippery underfoot. I turned to pull him back inside, but he let go of my hand, tipped his face to the sky and span around singing, 'Rain, rain, go away, come again another day!' I laughed as he stuck out his tongue and caught droplets. He grimaced as if they were the grossest thing he'd ever tasted, then grabbed my hands and said, 'Let's do ring-a-ring-a-rosy!'

We danced around singing at the top of our lungs, not caring about the rain or the fact that we were so loud. Out here Dad couldn't expect us to be quiet; the garden was our space and our only chance to be free and noisy. We collapsed on our backs and I pulled Eddie on top of me and tickled him until he cried out for me to stop. Giggling, he scrambled to his feet, span around and sprinted off towards the cliff. He was always very good at staying away from the edge, but I ran after him, afraid that he was going to slip and fall, that this time he wouldn't be able to stop. There was no fence across the end of our garden because it spoiled the view.

The rain bucketed down, and he moved further and further away, consumed by the downpour.

'Eddie – wait – slow down! Eddie!'

I slipped and righted myself. My hair fell forward and I flicked it back. When I looked up, he wasn't there. I blinked through the pouring rain and screamed his name, 'EDDIE!'

I scanned the garden. There was nothing he could hide behind – no trees, no bushes, no tall weeds, just barren grass. And the art studio. Dad kept it locked. Ever since Mum had gone, he'd not set foot in it. There was a slight chance my little brother was hiding behind it, in the narrow space that lay between the fence that bordered the sides of our garden and the back of the studio.

Knowing that was the only place he could be, I ran across the garden screaming his name. I was wearing jeans and a T-shirt and I was drenched. My limbs felt heavy, lungs tired as I ran towards the wooden building. He had to be hiding there. He had to be.

'Eddie? Eddie, come out. You're scaring me.'

I reached the building and darted around the side. Thrusting sopping hair out of my face, I peered into the gap between the fence and the studio: he wasn't there.

No – it wasn't possible.

I ran back around to the front of the studio and scanned the vast garden, trying to see through the rain. I needed help. I needed Dad to help me find Eddie. Not wanting to, but knowing I had no other choice, I ran back in the direction of the house screaming my brother's name.

The rain stopped. I blinked as the clouds parted and a dazzling ray of sunlight illuminated the coffin-shaped house.

Eddie was standing at the back door waving, soaked to the bone but grinning like a loon.

In front of him, arms folded, stood Dad.

Chapter 16

TWO YEARS AGO

ARRIETTY

I couldn't believe they'd hired him. I felt him watching me and angled my body away so that I was facing the back of the house. I'd asked Mum and Dad about Shane working for us, hinting at the fact that it was weird to have a convicted criminal doing stuff in your back garden, and they'd been all blasé about it, brushing my worries aside like they were as insignificant as dust mites. I knew they were doing this for Maggie but still...I didn't like him being here. It was probably my imagination wreaking havoc with my sense of logic, but there was something *dodgy* about him. Not dodgy enough to keep me from revising in the sun and improving my tan of course; just dodgy enough to make me feel uncomfortable.

Eddie was the opposite to me; he was totally into our new gardener. His little mind was blown by Shane's tattoos and skinned head – he kept trying to stroke the large man like he was a dog. Right now, my brother was dropping earth into the holes Shane had just created. I looked up to check Shane wasn't finding Eddie's attempts to help irritating. Everything seemed fine. Shane was laughing and pulling funny faces at my little brother. I knew it should have put me at ease, but it didn't.

When I'd finished this last bit of revision, I was going to do a mini easter egg hunt for Eddie. Dad was playing golf and Mum was shut up in her studio working, so I was on toddler watch until lunchtime. They'd told me to offer

Shane a cold drink and I hadn't done it yet. Grumbling under my breath, knowing I'd get in trouble if I didn't do as I was told, I pushed myself up, slipped my feet into my flipflops and ambled across the long garden to Shane and Eddie.

It was a scorching day. Sweat soaked the back of Shane's white vest. The band of his boxers was visible above his low-cut jeans. Compared to his head, his arms were hairy. He smelled musky and salty, and a tiny bit of weed. No surprise there.

Curiosity bit as I hovered behind him. There was something I needed to know. Eddie waddled across the newly dug bed, hunkered down and proceeded to pick up clumps of soil and rub it on his cheeks.

'Hey, little guy, don't do that,' Shane said.

'It's okay,' I said, 'my parents won't mind him getting messy.'

He jumped as if I'd caught him by surprise, clasped his chest and laughed. 'Didn't realise you were there.'

'Mum told me to ask you if you want a cold drink,' I said, trying to work out how to word my nosy question.

His eyes flickered down to my feet then back to my face. I folded my arms.

'Water's fine,' he said staring intently at me.

Was he weird or a creep? Whatever he was, he gave me the ick.

'Okay. Uh,' I couldn't stop myself, 'how do you and Mr Broughton know each other?'

He raised one pierced eyebrow. 'Why so curious?'

I shrugged. 'Dunno. Just am.'

He stood up and brushed off his jeans. I squinted up at him, feeling intimidated despite the fact Eddie was there.

'What will you give me if I tell you?' he said, tilting his head, face deadpan.

'What?' Oh God – he was a pervert.

He burst out laughing; a heehaw that made him sound like a donkey. 'I'm just pulling your chain.'

'Whatever,' I muttered turning away, tempted to call him a dick but knowing my parents would kill me if they ever found out I had.

'Wait,' he said, putting a sweaty, grimy hand on my shoulder.

I frowned around at his hand, and he immediately pulled it back. 'Sorry. So, Jay and I know each other from school. We were in the same tutor group all through secondary. That's how.'

'Were you best friends?'

'Mates. Shared a smoke every now and then.'

'Mr Broughton used to smoke?'

'Hell yeah. He was worse than me. But, don't get me wrong, he's not like that anymore. He's a 'responsible adult' now.' He made rabbit ear quote marks and rolled his eyes. His voice dripped with sarcasm and there was something in his eyes, something bitter maybe.

He lowered his voice conspiratorially. 'You know your mum used to babysit for him? We were all well into her back then, and she knew it.' He glanced towards Mum's studio, his mouth a grim line now, former jokiness gone.

I was annoyed by what he was implying about Mum. 'She couldn't have cared less about a bunch of eleven-year-olds fancying her. Just like I wouldn't.'

He looked back and gave a tight smile. 'Really? I think everyone likes to feel wanted, even rich people like your mum. We all need attention now and then, especially when we've not had any for a long time.' He had that distant look in his eye, that expression that meant he was about to talk about his childhood – like all adults do – so I hurried away to make his drink. I didn't know what to make of him, but at least I knew my crush on Mr Broughton didn't need to die. He knew Shane from school, not criminal stuff, which was good. I wasn't into bad boys.

Chapter 17

NOW

Dad's face was puce.

I jerked my head at Eddie, telling him to go inside. He got the hint and limped into the house. I hoped he'd go upstairs to get dry, out of Dad's sight and mind, because Dad was mad. I was supposed to be resting, not haring around outside in the pouring rain.

'What on earth were you doing?' he said, taking a step towards me.

I tried to work out what to say. A rainbow arced through the sky behind him and the house, conflicting with his anger. My breath hitched and I tilted my head to the side, a memory bursting up through the sludge of my brain, vivid as fire.

We were having a picnic out here on the grass in the middle of the garden. Dad had set it all up: red and white checked blanket, a bottle of fizz in a bucket of ice, coffee and walnut cake, ham sandwiches with the crusts cut off the way I liked it and juicy, fat strawberries with lashings of cream. It was heaven. I emerged from Mum's studio to see his display.

Laughter made me turn and there, playing in the sun –

'Go and get changed. You're soaking.'

Dad's voice cut through my reverie, snapping me back to the present.

'Why do you do that?' I said, irritation distilling my fear.

He frowned. 'Do what?'

'Speak to me like I'm a little girl. I'm almost an adult.'

He looked away. His teeth snagged the black stubble

above his lips. He exhaled as if trying to calm himself down and scratched the back of his neck then looked me straight in the eye.

I edged back. 'Why won't you tell me where Mum's gone? Is she having an affair? Are you two getting a divorce? Why did she leave and why hasn't she been in touch? Please tell me. I know you're hurting, but it's not fair keeping me and Eddie in the dark like this.'

His cheek twitched and his jaw worked. He was thirteen years older than Mum, but at that moment he looked far far older and more unknown to me than ever.

I shifted my weight, frightened I'd hit a nerve.

I said, 'I think I need to go and lie down for a bit. Eddie's inside getting changed. Do you think you could…?'

His eyes narrowed to slits.

'I'm sorry. It's fine. Don't worry,' I said.

I dashed away from him, legs wobbly, head spinning. I needed to lie down.

I hurried through the house, up the stairs and peered into Eddie's room. He was sitting on the floor looking at one of his dinosaur books. Like the good boy he was, he'd changed into dry clothes and they were on the right way, which was progress.

'I'm going to lie down in my room for a bit, OK? You can read or play in my room, or you can stay here.'

'I'll stay here. Are you tired?'

I nodded. 'If you need anything, come and wake me up.'

Feeling guilty, I ruffled his hair then hurried back to my bedroom.

I tried to sleep, but worries bit at me like fleas, stopping my brain from closing down. Why wouldn't Dad tell me anything? Where was Mum? What was making him so angry?

Chapter 18

TWO YEARS AGO

SOFIA

I felt bad about lying but Alec hadn't given me much choice. Humming softly, I added blusher to ensure I didn't look like death, brushed my hair, and checked the top button of my tea dress was done up. Satisfied, I grabbed my handbag and hurried downstairs.

Arrietty was over at Isla's revising. Eddie was in bed and Alec was watching the news on his laptop in the living space. I called bye, told him I'd be back between nine and ten 'o clock and hotfooted it out the back door.

It was a warm, close evening with no stars in sight. My studio sat proudly at the far-right corner of the garden, black and eyeless now that I'd locked it for the night. I smiled. For me it was a haven, a sacred space away from all distraction. My zone where I could zone in and zone out, be at peace while I lost myself in the obsession that was my art.

Sliding in behind the wheel, I jumped as a shadow appeared at the passenger side. It was Alec. His square jaw was hard and his expression was serious. I frowned, desperate to get going. He gestured for me to wind down the window. I obeyed, teeth gritted, hoping whatever he was going to say wouldn't keep me too long.

'Everything ok?' I said.

'Yeah. I was only half-listening when you said where you were off to tonight…'

'Oh. Right. I'm meeting Patricia for a couple of drinks

at the pub.'

'Which pub?' he said, adding quickly, 'just in case…you know.'

'The Red Lion.'

'Ah.' He scratched his neck, looked thoughtful. 'You don't usually meet her for drinks. Is there some special occasion or something?'

I sighed, smiled tightly. 'Nope. She just suggested it and I said yes. Look, I need to get going. I'm supposed to be meeting her at seven-thirty.'

He backed up with a sheepish smile, 'Sorry. Have fun. I'll stay up for you.'

'Great.'

I watched him walk back to the house, the sting of guilt sharp in my gut. I gave myself a mental shake and reminded myself why I was doing this. I nodded. I was doing this because I wanted to. Life was too short to deny simple pleasures. And besides, it was too late to change my mind now.

I pulled away slowly. Looking in the rear-view mirror, I saw Alec standing on the gravel watching me leave. My stomach churned. The problem was that he was a very intelligent man. If I wasn't careful, he would find out what I was up to. From now on, I'd need to sound a bit more convincing, cover my tracks. What he didn't know wouldn't hurt him, and it wasn't as if this arrangement was going to last forever.

Chapter 19

NOW

I'd lost Eddie. Again. He wasn't in my bedroom or any of the spare rooms and I didn't think he'd gone downstairs, which left the master bedroom. I thought he'd be wise to the fact that Dad wouldn't want him running around in there, but I'd clearly been wrong. Still, I couldn't bring Eddie down, not when he'd been upset earlier, so I tiptoed to the door and pushed.

The room was silent and seemed empty, but there were plenty of hiding places for a little boy to pick from. Eddie was good at hiding, which made the game more fun, and he was so tiny he could fit just about anywhere.

This was the first time I'd been inside their room since Mum left. It was enormous, big enough to fit a king-sized four-poster bed, a walk-in wardrobe and a two-seater settee that overlooked the long expanse of garden at the back of the house.

Satin curtains opened to lifeless sky and wet grass. In the distance, the hills sat dismal and dull, clouds dimming the countryside into a pigswill of murk. It was as though all colour had been bleached from the world. Like an artist with depression had painted through her tears.

My gaze fell on the closest bedside table and my heart stopped for a second. It was the only photograph in the room: the four of us, smiling at the camera on a sunny day, a selfie taken by Dad. Eddie was two and I was fifteen. We were in the back garden. Behind us, the sky was a delicate blue, grass green as a lime. Mum looked happy. So did Dad. That wasn't long after Isla and I had broken curfew after our trip to the fair. Dad had been furious with me and I'd been grounded for a month.

A lump blocked my throat. I stared at Mum's face, tried to work her out. The person I knew wouldn't just leave. It didn't make sense. I stared at Dad's face; he looked so much younger and happier. What had happened to him? To Mum? Why wouldn't he tell me what was going on?

I almost charged downstairs to bang on Dad's office and demand he tell me everything, but something held me back. What if it was better that I didn't know? Was Dad protecting me by keeping the truth to himself? Did he know what was going on or was he as clueless as me? He'd always had the attitude that adults knew better than kids. Maybe he thought I was too young and immature to cope with the truth. Maybe I was. Maybe I didn't want to know what had happened to Mum. Maybe Dad feared the truth would stop me from getting better.

Yes. That had to be it. Dad wouldn't keep me in the dark for no good reason.

Feeling better, I re-focused on the room and resumed the search for my little brother. The walk-in wardrobe was an obvious place. I checked under the bed first – no luck – but…what was that? Shock spiked my blood. I slid my fingers over the smooth silver surface, over the small silky device. Pink-cheeked, I slid my laptop and mobile out from under the bed. So this was where he'd been hiding them all this time? Feelings rushed me all at once: guilt, excitement, anticipation. Surely looking at my phone for a few seconds couldn't do that much harm.

I looked over my shoulder, certain Dad would be standing in the bedroom doorway, hands on his hips, glaring at me. But he wasn't there.

I chewed my lip and hovered my finger over the on button on my phone. If I did this, I was going against Dad's wishes and disobeying the doctor's orders, but I had to try to contact Mum. It had been too long, and this was my chance. Knowing Mum was OK was more important than making my condition worse.

I wiped a clammy palm on my leg and turned on my mobile. The screen flashed up, warm and bright as sunshine. Excitement bubbled around my tummy – I couldn't wait to check my texts and everything else. I'd been such a good girl. Not many teenagers would have managed to survive without their phone for so long, but I had.

I smiled at the photo of Eddie that I'd chosen for my background. He was wearing a baseball cap back to front and eating a piece of chocolate cake. Brown sponge blacked out his teeth and smothered his lips and most of his chin. He even had a chocolate stripe down his nose.

Knowing he was waiting for me to find him and that Dad could come upstairs and see what I was doing at any second, I entered my pin, but it didn't work. I tried again, certain I'd entered it wrong, and frowned. I remained locked out. I tried five more times before I gave up. Either I'd changed my pin and forgotten it, or someone had changed it instead of me. Feeling sick, I yanked open my laptop and tried that too. The same thing happened. Frustration flared inside me like a flame. What was going on? My opportunity to find out about Mum was ruined. I'd broken Dad's rule and subjected myself to harmful blue light for nothing.

Huffing, I placed my mobile on top of my laptop and shoved them back under the bed, unable to shake a nagging feeling that I would have remembered if I'd altered my code. If I hadn't, who had?

Dad.

But why?

To stop you doing exactly what you just tried to do, obviously.

Trying to work it out was pointless. There was no way I could ask Dad if he'd done it. Asking him would mean

71

admitting I'd gone behind his back and against his rules, which would get me in trouble and add to his stress.

Still, I couldn't stop wondering as I headed for the glorious walk-in wardrobe to look for Eddie.

Mum had a thing for heels; the brighter and more elaborate the better. It was the artist in her – at least that's what Dad used to say. Strangely, her artwork wasn't colourful at all. When she was younger it had been. She'd dabbled in vast watercolours of beaches and lakes, but as she'd matured, her preferred tool had become charcoal or black and grey ink, her work darker and more serious. I knew she liked her work to communicate moods, ideas and emotions. One of her goals was to evoke strong feelings in her audience. People who disliked her creations thought them too dark and dramatic. But I loved them. To me, the way she drew on artists like Hamilton Mortimer, whose Death on a Pale Horse was about the pointlessness of fighting in battle only to die, was brilliant.

None of her recent work was displayed in the house because Mum said it was too gloomy, and besides, she'd sold most of her stuff.

Since Mum left, I'd drawn with charcoal too. Dad had given me a box from her studio. Before, I'd sketched with pencil – animals copied from Google images and sometimes people's hands or eyes, but using cinder like Mum made me feel closer to her. I also liked the way the ash blurred and misted to form shadows, depth and mystery.

My fingernails were dirty, so I was careful not to touch the pastel blouses hanging from the rail. Her clothes were colour ordered from white to black. She owned few dark clothes. Only one black dress which she kept for funerals. My hand hovered above the black dress and pain splintered my temples. I gasped as if burned, the idea that Mum was dead stabbing my brain with irrational force.

After several seconds, the pain ebbed and the

ridiculous notion faded, and a thought pierced all else: *none of Mum's clothes were missing*. At least, I didn't think they were.

Forgetting my concerns about dirtying the garments, I yanked back hanger after hanger, each metallic shriek an alarm bell, to see if anything was gone. If Mum had left, she'd have taken a bag of stuff with her; she'd have taken her toothbrush for sure.

I ran out of the wardrobe across the room and opened the door to the en-suite. I scanned the sink. One blue toothbrush. One pink toothbrush. A make-up bag open on the side.

I stared open-mouthed, tried to wrap my head around this new information. Mum had left, but she hadn't taken anything with her.

None of it made sense.

Unless…

Pain flared in my temples again and I sat on the toilet lid and dipped my head between my knees. What was going on?

Feeling hot, I jerked up, darted to the sink and splashed my face with cold water. I felt for the hand towel, and dried my face then looked at myself in the mirror. I was very pale. Not in a beautiful Snow-White way. In a Frankenstein's bride way. I looked sick.

I shivered and looked away from the mirror. I saw Eddie's foot a split second before he whipped back the shower curtain.

'BOO!' His smile was so wide I worried it would split his cheeks.

I smiled, but my lips wobbled. Everything was upside down and inside out. Where was my mum? Why hadn't she taken anything with her?

Eddie touched my cheek. 'You look funny, like a sad clown.'

Chapter 20

ARRIETTY

'I've got a cunning plan,' I whispered the words into Isla's ear. The wispy bits of hair that always came out of her plait tickled my lips.

My best friend's white-blonde eyebrows shot up and her thin lips curled. 'Tell me more.'

I looked at Mr Broughton. He was leaning over Rosie, reading her essay on the computer screen. The lesson was nearly over. The computer room stank of boy B.O. We'd had PE the lesson before. Even though Mr Broughton had opened all of the windows, the air was muggy and gross. He'd taken off his tie and unbuttoned the top two buttons of his crisp white shirt. His cow's lick fell onto his forehead. I wanted to curl my finger in it. See what his hair felt like. My crush was growing stronger by the day. Isla liked him too, but I liked him more.

'We're going to follow him after school.'

'What?'

'You heard me. Mr B, we're going to follow him.'

Isla laughed. 'Stalker much?'

'I just want to see where he lives. Find out a bit more about him.'

She rolled her eyes and flicked her plait behind her shoulder. 'I know you fancy him, but you know you're never going to be together so what's the point?'

'You don't know that for certain. In three years' time I'll be out of this place and it won't be illegal for him and me to date.'

Isla laughed loudly. Mr Broughton's eyes found her, his glance stern. He put finger to his lips then returned to checking Rosie's work.

'You're living in La La Land if you think he'll date you after you finish here. Anyway, aren't we going to uni? You don't want to be tied down with an older boyfriend when you start university. You need to be free to kiss as many guys as possible.'

I sighed. 'You're probably right, but I just want to see his house.'

'What if he sees us though?'

'He won't. Trust me. It'll be so fun. We'll be like spies.'

'It won't be fun if we get caught…'

The bell rang for the end of the day. Chairs scraped across the sticky laminate. I shut down my computer quickly. It was Friday. Mr B never stayed after school on a Friday. He walked to and from school, that much I knew, which meant he lived close by.

I linked arms with Isla and pulled her towards the door. I was sleeping at Isla's tonight. Mum and Dad would never know what we were up to. I was so excited I could barely contain it.

*

Isla and I hid behind a silver Hyundai parked on the road outside school. The sun was hot on the back of our necks. I hitched my glittery pink backpack higher up my shoulder. My thighs were hurting from squatting for so long.

Isla poked her head out then whipped it back in, eyes wide. 'He's coming!'

'Great! Let me see.'

Staying low, we swapped sides. I watched the object of my love stride confidently through the school gates and turn left. As he walked, he slipped headphones on. He was moving at a pace, like he was running late for something.

I grabbed Isla's arm. 'Quick, he's motoring.'

We crossed to the other side of the road. Staying three cars' worth behind, we slipped on our sunglasses in unison and tailed him, giggling at ourselves.

'You're right,' Isla whispered, 'this is fun.'

'I reckon he's got a massive house.'

'On a teacher's salary? I doubt it.'

I wiggled my eyebrows. 'I wonder what his bedroom's like.'

'Arrietty Black-Hawkins! What would your mother say?'

'To be honest my dear, I don't give a damn.'

Isla laughed. I slapped my hand over her mouth for dramatic effect. She licked my skin.

'Gross,' I said, yanking back my palm.

'Look – he's crossing the road.'

'Shit. We'd better hurry.'

Clouds moved in front of the sun and the pavement turned three shades darker. We dashed across the road, narrowly missing an oncoming cyclist. Mr Broughton headed up Hill Street, not slowing at all.

'He's on a right mission,' Isla said whipping a banana out of her bag.

'I know.'

'What if he's got a girlfriend?'

I evil-eyed her. 'He hasn't.'

'How do you know?'

I shrugged and upped my pace a bit. 'I can tell.'

She snorted. 'He's too fit to be single.'

My smile wavered as I realised she was probably right. The best boys were always taken.

Mr Broughton stopped. Isla and I froze as he pulled his mobile out of his leather satchel, tapped the screen, slid the phone back into his bag and carried on walking.

'That was close,' Isla said, breathless.

'Tell me about it.'

We hurried after him shrugging our bags up our shoulders. Isla darted to the left and chucked her banana peel in a bin.

He crossed the street in a light jog then disappeared into an alleyway between a Chinese takeaway and a newsagents. I pulled Isla across the road.

At the alleyway, we peered around the side of the newsagents to see him plunged in shadow at the other end of the passage.

We waited until he turned left then jogged after him, scrunching our noses at the stink of urine dominating the narrow passage.

'He lives further from school than I thought,' I panted.

We reached the end of the alley and saw him a few houses up knocking on someone's door. This row of houses was pretty rundown. It was almost as if they'd been built there so they were out of sight and mind. Rubbish littered people's tiny front courtyards and there was a strong smell of marijuana in the air that made me think of Shane.

'That can't be where he lives?' Isla said.

Mr Broughton looked both ways then disappeared inside the house. I exhaled the breath I'd gasped in when he'd looked in our direction. Luckily, he hadn't spotted us peering around the wall.

I grabbed Isla's wrist and pulled her out of the alley towards the house he'd entered.

Isla dug in her heels two doors down and frowned at me. 'I don't like this place. It feels dodgy.'

I secretly agreed. This weird little back street felt like the sort of place where you got mugged, or worse.

Isla scanned the area, and I copied her, swallowing thickly, my heartbeat picking up speed. Graffitied swearwords smothered the rickety fence opposite the row of houses. The windows of the house Mr Broughton had entered were covered with newspaper and brown parcel tape, and the red door was scratched and peeling. A mangy cat scaled the gutter, pausing to stare down at us with piercing green eyes.

Isla nudged me and jerked her head. A group of men had rounded the corner at the other end of the path. They all wore baggy jeans and oversized T-shirts in grungy colours. One of them held a phone blaring rap music. They were heading our way.

'I think we should go,' Isla murmured, tugging my shirt sleeve.

Her face was usually pale but at that moment she looked like a ghost. My mouth went dry as scenario after scenario blitzed my mind's eye.

A frightened scream came from behind the newspapered glass. It sounded like a woman.

Isla jumped and grabbed my arm. 'Let's go. *Now.*'

Together, we whirled around and ran back the way we'd come. A wolf whistle travelled after us accompanied by laughter.

One of the lads shouted, 'Hey, where're you going girls? Come back – we wanna play with you!'

We turned into the alley and sprinted through the gloom out onto the street and the welcome sight of cars, people and shops. A toddler who looked a bit like Eddie waddled past with his mummy and an ambulance zoomed up the street.

I turned. No one had followed us.

'Phew,' Isla said.

'I know. Why do you think Mr B went there, of all places?'

She shrugged and pulled her plait over her shoulder. 'Maybe he lives there?'

'Why so circumspect though? It was like he was up to no good.'

'He might be embarrassed that he lives in such a dump.

Anyway, I'm starving. Can we go to mine now?'

I looked back up the alleyway and gasped – Mr B was walking across the space at the other end of the passage, dragging a pink-haired woman by her arm. She was trying to pull away. Mr B stopped in his tracks dead centre of the opening. I grabbed Isla and yanked her out of sight then peeked around the wall. My crush was stabbing his finger into the young woman's face. I strained to hear what he was saying but it was impossible to make out anything more than an aggressive tone. I felt Isla's banana breath on my cheek.

'Who's that?' she whispered. 'And why's he so mad at her?'

'I don't know.'

Our eyes widened as Mr Broughton grabbed the woman's upper arms and shook her roughly. She held his gaze for a second then hung her head. Releasing one of her arms, he dragged her away. This time she didn't fight back. She glanced up just before he pulled her past the end of the alley. She saw us and raised her arm as if to say *please help me*, but Mr Broughton yanked her out of view.

'Let's follow them,' I said.

'No way.'

'But, as much as I don't want to admit it, I'm worried about what he's going to do to her.'

'If that's the case, we can't put ourselves in danger. Should we call the police?'

'And say what? That we stalked our Art teacher?'

Isla slipped her thumb nail between her teeth and started to nibble. Her phone buzzed and she pulled it out of her Harry Potter backpack and rolled her eyes. 'It's my mum. She's wondering where we are. If we don't get home soon, she'll send out a search party.'

'But what about that woman and Mr B?'

Isla chewed her cheek. 'We just need to hope Mr Broughton's who we thought he was. I mean, you don't seriously think he'd hurt someone, do you? A minute ago, you were ready to marry him.'

I stared at the alleyway lost in thought, hoping there was an innocent excuse for Mr B's strange behaviour. Was he a bad boy after all? My heart screamed no, but my gut whispered yes.

Chapter 21

NOW

Dad was out and Eddie was still asleep in my bed. Maggie owned a key and had already let herself in. The sun was happy and shining into the house, making everything seem sunnier and brighter, but my mood was low, my nerves as brittle as glass.

'Morning, Maggie.'

'Good morning, dear. How are you? I didn't hear anything, so I came to do my duties like normal. I do hope that's OK?'

Maggie was what I thought of as a soft person: soft voice, soft body, soft nature, soft Irish accent. Her hair was light grey, white in some places, curly as a pig's tail, and her cheeks were round and pink. She reminded me of one of my favourite story characters from when I was small: Mrs Pepperpot.

I nodded. 'Yeah. I'm sure Dad won't mind.'

'Oh, your Dad's here is he? How lovely.'

'He's gone out, but I'm sure he'll be back soon.'

'Good, good.'

I made myself a bowl of cereal and a coffee. 'Would you like a drink?'

'No thank you, dear. One coffee in the morning's plenty for me, else I'll be popping to spend a penny every five minutes.'

Wanting to be sociable and enjoying the fact there was someone different to talk to, I sat at the kitchen island. Behind her, the sun sparkled like pirate gold, so I had to shield my eyes to see her properly.

'Anything new with you?' I said.

She pulled a face. 'Me? Oh no. Same old same old. Shane's up to his old tricks, I'm afraid to say – I barely hear from him these days, you know,' she stopped cleaning and eyed me, her gaze full of concern, voice soft and sad, 'and you, dear? How are you doing?'

I was surprised; I didn't know she knew Mum had gone. Had Dad confided in her about it? As far as I knew they weren't that close. Mum handled things with Maggie. Dad barely tried to talk to her when she came to clean.

I swallowed with difficulty. 'I'm OK.'

Maggie's eyes shone. Lowering her voice, she crossed herself and whispered, 'Life is plagued by the devil's will, but we must never concede defeat. We must battle the fetch and always *always* cheer on the clover.'

I knew about the four-leaf clover and how it was supposed to bring good luck to its finder, especially if found by accident, and Maggie had told me about the fetch before. According to Irish folklore, a fetch was a supernatural double or apparition of a living person. The sighting of a fetch was thought of as an omen for impending death.

I didn't believe in superstitions, heaven and hell, God or Satan, but I nodded, knowing she was offering what comfort she could. In a quiet voice I said, 'It's hard, but I'm sure she'll be back soon.'

Outside, the sun's light intensified.

'Yes. I'm sure she will, with God's good grace. As my dear old Ma used to say, *a good laugh and a long sleep are the two best cures.*'

She smiled kindly, patted my shoulder then got back to work, and I watched her, trying to understand what she meant. Was there something she knew about Mum that I didn't?

No. If Maggie knew anything, she'd be the first to tell you.

Maggie turned sharply, making me jump. I looked at

her, and she hesitated as if unsure whether she should say what she'd planned. My heart began to thump hard; was she about to tell me something bad about Mum?

'I have a question for you, dear.'

'Oh? What is it?'

'Well, it's a little silly, but I find wishing on things can do wonders for the spirit.'

I frowned, unsure where she was heading.

'When I was a little girl, I used to believe in leprechauns. They're supposed to bring good luck, you know. If one appears to you, it's said it will grant you three wishes.'

'Like a genie.'

'Just so. My question is this: if a leprechaun came to you today, what would your three wishes be?' She held up her small, weathered hands. 'Wait. Don't tell me. Keep it in your heart and pray on it.'

She turned back to her work and I thought about her question. Obviously, my first wish would be to have Mum back safe and sound with a reasonable explanation to give us. My second wish would probably be for my chronic fatigue to go away. My third wish…I couldn't decide. Possibly to be a successful artist like Mum one day or, actually, for Eddie to be unaffected by Mum's abandonment of us. Even if she did come home soon, I knew it would take me a while to get over what she'd done. And Eddie was so little; his mummy leaving him like this was bound to scar him.

Anger erupted like a dragon soaring out of its lair, beating my chest with insidious intent.

I placed my hand over my heart. How could Mum do this to Eddie? To me? What the hell was really going on?

*

'Rise and shine. I've got a surprise for you.'

Eddie beamed. 'Mum's here!'

I could have kicked myself. 'No, not Mum, but Maggie, she's here!'

His face fell and he yanked the cover up over his head.

I tried to pull it down, but he fought with me so I stopped trying. 'I thought you'd be pleased. You love Maggie.'

'But I want Mum. I don't want Maggie.'

'Come on, Eddie. We talked about this. Mum will be home soon but until then we have to be positive and make the most of things. Come downstairs with me and say hi to Maggie. It'll be nice for you to see someone new.'

'I don't want to.'

'But -'

'No. Go away.'

'Please, Eddie. Don't make this harder than it already is.'

He didn't say anything. I whipped back the cover. 'Boo!'

To my relief, he smiled. I tickled him all over until he squealed for me to stop. Out of his bad mood, he let me help him dress then we went downstairs to see Maggie.

We walked hand in hand past the living and dining areas, past Dad's office into the kitchen and stopped.

'Where's Maggie?' Eddie said, frowning up at me.

'I don't know.'

The kitchen was a mess. Maggie wasn't there but three of the cupboards had been emptied, doors flung open, contents covering the marble worktops. A bucket of steaming water with a cloth inside sat on the floor.

'Maybe she's cleaning the downstairs bathroom,' I said.

'Shall we go look for her?'

'Why don't I make you some breakfast first?'

I poured him a small glass of milk and popped two pieces of bread in the toaster.

85

'Where's Daddy?'

'I'm not sure. He wasn't here earlier. I think he's still out. Gone to the shops probably. We're pretty low on coffee. He might have forgotten to order more.'

Eddie climbed onto the kitchen stool and picked his nose while I buttered his toast. 'Don't do that.'

He yanked out his finger and pulled a cute face that made me smile. Seeing Maggie had cheered me up. I wanted Eddie to see her too. She was so warm and friendly and we were missing that with Mum gone.

'Here you are.' I slid a plate across the counter towards him.

He twisted his nose. 'Crusts!'

'Oh - sorry.' I pulled it back and cut off the crusts then handed him his plate, but it slipped through his fingers and hit the floor with a crash of breaking china.

'Eddie!'

He looked like he was going to cry, so I softened my tone and said, 'Don't worry. It was an accident. I'll clean it up and make some more.'

I grabbed a plastic bag and dropped all the broken shards into it then carried the bag through the house to the front door. On opening the door, I jolted; Dad was outside standing beside Maggie's car. She was in the driving seat talking to him through her open window.

Puzzled, I carried the bag to the wheelie bin and dropped it inside. Maggie's red Corsa drove away, and Dad turned and stared at me with his hands on his hips.

'Why's Maggie going?' I said.

Dad walked towards me and I tensed. He stopped three feet away. 'She's not feeling well.' He hesitated. 'Did she say anything to you?'

'About Mum?'

He ran his tongue over his front teeth. His face was pale, black shirt done right up to the top button choking his neck. Odd when it was such a sunny day. It was almost like he was in mourning. He shifted his weight and frowned harder. 'How are you feeling?'

I was surprised by his concern, even a little touched, but Mum's pink toothbrush flashed up in my mind. I almost asked him about it, but Eddie ran out of the house and pulled a face behind Dad's back. I shook my head at Eddie, warning him not to, but he wouldn't stop. Afraid Dad was going to turn and see him, I muttered 'I'm fine' and hurried towards my brother, who I grabbed on the way past and dragged back inside the house.

I thought our talk was over, but Dad followed us into the kitchen and made a cup of coffee. He glanced at me, 'Want one?'

I shook my head and knelt to mop up Eddie's mess.

'What happened?' Dad said.

Eddie sat at the kitchen island picking his nose again.

I gave him a warning look then said, 'I handed it to him and he dropped it. It was an accident.'

Dad stared at me for a beat too long. With a harsh sigh, he grabbed his mug and walked away. Halfway to his office, he stopped and looked over his shoulder.

I pretended not to notice he'd stopped. Eddie's eyes met mine and I tried to communicate that everything was OK, but he was frightened, as unnerved by Dad as me.

Chapter 22

TWO YEARS AGO

SOFIA

My hands clenched on the wheel and my tummy flipped at the sight of the grand estate ahead.

One week after the exhibition, I'd received an email from Hugo Grimes saying he'd like to commission some work from me and would be delighted to have me over to Emmetts Grange for coffee and cake to discuss his proposal.

So, a mere eight days after the event, I found myself driving along a magnificent entranceway towards one of the most impressive buildings I'd ever seen. A Georgian mansion set in (Alec looked it up when I told him) 894 acres located in the heart of Exmoor National Park with a range of outhouses, a swim-spa and tennis court. A nature lover's dream. If I was over-awed by Hugo Grimes before, that was nothing compared to how I felt now.

I looked at the unfamiliar dash and loosened my sweaty grip on the steering wheel. A few days ago, Alec had persuaded me to sell my car, arguing that I barely used it which, I had to admit, was fair, so now I inched his white Mercedes up the long, fir-lined drive listening to the crunch of golden pebbles beneath the car's tyres, wishing my nerves would disappear.

The closer I drew, the more impressive the farmhouse appeared. Unlike Alec's contemporary glass, the walls were a solid cream, creating a warm feel. The roof was slate-grey and the many windows were latticed and crisp white. I'd been expecting to see people milling about all over the place, but the estate seemed abandoned. Maybe it was no longer a working farm.

I wondered who Hugo Grimes lived with. According to Alec, the house contained nine bedrooms. Perhaps the man had a large family. I guessed he was in his late forties, so there was a high chance that he had four or more children and a wife filling up the huge house. Probably a couple of dogs too.

I parked outside the mansion beside Hugo's black Audi. Getting out of the Merc, I shielded my eyes and scanned the windows. It was as if no one was home. There was no movement, light or sound coming from the farmhouse. Puzzled, I crunched my way to the front door, an oak affair with a bronze ram's head knocker. I knocked three times, straightened my dress and told myself to be cool. My armpits were sweaty. I had a quick smell; luckily deodorant was working its magic. If I could show Hugo that I could deliver the art he wanted, I could be in for an exciting period of creation and a huge pay packet at the end. Even Alec was happy for me. To my surprise, he'd confessed that money was a little tight, so the more I could bring in the better. In fact, he'd actively encouraged me to work for Hugo. Sometimes Alec could focus on the negative in a situation but here, there was no downside, simply a great opportunity to keep producing and create something another person valued and loved. Hugo Grimes was a big personality and seemed to know his art. If he loved what I gave him, he might recommend me to his friends. I was probably getting carried away, but it was exciting to fantasise. One day, I might even get the chance to exhibit my work in London – imagine that!

Alec's mention of money nibbled at my mind, but the subject dissolved into thin air as the door groaned inwards.

Chapter 23

NOW

Dad was out again. I'd watched him drive off, Merc spitting pebbles, jazz music ear-shatteringly loud. He always went out in the afternoon at about this time. Where to, I didn't know and right then, I didn't care. Having him out of the house was good. Without him around, I could relax and stop looking over my shoulder every five seconds. I could also investigate Mum's disappearance.

I stirred the curry, tasted it, and added more turmeric. Curry was one of my favourites. Mum loved it too. She would have loved this one because it was extra spicy.

I glanced towards Dad's office, wondering if he'd locked the door. He didn't always lock it. Sometimes he forgot – or maybe he just didn't bother. Eddie and I weren't allowed in there. It was forbidden territory. Even when Mum was around, she didn't go into his sacred workspace for fear of *provoking the beast*. I used to think she was joking. Now I wasn't so sure.

I licked my lips, stirred the curry, thought about going in, looking around. A stern voice inside me yelled *no*. I couldn't do that. It was wrong. Sneaking into his office would be an invasion of his privacy. And yet…I needed to know about Mum. Eddie was suffering more each day. I owed it to him as well as myself to unlock the truth. If Dad wouldn't tell me, I needed to find out on my own.

I covered tonight's curry – which smelt amazing (even if I did say so myself) - and took off Mum's spotty apron. Licking my lips, I rinsed my hands, dried them and scurried across the room. I hurried through the kitchen

90

towards the only room in the house that I was not allowed to go in.

What I was doing was bad, but it felt so good, and it was time I found out the truth – for Eddie's sake more than mine. My little brother needed to know where his Mum was. So did I. Deep down, I was sure that Dad knew where she was. I just didn't know why he was hiding it from me. From us.

Adrenaline surged in my blood making me feel a little high. Not giving myself a chance to back down, I gripped the door handle, pushed down, slipped inside the office and shut the door behind me.

Straight away, I was overwhelmed by the pong of Dad's musty cologne and the sea of dullness: brown desk, towering brown bookcase, brown swivel chair, brown bin, brown floorboards. Brown, brown, brown. Dull, dull, dull. I yawned and scanned the bookshelves. Most were about architecture but some were about travel.

I scanned the walls. On the righthand wall was one of those maps where you scratched off where you'd been. I was surprised to see he'd visited so many countries. I counted them. When I reached twenty-two, I stopped, bored and aware that I was wasting time. He could come back any second. The thought sobered me up and I turned my attention to his desk.

I knew what I was looking for: a clue about Mum. Where she was, why she'd left, when she'd be back. I couldn't remember Dad and her arguing; couldn't recall her seeming upset. In fact, the more I thought about it, the less I remembered. My memory seemed fractured, incomplete, like a puzzle with missing pieces. When I tried to recall the weeks before Mum left my mind drew a blurry canvas, which was weird, but not something to worry about now. Before, I'd put it down to the chronic fatigue messing with my brain, but the doctor had never mentioned that the condition caused memory problems.

91

Or had he? That was the irony of it all. Maybe he had and I couldn't even recall that.

The first place I searched was his desk. It was one of those old mahogany captain's desks with lots of drawers and secret compartments. On top lay Dad's laptop. I pulled up the screen and tried Mum's birthday for the password. No luck. I sighed, bit my lip, thought. I tried Dad's birthday next. Nope. If I tried again would it lock him out? If it did, he'd know I'd been in here. I tried to predict what he'd do and a shudder gripped my body; I didn't want to make him angry. He might explode. I didn't think he'd hurt me, but sometimes it was like he wasn't *right* in his mind - like he was so sad and bitter he could do just about anything.

Feeling jumpy, I lowered the screen, deciding not to risk trying another password. It wasn't worth it. I'd find out about Mum another way. There were lots of places in this room I hadn't tried yet.

The desk had four drawers either side of the leg space. I yanked open the top right drawer, saw only pens and paper clips. The second drawer down contained a writing pad, a packet of lozenges and a small black stapler. Third drawer nothing but dust. The last one was also empty. I turned to the left side of the desk and pulled open the first drawer. This contained Dad's wallet and spare car key, which was odd given that he'd gone out, but maybe he hadn't gone out to buy anything. Maybe he'd gone to see someone.

I picked up the black leather purse and laid it open on the desk. A photograph of Mum when she was younger was slotted behind the clear plastic part of the wallet. She looked so like me, so young and happy. Her jet-black hair spilled over her shoulders, shiny and thick. My fingers found my hair and I frowned at its thinness. It wasn't as nice as Mum's. Not as thick or soft.

I slipped the photograph back into position and

checked the rest of the wallet, finding only bank cards. No clue about Mum.

Placing the wallet back exactly where I found it, I stared for a moment at Dad's spare car key. A stupid idea crossed my mind and I pushed it away and closed the drawer. No way. I couldn't drive. I'd had dreams about driving, yes, but driving for real, no.

I slid the drawer shut and it groaned in protest.

I froze and stared at the door. Listened and listened in case he was back. Nothing.

I returned my attention to the remaining drawers. The second one down I opened with extra care. It slid open without a sound and I looked inside, shocked to see a packet of condoms. Grimacing, I moved on to the third drawer; this held nothing but a dead woodlouse. Hastily closing the drawer, I tugged at the last one, which seemed a little heavier than the rest. The hinges squealed as it opened to reveal loads of paper – no - envelopes. Vanilla envelopes. Blank, vanilla envelopes. And a sweet, gorgeous fragrance. *Dolce Vita*. My perfume. The same one Mum wore. My lipstick print.

I grabbed the top envelope. The flap had been torn open, the paper shoved back inside with no care, leaving the letter inside crumpled.

My letter.

Something inside me tore. I snatched up the second envelope in the pile. This too had been opened, my letter read then shoved back. It was dated three days ago. It was the last letter I'd written to Mum.

Chills flared across my back. The next four letters were also from me to Mum. I had written six. Dad had not posted them. He'd not added a stamp. He'd not written an address. He'd made no attempt to post my letters. What he had done was open each envelope, read each letter and hide it away in his desk. He'd lied to me and broken his promise. He'd read my private letters to Mum.

In that moment, for just a beat of time, I felt like I could kill him.

The world tilted. My life felt like a lie. I thought I could trust him. I thought my mum would never leave. Both beliefs had been shredded. Did he even love me? Did he care? Did she? What kind of mother left their children without saying goodbye or giving some kind of explanation? What kind of father did something like this? How dare he read my letters.

I wanted to scream – find someone to tell what he'd done - but who was out there and how could I contact them? Mum was gone. Maggie was gone. Eddie wouldn't understand. I was basically on lockdown until I got better.

Half-blind with tears, I yanked open the thin drawer above the leg space. What else was he hiding from me?

I stopped: I'd talked about him in my letters. I'd described how distant and angry he was, how I felt uncomfortable around him and even a little afraid. I'd told Mum that if she wanted to leave him, Eddie and I would go with her, that I didn't want to live with this man who felt like a stranger. I'd mentioned how he ignored Eddie – and me. How he neglected us. In my last letter, I'd begged her to come and get us. To take us away from here. From him.

If he had read those letters…

I swallowed jerkily. Would my letters have hurt him or made him angry? He seemed angry. His hostility was clear, but I'd been unwilling to fully see the extent of it. I was angry, yes, but he was angrier. And he was finding it hard to control himself.

Struggling for air, I closed the drawer and backed away from the desk. I needed to leave. Now.

I bumped into the bookcase and glanced over my shoulder. There, leaning against the middle row of books was a small brown journal. My heart skipped. He was back. Footsteps; thudding closer, growing louder, and quicker,

94

as if he knew I was here.

Without a second thought, I grabbed the journal and dashed out of the room. In the hallway I froze, paralysed by fright, then shot into the kitchen towards the oven. Slipper soles clacking tile, I grabbed the wooden spoon, ripped off the lid and stirred the curry, once, twice.

Dad appeared at the other end of the room. I caught the jerk of his head and tensed, fingers tight on the spoon.

Fortunately, a moment later, he opened his office door and slipped inside, shutting himself in and me out.

Chapter 24

TWO YEARS AGO

ARRIETTY

I was home alone pretending to be sick. In a way, I kind of was. I felt sick when I thought about Mr Broughton dragging that woman by her arm, lovesick at the thought that he wasn't the perfect guy I thought he was. Isla said there was probably a reasonable explanation, but I couldn't think of one and neither could she.

I looked down at the pencil sketch I'd done of Mr B's face. With a growl I picked up a black marker and drew a big cross over the portrait. Looked like I was going to have to find someone else to crush on. I thought briefly about telling Mum what I'd seen, but the imaginary conversation that played out in my head ended with Mum telling me off for following my teacher and grounding me for a week.

A loud growling pulled my head up. I looked out of the window at the back garden. Shane was on the sit-down mower. He was topless even though it wasn't that hot. For a few moments, I admired his body: the broadness of his shoulders, the bronzed smoothness of his skin. A dragon tattoo spanned his back, the spiny wings unfurling across his shoulder blades like an extra pair of limbs. I wondered if Mr Broughton had any secret tattoos. Again, I tried to come up with a good excuse for his behaviour and why he'd gone to that dodgy house. Curiosity and frustration made me stand up, check my reflection, then hurry out of my room downstairs and out into the garden.

Shane was facing the house now. He clocked me and

gave a nod. I nodded back, hesitated then made my way towards him across the freshly cut grass. Overhead, the sky was silvery white, the sun in hiding. The air was two shades colder than mild, and goosebumps prickled my arms.

He stopped the mower, jumped down and grinned at me. His jeans hung so low that I could see the chiselled cut of his hip bones and the band of his Calvin Kleins. He'd lost the buzz cut and his sandy hair looked thick and glossy. Embarrassingly, butterflies danced in my tummy and I started to sweat. I avoided staring at his abs and stared instead into his sharp blue eyes. 'Hey. Want a drink?'

'Sure. Got any beer?'

I was taken aback by him wanting alcohol but realised that if he was tipsy he was more likely to open up about Mr B. 'Sure. Be right back.'

I jogged back up the garden and entered the house via the back door. I opened the fridge and pulled out a Brewdog – Dad's favourite. Turning, I found Shane standing right behind me, inside my personal space. I could smell his sweat and a musky aftershave. It actually smelled kind of nice. He looked healthier than the last time I'd seen him, and he didn't stink of weed, which was good. Maybe he was turning into a good boy after all.

'Bathroom?' he said.

'Oh. Upstairs, first door on the left,' I said.

I watched him stride out of the room, liking the swagger in his walk.

I looked down at myself. In my bleach-stained T-shirt and joggers I looked like something a dog might sick up. I hadn't even brushed my hair. Worried he'd be back any second, I sprinted out of the kitchen, through the middle of the house, up the staircase to my bedroom. I was yanking on a red crop over leather-look leggings when I heard the bathroom door open. I whipped a brush through my hair then stepped onto the landing to see Shane walking into my parents' bedroom. My heart somersaulted – what on earth was he up to?

I tiptoed along the landing and peeped around the door. Shane held a photograph of my mum in both hands. It was the one of her on the beach when she was about my age. She was lying on her side on the golden sand wearing a white bikini, one hand propping up her head, her long, dark hair cascading down her back, gleaming like silk beneath the Grecian sun. I watched, unable to look away as he replaced the photograph exactly where it had been. His gaze shifted to the bed. He cocked his head then wandered towards it, hands in his pockets, steps slow, as if what he was doing was completely normal. I almost said something. But I stopped, remembering that he had information about Mr B and Mum. Stuff I needed to know. Besides, it wasn't as if he was doing anything really bad like stealing my mum's jewellery or sniffing her underwear. He was probably just one of those people who got a kick out of nosing around other guys' houses.

I turned away from the bedroom door and crept down the stairs. Heart racing, I ran back through the house, turned right and hurried back to the fridge.

A few seconds later, Shane sauntered into the room.

I grabbed a beer out of the fridge and handed it to him. He crushed the first Brewdog in his large fist and dropped it on the counter with a grin.

'Thanks, Sweetheart,' he said, moving confidently to the bench. He opened the can, took a swig and tilted his head at me. 'Not having one?'

'I'm only fifteen,' I said, heat rising to my cheeks.

He laughed and swigged more beer. 'The first time I got pissed I was twelve. Stole a load of my old man's beers.'

'Really?'

'Yup.'

'How old are you now?'

'Twenty-three — though sometimes I feel twice that. So, what did you want to talk about?'

I poured myself a glass of water then joined him at the kitchen bench. It seemed intimate, just the two of us sitting there together.

'How did you know I wanted to talk?' I said.

He tapped his temple with his index finger. 'Not as dumb as I look.'

'Oh. Um, well, there is something I wanted to ask you. It's about Mr Broughton. I know he's your friend and well, I wondered -'

'What he and your mum are up to?' he said with a slight smile.

I frowned, head spinning at his words, but said, 'Yeah.'

He looked down and turned the can around and around. Condensation dripped onto the work surface. The giant copper clock ticked loudly into the silence. A strange smile played at his lips. I fidgeted with my red T-shirt.

He darted his head up, leaned across the table and gently moved my hair behind my ear. I flinched at his touch, half-scared, half-electrified. In my ear, he whispered, 'I'll tell you what I know if you promise me one thing.'

He pulled back, eyes locked on mine.

'What?' I said.

'That you'll come on Friday night.' He slid a colourful flyer across the table. Vertical ridges lined his fingernails but his hands were clean.

I picked it up. It was a handout advertising the local fair. I'd been before, but never on my own. I loved the fair, especially the hot doughnuts. A frisson of excitement scuttled through me followed by a beat of suspicion. 'Why?'

'Because it'll be fun. Also, your parents could be home any second. We don't want Mr or Mrs Black-Hawkins bursting in when we're discussing such a...*delicate* matter.'

'I'm not sure they'll let me go alone.'

'Bring your blonde friend with you if you want.' He downed the rest of his beer, hopped off the stool and headed for the back door. Over his shoulder, he said, 'Meet me at the waltzer at seven. Don't be late.'

I nodded, a mixture of emotions rendering me mute. Was Shane trustworthy? And what was going on between my mum and Mr B? One thing I knew for certain was that he didn't give me the ick anymore.

I licked my lips and stared out of the huge glass panes at Shane. With the agility of a gymnast, he mounted the mower and brought it back to life. The horrid growl ground against my temples and my mouth turned dry. I couldn't – wouldn't let myself think the worst. Mum loved Dad. She'd never do anything to hurt him. Then again…they'd slept in separate rooms the other night.

I put a hand to my abdomen. Anxiety churned my muscles like metal churning cream. Telling myself that no matter what, I needed to know the truth, I turned away from the window and headed back upstairs to text Isla about Friday night.

Chapter 25

NOW

My untouched bowl of curry sat on my dressing table. A fly landed on the coagulated sauce and began to eat – or lay eggs – I didn't know which and didn't care.

I sat cross-legged on my bed and looked down at Dad's journal. If I read this, I'd suffer more. Guilt had a nasty way of invading my mind and body and staying there for months on end. When sleep ran away, guilt slithered around like a slug, sliming my thoughts and making my chest ache. I already felt guilty for taking Dad's journal, let alone seeing what he'd written inside on those pages.

But he'd read my letters. He'd betrayed my trust in more ways than one. I didn't know if I'd ever be able to forgive him. The knowledge made my insides tear a little more.

A headache was building and I could tell it was here to stay. I took a sip of water. Exhaled a hot puff into the humid air.

Looking at my bedroom walls had a calming effect. There were photos of Isla. Us in our school uniform taking a selfie. Us in the living room, dressed up to go to the prom. Us having a picnic in the back garden, Eddie only two, holding a leaf up to show Isla. I remembered those moments but they were blurry, darkened by the ugly truth that life was good back then. I got to see people, go out, go to school, and Mum was here looking after me and Eddie, loving us, protecting us.

Dad had told my friends I couldn't use devices, but they had our address. They could have written to me. I'd nearly written to them loads of times but didn't have anything interesting to tell them, and the fact they'd not bothered to write to me hurt more than I'd ever thought it would. They were probably busy with their lives. Both were still at school doing their A levels but I'd had to leave because of my chronic fatigue. I'd repeat the school year when I got better. Dad said the more I rested, the quicker I'd feel my usual self. And I did suffer from strange bouts of exhaustion. As much as I tried to deny it, Dad and the doctor were right: I wasn't well.

My gaze hovered on my favourite picture. Mum had drawn it; a pencil sketch of my baby feet. At the bottom right-hand corner of the canvas, she'd written: *For my perfect little girl, Arrietty, who I love so much.* Her handwriting was so familiar, her words distant.

My chin trembled and I grabbed one of my fluffy cushions and hugged it to my chest. The hole in my heart was widening.

I needed to find Mum. Help her. She'd never leave like this unless something was wrong or…I couldn't – *wouldn't* – complete the thought.

A wave of terror washed over me, blistering as pan oil. One day she was here then she was gone. Vanished without a trace, just like that. What if…

No.

I stared at Dad's journal. It was in my hands and I didn't remember picking it up. The leather melted in my fingers and the smell of dead, dried-out skin tickled my nose.

I moved to flip back the front cover and guilt pinched my chest with razor-sharp nails. I couldn't do it. Dad had read my letters but I wasn't him. The journal might say something about why Mum had left or where she was, but I couldn't make myself turn the page. Guilt like that would be too great a burden for me to bear. There had to be another way.

I hid the journal under my pillow then left the room to brush my teeth. Tomorrow, I would find out what had happened to Mum, but I would discover the truth a different way. As soon as the coast was clear, I'd put the stupid journal back before he noticed it was missing.

*

On the landing, I stopped at the sound of Dad's voice. He was talking to someone – Mum? Was she back?

I dashed to the banister and peered down into the vast, shadowy living space. Lit by one table lamp, Dad sat in his armchair facing the black night sky holding his mobile to his ear. Disappointment made me queasy. It wasn't Mum. No-one was here. He was talking to someone on the phone. Maybe, just maybe, he was talking to her.

I crouched down and watched through the wooden poles, listening as hard as I could.

Dad went quiet. The person on the other end of the line spoke for a long time. I stared at the black thatch of his head. His skull was large. What was going on inside his brain? What was he thinking? Who was he talking to? I wanted to know. Needed to know. I strained my ears, caught snippets of white noise, but nothing that could help me.

Finally, he growled, 'I don't know how much more I can take. Sometimes I'm so angry, I worry I'll -'

Silence. A scrap of white noise.

'No. No way. I'm not that bad. I'm just -'

Tapping knuckles against the chair.

'And you're absolutely sure this is the right course of action?'

More tapping. A sigh. 'Yeah. I know. Deep down I know you're right. It's not worth it.'

White noise.

'All right. Yeah.' He hung up.

For a long time, he sat in absolute silence, motionless, so still he could have been dead. I watched, skin prickling all over.

He jerked to his feet, lurched forward, picked up the glass coffee table as if it weighed no more than Eddie, and launched it at the wall. The table shattered into a million sparkling fragments that resembled fallen stars. He stood and stared at the destruction, immobile once more, chest heaving. 'What a *fucking* mess.'

I gasped.

His head snapped around.

Eddie's voice echoed towards me and I ran to his bedroom.

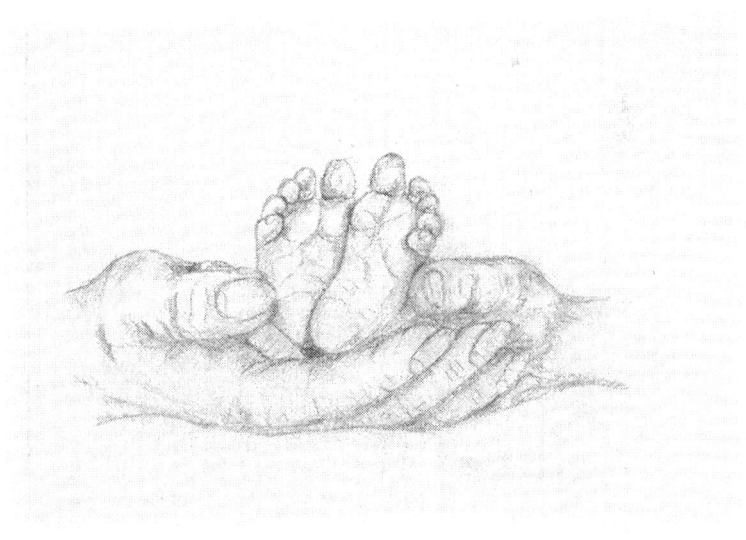

Chapter 26

TWO YEARS AGO

SOFIA

'Welcome to my humble abode,' Hugo said. He looked good in a mint-coloured shirt and cream chinos. His white hair had been gelled and parted in the middle, giving him a schoolboy look that was unexpectedly endearing.

I echoed his smile, wishing my teeth were as white as his. 'Thank you so much for inviting me.'

'You're most welcome, my dear Sofia.'

I followed him into an expansive foyer. Art smothered the walls, choking and impressive in its coverage. Most works were gold-framed pencil sketches of sparsely clad young women in varying poses. Some were almost obscene, revealing far too much.

I cleared my throat and pointed at one of the less crude drawings. 'These are interesting. Who's the artist?'

Hugo raised an eyebrow and puffed out his chest, making his shirt stretch unflatteringly. 'That would be me. You like?'

'What? Really? Wow – you're really talented. They're stunning.' Not to my taste, at all, but I wasn't going to confess that.

'Thank you. I like to capture my sexual conquests in more ways than one before they realise I'm a dirty old man and scarper.' He belly-laughed at my startled expression and added, 'I'm just pulling your leg, Sofia.'

I managed a fake smile and told myself to relax. He didn't want me for that – he wanted me for my art.

'Let's give you a tour before we settle down to business, shall we?'

'I'd love that. You have a truly beautiful home.'

'I know,' he said with a wink.

Hugo beckoned for me to follow him into a vast living room styled tastefully with vine-patterned wallpaper in sage and cream, leather settees and ornate furnishings. A grand piano sat at the back left of the room in front of a gigantic bookcase.

'You play?' I said.

'No – it's for show,' he said with another wink.

He led me around the ground floor, pointing out some more reserved artwork, watercolours that mimicked Monet. I commented on these, expressing my admiration. They were the work of another local artist – a woman by the name of Olive Brook.

'I had these commissioned ten years ago. Sadly, Olive moved away shortly after completion. She was a real firecracker, that one,' he sighed, scratching the back of his neck. 'But now that I've found you, all in the world is good again!'

He led me up a creaky, oak staircase. Again, the walls were lined with art. This time, Picasso-esque faces in black and white that were distinctly eerie.

'My work again,' he said over his shoulder before I could ask.

'They're splendid. So dynamic and, I hope you don't mind me saying, a little unnerving.'

He chuckled. 'I have a rather warped mind, don't I?'

'No, no. It's just…you seem to be able to turn your hand to anything. And your taste is so eclectic. I've never known anything like it.'

He stopped on the top step and turned to look down at me. His smile was gone. There was a certain sadness in his eyes. 'I get bored easily I suppose. Did you know I've been married three times?'

I tried to hide my shock and said, 'Do you have any children?'

'No,' he said rather sharply, 'I'm too selfish for that.'

An awkwardness tainted the air between us.

He turned away, barked out a laugh and beckoned me to follow.

We moved along a lengthy landing stopping at each bedroom room so that Hugo could show off more of his own artwork and the work of others he'd commissioned over the years, every artist of whom was female.

'And this, my dear Sofia, is the grand master bedroom. The room I wish you to decorate.'

'Decorate?' I scanned the enormous room; the four-poster bed, plush navy carpet, and white, clean walls. The scent of fresh paint flavoured the air.

'Why yes,' he said, wrapping a heavy arm around my shoulders, 'I want you to draw directly onto the walls, to enliven this blank canvas with your own exceptional vision.'

'Oh.' My mind whirled with the strangeness of his proposition, yet a delicious shiver of anticipation sparked in my heart making my fingertips tingle with the urge to draw.

Hugo hugged me closer and turned his face to mine. This close, I could smell a faint sourness on his breath, and see a mass of fine, red veins scattered across his nose. His nostrils flared, and he grinned, displaying those too-white teeth. For a worrying second, I wondered if he was inhaling my perfume. I'd spritzed on Dolce Vita – Alec's favourite – just before leaving home. Now, as his gaze lingered on my neck, I wished I'd not bothered.

He continued to hold me to him, and my muscles tensed. His body felt hard and strong against my side, his spicy aftershave overwhelming. His hand moved down my back to rest an inch above my right hip. Inside, I squirmed. I wanted to pull away but didn't. I couldn't appear cold or ungrateful. Hugo was clearly a tactile man - the opposite to Alec. I needed to loosen up. If I didn't, I might lose this job, and we needed the money.

After a playful smile, he released me and gestured towards the white walls.

'I want you all over my room,' he said brightly, eyes glinting, clapping his hands like a little boy.

I smiled and followed his gaze, glad we were back to business. Ideas were already fluttering around my head like escapee butterflies, each one more intricate and intense than the last. My fingers twitched.

'I've never done anything like this before, but I'm up for the challenge. Is there a particular theme you have in mind? And a deadline – when would you like the work completed?'

'I want it to be a celebration of the human form – male and female – hands, feet, buttocks, thighs, the whole shebang! Oh, and take as long as you need. I'm thinking £200 pounds a day or thereabouts. How does that sound to you? And, of course, you're more than welcome to stay here to avoid the commute. I have eight free rooms for you to choose from.'

I was taken aback by his generosity but knew there was no way I could accept an offer to stay overnight. Alec would have a fit at the idea and then there was Eddie and Arrietty to think about. The longest I had ever been away from Eddie was two nights.

'Thank you for the offer, but I wouldn't want to intrude on you like that. If you're happy for me to get here for about 9.30 and stay until 5pm each day, that would be perfect.'

'Absolutely,' he said nodding vigorously. A delighted smile lit up his face making him look ten years younger and more charming than ever. 'When can you start?'

I shook his hand and smiled. 'Tomorrow.'

As I walked back to my car, I pushed down the

memory of his index finger stroking the back of my hand in a highly inappropriate way, and pictured myself cracking on with the project. I couldn't wait to get started.

Chapter 27

NOW

Dad's journal lay beneath my head throbbing like an infected gash. I imagined its words carving through my flesh, cutting past bone, infecting me with a darkness that made its bed and never left. Guilt pulsed and the wound grew deeper, the urge to read his private thoughts more intense. I had stolen his journal; he had read my letters. I wasn't a tit-for-tat type of person, but I needed answers and I would probably find them inside that little brown book. I could feel myself wavering; angel versus devil. Good versus evil. The kind, compassionate, happy-go-lucky me versus the frightened, desperate, confused version. My morals were shifting, my priorities unfamiliar territory. Mum leaving was changing me too. I never, ever would have considered stealing someone's journal before this – but my mum could be in trouble. She might need my help. I couldn't bury my head in the sand, not when it came to this.

What would Mum do?

Read it.

No, she wouldn't. She'd put it back.

I wanted the truth. I needed answers. And yet, if I did this, I'd lose another part of myself. Already, I felt like a shadow. A girl living a half-life. A hermit with no friends, nowhere to go and no-one to confide in. I had Eddie, but he wasn't enough. I needed more. I needed my mum back. If she was around, Dad wouldn't seem so…strange. Things would go back to normal. Mum would restore order and sanity to the house. Our home would feel warm

111

and happy again, and this constant ache in my chest would disappear.

The journal was in my hands. My fingers trembled. I touched the soft leather cover, the word *Journal*. I'd never kept a diary. Neither had Mum as far as I knew. I was surprised Dad kept one. It didn't seem like the kind of thing he'd do. Then again, he wasn't the man I thought he was. I was beginning to think I never knew him at all. Maybe Mum had kept his demons at bay. Maybe he was a demon Mum had kept at bay from us. When I was little, I believed my parents told me everything, but they had their secrets too. Were there problems in their relationship that I wasn't aware of?

I thought about his phone call. He'd said *I'm not that bad.* But what if he was? What if Mum leaving had opened the door to a crazy part of his brain that had been closed before? What if he was unstable? Disturbed in some way? Smashing the table was an insane thing to do, not to mention violent. He'd talked about being worried he'd do something. That he was so angry – too angry to control himself. And I'd felt his rage. I felt it every time he looked at me. Like I was responsible for Mum leaving. As though I was the cause of every bad thing that had ever happened to him. What if, one day, he couldn't control his fury anymore? What if he let it out on Eddie?

The thought froze my blood. A vision so horrific I had to fight with every ounce to push it away, played in my mind's eye. No. Dad wouldn't hurt Eddie. I was letting my worries spiral out of control. My imagination was going into overdrive and that was never a good thing. I needed Mum to even me out, tell me the rational side of the story.

But she's not here, is she?

I tore at my nail, tasted blood, winced.

Put it back. Put it back. Put it back.

It was wrong of me to think so badly of Dad. Wrong of me to take his journal. Awful of me to even consider reading his private thoughts.

Shame surged like a tidal wave and my angel lunged forward and shoved the devil off my shoulder. He clung on with tight, black claws, taunting and teasing despite his perilous position. My angel stamped on his fingers and he let go. I let out a huge, shaky sigh, mind made up.

Cringing with guilt, I got out of bed, determined to find the key to Dad's office and put the journal back. It had to be tonight or there was a huge chance he'd go into his office tomorrow morning and realize it was missing, and that was something I needed to avoid at all costs.

Chapter 28

TWO YEARS AGO

ARRIETTY

The fair was in full swing when Isla and I arrived. Music from different rides fought with one another, screams of fear and delight filled the darkening air, and neon lights radiated off the wide eyes of tons of little children stuffing their faces with candy floss and sweet treats. Eddie would have been utterly blown away by the whole thing. Part of me wished he was here, that I could try to win him one of the cuddly minions from the ring toss or buy him a huge cloud of candy floss while he giggled with glee, but another, bigger part of me yearned to talk to Shane and find out what was going on between my mum and Mr Broughton.

Isla hooked her elbow through mine and marched me towards the waltzer, her fruity perfume wafting up my nose and making it itch. We'd both dressed up for the occasion, knowing fit boys from our school would probably be here. I wore a pink crop and tiny denim shorts, and Isla wore a grey crop and a denim skirt. We'd used fake tan, curled our hair into loose waves and applied a ton of makeup – far more than Dad would have let me wear. Luckily, we'd got ready at Isla's house, and her mum – who wasn't bothered about how much makeup we wore – had dropped us off. She'd given us money to get a taxi back and I was sleeping over. Isla's mum was recovering from chemo so needed an early night. Our curfew was 10.30pm. If we weren't back within a ten-minute window, we'd be grounded for a *month* – our mums had chatted over the phone and agreed the penalty, much to our horror and outrage – the end of year school disco was in two weeks' time – there was no way we were missing that. My dad had also warned me that he'd confiscate my phone for a week, which didn't bear thinking about.

We reached the waltzer and looked about for Shane. People bustled past us making it hard to see. I stood on tiptoe and turned around slowly, scanning the sea of bodies. I'd applied so much mascara that I had to squint through my gluey eyelashes. It was really annoying.

'Shane's pretty hot, even if he's a bit weird,' Isla said, checking her makeup in her phone.

'You haven't seen him topless,' I said.

She pouted and applied more lip gloss. 'Oh – there he is!'

'Okay, be cool,' I said, exhaling nervously.

Shane was standing at the back of the waltzer a few metres away from the edge of the field. Behind him stood the woods, which looked particularly dark and creepy beneath the moonless night. He wasn't alone.

'Who's that with him?' Isla whispered.

I shrugged. The guy he was with was shorter than Shane with gingery hair and a stocky body. Like Shane, tattoos covered his arms. Both guys wore jeans and slim-fit T-shirts that clung to their muscles in a way I liked. They held cans of Stella. Shane had a black backpack slung over one shoulder.

'Ah, here they are. Girls, this is my mate, Johnny. Johnny, meet Arrietty and – er?'

'Isla,' I said.

'Hey,' Johnny said, not meeting my eyes. Closer now, I saw he had greasy skin, a mass of yellow heads on his chin and weirdly pale green eyes.

I was disappointed that Shane wasn't alone – talking about Mum wasn't going to be as easy if his friend was around.

Johnny jerked his head towards the woods and said, 'Fancy hanging out for a bit?'

Shane shrugged and raised his eyebrows at me. I shrugged and glanced at Isla, wanting her to say no. I'd envisaged us going on rides, eating tons of sticky sweets and getting high on sugar and fun, as well as getting a moment to discuss Mr B and Mum with Shane. Unfortunately, Isla thrust her size A boobs out and gave Shane a cute smile. 'Sure. Why not?'

'Good girl,' Johnny said, licking his lips in a creepy way.

He already gave me the ick, but Isla seemed to like the attention. Linking arms with me, she tugged me over to the kissing gate. In my ear, she whispered, 'I like Johnny. He's short but he's got cool eyes.'

Rather you than me. 'He's way older than us.'

'That doesn't stop you fancying Mr B.'

She had me there. 'Good point.'

Shane and Johnny trudged after us. Isla half-dragged me further and further into the woods. A slimy, hot feeling writhed in my tummy like a baby alien. We were so far from the fair now that the tinkle of laughter was gone. Only a very faint wisp of fairground music reached my ears. It was so dark now that Isla switched on her phone light. We weaved in and out of monstrously tall trees, ankles snagged by thorns, arms scratched at, clothes tugged and nipped. Finally, we found a clearing with a strange, mini Stonehenge arrangement of upended logs.

'Perfect,' Isla squealed. She kicked over the smallest log, giggled and dragged it away from its position, breaking the circle.

My skin prickled and I couldn't help feeling that she shouldn't have done that. The writhing in my belly intensified. I gasped as pain rippled through my abdomen.

No-one noticed. Isla patted the log beside her and

Johnny sat down. Shane had copied Isla and patted the log next to him.

The pain passed as quickly as it had come. Shaking off the feeling that Isla had set something bad in motion, I perched on the rough bark beside Shane. Johnny slid out a bottle of vodka and passed it to Isla. She glanced at me through the darkness as Shane used a lighter to create a fire in the centre of our little gathering. She looked ghostly, her eyes huge as saucers in the flickering flame-light. I shook my head to say *don't do it*, but the bottle was already at her lips. She took a swig of the clear liquid then scrunched up her face into a hilariously, grossed-out expression. We all laughed when, after a few seconds of coughing, she said, 'Well fuck me, that's nasty.'

The tension seemed broken. Isla was tipsy from one swallow and motor-mouthed about how much school dragged, how she couldn't wait to leave, and what was it like Johnny, to be out in the real world? I felt for her, and understood why she'd caved and given in to the temptation to drink. Her mum had suffered immensely the last few months, and Isla had held it together. It was hardly surprising she was letting loose tonight.

When Shane offered me the bottle of vodka I declined. He laughed, glugged a load without even wincing then offered me a drag on his cigarette. I declined that too. He laughed again, but not in a nasty way. 'I forget how young and innocent you are. Not sure I can say the same for Isla though.'

Isla was trying to get Johnny to dance with her. Her playlist sounded tinny coming out of her phone, and her favourite song was on; the one she always said she wanted to have on when she had her first proper snog.

Reluctantly, Johnny stood and allowed her to twirl him around. He was clumsy and drunk too, which made for a funny show.

I looked directly into Shane's eyes. 'So, Mr Broughton

and my mum…what's the deal?'

My heart drummed as I waited for him to speak. Annoyingly, as if enjoying my torture, he took a long, slow drink of vodka then said, 'I dunno. You'll have to ask your mum. All I know is, James is a charmer. Can charm the pants off anyone he turns his eye to if you get my drift?'

I wrinkled my nose. 'My mum would never…I mean, she's married! And she loves my dad.'

Shane raised an eyebrow and drunkenly slammed the bottle of vodka onto the ground. 'You sure about that? I heard them arguing the other day. Not 'xactly what I'd call a match made in heaven. And your mum…she's a right MILF…right bloke comes knocking –'

'She's not like that,' I said hotly.

'Then there's that Hugo wanker she's creeping off to see.'

'Who?'

'That arty bloke – creepy as fuck you ask me.'

'What about him?'

'Dangerous. She shouldn't mess with him. She don't know what he's capable of.'

'Who's dangerous? Mr B? Or the art guy?'

Shane frowned in an effort to focus, lunged for the vodka and managed to knock it over. 'Shit!'

He went for the bottle again, but I grabbed it and held it out of his reach.

'Give it,' he half-growled.

'Not until you tell me the truth.'

'What truth? Like I said, Alec's got a temper on him. I wouldn't mess him, that's for sure. And your mum's hot. Great arse, great tits, what's not to like?' He leaned close to me and slurred into my face, 'Few years' time, you'll be even hotter.' He gave what he probably thought was a sexy grin, then snatched the bottle out of my hand and downed the contents.

'You're not making sense,' I said.

He picked something out of his eye, belched garlicky fumes, patted my thigh, then lurched upright and staggered away into the woods. I marched after him, angry and confused, not sure what to believe or think, what to be worried about, whether everything that came out of his mouth was crap or there was some truth to what he said. I remembered how rough Mr Broughton had been with that woman when Isla and I had followed him home, and I thought about how angry Dad could get. I didn't know anything about this other man, but if Shane thought he was dangerous...

I reached out to grab Shane's shoulder and realised he was relieving himself.

Feeling dirty and anxious, I checked my phone. It was 10.33pm. Past curfew. Crap.

Chapter 29

NOW

I dropped the journal and it thudded to the floor like a grenade. Pulse blasting, I grabbed it up, squeezed the buttery leather in both hands and sprinted down the stairs, breathless when I reached the bottom. Pausing, I glanced up into the gloom; no Dad. I was safe, my stupid fumble hadn't roused him from sleep.

My tummy pitched as I ran through the obscenely long living space, along the central thoroughfare past the vast dining area. I stopped outside his office. Tried the door. It was locked.

I looked around, inhaled shakily. The house was quiet and gloomy. I swiped perspiration off my forehead, licked my lips and reasoned. He'd keep the key somewhere close – kitchen, maybe.

Sweaty-fingered, I flicked on the oven light and searched the kitchen drawer – the one that housed every bit of excess crap you should throw away but never did. There was no key, only the usual detritus; receipts, elastic bands, paper clips, shopping lists, scrunchies, a plastic dinosaur with its tail lopped off, a battered peach lipstick. Mum's lipstick. I clutched it awhile, aware I was losing time, caring little. Something about holding that golden tube warmed me. Thinking too long about her make-up bag, I stuffed the lipstick in my pyjama pocket, closed the drawer and switched off the oven light. Nowhere else to look in here meant next stop: dining area. There was the grey dresser. The grey chest of drawers. A slight chance. Worth a check.

In the dining room, I switched on the flamingo lamp – Mum's birthday present from me and Eddie two years ago. Beneath the bird's metal feet, lay three drawers. Top: old magazines. *Vogue. Good Housekeeping. Women's Health.* Middle: wrapping paper, bows, tags, sparkly tape. Bottom: a letter writing set, unopened set of tealights and earphones with crud in the buds.

I turned to the huge dresser. A memory of painting it with Mum flashed. Up and gone. Lightning flashes and rolling thunder. Her hand, my hand. Grey paint. Laughter peals ringing through the house. I tried to hold on to the memory, pull out the moment, extend the feeling, but it vanished.

Pain squeezed. I told myself to calm down. The pang of loss weakened but lingered, pressing tight, gripping for too long.

I opened the left-hand cupboard knowing what I'd find. Mum's orchid tea set. A gift from Grandma the year before she died when I was just five, too young to remember her and yet something lingered as my fingers brushed cold china. Grandma always smelt of vanilla. Yes. I knew that much. They'd not been close, she and Mum, not like us. From bits I'd picked up here and there, I knew Grandma had been a cold woman, someone hard to love.

I wondered then if Dad had noticed it. My memory. There was something more wrong with me than bad fatigue, I felt it more with every passing day. Tiny pieces were missing from my mind. It felt like somebody had smudged parts of my brain with dirty fingers.

With a frown, I moved on. The right-hand cupboard was filled with random mugs; souvenirs from trips abroad when my parents were young. I picked up one with a wooden Buddha on, stared at him blankly then put it back. There was no key here.

I closed the door and rifled through each of the drawers in the bottom half of the dresser. No luck. A yawn cracked my jaw. I rubbed my back and headed to the living room.

The room looked like an immense black cave. I hesitated before flicking on the small lamp beside Dad's armchair. Not much light emanated due to the charcoal shade, so it was safe to say it wouldn't travel far enough to slip under the crack beneath the master bedroom door.

Light on, the huge panels revealed the garden and the velvet sky that loomed above. The stars were out tonight, the moon a slice of silver. Vast as the ocean, outside had never felt so oppressive and endless. I shrank away, turned my back on the walls and searched the drawer of the smallest of three coffee tables. These were mahogany, not glass. The remains of the table Dad had smashed were gone; the glass cleared. No trace of his temper fit remained. If I hadn't borne witness, I'd have come down in the morning, noticed the glass table was gone and wondered. I probably wouldn't have even bothered to ask. But he knew I'd seen him throw the table. When he'd stared up at me, he'd glowered. No guilt. No shame. Just pure vexation, as if it was my fault that he'd lost his temper and smashed up a table.

I swore, rubbed my arms, placed the journal on the arm of Dad's chair and kept looking. The nest of tables revealed more magazines, five coasters, a couple more of Eddie's plastic figures. No key.

I ran my fingernails over my tense scalp and gritted my teeth, felt enamel scrape. This was useless. A waste of time. I racked my brain and...pop! I hadn't checked the most obvious place yet – the big key-shaped row of hooks on the wall next to the front door. Tutting at my stupidity, I flicked off the lamp, moved out of the living room, through the coffin of the house, took a left at Dad's office and followed the hallway up to the front door. There, on the wall above the shoe rack, was the key holder. I stared: Dad's bunch of **keys** was on the first hook. I plucked the ring off the wall and identified one that looked like it might be the key to his office. The other keys were clear: his car key and house key. Excited, I stopped. Stared at the ring of keys on the end of the holder. My jaw dropped.

Mum's keys.

Icy sweat soaked my spine as I lifted them off the hook. Mum didn't have a car so there was no car key but her house key, studio key and gold S-shaped keyring were all there. S for Sofia. A stocking filler from me a long time ago.

My head created a list, each item a kick to my already winded gut.

Things Mum Left Without

1. Toothbrush
2. Make-up bag
3. Clothes
4. Shoes
5. Keys

I sagged against the wall and stared at nothing. For a long, strange while I felt like I watched someone who wasn't me, a girl who sagged and deflated like a punctured balloon, hollowed out by longing and fear.

The girl's face paled to ghoul-white and her small hands curled into balls. She replaced both sets of keys, span around and beat her fists against the wall until pain forced her to stop. Then she sank to the floor and wrapped her shaking arms around her knees and hid her face. Her shoulders shuddered and she remained on the ground like a little lost orphan for a long, long time, so long that when she stood up, a head rush attacked and she lost her balance and staggered into the wall.

I no longer felt the urge to put Dad's journal back.

Anger rode my veins, hot and unforgiving, murdering any remaining twinges of guilt. I strode away from the front door, fists clenched. Dad read my letters. Mum was gone and he knew where and why and how but he wasn't saying. I needed to know. I'd had enough of his lies.

In the living room, I switched on the light and reached for the arm of Dad's chair where I knew I'd left it, but the journal was gone.

Part 2

NOW

Chapter 30

I woke in the night with my heart in my throat and stared into the pitch black of my bedroom, arms frozen to my sides beneath the cover, skin soaked in sweat.

A nightmare was retreating, creeping down into my subconscious mind, recoiling like a vampire from sunlight, yet leaving its toxic taste injected into my heart like venom.

For some indefinable reason, I clung on and tugged the nightmare back.

I squeezed my eyes shut and fought to re-live the story, certain there was something there, something important. An image or idea that would tell me something vital. A sliver of information I needed to know.

I concentrated hard and kept pulling.

Little by little, soft, slippery shadows rose, taunting and teasing, just within reach. I gripped them with both hands and held on for dear life even as they tried to slip away.

Mr Broughton, my art teacher, smiling...playing with himself...watching while someone – a man I can't see - pins Mum down on the table in her art studio. I'm watching from above and below, almost like I have two heads; it's terrifying – I/we can't move and he's about to...

It was gone. *Shit.*

I gulped a load of water and tried to understand what, if anything, the weird dream meant. I used to have a crush on Mr B, so I didn't think it wasn't that odd for me to have a sexy dream about him, but the fact that another man was in it and Mum was being attacked while James Broughton watched was, well, disgusting, not to mention superwarped. Mum knew James from her babysitting days, and they'd bumped into each other at the gallery a while back.

They'd met up a few times after that because he was a fan of her art...why was I dreaming about him now? And who was that other man in the dream?

I rolled onto my side, unable to shake the feeling that my brain was trying to help me understand what had happened to Mum. Mr B's good-looking face flashed into my mind. Could he have something to do with her disappearance? Was that why Dad was so angry? Was that what he was hiding from me?

*

Eddie and I were eating breakfast in the kitchen when Dad emerged from his office. He hesitated then strode into the room. Halfway across the vast space, he stopped, put his hands on his hips and stared at me. After what felt like forever, he strode over to the island and hovered next to my little brother. The atmosphere shifted. For a second, I thought of a giant leech, sucking happiness from the room like blood from skin. Eddie looked around at him and smiled. Dad ignored him.

Rage came, hot as a rash. I wanted to scream at him to smile at my little brother, to make Eddie feel loved for just one second. I also wanted to demand to know why he'd read my letters and hadn't sent them, but I didn't want to upset Eddie and I was too tired to fight. A sleepless night had left me zombified, barely able to function let alone attempt a heated debate. And anxiety slinked into my fingers, making them shake; he knew I'd taken his journal. He was probably even angrier than me.

He raked his hand through his hair and moved to the sink where he pressed his knuckles into the counter and stared out at the back garden.

The sun was a golden pearl on a pristine canvas; the one thing keeping me afloat. I was glad it was summer rather than winter. Just thinking about short days and cold nights brought a chill to my bones. Imagining them without Mum made my stomach ball into a knot so tight I pushed my toast away. I stared at Dad's broad back as he looked out at the pearly sky.

'What's he doing?' Eddie whispered, darting fearful glances from me to Dad.

I shrugged, grabbed a wet wipe and dabbed milk off his chin. I smiled for the both of us and smoothed his hair. Eddie dropped his head and focused on his cereal. No matter how hard he tried, milk always leaked out of the corners of his lips. It was sweet but annoying. I reminded myself he was only four and mopped him up again. He looked up and stuck out his tongue; a chocolate hoop looped the end. I wrinkled my nose and poked his tongue. He giggled then shoved his hand over his mouth and glanced at Dad.

I followed his gaze. Dad had turned to face us. His stare was so intense that I had to look away. 'What?'

'I'm taking you to see someone about your memory.'

My heart leapt and stung at the same time. 'You've noticed?'

He nodded, scraped a hand through his hair. His Adam's apple bobbed. He licked his lips, sour-faced, unsmiling. 'The doctor thinks it's a good idea.'

I thought about it. It wasn't as though I had a choice. He said he was taking me, which meant he'd already decided.

In my head I phrased and rephrased my next question. 'Does Mum know?'

'No.'

'Please tell us where she is. Take us to see her. We miss her. We need to know she's OK.'

His voice was so dead I flinched. 'I've already told you I can't.'

'But why? I don't understand.'

'It will only upset you, make you feel worse.'

'It won't. I'll handle it. I'm not a little girl anymore. I can cope.'

Eddie tugged my sleeve. I looked down. He was on the verge of tears. My heart hammered. I wanted to press further but the conversation was upsetting Eddie. I bit my lip and flapped the top of my T-shirt, suddenly too hot. Dizziness swirled. I murmured, 'When?'

'Now.'

*

I strapped Eddie in while Dad tapped his knuckles against the steering wheel and clenched his jaw so hard I thought it might break.

Instead of sitting up front beside Dad, I sat in the back with Eddie and held his hand. My little brother's legs kicked and hopped with excitement. It was the first time either of us had left the grounds for two long weeks. About time too.

I felt high as well. My body felt lighter for being a hundred metres away from the house. Air-con blasted into the car offering welcome relief. A smile played at my lips as I watched Eddie point at a field dotted with sheep. My brother began to whisper 'Baa Baa Black Sheep' but Dad put jazz music on and turned the volume so loud that it drowned out Eddie's voice. I scowled at the back of Dad's head and gripped the seat so hard that I cut grooves into the cream leather.

Telling myself to calm down, I watched the passing fields and let my mind drift to happier times when Mum was around – us playing on the sand on holiday, building castles, eating sandy ice-cream, Dad smearing cream on my nose, on Mum's and Eddie's noses too, and belly-laughing, the sound so rich and happy and contagious that we all fell about giggling.

I blinked and the vision morphed into a grey, blurry

room. Panic skewered my ribcage, and I whipped my head to Eddie. He was grinning at me, cheeks rosy. I put a hand to my racing chest. The longing was there again, thick and aching and stabbing all over. I needed my mum back. Eddie needed her too. When this was over, I'd go back home and do whatever it took to find out the truth. Until then, I would go along with Dad's decision, try to be a good girl.

I turned from my brother, looked out of the window. Jazz throbbed. Dad's knuckles tapped and cracked. I ached and stared and tried not to worry.

Fields turned into houses and industry razed all beauty from the view. Smoke curled into the air from a factory chimney spoiling the sky. Scruffy houses lined both sides of the road, watching on with peeling faces, their front gardens messy, littered with overflowing bins and rubbish. An elderly man staggered along the road rather than the pavement. Dad cursed and overtook with an unnecessary roar of acceleration. I turned and watched the old man swear with two gnarly fingers. I wanted to high-five him and mirror his sentiment behind Dad's head, but worried Eddie might notice.

And then there was a woman – short, slim with long black hair shining in the sun. For a split second, I saw Mum and my chest spasmed and I dared to hope, but Dad drew alongside her and I saw she was younger, more my age and pregnant, her bump perfectly formed, hand resting on it as she walked.

I cleared my throat and battled a wave of longing.

Dad turned and took the Merc up a steep hill, away from the rough neighbourhood and out once more into meadows and fresh, unspoilt air.

Eddie grabbed my shoulder and pointed at a field with a handful of cows and a calf whose mum stood by, close enough to keep watch. I smiled then withdrew into myself, keen now to reach wherever it was we were going and get this whole thing over with.

Up and up we climbed, past woods, under a bridge, over a river, along a winding road so narrow I feared for our safety. A tractor could come and swipe us from the earth within moments; a van or a lorry might even try to traverse this country road - blind to the Merc's speedy passage, a driver fiddling with the radio or sneezing or squinting because of the sun wouldn't have time to notice, kill the engine, avoid impact.

Eddie was oblivious to the danger while my buttocks gripped the seat and my palms sweated.

Finally, Dad cut the engine plunging the car into uncomfortable silence. 'Her name's Rose Weatherby. Your appointment's half an hour long. I'll wait here.'

I stared at the large yellow house and battled the desire to ask Eddie if he was going to be OK staying in the car with Dad. I had to get this done, and it was only thirty minutes. Eddie would be fine. I kissed his cheek and clambered out of the car. He followed my movements with large, sad eyes.

The second I was outside, Dad switched on the ignition. Jazz burst from the Merc sending two pigeons fluttering out of the apple tree in Rose Weatherby's front garden and making my tummy flipflop.

I opened the white gate and approached the house with Dad's eyes burning my back.

Chapter 31

A middle-aged woman opened the door and smiled at me. She was big-boned and attractive, dressed in a simple yellow smock with her feet bare. I tried to smile at this stranger who was about to ask me personal questions about myself and my life, tried to bury worries about Mum. Both acts were impossible.

'Please come in,' she said, her voice husky and warm, "don't worry about your shoes. I'm Rose. It's lovely to meet you.'

I nodded, all too aware that she was probably analysing everything I said and did.

I followed her up a wide hallway painted lemon, across white-washed floorboards. The house smelt clean, like freshly laundered clothes. The walls were smothered with photographs of two beautiful Labradors, one chocolate, one golden. I admired them as I walked and looked for signs of dogs but saw none. As if reading my mind, she said, 'Ah yes. Millie and Bruno are out at the moment, otherwise they'd be barking the house down trying to say hello.'

She led me into a large room with a golden carpet and two peacock-patterned tub chairs. Between the chairs sat a small round table on which stood a glass jug filled with iced water, two glasses and a bowl of mints. The cream walls were blank save for two framed qualifications.

Rose gestured to the chairs and I sat on the left facing the window which looked out onto open fields. She sat down, crossed her long legs and arranged her skirt so that it fell evenly across her knees. With a warm smile, she leaned forward, plucked a mint out of the bowl and popped it on her tongue before offering me one. I shook my head and fidgeted with my shorts, not sure how to behave or what to say.

She filled our glasses from the jug, settled her skirt again and rested her hands on her lap. Her nails were manicured in pearl pink. I glanced down at my own, which were rimmed with charcoal, and curled my fingers inwards.

Rose smiled revealing straight teeth. Her eyes were slightly bulbous, like two pale brown acorns, her lips plump and pink. 'So, the first thing I want you to know is that everything we talk about will be strictly confidential. The only reason I would ever break that pact is if I thought you posed a threat to your own or another's safety.'

I nodded. Picked up my glass and took a sip.

'Before we begin, I'd like to tell you a little about myself.'

'OK.' I waited, leg jiggling, expecting her to reel off a factual spiel about her education and qualifications.

'I'm forty-two, and recently, but happily, I might add, divorced. My husband was a controlling man with anger problems, so I'm well out of that relationship!' She laughed, and I smiled, uncomfortable with the personal nature of her words – was it normal for therapists to do this?

'I'm sorry,' I said.

She plucked a mint out of the bowl and slipped it between her lips. It created a hamster-like bulge in her right cheek. Her eyes shone mischievously and she leaned across the table and patted my hand. 'It's fine. I'm better now. Brilliant in fact,' she paused and lowered her voice, 'now that a new man has entered my life.'

'Oh. That's great.'

'It is, isn't it?' She held my gaze a moment longer than necessary. I looked down at my hands, feeling awkward, wondering if telling me stuff about her life was her way of letting me know I could trust her.

'Anyway, enough about me,' she said with a light chuckle, 'time to get started. Now, before we talk about you, I'd like you to fill in this form for me.'

She opened a drawer in the round table and withdrew a piece of paper which she handed me along with a pen. I filled it in: name, date of birth, address, next of kin – I hesitated, wanting to put Mum, knowing Dad would be the better choice. Not wanting to take too long, I wrote Alec Black-Hawkins as next of kin, ticked the chronic fatigue box in the medical conditions list then handed her the form. Rose scanned it, nodded and slid the form back inside the drawer. She closed the drawer, rearranged her skirt and tilted her head. The light above made her copper curls glint like new pennies.

'What would you like me to call you? I'm very happy for you to call me Rose.'

I spoke in a cracked voice. 'Arrietty, please.'

She nodded. 'OK. Arrietty. Now, Alec contacted me because he's concerned that you may be experiencing memory problems, which is one of my areas of expertise. Would you say you've noticed anything different about your ability to recall events?'

'I – yeah. A bit.'

'Can you tell me when you first noticed this?'

'Yeah. I think it was about two weeks ago. I tried to think back and my mind sort of closed off. It was really strange, and it's happening more and more.'

Snippets of memories came to me; the picnic in the back garden; the snapshot of us with ice cream on the beach - but the memories didn't feel concrete and they were always incomplete, blurring and trailing off halfway through like they'd been dipped in sludge. Sort of how I'd felt ever since Mum left. Sludgy and mixed up. Half a person. Someone who was weak and broken and always on edge. Like I was standing on the cliff with my toes over the edge, peering down into murky, grey rocks that never offered clarity or reason. I shuddered. Picked my nails.

Rose took a sip of water then rearranged her skirt. Her voice was gentle. Lulling. 'Did anything change in your life two weeks ago?'

A spasm of shock hit. It was as if she knew. I made myself look up, but couldn't meet her eye. Had Dad told her? I looked back down at my bare knees. Stared at a blackish bruise on my thigh I couldn't remember earning. 'Yes.'

'Can you tell me about it?'

Nausea knotted my throat and my face grew hot. I fought the temptation to tell her everything – how Dad wouldn't say where Mum had gone or even why, how sometimes I felt like he was lying, that he was hiding something about her, how he'd kept my letters instead of sending them. I didn't want to betray him – he was my Dad and I'd already taken his diary - but the desire to spill my guts to someone plucked at me like tweezers and anger at his actions tugged me closer to disclosure.

'My, um…'

'It's OK. Take your time.' She rested her hand on mine and stared into my eyes. Laughter lines creased her skin. Her hand was soft, cool, comforting. Her thumb stroked mine and I felt a tingle of electricity spark in my skin. After a few seconds, she moved her hand away and waited, her expression one of practised patience, gaze gentle and encouraging.

I realized I could tell her the facts. Maybe that would be enough. Maybe she could help me. The words exploded from me. 'My mum left.'

Rose's face was impassive. She nodded and took a sip of water, waited for me to continue.

'That's it,' I said, confused by her lack of reaction. 'She left. We haven't seen her since.'

'When you say we, who do you mean?'

'Me and Eddie. And Dad.'

135

'Hmm. That must have been difficult for you. And for Alec.'

'Yes, more so for Eddie though. He's only four.' I glanced back at the door, frowned. Wondered how Eddie and Dad were getting on in the car.

'Is everything all right?' she said, looking at the door.

'Yeah. It's just, I worry about leaving Eddie alone with Dad.'

'And why is that?'

I struggled to explain. Guilt skittered across my chest. I fidgeted with my shorts. It felt wrong to talk badly about Dad. I shrugged, picked my nails. Realized what I was doing and stopped.

'Arrietty?'

I looked at her, held her gaze for the first time since entering her house. 'Since Mum left, he's...changed. I feel like I don't know who he is any more.'

A frown creased Rose's brow. 'I see,' she murmured – even though she couldn't; I hadn't explained anything yet. I hid my annoyance by ripping a thread from my shorts.

'Can you elaborate on that feeling?' she said.

'About Dad?'

'Yes.'

I chewed the inside of my cheek. 'Not really. He's just...different. Moodier. But that's probably normal, given the circumstances, with Mum leaving and everything.'

'Did you see her leave?'

'No. I heard the door slam at around midnight. I didn't go and check.' Guilt rushed at me like a tsunami. 'I should have checked she was OK. I should have been there.'

Rose scribbled something on her pad. I tried to read it upside down. She'd written BLAMES HERSELF. She looked up, eyes piercing, 'Where do you think she is now?'

I shrugged. "Honestly, I don't have a clue, but I feel like Dad's not telling me something. And,' I hesitated, wondering whether I should confide in her about him reading my letters and not sending them when he'd said he would, and about the fact that none of Mum's things were missing, 'and...well, he...' I stopped, heat flooding my cheeks. It was too early to tell her things like that. I didn't know if I could trust her yet, and it was personal, private. Even though Dad had betrayed my trust in such a horrid way, there must be a reason he'd read my letters and not sent them. There had to be. The alternative was unthinkable. I just couldn't for the life of me work out what that reason was, and I was too afraid to ask. I'd invaded his private space by going into his office. I'd done wrong too. And he'd read my letters, which meant he knew the negative things I'd said about him.

Rose was speaking, her voice a distant vibration. I tuned back in with difficulty. My head was pounding now, and I felt weak with exhaustion.

She smiled gently and said, 'You look pale. I think we should cut this session a little short, but I'd like to see you again soon. How about Friday?'

I hesitated and stifled a yawn. 'OK.'

'Good. Well done today. I know it's not easy. Now, because you're experiencing memory loss, I'd like to suggest we try hypnotherapy.'

I frowned, more alert. It sounded invasive. 'How does it work?'

'In cases such as traumas, the mind can block some memories for survival, so much so that the unconscious mind doesn't allow the conscious mind to have access to particular memories. As a result, the wound is still there, and it can manifest into unwanted, and sometimes harmful behaviours and emotions. What hypnotherapy aims to do, is to help someone recall certain painful memories in a safe way that neutralizes them.'

'But if my mind has gotten rid of these memories, how will you bring them back?'

She smiled. 'That's a question many people ask. The reason hypnosis can help with memory is that everything you've ever experienced is still there in your memory bank. I know it's hard to believe, but no-one ever truly forgets anything. Every single thing that we pass through in our lifetime makes an impression on us and remains stored in our brains. When we say we can't remember, it's because we don't have access to that particular memory in that moment. However, when a person's awareness is sufficiently increased, we can pull that little remembrance out of its hiding place. Memories of every type - from trivial ones, like where you put a photo album to significant ones involving something more impactful and emotional are concealed within you.'

I shifted my weight and chewed my thumbnail. 'But if my brain has chosen to hide something bad from me, is it a good idea to bring it out into the open?'

'That's a good question. Ultimately, it's up to you. What do you want to gain from these sessions?'

I thought for a minute. She couldn't give me what I really needed: Mum. But maybe she could help me remember more about Mum, about before, about why Mum left or where she was, or why Dad was acting so strangely. Maybe Rose could help me feel whole again. 'I want to feel normal. Since Mum left, I've felt all jumbled up and really tired. And confused. I think I can remember something then it sort of…fizzles out. Like a candle. It's weird. And I keep having these strange dreams. Nightmares more than dreams. I wake up feeling awful. And, as I said before, I feel like Dad's different.'

To my surprise, she leaned forward and took hold of my hands. Looking directly at me, she said, 'It sounds like you're going through a tough time, but the root of some if not all of these problems most likely lies in an experience you've been through that needs to be carefully and safely worked through. As you said, your loss two weeks ago has hit you hard. This may have worsened an already deep wound. Hypnotherapy can help us expose and treat that wound, so to speak. But it's up to you. We do not need to try it. Why don't you have a think about it and let me know on Friday?'

Avoiding her gaze, I told her I would. She patted my hand and gave me a warm smile then led me out of the house. Halfway down the path, she stopped walking and beckoned to Dad. He got out of the car and went to speak to her.

I walked back to the car wondering what she thought of me and whether she was right; did I have a deep wound that needed to be excavated? The thought made my spine prickle, but curiosity swamped my mind. If I wanted to work out what had happened to Mum and find a way to help her, I needed to be able to remember everything that had taken place before she left. The two were somehow interlinked. They had to be – either that or I was losing my mind.

As I slid into the car, I glanced back at Dad and Rose. She was rubbing his arm, talking intently to him, standing close. Their shadows stretched behind them on the bright grass of Rose's garden, merging into a formless black mass. Rose's eyes shifted focus and locked on mine, and she moved her hand off his arm, stepped back and waved at me, a broad smile on her face, curls glinting icily in the sun. Their shadows sprang apart, his bigger and broader but only just.

I held up my hand in response, an uneasy feeling stirring. Rose had said everything I told her was confidential, so what was she talking to Dad about?

Chapter 32

I slid inside the car surprised to see Eddie fast asleep with his chin on his chest, dribble leaking out of his mouth.

'You can sit in the front, you know,' Dad said, darting a glance at me in the rear-view mirror.

I opened my mouth. The words *I'd rather not* tingled on my tongue, but sense dislodged them and I snapped my lips together and wearily stared out of the window at the silvery, drifting clouds. Like me, those clouds were wispy and fractured. I wrapped my arms around myself and bit my lip as a wave of longing flooded my body like hot oil.

'How'd it go?' he said, watching, tense.

He drove slower than he needed to and I was glad for that. I didn't trust him as a person anymore, let alone as a driver. My life was in his hands now. I supposed it always had been, but before, things were different. Mum had been around to make me feel safe and loved. We'd baked together, chatted art, lain in the sun eating cookie dough ice cream until we felt sick…

'You don't have to tell me,' he grunted.

I agreed with him on that point. No, I didn't have to tell him, so I wouldn't. If he wouldn't tell me anything about Mum, I wouldn't confide in him about my private meeting with my therapist.

'At least tell me how you found Rose.'

His use of her first name jarred. The familiarity was strong; did he know her from before? Could I trust this woman? And then there was the question of hypnotherapy. If I agreed to that, she'd gain access to my deepest, darkest thoughts. Memories my brain had *chosen* to bury.

I cleared my throat. 'She's nice.'

I felt a spark of pleasure at the irritation that flashed in his eyes. I wouldn't give him more than that, even if he begged.

Neither of us said another word for the rest of the journey.

Dad's music was too loud, digging into my skull like a pneumatic drill. I stared out of the window at the green wash of countryside. He was driving faster than earlier. Too fast.

I avoided the whizzing view, rolled my shoulders and focused on what to do about Mum. I might have found her make-up bag, but I hadn't found her mobile, purse or handbag, which gave me hope, because it suggested she'd left voluntarily. In a mad rush, yes, but with her senses intact. If she'd taken her phone and purse with her it meant Dad hadn't done something bad.

A chill swept my skin and I stared at the back of his head, wishing I could see inside and read his mind. I didn't want to let my imagine continue down its murky path, but fears trickled through my thoughts like poison. Dad could have forced Mum out without her possessions. Guilt might be what was keeping his mouth shut. That might be why he hadn't sent her my letters. Even worse, they could have argued and fought. He could have struck out, hit her, made her fall…

No. I blinked and forced the image away.

Another came in its place; me unconscious, head wet with blood. My ears roared. Where had that come from?

Feeling sick and shivery, I looked at the house. We were home. Time had flown too fast.

Golden pebbles crunched beneath the Merc's tyres as Dad drove the long path that led down the side of the house.

Above, the sun was a burning opal in a too-pure sky.

On either side of the house rose the olive fence that

141

enclosed our huge plot of land.

I leaned across the middle seat and ruffled Eddie's hair. 'Time to wake up, little bro.'

I prodded his shoulder. No response. Dad turned off the ignition, plunging the car into silence, and got out. I shook Eddie again, a bit harder this time. Still no reaction.

'Eddie,' I said, 'wake up.'

But he didn't move. I undid his seatbelt and shook him again.

This time his eyelids fluttered like a moth's wings. Relief made me lightheaded.

'Where are we?' he said, frowning at me.

'In the car. We're home now.'

'Is Mum here?'

'No.'

'When's she coming home?'

'I don't know. Soon. I hope.'

He nodded, rubbed his nose and climbed out of the car.

I hesitated before following him, attacked by the feeling that I was returning not to my home but to a prison. Without Mum, the house was a glass cage with me and Eddie its prisoners. We could use the back garden and roam the house when and as we pleased, but we could not venture away from the grounds without Dad's help. My eyes locked on the steering wheel. My fingers tingled. I scratched my head and wondered whether I had been learning to drive. A wispy memory of sitting behind the wheel of a car came; I could feel the hard, smooth wheel in my palms, the grumble of tyres beneath me. Suddenly, I felt certain that I had experienced at least one driving lesson. Somehow, the memory had been scrubbed from existence – until now.

Frowning hard, I got out of the car and jumped: Dad was standing at the front door watching me. Waiting for me to get inside, so he could close the door and lock me

142

in.

Avoiding his cold glare, I hurried past him into the hallway and rushed to the kitchen. Eddie wasn't there. Assuming he'd gone to his bedroom, I poured myself a glass of orange juice and stared out at the long, flowerless garden. Beyond the cliff, the world stretched on, mysterious and tempting, but untouchable. As I watched, the crooked-footed blackbird limped in front of Mum's studio.

I pressed a hand to the glass. Longing for Mum dragged me back to the idea that Dad was hiding something. There had to be a way to find out the truth.

My gaze fell on Mum's studio. She always kept it locked, but if she hadn't taken the key…

I nodded sharply to myself as an idea formed. I was going to solve this mystery. I was going to find my mum and get her back, whether Dad liked it or not.

*

I waited until Dad left the house and Eddie was engrossed in an imaginary dinosaur game before sprinting downstairs. I didn't know where he'd gone or how long he'd be out, so I needed to be quick, but when I got to the front door where I'd found Mum's keys before, they were gone. Dad must have moved them. Hidden them – *from me.*

I battled the need to swear and turned my back on the empty key hooks. With a sour taste on my tongue and an even stronger determination to find her studio key, I ran upstairs into the master bedroom.

Their bedroom was neat as ever, the bed made, corners tucked in. I searched high and low; in the walk-in wardrobe, in the bedside tables, under the bed, under both pillows, in the pockets of Dad's jackets and trousers. Nothing. I checked the en-suite and was startled to see that

Mum's make-up bag and toothbrush were no longer there. Had Dad hidden them too?

He's hiding the evidence.

No.

Yes.

I checked the medicine cabinet and found nothing except for the usual stuff. No studio key here, but there were many other places to check.

I ran downstairs through the house.

To my utter disbelief, Dad had left his office unlocked so I slipped inside, pitting hope against hope that I could find his journal. If he wrote in it regularly, there had to be some indication in those cream pages about Mum's whereabouts.

I checked every shelf of the enormous bookcase, but there was no journal. In the drawers, again, no journal and no key.

I plonked myself down on Dad's chair and kicked the table. My toes screamed in pain and something thudded to the carpet. I couldn't believe what I was seeing; it was a phone. A wave of horror hit me. The mobile was covered in thick brown sticky tape; it had been stuck to the bottom of his desk. Shaking my head at the weirdness of the discovery and Dad's slyness, I picked it up and began to peel off the tape, but my blood froze as recognition sizzled in my brain. It was Mum's phone. Dad had taped her mobile to the bottom of his desk.

The case was cherry-red. My favourite colour. Mum's too. I swiped to unlock and stared at the numbers. Before I knew it, I was typing in the four-digit code: 1209 – Eddie's birth date and month. It worked.

I grinned and stood. The WhatsApp icon showed no unread messages. I tapped the green box and stared, shocked to see that the most recent message was from Shane, sent almost two years ago. A frown made me almost cross-eyed – why was her most recent message from so long ago? Had she deleted more recent ones? Had Dad? Why did he even have her phone taped under his desk in the first place?

I swallowed thickly, heart walloping in my chest. The grey text underneath Shane's name read *RICH BITCH. YOU'LL PAY FOR THIS*. Staring down at the screen, I shuffled out from behind the desk. There were other messages from Mr B, and Hugo Grimes.

Excited to delve deeper into the phone, I rushed out into the hallway about to tap the messages icon, and my neck tingled. I glanced up; Dad stood in the back doorway.

*

Dad closed the front door behind him. His eyes were on my hand. On Mum's phone. I gripped it harder and took a step back.

His chest rose and fell rapidly. Sweat smeared his upper lip. His grey T-shirt was black under the armpits, and a sour smell wafted from him.

'Give me the phone,' he said, taking a step towards me.

I stared at him and tried to tell myself everything was going to be OK.

He took another step closer and another. I took a small step back. His jaw clenched and a muscle in his cheek twitched. He held out one large, rough hand.

I tried to steady my nerves.

'You don't need it. Give it to me,' he growled.

I looked down at the phone then glared up at him. 'If you tell me where she is, I'll give it to you.'

He exhaled through his teeth. 'I can't.'

I stared at him in disbelief. 'Why can't you? You're not making sense.'

He ignored my question. 'Give it to me or I'll take it off you.'

I shook the phone at him. 'Have seen it? Shane's text?

I think he's -'

'He was angry I fired him, but he's got nothing to do with this. Remember the night of the fair?'

I scrunched up my nose, shook my head. Was that what happened? I couldn't remember. Everything was foggy.

'But...how can you be so sure? And why have you taped Mum's phone under your desk? Where have all her recent messages gone? Nothing makes sense!'

He closed the distance between us in three strides and stopped a metre away. He was a head taller than me. He made me feel like an ant. My mouth went dry, and I tried to think of something to say – anything that would calm him down and make him tell me about Mum. But I couldn't be logical. Words burst from my lips, shaky and poisonous. 'You've done something to her, haven't you?'

I instantly regretted the words. He cast his glare to the ceiling and scratched at his stubble, breaking the skin. When he looked at me, I saw such intense resentment that I shrank away, but I was not ready to give up the phone, so I turned from him and walked as calmly as I could back through the house heading for my room where I could find refuge from him and his rage.

For a few seconds, I thought I'd won. The house remained quiet except for my frantic breaths and hurried footsteps, but then his heavy footfall joined mine; his steps faster and angrier.

I glanced over my shoulder and saw him running after me, reaching out to grab me, and I raced past the dining room, too terrified to look back, knowing that I was fast but he was faster.

At the foot of the stairs, his fingers found my arm and held on like a vice. He spun me around and tried to rip the mobile out of my grasp, purple with rage. I struggled and clawed at his face and he gasped and pushed me away. I staggered backwards and tripped, crashing to the floor with a bone-shattering thud. He glared down at me glassy-eyed. With a grunt, he lunged forward and tore Mum's phone out of my hand. I stared up at him, tears brimming, and he dragged his hand through his hair, muttered, 'Crazy', hesitated as if he was about to do something else, then shook his head and strode up the stairs without another word.

Chapter 33

Despite everything, it was a beautiful day. The sun was smiling, the sky a melty cornflower blue. There were no clouds or darkness. No promise of rain. But looks could be deceptive.

Dad drove in stony silence. I half-wished he'd play his horrid music, but he didn't. Instead, he drummed his nails against the steering wheel the whole way there and ignored both me and Eddie. Even when Eddie asked him if he could put on nursery rhymes, Dad just grunted. It made me angry, but I was too shaken up by our fight to say anything. For days, I'd been unable to muster up the courage to meet Dad's eye, let alone exchange words with him, and fear had halted my investigation into Mum's disappearance.

I reached out to stroke Eddie's cheek, but he pulled away and turned to face the window.

Worries tore at my chest. The only thing that had kept me going these last few days had been the knowledge that I'd get to escape the house to meet with Rose. What with Dad's ever-expanding hostility and Mum's absence, I was feeling lonelier than ever. Even Eddie seemed to be pulling away from me now, speaking less and less and sleeping for longer periods of time. I thought he was probably grieving for Mum, so I let him sleep until mid-morning before waking him and helping him dress. A small part of me worried that he blamed me for Mum's disappearance, but there was little I could do about that. All I could do was continue my lie – she'd gone to take care of her friend Patricia and that was that. I'd decided to stop asking Dad; it was clear he was never going to tell me. The need to know burned, but I was too afraid to snoop around. When Dad had pushed me over, I'd bruised my lower back. It still hurt.

If I pushed the wrong button, he might snap.

Like he did with Mum.

No. Dad hadn't done anything bad to her. He couldn't. And yet, he'd hurt me. If he could bring himself to harm me, could he have harmed Mum? Was he right about Shane? Shane was a bit strange, but I didn't think he'd be capable of hurting anyone. Then again, he had spent time in prison for GBH. And I remembered the way he used to look at Mum, a bit like she was a piece of meat he wanted to sink his teeth into.

I frowned heavily, so hard my head began to pound. Where did Dad go every afternoon without fail? Why was he so afraid for me to read Mum's messages? Why had he taped her phone to the bottom of his desk? Who was he having secret phone calls with? If anyone was hiding something, it was him. Shane hadn't been in the picture for ages. I couldn't even remember the last time I'd seen him. Had it been on the night of the fair when Isla and I had missed our curfew? No matter how hard I tried, I couldn't remember.

There were so many unanswered questions. Too many. I was weak and out of my depth, but the need to keep digging scratched at my brain like a thousand lice.

Sometimes I worried Dad was right. Maybe I was crazy. Why else would I be going to see a psychiatrist?

Because you've got memory problems. That's all.

Dad cut the engine.

But what caused these memory problems?

I felt Dad watching me and scrambled out of the cool car into the baking sun. As I passed his window, the glass descended an inch and he murmured, 'I'm going to town.'

I acknowledged his words with a quick nod, anxious about leaving Eddie with him, but eager to see Rose

Weatherby. If she could help me revive lost memories, maybe she could help me find Mum.

A warning voice whispered that Rose might not be trustworthy, but I beat it away and knocked on the door, determined to be open and co-operative.

Rose opened the door and welcomed me in. She wore a blush dress and scarlet nail varnish on her bare toes. On anyone else, the pink and red might have looked tacky, but she managed to pull it off. I was less shabby today in a red maxi dress. Not getting out much these days, I'd decided to make more of an effort. It seemed rude not to, especially when Rose was so well-dressed and her house so beautiful. It was what Mum would have wanted from me too. She always dressed appropriately for whatever she was doing. I remembered that much.

Somehow, I managed a small smile as Rose beckoned me up the hallway. I heard the dogs before I saw them. One yellow, one chocolate, tongues lolling, they skidded out of the kitchen and bounded up to her. She laughed and stroked them, chastising the blonde lab when it tried to lick. After greeting their mum, they turned their enthusiastic welcome to me. I laughed for the first time in ages as they sniffed and licked me. A warm bubble rose in my body and I floated on the feeling, not wanting it to end. The dogs were so friendly and simple. I stroked behind their soft ears and ruffled their fur. A tingle on my neck made me look up. Rose was watching me, head tilted.

'You don't have a dog, do you?'

'No. I've always wanted one, but…'

She nodded as if she understood. 'They're good for the soul.'

'Have you always had dogs?'

'Yes. Even as a little girl. My father was dog-obsessed. In fact, sometimes I think he liked his dogs more than me.' A dark look clouded her eyes and she scratched at her neck so roughly that red marks appeared on her skin, but a split second later she laughed and shook her head as if dispelling the bad memory.

She focused on me again. 'At one time we had four. A cocker, a springer, a black lab and a golden retriever.'

'Wow.'

'My father shot them when they were too old. I was only five when he put Sandy to sleep. He didn't mean for me to see, but I did. I was watching through my bedroom window. I was supposed to be asleep, but I heard Sandy whining. I think she knew what he was going to do.'

I swallowed. 'Gosh, that's...'

'Terrible? At first glance it is, but he was just putting her out of her misery, exactly as a vet would have done. Sandy's hips were causing her so much pain. Sometimes in life we must be cruel to be kind. It was unfortunate that I saw it, of course. No five-year-old should witness something like that.'

I swallowed uneasily. Tried to imagine how Eddie would react if he witnessed Dad shooting an animal dead. It would scar him for life. I glanced at Rose. She had a faraway look in her eye. A slight frown squinched her brow.

'On the plus side,' she said, 'I think that's why I gravitated towards psychology. I wanted to help those who'd experienced trauma, especially those who craved the love of their abusers, like I did.'

Desperate to change the subject, I ruffled the brown one's hair and said, 'Eddie would love them. Mum too. We've never had a dog because Dad doesn't want one.'

Rose frowned. 'Really? Why on earth wouldn't he want a dog?' Her voice was brittle, as if the very idea that someone wouldn't want a dog was a personal offence.

'He's house proud. Doesn't want a dog eating the furniture or weeing on the floor, you know?'

She didn't seem to be listening. Her eyes were distant, a trace of a smile on her lips. 'Well, that is interesting.'

151

I wanted to ask what she meant, but she dragged her gaze up to mine and grinned. 'Two's plenty for me. I think anyone can live with two. Now four, that would be a handful.'

I petted the blonde one's head. 'Sorry. I can't remember. Which one's which?'

'Millie's the gold. Bruno's the chocolate.'

'They're gorgeous.'

'Thank you. Millie's seven and Bruno's six.'

'Your children must love them.'

A shadow crossed Rose's face. She masked it with a smile. 'Sadly, I don't have any little ones. I never could.'

'Oh. I'm sorry.' I could have punched myself. Tact wasn't my strong point, but still.

'Don't worry. These two keep me happy.'

I forced a smile as she called Millie and Bruno and shut them in the kitchen. She walked back across the white-washed floorboards and opened the door to her treatment room. 'Shall we?'

I nodded and followed her inside. Today, light sparkled onto both peacock chairs making their bold colours all the more mesmerising. My gaze lingered on the black buds in the centre of the green-blue pattern. They looked, for a second, like hundreds of beady black eyes. A shiver traced my shoulders as Dad's explosion burned a hole in my memory. I touched the base of my spine and winced, fingers making contact with the bruising. I thought about telling Rose what had happened, but shame bit and I shoved the urge away. Dad had hurt me, but he was, at the end of the day, my dad. And I wasn't really sure if he'd intended to push me over. It could have been an accident.

Rose arranged the pleats of her skirt into a neat waterfall over her legs and took a sip of water. 'Have you decided whether you'd like to give hypnotherapy a try?'

'Yes. I need to remember…things.'

She beamed. Her shoulders relaxed. 'Great, that's great. Right. I'm just going to close the curtains.'

She stood and moved to the window. Scraped them closed. The sound made me wince. I swallowed. Ignored the rapid scaling of my pulse. She returned to her seat. Around her, shadows settled and the room cooled a little. She told me to get comfortable. To close my eyes and focus on her voice.

I rested my head against the padded chair. I felt her watching me, heard her voice, registered instructions.

I battled a while, clinging on to the present like a rock climber on a cliff edge, but my fingertips were weak, my grip tenuous, and within moments I felt my brain do something strange, but good.

The sensation of someone massaging my mind with warm fingers came and Rose's voice grew softer, more distant as she told me calmly and firmly to relax, think back.

With each descending second, my muscles unclenched and my consciousness peeled away from the room. Unable and unwilling to fight, I let myself free-fall into the warm embrace of nothingness, and after not very long at all, I was deep down in a bland, unthreatening place, my body numb to my surroundings, mind softened and kneaded and comforted by the unrelenting rhythm of her commands, fear assuaged by the distant knowledge that I was safe here. Closeted in the blackness of my own subconscious, I was away from danger in honest hands.

*

I was back in the room with Rose. She was watching me closely. I remembered nothing about what had happened while I was under hypnosis. The fact was chilling.

I looked at the woman sitting opposite me. She was a stranger. An outsider. What personal thoughts had I

153

spilled to her? Had I said anything about Dad? Mentioned my growing suspicion that he'd done something awful?

'How are you feeling?' she said.

'OK. Sleepy.'

'You did well. You have an exceedingly high level of hypnotic ability.'

I frowned. 'What does that mean?'

'It's nothing to worry about. On the contrary, it's a good thing. Makes my job a lot easier. It means that you're highly hypnotisable.'

'Easily controlled then,' I said.

'No. Just open to hypnotic suggestion. This implies that just as suddenly as you lost your memories, you may also recover them.'

'What did I say? Why can't I remember anything?'

Her eyebrows rose a fraction. 'You remember nothing?'

'Nothing.'

Her tooth snagged her lower lip. 'I think you're experiencing something called posthypnotic amnesia, or PHA for short. Typically, a hypnotherapist needs to suggest that you forget events or material. He or she will then later cancel this suggestion and the patient's memories will come flooding back. I have not induced PHA, of course. My goal is to help you recover memories in a safe, controlled way.' She paused to let me digest her words. 'The good news, however, is that PHA reflects only a *temporary* inability to retrieve information that is safely stored in your memory.

'Indeed, from our session, it's now clear that you have functional amnesia, a rare condition where a person develops severe memory loss instigated by personal trauma. A trauma which you can't yet recall. This can also result in confusion and changes in behavioural patterns. However, in our next session, I'll take you closer to that trauma. It's important that such memories are exposed

154

slowly or else you may become overwhelmed and your mind could further repress that information.'

Most of her words flew over my head. All I really heard was the word trauma. 'Is Mum leaving the traumatic thing you're referring to?'

She rearranged her skirt, and I had the feeling she was stalling, giving herself a moment to think through what she was going to say, how much, maybe, to tell me. 'According to what you've revealed so far, I think your trauma goes further back.'

I frowned. Curiosity bit like a snake. 'What have I revealed so far?'

'I'm afraid I can't tell you that at this stage. It's safer for you to recall material on your own, in a safe space, post-hypnosis.'

'But if I have this PHA thing this time, what's to say I won't have it next time? And every session after that? What if it stops me from ever remembering?'

'I'm quite confident that it won't work like that. With every session, I'll coax your mind to loosen its grip on specific events and eventually you will recall what we need you to.'

I stared at her, angry words on the tip of my tongue. I wanted to demand she tell me what I'd said. If I'd recalled anything about Mum I needed to know, but she stood up. 'I'm going to have a word with Alec before you go.' She left the room quickly.

I stared after her, open-mouthed and suspicious again. What was she going to tell Dad? What had I said?

I hurried out of the room, up the hallway and out into the smouldering heat. Sun blinded me and I blinked to clear my vision. Rose was leaning over speaking to Dad through the car window. I hurried down the path towards them and froze, shocked to see her push her head inside the car and peck him on the cheek. He pulled away quickly, and she straightened and turned to face me. Acting like

155

she'd done nothing out of the ordinary, she offered a brief smile and suggested I take it easy for the rest of the day, then left me to face Dad and the long drive home.

Chapter 34

I dragged myself out of bed, foggy-headed from my nap. With a yawn, I sat at my desk and eyed what I'd drawn the other day. It was a face, a nightmarish face that part-resembled my dad's. The portrait had the same shadowy, hooded eyes, an identical slash of thin lips. What was different was his nose; in reality, Dad had a hook nose, rather like a beak, but in this impression his nose was upturned like a pig's snout, the nostrils open and flaring. It would have been comical if not for the black splodges that dripped down his cheeks. Tears or blood, even I wasn't certain what they were supposed to be. The drawing was frightening, like a Picasso dragged through hell.

I looked away and suspicions rose black and ugly in my mind, pricking like thorns. Dad wouldn't say where Mum was. He wouldn't tell me the truth. He was hiding something. What role had he played in Mum's disappearance? Why had he taped her phone to the underside of his desk?

Were Eddie and I at risk?

I glanced over my shoulder. Eddie was asleep. He'd slept the entire way back to the house. I'd carried him up the stairs to his bedroom and tucked him in. He was sleeping far too much.

Dad hadn't spoken a word to me. He'd avoided all eye contact too.

I wondered whether I should have confided my fears in Rose, then recalled the familiar way she'd said Dad's name, the way she'd draped herself against his car window and kissed his cheek and whispered words she didn't want me to hear.

Dad had muttered that I was crazy, but I wasn't. The more I thought about it, the more I feared it was the other way around.

He was out again this afternoon. Out where, I didn't know. It was one of a million things he hid from me. And that didn't make sense either. Why did he need to venture out every afternoon?

I shoved myself away from the vile portrait and dusted my hands on my thighs. With a jaw-breaking yawn, I stood and froze at the sound of the car door. He was back.

I peered out of the window and bit the inside of my cheek; Hugo Grimes, Mum's old client, was walking towards the back door. What was he doing here? I glanced at his black Audi sitting beside Dad's white Merc.

Dad marched out of the house across the gravel, heading straight for Hugo. The white-haired man stopped in his tracks. He was dressed in cream chinos and an ice-blue polo T-shirt, his thick hair parted neatly down the middle. Stood together, they were so similar in age, height and physique they could have been brothers.

Dad started speaking, each word clipped and rough. 'You shouldn't be here. You need to leave, *now.*'

He looked back at the house; I darted away from the window. I waited a few seconds then risked another peek. Dad's face was on Hugo's again. Hugo's hands were on his hips. He was frowning heavily. He began to say something. I tried to catch what he was saying, but Dad grabbed his upper arm and steered him away from the house across the lawn towards Mum's studio. They were clearly arguing about something. I sighed in frustration, wishing I could hear their conversation. Desperate to know, I left my room and dashed along the landing. The tulip painting hung there, forcing me to look at it. I stopped and stared, took a step closer to the painting. A queasy sensation fluttered up my throat and I leaned against the wall as dizziness and fear gripped me and made my blood pound. I felt something stir in my mind, like the unexpected remembrance of a dream, or in this case, a nightmare. The fragment was thin and wispy and hideous, but I clung on desperately and tugged it forward. It began to fade, but I concentrated and focused harder, and the tendril solidified into something more, something dark and twisted but horribly real.

Dad – screaming - face distorted, towering, bitter, hateful - so full of hate – and I was watching – from somewhere – small and hunched up - and then –

And then…

No. I slumped against the wall. It was gone. I'd lost it. But the feelings the memory had given me remained. In equal measure: fear and dismay. So did a horrifying certainty. Dad was not to be trusted; I already knew that. But now I knew something else. Knew it better than my own face: he had done something to Mum. Something nasty. Something unforgivable.

The certainty crashed into me, knocking the wind out of my body.

A high-pitched whine electrified the air. I lurched away from the painting towards the banister. Nothing was down there, but the sound continued. I poked my head into Eddie's room – he wasn't there. Where was he? What was making that awful noise? It sounded like an animal in pain. What if my brother had gone downstairs and –

I tore myself away from the railing and sprinted along the landing. Seizing the banister, I propelled myself around the corner down the stairs. The racket I was making was great, but at that moment I didn't care, because the terrible whining continued.

Dread smothered my lungs, but I forced my legs to move, sprinting through the living space, past the dining room, up the endless tomb of the house.

At the end wall, I stopped. Listened. Trained my ears on the sound. I glanced at the glass wall. Hugo's car had gone.

The whining grew more urgent; higher, faster, needier.

I turned right and dashed towards Dad's office. The door was closed, but someone was in there.

Heart thrashing, I stared at the solid wood, certain the dreadful sound was coming from inside that room.

Chapter 35

Despite every instinct in my body telling me to stop, I pounded on Dad's office door. 'Eddie! Eddie, are you OK?'

The high-pitched whine stopped, and I pictured Dad standing over Eddie's unconscious form, my brother's head wet with blood.

'Open the door! Let me in!' I screamed and smashed both fists against the wood until pain burst into my hands.

'Hold on,' Dad grunted. The lock scraped. The door opened.

He stood in the doorway, frowning down at me, face red. 'What's got into you?'

A strange, hamster-like smell hit my nose. I ignored him and tried to shove past, but his fingers pincered my arm. 'Hey, what are you doing?'

Staring around the room, I saw nothing. Heard nothing. There was no Eddie. Only a sea of books and brown furniture, laptop open on the desk.

I frowned. Had I imagined the terrible sound? Surely not. Had he been watching something on his laptop?

Whirling around to face him, I said, 'Where's Eddie? I thought he was in bed, but then I heard this horrid screeching sound...'

He sighed and released my arm.

I rubbed the sore spot. 'Where's Eddie? He isn't in his room and he's obviously not in here.'

Dad's jaw clenched. He stared at the ground. 'Gone.'

'Gone where? Why?' I said, head roaring. The way he'd said it sounded so final. 'What do you mean?'

'I – it's best you don't know.' He pressed his hand

against my lower back and, glancing over his shoulder, pushed me out of the room. 'Rest now. I'll be up soon to bring you something that'll cheer you up.'

'What? No. Dad, please, where's Eddie? Does this have something to do with Hugo? I saw him just now. You two were arguing. Why did you tell him he shouldn't be here? Is that where Mum is? With him? First Mum and now Eddie. What the hell's happening?'

'This has nothing to do with that vile man. Now, do as I say. I'm beginning to lose the will -'

'*You're* beginning to lose the will? What about me? You won't tell me where Mum is and now Eddie's gone.' I took a deep breath, fired myself up. 'You've done something to her, I know it. And I'm going to find out if it kills me.'

'Just go.'

'No. Tell me where they are or I'm leaving.' I folded my arms and raised my chin, trying to conceal the fear vibrating through my body.

He stared at me then, eyes unreadable. "I can't tell you, so just leave it."

The veins in his temples pulsed savagely. I took a step back.

'Tell me or I'm going,' I said.

For a moment, I thought he was going to hit me. He stared for what felt like hours, and I glared back. Behind him, the office blurred into a meaningless void. There was only him and me. Once upon a time, he'd been a good man, but something inside his mind had shifted, snapped. He was a stranger to me now. A stranger capable of unknowable things.

I jumped as he laughed and leaned low. In my ear, he whispered, 'Rest,' then shut the door.

I stared open-mouthed at the door. The lock crunched. His laugh rang in my ears and I squeezed my nails into my palms, rage flushing my cheeks. He'd actually *laughed* at me when I'd threatened to leave. It was as if he

163

didn't think me capable of going anywhere on my own. The thought made me mad, madder than I'd ever been.

Head burning, I raced up the hallway to the front door and snatched Dad's car key off its hook. There was no way I was spending another second stuck in this house with that man when he'd clearly done something to my mum, and possibly my little brother too. I was going to drive away and track them down.

*

Stood by the front door, my adrenaline fizzled out and I realized I couldn't just leave. For starters, I didn't have a phone. Secondly, I didn't know how to drive, but how hard could it be, really? In the car the other day, a flash of driving had come, making me think I'd been learning to drive before my memory had turned to scrambled egg.

I bit my lip, tried to recall sitting behind the wheel of a car, using the accelerator. Nothing came. No blinding vision of insight. But driving was easy. I was sure I could figure it out. I'd have to drive to get anywhere. Our house was in the middle of nowhere, a long hike from the closest town. If Dad thought that I'd left on foot, he'd hop in the Merc and track me down. I wouldn't get far.

Dad's car key dangled from my fingers. I pocketed it and thought about other obstacles to leaving. My phone was blocked to me, as was my laptop. But Dad hadn't taken my purse. My card was in my purse. I could use it to buy a phone when I got to town. But calling Mum would be pointless as she didn't have her mobile – he did.

Because he hurt her.

No.

Yes. That's the trauma you went through. You saw him do it.

But, in that case, why is he making you see a therapist? Wouldn't he be worried the horror would come crashing back into your psyche, revealing the truth? It doesn't add up. Unless...

Rose Weatherby's face entered my mind. I saw her smile, so bright and...*fake*. Were they having an affair? Was that where Dad had been going every afternoon for the last two weeks? She'd called Dad by his first name, acted so familiar with him, like she knew him. Had they planned this together? Conspired to get rid of Mum? Maybe Rose was deliberately manipulating me to make these memories regress deeper into my brain, so that I'd forget what I'd witnessed.

Am I making a crazy leap? Maybe they're just friends, maybe
-

And what about Eddie?

My brain felt like it was curdling. A wave of exhaustion attacked. Still, I tried to think. Work out what was happening.

If Dad and Rose were in this together, why would they take Eddie away? Where would they send him?

Maybe he's at Rose's house. Maybe Hugo took him.

Why would Hugo look after Eddie? That's a stupid idea. Dad hates his guts by the looks of it.

No, it must be Rose. Rose and Dad.

My head cleared a little. Yes. That could be it. I couldn't think of anyone else Dad could send him to live with. My parents had no siblings and my grandparents were dead. Dad used to play golf with two work associates, but gave it up years ago because of a dodgy shoulder. There was nobody else he knew who'd be willing to take care of Eddie, and besides, what explanation would he give? That his wife had left us and he couldn't cope on his own? That would lead to questions and more lies. Social services might get involved. Someone might even grow suspicious enough to call the police regarding Mum's disappearance. And Dad wouldn't want that.

No. Eddie had to be at Rose Weatherby's place. They were probably worried I was going to say something to Eddie about Mum, turn him against them. Or maybe during my session, I'd said something about him, and now Rose was using her psychological expertise to twist his mind against me, possibly against Mum too, so that he'd move on and accept her as his new mother.

I slid down the wall. Dug in my jeans, stared at Dad's car key.

Am I leaping to conclusions too quickly?

No.

Putting two and two together and getting twelve?

No. You're onto something. He's hiding too much. Only guilty people have so much to hide. And there's something weird about Rose.

It was all so far-fetched, but fear that I was letting my imagination roam too far bounced off my mind and out of the house, and the feeling that I was close to the truth slipped under my skin and latched on like a leech. Crazier things had happened. Mum wouldn't have left us for this long and not got in touch. Eddie had to have gone somewhere. Dad said he couldn't tell me where Eddie had gone, which meant he was keeping things from me. He'd hidden Mum's phone under his desk, read and never sent my letters. He was so strange and angry, and that memory – the one where he'd been screaming, his face bursting with hatred...

Pushing myself to my feet, I replaced Dad's car key on its hook and hurried back through the house to my bedroom. I needed to see Rose Weatherby again. I needed to get into her home, snoop around, see what she was hiding about Mum and Eddie, and the only way I was going to do that was if I stayed put with Dad and played along.

Shielding my eyes from the tulip painting, I entered my room and closed the door. My bed looked so inviting and my body and mind were so tired, but the compulsion to spill my emotions onto the page sucked me towards my desk.

With quivering fingers, I drew.

166

Chapter 36

Footsteps outside my bedroom had me grabbing *Emma* off my pillow and shoving it over my drawing. Dad couldn't be allowed to see this sketch. It would clue him into my suspicions about him and Rose. It would also make him angrier than he already was.

To make it look like I wasn't just sitting there doing nothing, I leapt off my chair, curled up on the bed and pretended to be asleep. Hopefully, he'd look inside, see me dozing and leave. I needed to keep out of his way as much as possible. There was no way of knowing whether he was crazy enough to hurt me.

Deep down, I knew he'd never hurt Eddie. My brother was too small and weak. He didn't pose any threat to anyone. But I did. And it was growing clearer with every passing day that my dad's patience with me was ebbing away. I'd pushed it too far earlier by accusing him of harming Mum. I regretted those words now. He couldn't know I was suspicious. If he thought I'd go to the police, he might take matters into his own hands. Luckily, he'd laughed when I'd said I was leaving, which made me think he hadn't taken my threat seriously.

I told myself all I had to do was play nice. Be obedient and agreeable. Feign ignorance. Pretend Mum's and Eddie's disappearances weren't all I could think about.

A light knock on the door made me jump. I faked sleep and prayed he'd go away.

For a while, nothing sounded, then he knocked again. Louder than before.

Worried his temper would fray, I sat up and murmured, 'Yes?'

A whimpering sound not dissimilar to the one I'd heard coming from his office erupted from behind the closed door. Eddie! Was Eddie back? Was he in pain?

I scrambled off the bed, ran to the door and yanked it open.

Dad held a ball of sandy fluff in one large hand. 'I got this for you,' he said, watching me.

I stared at the adorable puppy, unable to believe it. The puppy stared back and tried to wriggle out of Dad's grasp to get to me.

'This was what you heard earlier. I trod on his tail. I wanted him to be a surprise. He's a cockapoo, like you always wanted. Here. Take him. I don't think he likes me very much.' He handed me the puppy, gave me a strange smile then backed out of my room and closed the door.

In spite of everything, my heart swelled with delight and I hugged the tiny puppy to my chest. 'Oh my God. You're gorgeous!' I whispered into his soft, yellow fur.

His body wagged as he scrabbled up my neck and licked my skin. I giggled and let him lick on, knowing it was gross but loving it all the same.

'What shall I call you?' I said, admiring his cute little face.

I allowed him to scamper across my duvet. Once he reached the pillow, he tottered onto the bedside table then bravely leapt onto my desk, where he plonked his fluffy bottom on top of *Emma* and stared at me, tail wagging.

I smiled and picked him up. 'I know. I'll call you Knightley. The perfect name for a brave little pup like you.'

Cuddling Knightley, I tried to linger on the warm sensation of happiness he brought, but my thoughts trailed into murky waters.

What was Dad up to? He'd always refused to get a dog, saying they were too needy and time-consuming yet here he was, offering me one up with a smile. I frowned and scratched my neck. Knightley threw himself into licking my hand. Absently, I stroked his fur, frown deepening as I realized what this was about.

The puppy was the perfect bribe. A way to keep me happy. Eddie's replacement. Without my brother to look after, I'd have little to keep me distracted and, more importantly, nothing to stop me from prying into Mum's disappearance.

This wasn't a kind, loving gesture designed to make me feel better. It was calculated. A tactical move designed to make me easier to control.

Dad's deviousness cut out another piece of my heart. I tried to remember the daddy I used to love, and drew a blank. What had happened to him? Why was he lying to me?

And why couldn't I remember the things I needed to most?

*

Not only had Dad bought me a puppy, he'd purchased the things required to go with a new dog.

Down in the kitchen near the back door I found a small dog bed, two silver bowls, one overflowing with dog food, the other with water, a towel, a navy collar and lead, a chew toy and a tennis ball. He'd gone to town.

As I inspected each object, I couldn't help feeling a trickle of doubt, wondering if I was way off base about Mum and the role Dad had played and was still playing in her disappearance. He was, after all, my flesh and blood. My Dad. But there was no denying he'd changed. He wasn't the person I used to know. It was as if he'd morphed into another human being overnight. Worse than that. An impostor. He didn't even look like himself anymore. His edges were rough and hard. Gone was genuine care and fatherly love. In its place was my frightening memory of him in a terrible rage, of him

169

screaming at Mum while I cowered in the corner. It was a bloody stain inked inside my brain. No amount of scrubbing would make it disappear. And his viciousness on the stairs – snatching Mum's mobile and knocking me over – that wasn't a person I knew. That was a disturbed and horribly altered creature I no longer recognized. More monster than man. There was nothing innocent in his actions. He'd realized avoidance tactics and intimidation weren't going to work, so now he was playing a different game altogether, and he was good at it. Getting me a puppy would win me over – or so he thought.

Intent on playing along, I knocked on his office door. Without waiting for an answer, I said, 'Thank you for the puppy and everything. I'm going to take Knightley outside now to do his business.'

I heard movement from within. A second later, he appeared. Looking down at me with suspiciously soft eyes, he said, 'Knightley is it? Great name.'

His acting was so good. Worryingly so. I couldn't let him manipulate me. I needed to get away.

'Like him then?' he said, a faintly smug smile on his lips.

'Yeah. He's cute.'

'Good. You've always wanted one. I thought this was the perfect time…'

I gave him a thin-lipped smile and headed outside before he could say anything more.

Knightley darted ahead of me, keen to explore the large space.

Above us, the early evening sun was warm and bright. I followed my little friend closely, worried he might stray too close to the cliff edge. He yapped a few times at nothing then circled back to me for attention. On my haunches, I enjoyed rubbing the soft spots behind his ears for a while before tossing the tennis ball a short distance. Knightley gambolled after the ball then pawed at it.

Unsure what to do, he grew bored and bounced off in search of something more interesting.

Watching him, I felt something shift in my chest. The knots in my shoulders seemed to be loosening, my tummy uncoiling. Dogs were supposed to be great therapy, weren't they? With their unconditional love, bonny personalities and inability to criticise or pass judgement, they offered something humans couldn't. Already, I was in love with this little bundle of cuteness.

Knightley drew closer to the art studio and I followed him, keeping a close eye, just in case he headed for the precipice. The drop was deadly; thirty feet onto jagged rock. If you were lucky, you'd escape the fall with two shattered legs, but death was a far more likely ending.

Knightley yapped excitedly and I watched him. With a start, I realized he was a canine version of Eddie. He was cute, lively, playful and affectionate – a joy to be around - but nothing could ever replace my brother and nothing would make me forget that he and Mum were missing. Dad was an idiot if he thought a puppy could win me over. He clearly thought I could be controlled, but he was wrong. Dead wrong. There was *nothing* he or Rose Weatherby could say or do that would make me accept Mum and Eddie's absences in my life. If they thought getting me a puppy would persuade me to drop my investigation and move on, they were crazier and stupider than I thought. I'd sooner die than accept that I couldn't know where my own mum and little brother had gone because, in Dad's words, it'll *make you feel worse*. What a load of crap. He was using my chronic fatigue as a convenient excuse to avoid telling me the truth. In reality, being unable to see or talk to my loved ones was the only thing that would make me feel worse; it already was; and if he really cared or didn't have something terrible to hide, he'd tell me where they were immediately. So would Rose.

Raw with emotion, I picked up Knightley and carried

him inside the house. A vacuum of silence descended on us. Nothing stirred from within Dad's office.

I jumped as a presence prickled my neck; Dad was sitting at the kitchen island watching me. My muscles bunched up again. I waited for him to speak, but he wasn't looking at me, but through me, as if I was nothing more than an apparition. Abruptly, he blinked and directed his cold gaze onto mine. I stepped back and hugged Knightley tighter to my heart. Fear erupted in my belly at the way he looked at me. It was like the man I'd spoken to minutes earlier had been painted with tar. Like the effort of being nice had been too much for him. Anger stiffened every angle of his body. With jerky movements, he got up and strode to the kettle. He stabbed it on then barked, 'Want one?' without looking at me.

I glanced over my shoulder to check no one else was there. The hallway remained empty. No Rose. No Eddie. No Mum. Just me and Knightley.

The idea of spending another second around him rammed nails into my gut.

Avoiding eye contact, I shook my head and returned to my bedroom as quickly as I could.

I spent the rest of the day and most of the night reading, too worried to eat, too shaky to draw and too scared to sleep.

Chapter 37

It was my session with Rose today, a chance to do some digging. Nerves tingled at the base of my spine as I allowed my imagination to roam, pictured myself finding Eddie in someone else's home, held there against his will, hugging his knees to his tiny chest.

Closing down the image, I took Knightley outside. He sniffed the warm country air, then wandered off towards Mum's studio.

Above me, the sky shimmered with promise, mocking my situation. I inhaled deeply and rolled my shoulders to a chorus of clicks and crunches. I was bone-tired, and my brain raced along like a freight train. Would I find any evidence in Rose's house? Would I even get the opportunity to look? Was I barking up the wrong tree?

Knightley ran back to me and leapt at my ankles. I scooped him up, cuddled his warm body against my chest, turned and went back inside the house.

Once my little buddy was curled up on my bed, I crept out of the room, along the landing and slipped inside Eddie's bedroom.

The room looked the same as the last time I'd set foot in it, before Eddie had gone. Light streamed through the windows highlighting my brother's carefully arranged set of dinosaur rubbers. I picked up a yellow stegosaurus and held it to my cheek. With a thick swallow, I slid the rubber into my pocket, wanting to have something of him close.

Slowly, I scanned the room. If Eddie had been sent to live somewhere else, it made sense that Dad would have sent a bag of clothes with him, maybe some toys as well. But no toys appeared to be missing.

The sound of movement made me freeze. Dad was awake. I listened and waited until I heard his heavy bulk descending the stairs.

I hurried to the baby blue chest of drawers, opened the top drawer and rifled through my brother's underwear and socks. Nothing missing. The other drawers told the same story. I rifled through his wardrobe. I couldn't find his green and blue stripy hoody or his Clarks dinosaur trainers anywhere. What did that mean?

*

The journey was filled with roaring jazz.

I tried to sleep, but my mind spun.

Dad had told me to leave Knightley at home, so I'd left to the horrific sound of my puppy screaming and scratching frantically at the back door. Dad hadn't even batted an eyelid. It was another sign that he'd changed. How anyone could listen to a baby animal cry like that and not be moved was incomprehensible. It made me wonder how much empathy remained in his heart and what had happened to make him so cold and cruel.

After what felt like for ever, Dad pulled up outside Rose's house behind her cream Figaro. He cut the engine and glanced at me in the rear-view mirror.

I pretended not to notice, opened the door and slid out into the baking air. The sun was a blinding coin, too hot and glaring. I wore denim shorts and a white top but would have been better off in a floaty dress. Rose, barefoot as before, dressed in an indigo shift that skimmed her curves, was already walking down her front path towards me. Behind her, the door stood open. The entrance to the temptress's lair? Maybe. Maybe not.

'Go in. Make yourself comfortable. I just need a word with Alec,' she said, touching my elbow. There it was again. Calling him by his first name.

I managed not to flinch at her touch and slowed my pace, pausing at the door to watch as she bent over to speak to Dad through the passenger window. A moment later, he got out of the car. Today he wore a grey T-shirt and navy combat shorts. Sweat patches bloomed beneath his armpits. The rings under his eyes were dark, almost purple, and he'd not bothered to shave.

I entered the hallway and checked for my brother's shoes. Nothing. I wasn't surprised. Rose had probably hidden them.

My skin prickled and I listened for Eddie, but the house remained silent. Maybe they'd started sending him to a nursery? The term wouldn't be over for a couple of weeks. Had they decided to cart him off when I was here, so that I wouldn't see him?

Feeling sick, I pressed my back into the wall and watched open-mouthed as Dad and Rose embraced. She rubbed his back and whispered something in his ear before standing back. They spoke for a few moments and Rose said something that made his face change from its usual sour expression to one of pleasure. I couldn't believe it. It was more evidence of their deceit. Like they didn't see the point in hiding their relationship any more.

They turned as one and began to walk up the path, so I hurried after them, took a right and entered Rose's office. Instead of sitting on one of the peacock chairs, I scanned the space for anything incriminating, tensing as Rose popped her head into the room.

'I'm just going to make Alec a cup of coffee. Would you like one too or is water OK?' she said. Her cheeks were flushed, eyes bright.

'Water's fine,' I said, pleased I'd be alone for another few minutes.

As soon as she left, I dashed over to her desk. Like the peacock chairs, the desk was stunning to behold. Painted black with gold filigree decorating the top and twisting legs carved with spirals of ivy, it made me think of Mum. She would have loved such a unique, eye-catching piece – not that Dad would have let her have it. It was far too flamboyant for him, too adventurous. The fact made me realize how different they were to one another. Had they separated? Had Mum moved out and then something bad had happened to her? Was Dad actually innocent in all this? Was he keeping quiet because I was ill and he didn't want to upset me further by telling me they were getting a divorce or that, God forbid, Mum was hurt? Could Mum have run off with another man? Was she not contacting me because she felt guilty?

No. Don't be so stupid. Something happened two weeks ago. Something so traumatic it messed with your memory. Rose Weatherby might be lying about a lot of things, but you can't deny she's hit the nail on the head about this. Your memory's been playing up ever since Mum vanished. Don't lose focus. Dad and Rose are in this together. They've done something to her and Eddie. You need to hurry up and find out what.

Heeding my own advice, I attempted to open the top drawer but it wouldn't budge. I tried the other two drawers. Again, no luck. Keyholes indicated they were locked, so I checked the golden tiger pot on the desk for a key, but came up empty. There was no laptop in sight – not that I'd be able to get in without a password anyway.

With a frown, I surveyed the rest of the room. Behind the desk stood a sideboard cupboard that had also been painted black. On top of the cupboard was a framed photograph of Millie and Bruno beside a spiky potted plant.

I opened the cupboard doors and looked inside. It was filled with stacks of alphabetised files. Frantically, I flicked through the 'B' files until I reached Black-Hawkins – me. My fingers lingered on the slim, cream folder. I couldn't decide what to do. Should I open it and look inside? Would it tell me anything useful about Mum or Eddie? I did a double-take. The initial next to my surname on the divider was S. S for Sofia. Mum's name. But that wasn't right. It should say A for Arrietty. Had Rose made a mistake or had Mum seen this woman before? Was that why Dad was familiar with her? Was she an old family friend? Had she treated my mum in the past? And where was my file? Questions, questions, questions. I wanted to scream.

Panicking, I rifled through the B files again – bingo! My file had been put in the wrong place, but there it was: **Black-Hawkins, A**. A for Arrietty. But that didn't explain why there was a file for Mum here too.

The creak of the door made me straighten. Hastily, I shut the cupboard doors and picked up the picture of Rose's dogs.

Chapter 38

Rose stared at me from the doorway, eyebrows raised.

'Sorry,' I said, replacing the photograph, 'I was just admiring the picture. Millie and Bruno are so gorgeous.'

'No need to apologise. They are rather, aren't they? Please, take a seat. Get comfortable.'

I analysed her tone and body language as she spoke, desperate to work out if she'd seen me snooping, but she sat down and smiled as if she hadn't a care in the world.

Phew. That was close.

The need to blurt an accusation stung the back of my throat. I forced myself to stay calm. I had to be clever and careful. Work out what, if anything, she was hiding. She might not be involved at all. I could be wrong.

'Where are they now?'

'Who? Oh – Millie and Bruno?'

'Yes,' I said, forcing a smile.

'With my friend. He takes them for walks sometimes. Call it a labour of love.' She leaned forward with an excited smile and clapped her hands. Her overly sweet perfume almost made me sneeze. 'I hear you just got a puppy?'

'Oh. Dad told you?'

She nodded. 'What's his name?'

'Knightley.'

'What a lovely name. From Austen? Alec showed me a picture on his phone. He's adorable.'

'I – thank you. Yes, he's perfect.'

Rose smiled and re-crossed her legs. 'Right, let's get down to business, shall we? Now, since our last session, have you been able to recall anything at all?'

I hesitated, tried to decide what to tell her. Instead of

answering the question, I blurted, 'Eddie's gone. Did you know that?' I could've slapped my own face – so much for self-control and playing things with care.

I watched her reaction. She blinked, nodded, took a sip of water and smiled tightly. 'Why yes, I did know that. Alec told me he'd told you. How are you feeling about it?'

'How do you think I'm feeling about it?' I snapped.

'Upset? It must have come as a shock.'

'Do you know where Eddie is?' I said.

Her eyes wandered away from mine and landed on the floor. She slammed her glass down on the table. 'Alec shouldn't have said anything about Eddie. Not yet.'

'What do you mean?'

'I don't believe you're ready. We still have work to do. It will be far better for you if you gain a better understanding on your own, in your own time, so to speak. Memories need to be drawn out of you safely and slowly, not dumped on you from an external source before you're ready to receive them.'

I frowned, puzzled and irritated. 'Memories? What do you mean? It's only just happened. Eddie's only been gone for a couple of days.'

She shifted. 'If Alec won't tell you where Eddie's gone, I expect there's a very good reason.'

My heart jolted – had Mum asked Dad to send Eddie to live with her, but didn't want me to go too? Was she angry with me about something? Was that why she was avoiding all contact? Was Dad simply trying to protect me by not telling me the truth? Or was Rose lying?

More confused than ever, I stared at my hands, shocked to see them shaking.

'So, have you remembered anything since we last saw each other?' Rose said, watching me closely.

In my mind, I replayed the frightening vision of Dad looming over Mum. There was no way I was telling her I'd remembered that. 'No. Nothing.'

179

She frowned and sighed. Was that relief or disappointment? It was impossible to say. She was so hard to read.

Feeling increasingly desperate, I blurted, 'Have you treated my mum in the past?'

Her eyebrows shot up in surprise, but she recovered quickly. 'I'm afraid I can't disclose that sort of information due to confidentiality issues.'

I watched her, wondering what was going on inside her brain. She was so good at avoiding my questions, so talented at side-stepping.

'Are you ready to get started?' she said.

'Why's my dad in your house?'

She sipped her water. Looked me in the eye. Smiled. 'It's so hot today. I thought he'd be more comfortable waiting in here.'

'He usually drives into town,' I pointed out.

'I thought he might like a drink. I often invite people in to wait. Why do you ask?'

'Just curious.'

She smiled. This time the smile didn't ring true. Her lips moved, but her bulbous eyes were cold and unblinking. After rearranging her dress, she said, 'Shall we begin?'

I hesitated, torn. If she was genuine, this hypnotherapy session might allow me greater insight into Mum's disappearance. Then again, if she was in this with Dad, and intent on keeping unwanted memories locked inside my head, letting her put me under might give her the chance to do more damage. In fact, she seemed especially keen to get started, which made me more suspicious.

Unwilling to decide yet, I downed my glass of water and said, 'Do you have any idea where Mum's gone?'

Again, she hesitated, frowned, re-crossed her long legs, scratched her ankle. 'I really think it's best we begin.' She glanced at her watch.

Her non-answer made my blood boil, and my decision was made. She was hiding something. They both were. There was no way I was letting this woman poke and prod my brain ever again.

'Can I use your toilet first?'

'Yes. Of course. Let me show you where it is.' To her credit, she hid her frustration and led me into the hallway.

I followed her deeper into the house, ever-conscious that Dad was in here too. Snooping would be tricky with both of them around, but I wasn't going to let it stop me.

She opened a door on the right. 'I'll wait for you in my therapy room.'

*

I closed the door and waited until Rose's footsteps were out of earshot. My pulse was already racing, palms sweaty. I smeared my hands on my shorts and inched out of the bathroom, not even bothering to look around; I wasn't going to find anything in a downstairs toilet.

The house was quiet. I peered up the hallway to the kitchen, wondering if Dad was in there or in the living room. Knowing I couldn't waste any time, I crept towards the kitchen and stopped outside the door, which stood ajar about a head's width. The room was empty. It was a large, bright kitchen with red granite counters and retro accessories. I scanned the space for anything Eddie-related. The fridge was smothered with magnets and postcards and…was that what I thought it was? I dashed over to the Smeg fridge-freezer and stared at what appeared to be a child's drawing of a stick man, a stick woman and a stick boy. My head began to roar. Swallowing a wave of acidity, I backed away from the image, turned and hurried out of the room. The feeling that I was bang on about Rose and Dad solidified as, throwing caution to the wind, I dashed past Rose's office to the front of the house, took a left and tiptoed up the stairs.

The floor creaked horribly when I touched the landing, and I hesitated and looked back down the staircase, certain I was going to see Dad standing at the bottom glaring up at me. But the stairs were empty.

Aware I'd already been gone a couple of minutes, I opened the first door and poked my head inside. It was another bathroom. I dashed into the room and opened a white cabinet, finding only adult things. There was another cabinet which held cleaning products, but no bath toys of any description. Feeling disappointed, I left the room and opened the next door. This was a bedroom. Large and exquisitely decorated with vibrant tropical wallpaper covering the wall behind the headboard of a king-sized bed, and ornate oak furniture, I assumed this room belonged to Rose. I dashed inside and yanked open the bedside table drawer. There were a pair of glasses, a lip balm, hand cream and a book. Nothing incriminating. I hurried around to the other side of the bed and opened the second bedside table. My heart fluttered unpleasantly as my eyes landed on a photograph of my dad. It was a passport sized photo. A thumbprint. It was the one he had on his current driving licence and passport. I picked up the image and eased the drawer shut. My heart hardened. There was only possible explanation for Rose having a photograph of my dad in her bedside table: they were having an affair. I was right. Right to be cautious, right not to trust her.

A sound behind me made me whirl around; Rose was standing at the top of the stairs staring at me, head tilted at an odd angle.

'Everything OK?' she said. Her voice was flat, face neutral.

Colour flooded my cheeks. I closed my hand around the photograph and said, 'Sorry. I'm so nosy! I just wanted to have a peek upstairs. Your house is so beautiful.'

To my relief, she smiled. 'Thank you, and there's no need to apologise. I love a good nose around other people's homes.'

A memory flickered in my mind; of Shane nosing around our house. What if Shane had something to do with Mum's disappearance…he'd vanished not long before Mum. And he'd sent that nasty text. Was I barking up the wrong tree? Or were Dad and Shane in this together?

Rose scanned the room quickly then headed back down the stairs and I reluctantly followed, wishing I'd had time to explore the rest of the house. Maybe next time I came here, I'd get the chance. I thought about challenging her about the photo but bit my tongue. It was clear they were having an affair now, which meant I couldn't trust her, because I couldn't trust him. She might be innocent in most of this, but I couldn't be sure, so I couldn't let her get inside my head again. I thought about Shane again. There had always been something off about him…

Back in Rose's office, she told me to get comfortable and began her usual routine. Determined to pretend to be hypnotized so that I could find out what she was up to, I closed my eyes and tried not to follow the rhythm of her voice, but it slipped into my mind like honey.

Before I knew it, despite all my efforts, she took me under.

Chapter 39

The whole journey home I berated myself for letting Rose hypnotize me. Who knew what damage she'd done this time? I was almost certain now that she wasn't trying to help me remember; she was trying to make me forget. The drawing on her fridge proved she was in this with Dad - Eddie had drawn that picture, I was sure of it. And Rose had admitted to me she didn't have any children, which led to one conclusion: Eddie was being kept there. But why?

I thought about how long they'd embraced one another, how Rose's hand had lingered on Dad's arm. How could I have been so blind? It was obvious she and Dad were having an affair. Had they worked together to get rid of Mum? As much as I wanted to ignore it, the idea that Dad had hurt her was growing stronger by the day. If that was true and she was in danger, I needed to act fast. My plan was simple. The next time Dad took me to Rose's house, I'd use her house phone to call the police and tell them that my mum, Sofia Black-Hawkins, disappeared three weeks ago and that my little brother vanished this week. I'd also tell the police that I was pretty sure my dad was to blame for my mum and brother going missing. I wondered whether to mention Rose too. If she wasn't involved and I accused her of a crime, would I get in trouble for something like slander? I didn't know. Maybe it would be best to keep her out of it, until I was sure she was involved in Mum's disappearance.

Calling the police meant waiting until my next session, but I had no other choice. I was annoyed at myself for not doing it today. In Rose's kitchen I'd spotted a house phone on the windowsill. I could have phoned then instead of mucking about playing amateur detective.

Back at the house, I mumbled to Dad that I wasn't hungry and was going to bed for the rest of the day. He acted concerned, and offered to bring me up a jug of iced water, but I hastily poured myself a pint of orange juice and said that I didn't want to be disturbed.

Knightley was delighted to see me and vice versa so, after cleaning up his little accident, I played with him in my bedroom for a while then we snuggled up in bed together.

At the same time as always, the Merc rolled away from the house and Dad went wherever it was he went every afternoon. *Maybe to see Mum?*

A horrific thought pierced all else – was Dad keeping Mum somewhere? Was he visiting her every afternoon, taking her food and water to keep her alive, because she was locked up in some nasty little shed?

Shaking my head so hard my neck cracked, I pulled Knightley in closer and tried to visualise happy images of Eddie playing in the garden, but a vision of Mum tied and gagged, her face swollen with bruises, invaded every thought.

Was Dad capable of something like that? Why would he even do it? Why not just ask for a divorce if he was so desperate to be with Rose? Rose was clearly keen to be with him. I thought about all the times she'd touched him, got too close. Was she to blame? Had she tried to get Mum out of the way so they could be together? Was she the one I needed to worry about rather than Dad?

No. No. No. No!

I was letting my imagination go crazy. There was no way he or she would do something like that. No way. Never. I didn't even have any proof that Mum was even in danger.

So where's he going every afternoon? And didn't he start doing that about the time Mum disappeared? And you have this feeling – this instinct that she's in trouble – your brain's trying to tell you something. Don't ignore it.

Don't forget about Hugo and Shane. They could be involved in this too.

Feeling like my head was going to explode, I grabbed *Room* by Emma Donoghue off my shelf and started reading, but the story was written from a little boy's point of view. It reminded me too much of Eddie so I set it aside for another time when things were back to normal.

If they ever get back to normal…

I decided to try drawing and sat down at my desk. Knightley curled up on top of my feet.

I removed my book from my last sketch and stared at my work. Rose and Dad stared back at me with gaping black eyes and cruel grins. Their faces were skeletal, jaws elongated and lopsided as if they'd been dislocated. For a second, I couldn't believe I'd drawn such a ghastly vision.

In a sudden fit of rage, I grabbed the paper and ripped it to shreds.

Blind with tears I picked up a piece of charcoal and drew Mum cowering in a hole, hand up in self-defence.

Horrified by the drawing, I tore that up too then, without conscious decision, found myself sketching the vase of tulips mounted on the wall outside my bedroom. I hated that painting with a passion yet, as my fingers worked, I started remembering something and then, without warning or reason, a voice shrieked in my head: *'hurt…your fault -'*

I shot away from the desk, the words ringing in my ears like screams in Hell. Desperate to pull the memory upward and remember exactly what had happened and who had uttered those hateful words, I sent my mind back. The words 'hurt' and 'fault' repeated over and over and over again, combining with a flash of red tulips and Mum's terrified face and Dad's scowl…

It was gone. The images recoiled as quickly as they came, but the feelings they'd evoked remained, stronger and more alarming than ever.

Adrenaline brought me to my feet. Knightley scampered away and I scooped him up.

Suddenly, I knew without a shadow of a doubt that I couldn't wait for my next session at Rose's house. Mum needed my help. I didn't want to believe it, but my dad had hurt her. My mind was trying to show me what he'd done and while it hadn't revealed everything, it had shown me enough. Mum was in danger.

Chapter 40

I couldn't leave in daylight, so I decided to wait until the sky turned black. Dad usually went to bed at ten-thirty, so I chose to wait until midnight, just in case it took a while for him to fall asleep.

The evening dragged like a cart loaded with the dead. My tummy rumbled but I couldn't eat and didn't dare leave my room for fear of seeing Dad. One look at me and he'd know I was up to something. I was as transparent as glass.

A tension headache straddled my skull and I curled up in a ball on my bed with Knightley in my arms and pictured myself reaching the police station and telling them everything. The relief would be immense. Imagining a kind, portly policeman nodding and smiling at me encouragingly, I closed my eyes and the aching in my head began to ease. But, no matter how exhausted I was, sleep evaded me.

Using an old spotty sock, I played tug of war with Knightley on my bedroom floor. His unabandoned joy reminded me of Eddie. My resolve hardened. At midnight I was going to leave this house and tell the police everything. They'd believe me. I was Mum's daughter. All they needed to do was come to the house and see that Eddie and Mum were missing. That was evidence enough. I imagined lies spewing out of Dad's mouth then pictured him clamming up and not saying anything. Would the police wrestle the truth out of him in time?

It was something I had no control over. I'd failed to find out what he'd done to her, but the police were experts. Where I'd failed, they'd succeed. They had to.

*

I looked at the clock: it was nearly midnight.

Money. Car keys. Knightley. Clothes on my back. That was all I needed. I grabbed my purse and shoved it in my backpack, took off my pyjamas and dressed in jeans, a T-shirt and trainers, scraped my hair into a ponytail and lifted Knightley off the bed. Praying he'd be quiet, I held him to my chest and slipped out of my bedroom into the blackness of the landing.

The house was silent. Every light was off. Holding Knightley in one arm, I felt for the banister then edged along the landing, wincing at every single noise. Outside the master, I paused, listened to the sound of Dad's breathing. He was asleep – thank God.

Breathing a little easier, I carried Knightley down the stairs and stopped at the bottom. The moon shone into the living space offering respite from the dark. I hurried through the house as fast as I dared, checking behind every few seconds despite the vacuous silence.

Knightley squealed and wriggled out of my grip, hit the ground and scurried away under the dining room table. I knelt and whispered his name. A moment later, a potent urine smell tainted the air and a small wet nose touched my hand. I picked him up, undid my backpack and slipped him inside, doing up the zip partway so he wouldn't suffocate. Putting him in my bag felt wrong, but I was going to need both hands soon. Hitching the bag onto my back, I jogged through the house towards the front door.

My hand found Dad's keys and I grabbed them and headed for the back door. Dad parked around the side of the house. Leaving via the back door would get me to his car more quickly.

My hands shook as I fumbled for the right key. There were so many and it was too dark to see.

As if he could sense my distress, Knightley whimpered

and pawed my shoulder. I shushed him and shoved what I hoped was the right key into the keyhole. I didn't turn on the lights, paranoid that if Dad went to the toilet and light somehow found its way through the vast tunnel of the house, he'd know something was up and come to investigate.

Knightley crawled onto my shoulder, making me drop the keys. The clatter of metal hitting wood shattered the silence like a broken glass in church. I grabbed Knightley before he fell and held him against my pounding chest, terrified he'd run off again. Crouching down, I felt for the keys and froze as the rapid thud of feet met my ears.

Chapter 41

There was nothing else do to but go for it. I stood up, shoved the key into the hole and twisted. Click. Glancing over my shoulder, I yanked open the door and sprinted out into the darkness. The night light sensed my presence and came on, bathing me in yellow and rendering me as conspicuous as a snowman in summer. I looked back, frozen in panic. In the doorway, chest heaving, stood Dad.

'What are you doing?' he snarled.

I ignored him and sprinted around the back of the house.

'HEY!' He was coming after me.

Lungs burning, I turned the corner and skidded. Knightley fell out of my grasp with a yelp, then scampered away to smell something. I had to make a split-second decision. Hard as it was, I had to leave him.

Dad rounded the corner as I reached the Merc. Frantically, I pressed the button on the key fob. The car beeped. Lights flashed. I yanked open the driver's door and slid behind the wheel then stabbed at what I hoped was the door lock. Something clicked. Jabbering incoherently to myself, I slotted the key into the ignition and turned. The engine came to life and I adjusted the rear-view mirror, horrified to see Dad standing behind the car with Knightley in his arms.

His voice roared above the Merc's purr, 'Get out now. Come back in the house.'

I looked down at the gearbox. It looked simple. On the right side of the gearstick were three letters: R, N and D. Reverse. Neutral. Drive. My hand found the gearstick. The smooth, roundness of it felt oddly familiar – had I been learning to drive in this before everything went upside down and inside out?

I jumped as Dad smacked his fist against the window and gestured for me to get out. I glanced at Knightley, frightened for a moment that Dad would use him against me, but the thought clearly hadn't occurred to him. Yet.

He gestured for me to wind down the window. I shook my head and tried to work out which device would make the car lights come on.

I tried one, but it switched on the front wipers. The next turned on the indicator.

Dad tried opening the door. I flinched at the scorn in his eyes when he realized that I'd locked the doors.

He slammed his palm against the window and shouted, 'GET OUT! THIS IS CRAZY! GET OUT NOW!'

'NO!' I screamed back.

There – I found it. The lights flashed on, revealing the golden driveway that led away from the house towards freedom. That path was my yellow brick road. My salvation. My route to the police. To Mum and Eddie. Nothing was going to stop me now.

I slid the gearstick into drive. Glanced at Dad. Understanding dawned in his face and he looked scarier than I'd ever thought possible.

With a lump in my throat I took one last look at Knightley.

I lowered my foot to the accelerator, surer than ever that I'd done this before, but froze as Dad dashed around the bonnet and stood in front of the car, blocking the way.

I slammed my hand on the horn. Poor Knightley leapt out of his skin and turned to stare at the car.

Shielding from the lights, Dad yelled again, demanding I get out and go back inside the house.

'GET OUT OF THE WAY!' I screamed, reluctant to beep the horn again because of Knightley.

'GET INSIDE!' he screamed back.

His face was florid. Livid.

'I'M GOING TO FIND HER. AND EDDIE. I'M CALLING THE POLICE!'

His eyes widened for a fraction of a second in what seemed like shock, but he didn't move out of the way.

I sighed in frustration and looked down at the gearstick. R. Reverse. Of course!

Without further thought, I slid into reverse and slammed my foot on the accelerator. The car whizzed back so fast that I gasped. Dad shot forwards, chasing the car. I shifted into Drive, yanked the wheel to the right and swerved off the path onto the grass, narrowly missing him as I raced away.

In the rear-view mirror, I saw Dad gaping after me, Knightley clutched under one arm.

Relief sang in my veins. I'd made it. There was no way he could follow me...unless. Oh God. His motorbike. Was it working? He hadn't ridden it for ages. I faintly recalled him telling Mum it was on the blink and I was pretty sure it hadn't been fixed yet. I licked my lips and prayed I was right.

Chapter 42

Every other second I glanced in the rear-view mirror, worried I'd see Dad motoring after me on his Yamaha, but the night was empty and dark, and I began to relax a little, thinking the bike was broken. Even so, anxiety gnashed its teeth when I thought about Knightley. Dad hadn't used him to stop me leaving which gave me hope that he wouldn't hurt him. He'd gain nothing by hurting my puppy, but I couldn't quell a sickening niggle of doubt. I didn't know this man anymore. He could be capable of anything. Knightley was so small and sweet, and Dad was angry.

A scene played out in my mind. Dad kicking Knightley, my puppy whimpering and scampering away to hide under the table, tail between his shivering legs. Dad shutting him out in the back garden for the entire night; Knightley falling off the cliff...

I smeared cold sweat off my forehead with a trembling hand and tried to concentrate on driving. The road was narrow, winding and black, lined by high bushes that seemed to press in on the Merc with vicious intent. My hands were clamped on the steering wheel like vices, my elbows locked out so hard they almost bent inwards.

Despite the heat, my teeth chattered. With no streetlights or cats' eyes it was hard to see and I kept veering too close to the bushes then swerving back towards what I imagined to be the centre of the road. I saw a light behind me, speeded up and swerved onto a side road which led uphill to where I didn't know. Terrified I was going to crash, I waited another few seconds to create distance between me and the vehicle that had been behind me on the main road then slowed to 35mph and drove as carefully as possible. Thankfully, whoever it was hadn't followed me.

This road was even narrower than the last and as bumpy as a grater. I didn't care about the car, but if I had an accident and got hurt or wrecked the Merc, I'd have to run to town and by then it might be too late. Which direction was town now? My heart hammered against my rib cage. When I was on the bigger road, I'd known where I was, but now I was following a rake-thin country lane to the middle of nowhere.

It was a maze of tiny channels out here, a random network of ancient, higgledy-piggledy lanes that shouldn't exist these days with cars, vans, buses, lorries and tractors needing to use them. There were no streetlights, no houses – nothing but the black cloak of night made blacker by the absence of man-made light – meaning I had to rely solely on the Merc's headlights. As it was, I was perched on the tip of the seat so that I could reach the pedals, my face poking over the wheel into the inky blackness to see what lay ahead before I crashed, missed a bend or clipped a tree. The lane wasn't even wide enough for two cars; it was barely big enough for the Merc, but every now and then a passing place appeared on the verge. Trust me to take a weird diversion onto a single-track road and get lost. I bit off my pinkie nail and winced. I'd panicked and screwed up. Was Dad panicking right now? I pictured him phoning Rose and telling her what had happened. Imagined how their conversation would play out. She'd probably tell him to go after me, and he would. I glanced in the mirror but the road was abandoned. He couldn't follow me; his bike was broken. Exhaling shakily, I tried to guess their next move. Would he and Rose grab Eddie and rush to the airport? Fly somewhere to escape the police? Or had Dad somehow covered his tracks enough to stay put?

The thought that they'd take Eddie with them made

me grip the steering wheel so hard my knuckles went white. It also tripled the need to contact the police as soon as possible; the longer the delay, the more likely it was that Dad would disappear with Eddie and, if he had done something awful to Mum, what then?

I shuddered and blinked back tears, telling myself she wasn't dead. If she was, I'd feel it. Wasn't that a thing? If Mum died, some sixth sense would tell me. I'd know. And she felt alive. I had to believe she was, and that Eddie was OK, or I'd crumble. And if Dad had done something that terrible, I'd know. I'd feel that too. Wouldn't I?

A sudden bend caught me off-guard. I gasped and managed to avoid driving into a ditch by the skin of my teeth. Shaking my head, I focused on the road ahead and slowed to 25mph, knowing I needed to hurry but too scared to drive faster. I didn't know where this road was taking me; I could be driving further away from Shepton rather than towards it. In fact, I probably was. The time on the dash said it was twelve-fifteen. At least the police never slept. I didn't know where I was or how to get to the police station from here, but there was a SAT Nav in the Merc. If I could work out how to use it, I could find out the address, tap it in and hey presto!

The road straightened out but remained just as narrow, lined by fields that resembled black lakes. There was no sign of human life out here and I was aware of how vulnerable I was; if Dad found me, what would he do? He hadn't hurt me so far – apart from the push on the stairs – but what if he'd reached the end of his tether?

No. Dad wouldn't hurt you. He's trying to manipulate and control you, that's all. If he found you, he'd drag you home and start all over again, and you'd need to play nice, make him think you felt sorry for running away.

I sighed and rubbed my neck. Confusion made me dizzy. The truth was that even with all the evidence piling up against him, I still couldn't entirely accept that Dad could do something so terrible, yet the facts spoke volumes and the police needed to know everything I'd discovered because Mum wasn't safe. She was missing and Dad knew things he wasn't telling me. He was hiding something awful and the police would find out what. They had to. I couldn't do it alone.

I drove until I reached a passing place then pulled in, put the car in neutral and turned my attention to the screen.

It took me ages to work out how to turn on the stupid device. Once I was in, I searched 'police station Shepton' and the address came up immediately. I tapped the postcode and a map appeared. With a huge sigh of relief, I slid the gearstick into drive.

The roar of an engine made me jump. A car had parked up behind mine. I glanced in the rear-view mirror to see a tall, broad man climb out of the vehicle. It took me a few seconds to register that it was someone I knew – not Dad, thank God, but Mr B. James Broughton. My art teacher. Mum's friend. What was he doing here? How did he know – Dad must have sent him!

Mr B jogged over and raised his hands as if to say 'I come in peace.' He looked worried. He gestured for me to unwind the window. I shook my head. Shouted, 'Get out of the way! Leave me alone. I know Dad's sent you.' It was too much of a coincidence for Mr B to stumble upon me out here. Dad must have known he lived this way and rung him, told him to stop me. My heart skipped. Did that mean Mr Broughton was involved in all of this? Were he, Dad and Rose working together?

'You need to listen to me,' Mr B said.

'Get out of the way!' I repeated, pressing the accelerator to emphasize my words.

'I'm not moving until Alec gets here,' he said, shaking his head. He pulled out his phone and started tapping at it.

'Don't!' I screamed. 'I mean it!'

Mr B ignored me. He put the phone to his ear.

I gave him the finger then slammed my foot down on the gas and zoomed away, forcing him to stumble backwards and fall over. I glanced in the rear-view mirror to see him searching for his phone. Heart thumping madly, I looked back at the road ahead, wondering how on earth Mr Broughton was involved in this madness. Did Dad have something on him?

A mechanical growl pulled my focus to the rear-view and I stared in horror at a spot of light behind me that was growing closer by the second.

The blinding ball of light wasn't big enough to belong to a car and the aggressive roar of the engine wasn't coming from a four-wheel vehicle.

My breath hitched and I stamped on the accelerator.

Dad was coming.

Chapter 43

I no longer cared about driving safely; all that mattered was getting away.

The Merc zoomed forward and I leaned over the steering wheel as if that would make it go faster.

The road was straight for a while, but a quick glance at the map told me a sharp bend to the left was coming up. I bit my lip, told myself to hold my nerve. This was risky, but slowing down wasn't an option.

My pulse accelerated along with the car as I took her up to forty, fifty, sixty, seventy miles per hour, glancing at the mirror, throat pulsing hard as Dad's motorbike drew closer and closer, cutting the distance between us with hideous ease.

The countryside turned into an indecipherable blur as the Merc hit eighty. One hundred metres and I'd reach the bend. Eighty. Sixty. Fifty. I slammed on the brakes, taking her down to forty and swerved around the corner, wheels squealing in protest, arms rigid, hands clenched on the wheel. Luckily, the car held ground and I sped her back up then braked harshly at the next bend, leaning into it like a race car driver. Behind me, Dad kept coming. The Yamaha's engine buzzed like a gigantic wasp, not giving up, barely slowing for each bend.

And then, to my absolute shock, the bike's lights turned blue and a siren belted out into the silent morning.

I frowned, glanced round, wondering if this was some kind of trick. But no. It wasn't. I wasn't being chased by Dad. I was being chased by a police officer.

Cursing my stupidity, I slowed the Merc to a stop and eyed the mirror nervously. Oh God. I didn't have a driving licence and I'd been speeding. Was I going to get arrested? And what then? Maybe if I explained to the officer what I'd been doing, he or she would understand and offer to help.

The motorbike pulled up in front of the Merc and the siren stopped. A male officer pulled off his helmet, placed it on the bike and walked over. I unwound the window and waited.

'Get out of the vehicle, please Miss. I'm PC Roberts and...'

The officer's words came and went like static. All I took in was the seriousness of his tone and the words 'stolen' and 'speeding'. I shook my head and tried to interrupt him and explain about Dad, but he wouldn't listen.

Two minutes later, a police car pulled up and I was escorted into the back of the vehicle by PC Roberts and a female officer. The first officer handed the new officers a slip of paper and Dad's keys, then wandered back to his motorbike.

The police car pulled away with me inside. The driver introduced herself as PC Clark and her colleague as PC Budd. I stared into the mirror and met the female officer's eyes. 'Please, you have to listen to me -'

I tried to explain what had happened, but she warned me I could harm my defence – blah blah blah. Budd mirrored her sentiments, turning to give me a hard stare. Neither of them would let me speak.

'But, please, my Dad, he's done something to my mum and -'

PC Clark's eyes flickered with what I thought might be concern, but she held up a hand and said, 'When we get to the station you can tell me your story. OK?'

I nodded weakly. I wanted to smash my fists into the glass divider and demand they listen to me now, but her no-nonsense tone told me it would be futile. If I was going to convince them I was telling the truth, I had to play ball and follow their lead.

*

The station was eerily quiet, the officers at my side even quieter.

The officers booked me in at the high reception desk, then sat down to wait for whoever was coming to fetch me and take me to God knows where. They weren't going to listen to what I had to say until they'd processed me, which could take ages. With rising panic, I registered the futility of my situation, but gave it one more try.

Keeping my voice low, I said, 'Please. It's not what you think. I thought I was being chased.'

PC Clark shifted subtly in her seat and scanned my face. I held my breath, hoping, praying she'd listen to me now. She rolled her tongue around her lips, glanced at her colleague once, then twice. In a loud voice she said to her partner, 'Go grab a coffee. I'll deal with this one.'

Almost too grateful to speak, I swiped at my cheeks and said, 'Thank you. Please, I need to get out of here. He's dangerous -'

She held up her hand and I stopped. Her voice was softer now, eyes kind. 'Tell me everything slowly and clearly and I'll see what I can do.'

'My dad, Alec Black-Hawkins, the man who pulled up on a motorbike as we drove away, has done something to my mum. Something bad. She disappeared about three weeks ago and I haven't heard anything from her since. None of her stuff's gone and Dad won't tell me where she is.'

'Has he hurt you?'

'No, but -'

'Threatened you?'

'No, well – that's not the point. I was driving here to speak to you, the police, to tell you to look for her before it's too late. My memory's been messed up recently, but I keep getting these flashbacks and seeing him towering over her and -'

Lines furrowed the fair skin between her eyebrows. She scratched her forehead then said, 'Have you any evidence to prove he's harmed your mother?'

I swallowed nervously. 'Isn't the fact that she's gone and he won't tell me where or why enough? Surely that warrants an investigation.'

'Well, of course, if you give us her details, we'll look into it. But I'm sure that if your Dad was worried, he'd have reported her missing by now.'

'But that's just it!' I said, standing up, 'he's not reported it because he's involved. He's done something to her. Rose Weatherby too.'

'Who's Rose Weatherby?'

'My therapist, but they're having an affair. They're in this together. And that's not all – I think they've taken my little brother too. His name's Eddie and -'

'Sit back down,' she said.

I sat down and twisted my hands together. 'Why aren't you listening to me? He's dangerous.'

She shook her head. 'I'm sorry but I have to be honest. So far, what you've told me is sketchy at best and there's absolutely nothing to suggest Mr Black-Hawkins has done anything wrong. In fact, he's the one who reported the car stolen, and PC Roberts found you driving at upwards of seventy miles per hour in a thirty zone without a driving licence.'

'I thought he was chasing me,' I said, 'please, you have to help her. Please.'

She sighed, pursed her lips and thought for a moment. I waited, terrified she was going to say no.

Finally, she withdrew a pad and pencil from her

pocket. 'Give me your mother's details and I'll get someone to look into it. I'm afraid that's the best I can do at the moment.'

'OK, good. That's great, thank you.'

She looked at me. 'Your mother's full name?'

'Sofia Black-Hawkins.'

'Age?'

I hesitated, stuck for a second. Was she thirty-eight or thirty-nine?

'Age?' she repeated.

'Thirty-nine,' I guessed.

Her hand froze above the writing pad.

'What? What is it?' I said.

She cleared her throat and stared at me for a beat then looked towards the station entrance. I followed her gaze and my eyes locked with Dad's. He was standing with PC Roberts, the officer who'd caught me speeding. On seeing me, he hurried over and stood far too close.

'Oh, thank God, you're OK,' he said.

PC Roberts walked over and looked down at me sympathetically. He gestured with his head to PC Clark. She moved away from us to speak to him. Heads bent together, Roberts whispered something in her ear and she pulled back, gave me a strange look, handed him Dad's keys and walked away.

'Wait! What?' I stared at PC Roberts.

He passed Dad the keys, smiled gently and said, 'Mr Black-Hawkins has explained your circumstances. I've also spoken to your therapist on the phone. They both assure me that you're unwell and so, given this, I've decided to write this off as an exceptional case, which means you're free to go, uncharged.' He glanced at my Dad and said, 'Just make sure this doesn't happen again.'

He and Dad shook hands and I watched, too shocked to speak.

Dad reached out a hand to me, 'Come on. Let's get

you home.'

I recoiled and said, 'I'm not going anywhere with you. You hurt Mum.'

PC Roberts's eyebrows shot up.

With a desperate cry, I ran for the door, but two officers were on the other side and stopped me in my tracks. Dad and PC Roberts appeared a moment later, and Dad cupped my face in his hands and said, 'If you don't come with me easily, it'll only make things worse, darling.'

His threat was clear and hideous, but right now I knew I was fighting a losing battle. Dad, with the help of my 'therapist', Rose fucking Weatherby, had somehow convinced the police officers that I was unstable. I leaned against the wall, weak and defeated.

'Come on. Let's not make it worse than it has to be,' he said softly.

I latched on to his meaning with hope in my heart: if things could get worse, it meant they weren't as bad as they could possibly be for Mum. Not yet.

Fighting the impulse to run again, I allowed him to lead me to the Merc. There was nothing else I could do, but Mum was still alive. Dad might be taking me back to the house, but not for long. If the police wouldn't do anything to help Mum, it was up to me, and I wasn't going to give up until I found her.

I didn't think Dad would hurt me, but the look he gave me as he slid behind the steering wheel sent tremors up my spine.

Chapter 44

Dad said nothing the entire journey home. On the steering wheel, his knuckles were white and knotted, his arms locked out so tightly that veins swelled beneath the skin like eels.

I huddled as far away from him as I could and wondered how on earth I was going to save Mum when I was being taken back to that enormous glass cage. One thought overrode everything else: I needed to dig deeper. Search harder. There had to be something in the house that would give away where he was keeping her. Where hadn't I searched?

Mum's art studio.

My mind cleared a little. There was also the garage. Dad never parked in there but all his tools, including the sit-on lawn mower lived there. He'd used it last week. How he could go on with his life acting like everything was normal when he'd done something awful to his wife was beyond belief. I glanced at him and imagined grabbing the steering wheel, jerking it to the left, crashing us into a tree, leaping out and making a run for it, but I didn't. I wasn't that reckless. There was no way of knowing if I'd make it out of an accident like that unscathed. It was too risky.

Still, the urge to attack him clung on.

When had he changed? When had my dad become this dark, twisted stranger?

I forced my mind back as far as it would go and frowned. I remembered playing with Eddie, making dinner, cleaning, going to school in the Merc, seeing Isla but these were all random flashes. None of these memories unfolded into a longer story. They all lasted less than a second, like they'd been taken in the blink of an eye, stored there, but not really engaged with. There was nothing concrete about them. It was as if they were ghosts of memories rather than memories themselves. Polaroids that never developed. I tried to remember the last conversation I had with Mum. The last time I'd seen her. I'd been putting this off, ignoring how bad my memory was by not trying to remember things with any real effort, but now that I was really trying, it was frustrating and scary to realize how damaged my recall actually was. In fact, all I could remember was a vague feeling that my last conversation with Mum had been heated. We'd argued. That's all I could recall. How weird.

I rubbed my chest. Longing gnawed a hole. The yearning to have her hold me, tell me everything was going to be OK was so dizzying that I thought I was going to pass out.

'You OK?' Dad said. His face seemed fuzzy.

We'd reached the house.

I nodded and stumbled out of the car.

'You sure?' His words were distant.

My head felt like it was vibrating. I leaned against the Merc and rested my forehead in my hands, waiting for the vertigo to end, so exhausted I could barely stand. Dad's arm wrapped around my shoulders and I allowed him to guide me inside.

'It's the shock. You need to rest,' he snapped, half-carrying me through the house.

'No. I need Mum,' I croaked, hating the fact now more than ever that my life was in his hands.

Chapter 45

I was woken by Knightley licking my nose. I cuddled him close and started as Dad entered the room without knocking. I shrank into my pillow and turned my face away.

He placed a breakfast tray piled high with pancakes on my chair and said, 'When you're dressed, we need to talk.'

Without waiting for an answer, he left, closing the door behind him.

I loved pancakes. Mum and I used to call them heaven on a plate.

My stomach growled and I stared at the bottle of maple syrup he'd placed on the tray. This was clearly another ruse, a ploy to worm his way into my good books, make me think he was innocent in all this. But buying me a puppy and bringing me my favourite food wasn't going to cut it. I wasn't a four-year-old. And I wasn't stupid.

A memory of making pancakes with Mum and Eddie burst into my mind. *I was tossing a pancake, but I dropped it and -*

Knightley scrambled off me and headed for the pancakes. I caught him before he made the leap, reached over and grabbed the plate. Feeling guilty, I ate two then fed the rest to my puppy. To outwit Dad, I needed energy, and the shot of sugar helped to battle the weariness pulling at my limbs.

In the hallway outside my bedroom, I forced myself to stand in front of the tulip painting. The petals looked like droplets of blood. Feelings rushed through me – terror – helplessness – confusion. No memories flashed up from the sludge of my brain. I focused on the snippet I'd already remembered, tried to draw it forward, but it wouldn't come. Already, it was as if that tiny insight was fading, dissolving like sugar in tea without a hand to stir it. But suddenly, I felt oddly compelled to take the painting off the wall. The urge was overwhelming, as if I was a puppet being controlled by its master, and I found myself grabbing either side of the gold frame and heaving the picture off its hook. I laid the painting on the floor and then, in a zombie-like daze, returned my gaze to the white wall. A frown buried into my forehead as I stared at a crack in the paint. I ran my fingers over it, wondering, hoping a new awareness would form in my mind. Incoherent shouts echoed around me and I whipped my hand away, desperate to put words to the raging voices resonating from some distant, forgotten place. But nothing more came. Feeling disappointed and more confused than before, I replaced the painting, wiped my hands on my legs and turned away.

Knightley scampered along the landing. I scooped him up, went inside the bathroom and locked the door.

For a while, I rested my forehead against cool tile, naked and shivering, trying to work out where Dad might be keeping Mum. In a weird way, it comforted me to believe that Eddie was with Rose Weatherby rather than here, with Dad. Rose might be a husband-stealer and a liar, but she didn't seem capable of violence. She might well know what he was up to, but was keeping well out of it, not wanting to stain her hands with another woman's blood.

Of course, this was guesswork and assumption based on scant evidence. It was hardly surprising the police didn't believe me. I had no physical evidence of Dad's guilt, and my inability to recall key details slaughtered my credibility.

I rubbed my chest and turned on the shower. Knightley joined me before I could stop him. He yelped, backed away, then changed his mind and splashed about around my feet. Watching him, I gulped back a sob and scrubbed my skin harder than necessary, as if that would erase the soot clouding my mind and allow me to remember everything clearly again. If only I could remember exactly what had happened...

My head began to throb with frustration, and I switched off the water and strode out of the shower. Knightley continued to frolic, unaware of my distress. I brushed my teeth until my gums bled. Memories of trying to convince the police slammed into me; their refusal to believe anything I told them brought bile to the back of my throat. And the fact that Mr Broughton was clearly on Dad's side. Involved somehow. I'd thought I could trust him. Had he played a part in Mum's disappearance? Or was he simply trying to help, concerned that I was putting my health at risk by venturing outside – and driving without a licence? Dad could have lied to him too.

The knowledge that I was on my own made me feel like I was drowning. A scolding desire to collapse and break down took hold, but I pushed it away, turned from the mirror and left the room, telling myself I had to keep it together for Mum's sake.

*

The weather was muggy and oppressive. Storm clouds gathered, darker than ever. I dressed in leggings and a baggy T-shirt then carried Knightley downstairs. Dad had said we needed to talk, but talking to him was the last thing I wanted. Still, if there was a chance that I could trick him into revealing something, it was worth a shot.

I let Knightley out into the back garden. With a yap of excitement, he gambolled away. I was confident he wouldn't fall off the cliff edge. He was used to his surroundings already.

Shutting the door to make sure he stayed out long enough to do his business, I hovered outside Dad's office, chills of dread flaring along the back of my neck. There was no way of telling how angry he was about yesterday. He'd hidden it well when he'd brought breakfast to my room.

I raised my hand to knock. Before my skin touched wood, he opened the door and loomed over me. In one large hand, he held a cup of coffee. Shadows plagued his eyes. He nodded and gestured for me to follow him into the kitchen.

I poured myself a glass of orange juice then leaned against the counter. He sat down at the island with his legs splayed in a blatant show of dominance. I watched as he downed the rest of his coffee before slamming it onto the counter with unnecessary force. His eyes locked on my face and he cleared his throat.

I stared off into the distance and said, 'What do you need to talk to me about?'

'Why don't you sit down?'

I bit back a snappy response. Told myself to play nice.

I walked over to the island, dragged out the stool and perched on it, ready to spring off and run if needed. Reminding myself that he wanted to win me over, not hurt me, I told myself to relax, act cool.

'Good. Now, I think we need to talk about what happened yesterday.'

His voice was weirdly calm. I stole a glance at him.

'I'm sorry,' I said. 'I don't know what got into me.'

'You could have crashed. PC Roberts said you were driving at eighty miles an hour.'

'Like I said, I panicked. I thought...I don't know what I thought.'

'I know you're confused right now but driving off like that – telling the police that I -' He shook his head, drummed his fingers against the table. Suddenly, he looked up. His face was harder, voice raw. 'If you do something like that again, I'll be forced to take measures you won't like, and I really don't want to do that, but I won't have a choice.'

'Measures like what?'

'There's no need to go into the details now. As long as you behave yourself, I won't need to do anything.'

I nodded, pretending I understood. Inside, panic spiralled.

'I need to know you're not going to go haring off again.'

'I won't. I promise.'

He frowned. I wondered if he thought I was lying. Hoped he believed me.

'And this ridiculous notion you've got in your head needs to stop too.'

'What notion?' I said innocently.

'The notion that I've done something to...someone. That I've hurt someone.'

'Why won't you say her name?' I said.

'Alright. *Mum*. This warped story has to stop. If this carries on...' he hesitated, looked out of the window at the blackening sky. 'Rose thinks – *no* – that doesn't matter.'

'Wait. What were you going to say?'

His knuckles cracked one by one. He looked guilty. 'Nothing. She's just worried, that's all. We both are.'

Worried I'm going to find out what you've done.

'Maybe if you tell me where Mum and Eddie are, my *story* won't be so *warped*. And tell me this – where do you go every afternoon?'

His hands curled.

I tensed, afraid I'd gone too far.

He opened his mouth as if to shout. His eyes blazed.

Without a word, he stormed out of the kitchen, yanked open the door to his office and slammed it so hard that a photo fell off the wall and smashed.

Chapter 46

As soon as Dad went out, I set to work. First step: find the key to Mum's art studio.

It took me a while to find it, but I finally discovered the key hidden in a shoe box in Mum's walk-in wardrobe. I wondered if Dad had hidden it there, then dismissed the thought; either way, I had the key, which meant I could hunt for more evidence and hopefully find some clue about Mum.

Having only eaten two pancakes all morning, I made myself a quick snack of cheese and crackers and wolfed it down. Still hungry, I grabbed a banana. Aware time was ticking and that Dad's afternoon trips could last anywhere between one and three hours, I tidied my plate into the dishwasher, swiped my finger across the electric bin and dropped the banana peel inside. Before the lid dropped, I thought I caught a glimpse of a book in amongst the other rubbish. I swiped it back open, reached in and grabbed the brown leather book. I turned it over, ran my thumb over the imprinted word *Journal.* This was insane. Dad had thrown his journal away and I'd just found it.

Unable to believe my luck, I gawped at the book for a while before finding my way to the kitchen island.

I was almost unaware of Knightley begging to be picked up. Cold dread seeped into my veins as I stared at the diary. Dad's diary. The one I should have read weeks ago when I had the chance.

This was it. I felt certain. I was about to find out the truth. I was going to learn what he'd done to Mum and where she was, and where he'd put Eddie. And if that was the case, I could take the journal to the police and present it as evidence.

Realising the enormity of my find, I glanced behind me, worried that Dad had planted it there and was still in the house, waiting and watching to see what I would do.

But it was just Knightley and me. And the tinny click of the copper clock.

I focused on the evidence. This time there was nothing to hold me back. I thought about Dad's deviousness when he'd spoken to the police, how he'd pushed me on the stairs, taped Mum's phone under his desk, read my letters but never sent them…I owed him nothing. Horrid though it was to admit, any loyalty to him was a thing of the past.

With prickling fingers, I opened the journal and began to read.

1 June

I'm a monster. What I've done is unforgiveable. What I continue to do goes beyond that, but I can't seem to stop myself. Seeing her there in that room gives me something I need. It's like a drug. It's addictive and terrible and I know I ought to put her out of her misery. I've already hurt her so much and keeping her there is awful, but I can't do that. Not yet. Maybe not ever, which is possibly the cruellest course imaginable, but it gives me what I need. Is that selfish? Yes. But right now, it's a compulsion I can't fight. I need to see her there in that room, I need to keep her alive longer, watch her, keep an eye on her, gauge her reactions to every single word I utter.

Must go. Arrietty's calling.

8 June

God – if it wasn't for Rose, I don't know what I'd do. Rose says not to tell her anything, so I haven't, but if her approach doesn't work,

I'll only have one choice left and if that's what has to happen to give us a chance of moving on together, I'll do it. Rose is right. She's always right.

I love her so much it hurts. S

Frantically, I turned to the next page. There was nothing. I flicked through page after page after page, but every one was blank. There were only two entries in the whole journal.

I re-read the vile words several times, mind spinning like a tornado, snatching up thoughts and feelings and hurling them in random directions with zero care or mercy. Dad alluded to keeping my mum in a room, but he didn't say where this room was. Putting her out of her misery – did that mean what I thought? And Rose. Rose was worse than I thought. It sounded like *she* was the one convincing Dad to lie, persuading him to keep me in the dark and Mum locked up in that room, all so she could have my dad to herself.

My hands clenched as I re-read the final complete sentence. *I love her so much it hurts.* Bastard. Cheating, lying, psychopathic bastard. I shouldn't have been surprised – I'd already worked out they were having an affair, but this seemed worse - though not as bad as his sadistic need to keep Mum in a locked room. Nothing could ever be as bad as that.

My airway constricted as I zoned in on the most important, horrific fact: Mum was hurt. He said he ought to put her out of her misery, which meant she was in pain, that she was suffering. He'd even admitted he'd already hurt her a lot. That what he'd done was unforgiveable.

Worst fears confirmed, I felt so lost and frightened that I didn't know what to do. Cold, black dread enveloped me like the grim reaper's cloak.

My eyes fell on the word *room*. If this wasn't enough evidence for the police, I didn't know what was. The problem was that in the journal Dad didn't mention where he was keeping her.

I became aware of the studio key in my hand. Before I did anything else, I had to check the building, see if there was anything in there that might indicate where she was being held prisoner.

Leaving a whimpering Knightley in the kitchen, I tore out the page from the journal, shoved it in my bra, threw the book back in the bin, slipped on my trainers, closed the back door and headed for the studio.

Above me, clouds clustered like Hell's demons. They reflected my Dad. It was as if the daddy I'd grown up with had been possessed by the devil and reborn with a new and sinister intent. There was no real care, no love. A vague part of my mind remembered a warmer man who cared about me, but the present eradicated the past; he was a slave to his demons, whatever they were, and I was helpless to prevent him from travelling down the dark path he'd chosen. He may have been my blood, but in my heart existed no love, only hatred and fear and the horrifying certainty that he'd hurt my mum. I needed to act quickly before he decided he had no choice left other than to kill her. Enough with tiptoeing around on eggshells and trying to play nice. I was getting out of here. I just needed to make sure the studio didn't contain any clues that would point me in Mum's direction. And I needed to be quick. Having the key meant it would only take seconds to check.

I stopped halfway down the garden. The first droplets fell, warm and thick as blood. I shuddered despite the mugginess and closed off my imagination to a carousel of images too awful to name.

The art studio beckoned me closer.

I jogged the rest of the way and hesitated next to the door. I remembered men coming to put the building together, Mum taking them cups of tea, Dad chatting to them in a friendly way that didn't seem to tie in at all with the person he was now. Eddie wasn't born yet. He wasn't even a glimmer on the horizon. It was just the three of us. I was ten. It was the year we moved in. Before that, we'd lived in a semi-detached red brick house in Shepton. I remembered it with surprising precision. Could visualise every room, upstairs and down. How was it that I could recall the old house so well but not remember more recent events? I frowned, scratched my temple. A sudden memory of Maggie O'Connor mopping the kitchen floor in the Shepton house popped into my head. I remembered chatting to her, asking her about her hobbies. She liked arts and crafts and visited craft fairs throughout the year selling her handmade jewellery. She'd given me a bracelet one year as a Christmas present. She'd given Mum something too.

I wished I could talk to Maggie right now, confide in her about everything, ask her for help. She was a soft, motherly sort of person. She was also wise and kind.

But no. For now, at least, I was on my own. I needed to find out where Dad was keeping Mum. Once I knew more, I could leave and take my evidence back to the police. I already had Dad's written confession. If I could find a hint of where he was holding her, I could tell the police, they'd go there and save her. The problem was that I had no way of calling the police straight away and asking them to drive over here. But as soon as I'd finished checking the studio, whether or not I found more evidence, I'd get out of here. Once Dad got home, I'd snatch his car keys again and leave. An idea popped up and I smiled – before I drove away, I'd stab his motorbike tyres so he couldn't follow me.

Smiling at Dad's inevitable fury, I jammed the key into the slot and twisted. A satisfying click told me I was in. With a glance over my shoulder to check Dad wasn't back, I opened the door and stepped inside the studio.

The blinds were closed so I opened them, coughing as

dust flew into the stale air. How long was it since Mum had set foot in here? *Too long.*

The centre of the room was filled with a long wooden table which was empty, but the walls were smothered with charcoal drawings of Eddie and me - happy sketches of us holding hands on the cliff, sitting on a beach beside a sandcastle with waves lapping the shore behind us, walking hand-in-hand through a poppy field.

But as I followed the sketches around the room, they grew darker. Our faces turned sadder, vacant and staring, shoulders rounded. Dread stirred inside me as I stared at one of myself. It was a portrait of me looking out of the kitchen window at the cliff, my face mostly concealed by a swathe of black hair. In the distance, a white figure stood at the edge of the cliff watching me. Even though the figure had a skeleton's face, I knew immediately that it was supposed to be Dad. Just like in Death on a Pale Horse, a gaping black grimace lay where his teeth and lips ought to and pitted black holes that screamed of death burrowed in alabaster bone in place of his eyes. Was Dad dead to her? Was that what the drawing meant?

There was something so disturbing about the sketch that I recoiled. My thigh banged into the table, and I rubbed it and ran around in a whirl of frustration opening cupboards and drawers, finding only an array of art equipment, two coffee-stained coasters and a few art books. One of the art books was entitled 'The Art of the Nude'. The front cover was covered with pencil sketches of naked bodies. I felt like I'd seen the book before. Curious, I opened it. My eyes widened and I gasped. A note had been written in red ink on the introductory page.

Sofia, you have shown me your soul and made me the happiest man alive. As such is the course of true, artistic love, I shall never move on nor let you fade from view. And I promise you this: I shall preserve your unique beauty in my home, heart and mind forever. Indeed, you have captivated me. One day I shall return the favour, even if you are unwilling to accept. As you now know, I am not a man who accepts the word no xxx

My stomach dropped. I didn't recognise the handwriting. It wasn't Dad's. Was it Hugo's? Or Mr B's maybe? Either way, was I reading too much into the message, or was there a veiled threat in those words? I rubbed my eyes, mind spinning. I was overcomplicating things, trying to find someone else to blame for Mum's disappearance, but Dad had admitted in his own journal that he'd done something unforgiveable to her. I had to stop looking for other explanations and accept the truth: my dad was the guilty one here. No one else was to blame. Not Hugo and most certainly not Mr Broughton. Unless...no.

Yeah. Mr B liked her - too much. Maybe he took her for himself. Maybe him and Dad...

I shook my head, rubbed my eyes. Locked up these wild ideas in a box inside my head. They pushed against the lid, buzzed frantically, tried to hammer their way out like a swarm of trapped bees.

I re-read the message, swallowed a lump in my throat and nodded. It was probably written by one of Mum's ex-boyfriends, someone she dated before I was born. I snapped the cover shut and closed the cupboard. Determined not to think about the creepy note again, or the notion that Mr B and my dad might be more than acquaintances, I left the studio quickly and locked the door.

My pulse ramped up as I ran across the garden, feet squelching the wet grass, soaked from the crying sky. I had to get into the garage and disable Dad's bike before he got home.

222

Part 3

NOW

Chapter 47

I'm in a room. No matter how I struggle, I can't free myself. My entire body feels like a sack of coal, hot and dry and heavy; a thousand grains of sand pressing into my flesh suffocating my senses. I think about MasterChef and salted cod. That's me. Crusty scabs of sea salt are digging into my skin cooking me from the outside in. There is no pain - but the fear is agonising.

I see nothing except the blackness behind my eyes. I can't speak. Often, I hear nothing, smell nothing. Sometimes I begin to think I am no more than a cloud in the sky, but when I try to cry, tears won't come. I am as shrivelled on the inside as I am on the outside. A fossil. Will my body leave a print? How long will it take them to find me? Days, weeks, months, years, decades?

If I could shudder, I would.

My eyeballs feel like they've been stapled to my skull.

I don't want to die. I'm too young and there's so much to live for. I did something terrible, yes, but I don't deserve this. No one deserves this eternal torment. Not even him.

Chapter 48

By the time I reached the back door I was soaked. Knightley was curled up fast asleep in his puppy bed. I strode past him into the kitchen looking for the largest knife I could find.

The knife block was full. I grabbed the biggest handle, turned and headed for the front door. It was locked so I pulled Mum's keys off the hook and I hurried out into the downpour. There was no sign of the Merc making its way down the gravel path towards the house. I stared at the turning off the road. The road was mainly obscured by high bushes, but I hoped I would be able to see a glint of silver above them if he was coming. The rain made seeing difficult. I scanned the top of the bushes several times until I was sure the road was empty.

He'd been gone a while now. I wasn't certain for how long and felt annoyed at myself for not checking the time. Knowing there was nothing I could do about that now, I splashed my way across the paving stones towards the garage.

The blue door was closed. With slippery fingers, I hunted through my mum's keys for one that looked right. The first one didn't work and I realized I'd tried her studio key. The next one struck gold. On a small lift, the door rolled up. I hurried inside, relieved when a light automatically came on alleviating the gloom. Dad's motorbike stood front and centre, gleaming like a new pound coin. An array of tools lined the grey walls.

Rain hammered against the windows and walls making me even edgier. I glanced back. There was no Merc, only sodden grass, puddle-smothered stone and pounding rain that echoed the roaring in my skull.

HURRY, FASTER, YOU'RE BEING TOO SLOW.

I lurched towards the bike, crouched down next to the front wheel, gripped the silver handle of the knife in my right hand and clutched the tyre with my left. Aiming for the smoother section of rubber above the hub cap, I drew back my arm then stabbed the thick rubber as hard as I could. It made a tiny scratch on the black surface but didn't break through. I stabbed again and again and again, feeling like some kind of psycho serial killer. After the third stab, a hole appeared and air hissed out. The sound was heaven to my ears. All I had to do now was go back inside the house, wait until he came home, snatch his car keys and leave.

Pleased with my vandalism, I turned and ran out into the rain, freezing in horror at Dad, who stood on the paving stones three feet away from me.

His face was half-hidden by the navy hood of his raincoat. 'What the hell are you doing?' He glanced back and forth between me and his precious bike.

'Give me your car key. I'm leaving,' I said, trying to steady my voice.

He removed his hands from his pockets and dangled his keys in front of my face. 'This what you want?'

'Yes. Give it to me. I want to leave.'

'Where are you going?'

I licked my lips. I didn't have to answer him. He couldn't keep me here against my will. My fingers tightened on the knife.

'Let's go inside and talk about this,' he said forcefully, glancing towards the front door.

'No.'

'I'm not giving you the key, so you might as well do as I say.'

The knowledge that he was keeping Mum somewhere ticked in my chest like a bomb. Any second I was going to explode. I didn't want to hurt him.

I raised the knife and pointed it at his chest. 'Tell me where she is. I know you've got her locked up somewhere. I found your journal.'

Fear sparked in his eyes. He scanned my body as if looking for the journal. 'Put the knife down and go back inside the house. *Now.*'

I jumped and stared at the knife, which was shaking in my hand as though charged with electricity.

Mum's in danger. She needs you. Do something.

But I couldn't make myself stab him. I couldn't do it.

But you can pretend you're going to.

'Give it to me,' he said, lunging forward and grabbing my wrist.

'Get off me!' I twisted and plunged my teeth into his arm.

He roared, let go then darted forward and tried to grab me again; I jerked back and held the knife up with both hands. 'Come near me and I'll use it.'

He ignored my warning, strode forward and grabbed my wrists, squeezing them so hard that I screamed and dropped the knife. He kicked it out of the way, twisted my arm behind my back and frogmarched me into the house. 'I didn't want to do this but you've given me no choice,' he rasped, dragging me along the walkway.

Knightley followed us, yelping and jumping up at Dad's heels and Dad kicked out at him, sending him scampering away with his tail between his legs.

I was too scared to talk, too shocked to fight as he hauled me up the stairs and hurried me along the landing to my bedroom. He pushed me into the room and I stumbled forward and nearly fell. Swivelling around, I stared at him and he stared back, jaw clenched, chest rising and falling too fast.

'Stay in here. I'm warning you. Don't come out until I say you can.'

227

He slammed the door shut.

Shaking uncontrollably, I wrapped my arms around myself and dropped my head between my knees. Dad's footsteps thundered back down the landing, down the stairs, through the house.

I stared at the door, desperate to leave, but too frightened to disobey him.

After what seemed like less than a minute, Dad's footsteps pounded back up the stairs across the landing.

I huddled into the corner of my room, hugging my shivering body. He opened the door and dropped Knightley inside my bedroom then slammed the door shut. I scooped up my puppy and stared in horror at the door as the sound of a drill burst through the silence. What was he doing?

I was too afraid to speak; in my mind's eyes I saw a pathetic little piggy cowering inside its house of sticks; a powerless, cowardly creature not built for this kind of war. This was me. This was all I amounted to in such an important, life-changing moment. Mum needed my help and all I could do was hide inside my bedroom trembling like a new-born lamb.

I might have been weak, but thick I was not.

Understanding dawned in a streak of blazing light and terror seized every bone and muscle in my body.

My courage returned in one gut-wrenching kick, and I leapt to my feet, ran to the door a fraction of a second too late.

He'd already slid the bolt across and locked me in.

Chapter 49

My brain tells my eyes to open, but they won't. Not even a flicker. The blackness is deep, deeper than the ocean and just as terrifying. Fears roam my mind like sharks; any moment they could tear a chunk out of my brain and remove yet more of my self. It's like the darkness is eating me up, devouring my senses, consuming my memories. There are things I know, things I think I know and things I don't know that I should. Being cooped up with such a chaotic mess of knowledge is almost as frightening as being kept here against my will.

There's noise in the room. Movement. Shuffling. Feet.

I try to tense, but nothing happens. I beg my eyes to open: they refuse. I wonder who it is and then my thoughts dash elsewhere.

I am physically blind. Mentally broken. My head is a puzzle with missing pieces. Sometimes I picture my skull like an ostrich egg that has been cracked in several places, its insides gooey and half-formed. It's a hideous visual that reminds me I have an overactive imagination. If I wasn't in this situation, I would laugh at myself. As it is, I cannot cry, laugh, smile or frown. I am little more than Pinocchio with his strings cut. I'm a puppet that looks like it might leap to life at any moment but remains glass-eyed and practically dead.

But I'm not dead. Not yet. So, there's hope. Sometimes, in my more lucid moments, I think it is this hope that keeps me alive. But of course, my life is not up to me. I will die when he decides. He has made that clear.

A whisper of air against my arm. Someone's here. I don't know who. Sometimes I think it's just one person. Him. Sometimes I think it's more.

Oh God.

Chapter 50

I sat on my bed and stared at the door. I couldn't believe he'd attached a bolt. Fear locked me in its spiky embrace. At my back, rain pummelled the window like the hellish truth that pummelled my mind.

Dad was keeping my mum locked up and now he was doing the same to me. Would he hurt me too? I touched my arm, the one he'd twisted behind my back. It was painful and bruised. He'd already hurt me. There was nothing to say he wouldn't do so again. Especially if I put up a fight.

But there was a bigger fear to consider: if he could do this to Mum and me, could he do it to Eddie?

The thought of Eddie in pain made my stomach cramp. I curled into the foetal position and Knightley climbed all over me. I blanked out for a while.

*

The rain had stopped, and the house sat heavy with silence. Knightley lay on my pillow with his legs in the air. I tickled his baby-soft belly, grateful for such unconditional love, especially when Dad had clearly lost his for me – if he'd ever had any at all.

A car beeped. Still sodden, I rolled off the bed and dashed to the window, hope rising as I recognised Mr B's white Hyundai. What was he doing here? Was he here to be my knight in shining armour?

Mr Broughton pulled up alongside the Merc. While his car was tired and scratched, Dad's was pristine. Since my attempted escape, he'd had it valeted inside and out.

The sky was bluish grey, streaked with rays of sunlight that didn't seem real. A rainbow bowed over the hills and beyond like a bridge in a fairy-tale. Dad was the ogre hiding under it. I was the damsel in distress. Was James going to be my hero?

Blood pulsed savagely in my head as I began to scream.

Mr B got out of the car and slammed the door shut. Dad met him on the gravel, hand extended, smiling warmly. I stopped screaming, my mouth an 'o' of shock. I'd told myself my art teacher was innocent and here he was shaking hands with my dad. Smiling, nodding, handing Dad a piece of paper. Acting like they were best buddies.

Clinging on to the hope that James had been brainwashed by Dad and had nothing sinister to do with any of this, I smashed my hands against the window and screamed, 'Help! He's locked me in here – please – help me, Mr B…'

James glanced up at the window and looked back at Dad quickly. Dad waved his hand dismissively in the direction of my screams and they walked towards the back door and out of view, deep in conversation, neither of them taking any notice of me. A hand clenched around my heart. Was James buying Dad's story that I was crazy? Or was he working with Dad and Rose? I thought about the time Isla and I had seen him manhandling a young woman – I'd told Mum about it but she'd said it was nothing to worry about and told me off for following my teacher in the first place. But if Mr B could be rough with someone like that…

What the hell was going on?

Nothing added up. The only thing I knew was that I had to get away.

For ages, I hammered my fists into the bedroom door and screamed as loudly as I could but no-one came to my rescue. Exhausted to tears, I collapsed on the bed, hugged

231

Knightley to my chest and fell asleep.

*

After a long time, I came to, shivering and damp, clothes glued to my skin like cling film. With slow movements, I uncurled, sat up and got off the bed. Knightley was asleep, a fluffy ball on the pillow, unaware of the horror around him. Telling myself it was a good sign that Dad hadn't hurt my puppy, I pulled my towel off the door hook, stripped off my leggings and T-shirt and dried myself. My underwear was damp, so I tugged off my knickers and unclipped my bra. I dropped my clothes into the laundry basket and my eye landed on the page from Dad's journal that I'd hidden inside my bra.

Shit, shit, shit.

I glanced at the window. Rain pelted down.

I picked up my bra and laid it on the bed. The paper looked damp, but still intact. As gently as I could, I peeled the journal entry away from the bra cup and turned it over.

My heart dropped. The ink had run, turning every single word of evidence into unintelligible, black smears.

The evidence I was going to show the police was gone. I had nothing now, just my word against his and Rose's. And, possibly, James Broughton's. Everything and everyone were thwarting my every move.

My fists clenched. The locked door taunted me with its impenetrability. Anger beat in my chest and my vision turned black. I wasn't going to take this lying down. Even without evidence, if I could break out and leave the house, I could get to someone who would help me, someone credible who'd believe me and convince the police to question Dad and Rose and search for Mum and Eddie.

I turned my gaze to my dressing table. There had to be something in the room that I could use to help me escape.

I was about to open the drawer when I heard not one,

but two voices outside on the landing. A male voice and a female voice.

It was decision time, but I hadn't decided how to behave. Should I be difficult or docile?

With a metallic scrape, the bolt slid back. I backed into the dresser.

The door opened with agonising slowness.

I grabbed my towel and wrapped it around my naked body.

Without knocking or asking to come in, Dad and Rose entered the room.

Chapter 51

He's still here. My ears are wolfish, hungry. The slightest sound seems magnified. This is the best I've heard for a long time. I don't want him to know. I instruct my brain to make my body play dead and have no way of knowing whether it's obeying me — ironic because it's usually the other way around — but this time I need to be still as the slightest ear twitch might mean he detects I'm spying. He must have grown used to my inability to move or react. He seems to prefer me this way. He likes me to be his silent captive. A mute, helpless invalid.

I think it's him because of the sounds of his breathing. While his words come and go, too disjointed to make much sense, his throaty rasps scratch my ears. His breathing sounds more laboured this time. Maybe — dare I hope — someone saw him, followed him. Hope sputters like a flame, battling to stay alight against an ice-cold draught. If I'm right, does that mean my suffering is about to end? Has someone found me?

But the rest of the room is silent and still. No tick of a clock, no scrape of a chair, no hushed voices. There's no one else here, and his breathing is slower. Finding its usual pace. He's relaxing. Perhaps he's starting to enjoy himself.

For the millionth time I wonder. He must know what I've done or he wouldn't be doing this to me. Making me suffer. Making me lie in darkness like a hibernating mouse. Except I'm not in control of when I emerge from this black hole; he is. This unknown entity. A monstrous human being who, I hope, in a mad sort of way, is a stranger to me. In my bleakest moments, I think I know his identity, but I can't make myself accept it. His face simmers in my mind and dread uncurls its talons; if it is him, everything is worse. Unimaginable. What I've done is unforgiveable. I will never forgive myself and no one else should either, but what he's doing now is even worse. The guilty must be punished, but not like this. Never like this.

I try to hear him again. My mind darts in and out of awareness. I taste blood. Smell metal.

There's something on my arm. I try to brush it away, but I can't. My body is donkey-stubborn. Pathetically unresponsive. It scratches me, bites into my skin. I jump inside and wonder if he sees my response. If he does, he says nothing. Is he touching me or is it a mosquito? Or – God forbid - a spider? The thought makes my mind shiver. Spiders probably hover in every corner of this room. I imagine a lightless basement. A metal bedframe, dirty sheets, cobwebs, dust, grime, blacked out windows.

Where am I? Where is he? Is he still in here with me?

Suddenly, cold air rushes over me. A horrid thought pierces all else: am I naked? Has he touched me?

I can't contemplate that. No. Close it down. No point thinking about it.

With extreme effort, I switch lanes, hone in. Footsteps patter. They sound different, but that could be my imagination. At times, I fear this is all a nightmare and that I'm insane, trapped in delusion. But it's real. I know that really. My body might be untethered but my mind still stands. The bridge is leaning and crumbling, but holding. He won't let it break – not yet. The idea that he can smash it to pieces or rebuild it is too much, his power undeniable. I am Jonah and he is the Whale.

If I knew what his intentions were, would it make things better or worse? To know or not to know. Maybe being blind is easier than seeing what he has in store for me.

He is silent. There is no way to know whether he is still here. I can't remember hearing a door. I don't know whether my ears have stopped working again or whether he's covered them up or cut them off. He could be staring at me right now, his eyes inches from my own, a scalpel in his gloved hand. I think of the film 'Face Off'. He could be marking the outline of my face, connecting the dots, preparing to slice it off and start again. Maybe that's one of his fantasies. Cutting off women's faces. Carving fresh ones. Maybe he's trying to turn me into his bride. Like Frankenstein – or is it the monster? I'm so

235

confused.

Shadows crawl into my thoughts. I cling on but the glooms are winning.

I try to sniff the air and smell nothing. Nothing moves. There is no temperature, no motion. Only swelling blackness and the kind of stillness that comes with death.

Panic spits like oil - what if he leaves and never comes back?

It's all too much. My brain is sludge.

Him...me...room...why...Eddie...

Chapter 52

Rose eyed my bedroom. In a pencil skirt and silk top she looked over-dressed. A white lace bra was visible through the thin blouse. I wondered if she'd done that on purpose or didn't realise her bra was on show. It was like she'd dressed up for Dad and they were about to go out for a meal together, which they probably were – but in that case, where was Eddie? Who was looking after him?

Dad had changed into a white shirt and smart jeans. He'd even made an effort to shave.

Be calm. Play it cool.

Rose blinked when she saw I was wearing a towel. She trailed her gaze over my body then glanced down at herself. 'Oh – sorry – we'll let you get dressed first.'

Looking more irritated than embarrassed, Dad followed her out of the room. I heard their muffled voices outside my door. Caught fragments of what they were saying. *Seems better. Calmed down.*

Taking my time, I pulled on a pair of joggers, an old T-shirt and trainers then crossed my arms and waited.

A knock on the door. Rose said, 'You decent?'

I said nothing and they came in anyway.

'May I?' Rose said, gesturing to my bed.

'Go ahead. Make yourself comfortable,' I said.

She perched on my mattress, reached out and stroked Knightley, who remained asleep. The urge to whack her hand away from him hit hard. I pushed it down. Held it back.

Rose cleared her throat and looked up from Knightley. Her bulbous eyes bored into mine. 'Alec told me what happened. Would you like to talk about it?'

Dad shifted his weight and crossed his arms. He wouldn't look at me and instead fixed his gaze on the window.

'I wanted to leave the house,' I said flatly.

'And why was that?' she said.

'Because…' I trailed off, lost for words. They were in this together. The truth wouldn't go down well. Then again, Dad already knew why I wanted to leave, so what was this? Some weird control game?

'Go on. You can trust us,' she said.

I choked on a laugh. 'Trust you? You locked me in my room. You won't tell me where Mum and Eddie are. How on earth am I supposed to trust you? Is Mr B in on this too? I saw him earlier you know.'

Dad raked both hands through his hair. He met Rose's eye and they exchanged a look, which read as *she's onto us. What are we going to do with her now?*

'I want you to let me try hypnotherapy on you one more time. I really think we're getting close to a breakthrough,' she said.

'No way. I know what you're doing.'

She frowned. 'What do you mean?'

'You're not trying to help me remember. You're trying to make me forget. To make sure my memories stay buried.'

'You're wrong,' she said, her voice firm, harder than I'd heard it before, eyes piercing.

Was her façade beginning to crack? Had I hit a nerve? 'Then why can't I remember anything? Either you're manipulating me or you're shit at your job.'

She licked her lips. I could tell it was an effort for her to stay calm. 'Why don't you leave us alone for a bit?' she said, glancing at Dad.

'No. I don't trust her, not when she's behaving like this,' he said.

I snorted. 'You have to earn trust. Tell me where they

are and I'll be fine.'

Dad stared hard at me then looked away. His knuckles began to crack, and I tensed, knowing he was close to losing it.

As if sensing his anger, Rose placed her hand on his arm and said, 'Please, Alec. Let me deal with this. Let us talk, woman to woman.'

His jaw tensed. 'I really don't think that's a good idea.'

'What? You think *I'm* dangerous?' I said.

Neither spoke.

'TELL ME WHERE THEY ARE!' I screamed.

'You need to calm down,' Rose said, standing up from the bed, tone clipped.

Dad looked at her as if to say *I told you so*. She ignored him and stepped closer to me. 'Look, we can't tell you. When the time's right, and when you're ready, we will.'

'Ready? What are you on about? I'll never be ready to accept that he's locked Mum in a room and done God knows what to her. I'll never be ready to hear that you two have conspired to get rid of her so that you can carry on with your affair, so you might as well just tell me now. There's no way I'm getting out of here anyway.'

'You're not seeing straight, but if you trust me, I can make you understand. You just have to let me try. Open your mind up to other ideas,' she said, reaching out her hands to me.

'By getting inside my head and twisting my memories? Hell no. I found evidence. In his journal. I know what you've done.'

Rose seemed confused. She frowned at Dad, who shook his head and said, 'I've had just about as much as I can handle for one day. Let's try again tomorrow. Maybe she'll have calmed down by then and be more reasonable.'

'No. Don't go, not until you've at least told me where Eddie is and whether he's alright. Please. Please tell me what you've done with him.'

Rose and Dad stared at me, jaws locked.

'*No.* He's OK, isn't he? What have you done?' I cried, darting forward and thumping Dad's chest.

'Stop. Calm down,' Rose said.

'Fuck off!' I snarled.

Dad pushed me away and my back smashed into the dresser.

He left the room quickly. Rose shook her head at me as if disappointed, then followed him out of the door and called to him softly in a husky voice.

The bolt slid into place, leaving me and Knightley once more alone in our cell. I dropped to my knees, terrified that their silence meant they'd done something to Eddie.

Chapter 53

I'm choking like a fish out of water. I can't breathe. There's no oxygen, no air, nothing but a vacuum in my throat.

Has he buried me in the ground and smothered my body with soil? Is earth invading my lungs, running down my throat, compressing my airway? Am I about to die? Is he strangling me? I can't die. There are things to be said to those I love. I need to say sorry. I need to explain. Nothing will take it back, but I have to see them again, just once. I need to talk about Eddie.

Just breathe…

Every instinct in my body and brain tells me to fight back, breathe, live, but I can't move or speak. I can't fight him. I'm too weak, as insignificant and ephemeral as a fly.

My body is paralysed. I know this suddenly without a doubt. Has he severed my limbs? Or is it drugs? Am I a vegetable? Has he lobotomised my brain?

Please breathe…please…I need air…

Oh God. Was there ever a point in me at all? Yes. There was. I was a good person for a while. I helped others, worked hard to be successful. Then everything went to shit. I made a mistake. Everyone makes mistakes, but this was the worst.

Air air air please God please…

Please don't kill me. I try to say it. My brain barks at my lips. But they belong to a doll.

I see the Island of the Dolls. In Mexico. I drew it once. There are so many of them hanging from the trees by their throats, their hair, their chubby arms. Their eyes are glazed and empty as if they knew their fate all along. Will my eyes look like that when I'm dead? Will they be open or closed? Will he push my eyelids down with his fingers?

Do I even have any eyes left?

If I could be sick, I would. If I could scream and scratch and kick, I would.

Where are the police?

Please…

A light. Is this it?

Someone help me.

Chapter 54

Eddie's not dead. Eddie's not dead.

For a couple of hours, I paced my cell, back and forth, back and forth, trying to convince myself everything was going to be OK. Knightley scampered behind me, nipping at my heels. There was no way of telling what they were going to do to me. Regardless of that fact, I knew what I had to do: escape. If there was a chance that Mum and Eddie were still alive, I wouldn't stop until I found them, and it was impossible to find them locked in this room. Finding them meant getting away as fast as possible. But how on earth was I going to do that when the door was bolted shut?

The dressing table beckoned once more. I ran to it, yanked open the drawer and tipped the contents onto my bed. All I found was nail polish, fake eyelashes, a pair of gummy eyelash curlers, tweezers and a handful of tampons. There was nothing sharp or heavy. Nothing that could do serious damage to a door.

I tried my desk next, expecting to find nothing. To my surprise, alongside worn-down charcoal sticks and old, half-finished sketches of people's hands, I found a small pair of scissors and a packet of matches. My eyes went to the bookcase where a Buddha-shaped candle sat. A letter writing set leaned against the figure, and I frowned as the memory of finding out that Dad had never posted my letters to Mum splashed my brain like boiling water.

Knightley was begging to be picked up so I bent over and scooped him into my arms, unable to stop looking at the box of matches. Could I burn a hole through the door without burning the house down and killing myself and

Knightley in the process? Maybe, if I could control the fire and blow it out when it got too wild, it would work.

I put the idea to one side, deciding to use it as a last resort, and stared at the scissors. They were blunt with blue plastic handles, the sort of scissors primary school children used. I sighed and tossed them back in the drawer, knowing they wouldn't be any use. It would take a heck of a lot more than that to break through a heavy oak door.

My thoughts travelled to prison films and documentaries, and I pictured myself digging a hole in the floor and crawling out under the doorway. I looked at the thick cream carpet and wondered what lay beneath. Perhaps I could use those scissors after all. If I could pull up the carpet and dig down, maybe I could tunnel my way out. I rolled my eyes then, realising I wasn't on the ground floor, so it would be impossible.

I stared at the door and scanned every inch of it looking for a weakness. Maybe…

I put Knightley on my bed and moved to the door. It might be possible to break the hinges and pull the door off. Hope sang in my veins and I grabbed the blunt pair of scissors. I raised my hand, then realized that such a sound would create too much noise. If Dad and Rose heard, they'd come running. I glanced at my bookcase at my Apple iPod Nano. I'd got it a couple of years ago for Christmas. Mum had been so excited to give it to me; her excitement had almost outweighed mine. I'd wanted one for ages.

Mum always knew what I wanted and I always knew what she wanted, what made her happy when she was sad. We were similar in so many ways. Like mother like daughter. Two peas in a peapod pressed. Ice cream on a sizzling day, candle-lit baths, a great new book, roses, shopping, home-baked blueberry muffins, picnics, dogs, art. Loves we shared. Simple pleasures that cheered us up and chilled us out.

But the past was the past, and suddenly it felt like light years ago. We might never share those things again.

My throat closed. I massaged my chest and forced back tears, telling myself to focus, think logically. Music could help me.

I put on Rhianna's latest album on volume seven – not too loud, but loud enough to obscure the sound of me bashing the life out of the door. If Rose and Dad came to investigate the source of the noise, I could hide the scissors and act innocent.

Knightley jumped and whimpered when I started to hammer at the uppermost part of the hinge mechanism. I soothed him with a cuddle then got back to work.

Rhianna's voice blared into the room giving me a headache and making me think I didn't like her music as much as I used to. I put on Celine Dion – Mum's favourite - then hammered away, but within minutes it became clear there was no way a blunt pair of scissors was going to have any effect. It was a stupid idea. I frowned and sat back on my haunches. What now?

I turned around and stared at the window.

Maybe that was my only option.

I stood up, then stopped, aware of a change in the atmosphere. I paused the music, hoping my imagination was playing games, but Dad's voice told me I'd been on the money.

'I'm coming in.'

The bolt slid. Heart slamming, I pocketed the scissors and darted away from the door.

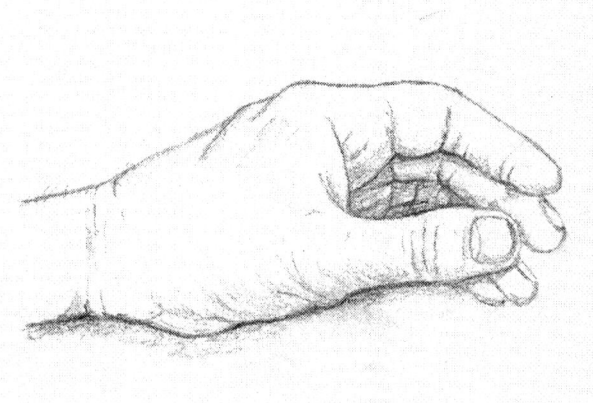

Chapter 55

Dad yanked open the door and searched my face. I averted my gaze and faked a calmness I didn't feel. It was important to act passive and meek. If he thought I was about to explode again, I wouldn't get anywhere.

'Dinner's ready. We're eating together,' he said.

He stood aside for me to leave the room. I wanted to refuse to go, but he was letting me out; I couldn't afford to lose this chance. It also sounded like I didn't have a choice.

'I need to go to the bathroom first,' I said, squeezing past him.

'Be quick.'

Feeling his gaze on me, I hurried down the landing into the bathroom. I locked the door, exhaled a shivery breath and explored the cabinets looking for anything I could use to help escape once he locked me back inside my bedroom.

Other than a pair of nail scissors, I found nothing. But they were sharp. They could prove useful. Pocketing the scissors, I used the toilet then left the room. Dad stood outside waiting for me. He scanned my face and body as if he knew I'd been up to something. I hurried past him and went downstairs. Every impulse screamed at me to make a run for it. My foot hit the bottom step and I stared out at the remote countryside and ominous-looking clouds. It was going to pour tonight. I jumped as Dad's hand fastened onto my shoulder and steered me through the house, past the double-breasted fireplace into the dining area. The way he guided me made it clearer than ever that I was a prisoner in my own home.

Rose already sat at the table. She offered one of her fake smiles and gestured for me to sit down beside her. Behind my lips I gritted my teeth. It was like she already owned the place. Mum was gone making her hostess and she was savouring her new part in this screwed up play. She'd even laid the table with our posh cutlery, the stuff we only used for special occasions like Christmas.

I sat and looked down at my plate of chicken stir fry. It smelt good, but the thought of eating something Rose had cooked brought bile to my tongue.

I scanned the table, unsurprised that Rose and Dad had glasses of wine while I had orange juice.

'To new beginnings,' Rose said, eyes twinkling.

She raised her glass. Dad hesitated and glanced at me then raised his. I ignored them and slugged back my juice.

Rose and Dad sipped their wine and began to eat. I forced mouthful after mouthful of food onto my tongue tasting nothing. My chest quivered with suppressed anger and I snuck glances at them, wondering what game they were playing now.

They chatted about simple things like the weather and books while I raged at their pathetic attempt to act like everything was OK. I stared at the silver knife in my hand and thought about the sharp scissors in my pocket. If I could catch them unaware, maybe I could get away.

'I think I'd like to try hypnotherapy again,' I said.

They stopped mid-conversation and looked at each other. Rose's excitement was clear, but Dad stiffened.

'Brilliant!' Rose said, clapping her hands. She rested her palm on Dad's arm and he moved away sharply, making her hand flop onto the table. Hurt flashed in her eyes, but she recovered quickly and pasted a smile on her face.

'On one condition,' I said.

'Condition? Jesus Christ,' Dad snapped.

'And what's that?' Rose said tersely.

'That it's just you and me. I can't relax when he's around.'

Rose looked at Dad, patted his hand. He seemed to tense at the contact but didn't move his hand away this time. 'Alec, I think that's an excellent idea, don't you?'

Dad didn't look up from his plate. His hand found the back of his neck and he rubbed it roughly. 'If you think it's a good idea, go for it.'

'Great. That's settled. When would you like to have your session?'

I frowned. 'Won't it be when I normally have it?'

'Oh no, that's not necessary anymore. Now that I've moved in, you can have your session whenever you want.'

I choked on a piece of chicken and glared at Dad. 'You've moved her in?'

'Yes,' Dad said, 'I have. She's here to help us.'

'Help *you*, you mean,' I snapped.

He pushed his chair away from the table and tossed his napkin onto his plate. With an angry wave of his hand, he left the room.

'When shall we have our session?' Rose pressed.

'Are you going to lock me in my room again?'

'That depends.'

'On what?'

'On whether Alec says we need to.'

'So he's the one calling the shots? I thought it was the other way around.'

Acting like I hadn't spoken, she slid her fork and spoon together and gathered up the dirty plates. 'Your session? When? I thought we could do it in the living space. It's more neutral than the bedroom.'

'Where are you sleeping tonight?' I said.

'One of the spare rooms, of course.' She said the words lightly, but a smile played at her lips.

I rolled my eyes.

'Look, you said you wanted to try again, so give me a

time and we'll make it happen,' she said.

'Tomorrow afternoon. When he's out.'

'Where would you like to do it?'

'My room.'

She smiled and reached out a hand to me. I recoiled. 'You know, he only wants what's best for you, don't you? He's a wonderful man. One of the most brilliant, thoughtful men I've ever met. Sometimes you must be cruel to be kind. Alec understands that better than most.'

'What, like your father you mean?'

Her eyes narrowed and colour heated her cheeks. There was anger there. I'd hit a nerve. Her hand clenched and unclenched on her fork. She exhaled heavily and placed the cutlery down, then picked up her napkin and slammed it onto the table an inch from my hand. I jumped and jerked backwards, but she merely smiled, unfolded the napkin and held it up. A dead spider was crushed into the white cloth. Rose sighed and neatly folded the napkin before placing it back on the table.

She looked askance at me and cleared her throat. 'Nasty little thing. It would be so easy if we could erase all of our problems so quickly, wouldn't it?' Crinkling her nose, she crushed the napkin in her fist.

I swallowed uneasily and stared down at my plate, willing for this weird dinner to be over. A banging sound came from above our heads and we both looked up. Rose seemed as surprised as me.

'What's that?' I said.

She shrugged and sipped her wine.

I watched her eat, sickened by how relaxed she seemed.

Minutes ticked by. Five. Ten. Fifteen. The banging above our heads stopped.

'Can I go?' I said.

Rose looked up. 'Better wait for Alec.'

'Why was James Broughton here?'

Rose brought the glass to her lips then lowered it an inch. She stared into the wine, swirled the red liquid around, and inhaled its aroma, nostrils flaring hungrily. Her gaze flicked to mine then back to her glass.

'He's concerned about your wellbeing, that's all,' she murmured.

She was clearly lying.

I considered sprinting to the front door, making a run for it, but Dad walked in and glowered at me. I glared back. He made to grab my arm and I darted out of reach. 'Don't touch me.'

Desperate to be free of them, I stalked away.

'What about dessert? I made Alec's favourite – blackberry and apple crumble.' Rose's voice floated after me, but I'd already made it to the stairs.

Dad followed two steps behind.

I pretended I didn't know he was there. Once I got to my room, I slammed the door in his face.

Through the wood, he said, 'You can come downstairs and spend the rest of the evening with us if you like. Despite what you may think, I'm glad you're giving hypnosis another try.'

'No thanks,' I said, hoping he'd leave quickly. I wanted to try to break the child lock off the window. From there, I'd find a safe way to lower myself to the ground. I thought I might have a skipping rope somewhere. Maybe, if I could tie it to my bedpost, I could climb through the window and down the side of the house.

I could feel him lingering on the other side of the door. I raised my voice. 'I'd rather rot in hell.'

There was a long silence. I imagined his scowl. Felt a spark of satisfaction.

At last, he said, 'Fair enough. Rose would rather I didn't lock you in, but I'm afraid your recent actions have scared me a great deal, so I'd prefer to play it safe. I'll bring you some dessert and a cup of tea and take Knightley out to do his business at nine. If you want to come out, just knock on the door. I'll come up.'

'This isn't going to work, you know,' I said.

'What?'

'Acting all nice. I know what you've done.'

He sighed. 'Once Rose has worked her magic, we'll be able to scavenge something out of this mess. Maybe, one day, we'll even carve out some sort of happiness again.'

I bit back a million responses and waited for him to leave, but no footsteps sounded.

'The quicker you accept this new situation, the better for everyone. I'm locking you in for your own good. I only hope you'll realize it soon.'

'And if I don't? What will you do? Hurt me like you hurt Mum? Or maybe you haven't actually hurt her yourself – maybe you've got someone else doing the dirty work for you.' *Someone likes James.*

'If I could trust you, I wouldn't need to lock you in,' he barked.

He bolted the door. The landing shuddered as he stormed away.

I spun around and raced to the window. Froze. Stared, unable to believe what he'd done.

A rectangle of metal had been hammered over the window frame, straight across the centre where I'd hoped to pry out the screws with the nail scissors. He'd even used several nails to make it doubly secure.

I grabbed the scissors out of my pocket and attacked a nail, which only served to bend the metal blades of the scissors out of shape. Through tears of frustration, I tried and tried, but there was nothing I could do to prise them out.

Although I'd known the window was a long shot, the fact that Dad had caught on before I'd had a chance to do any damage hit me like a fist. Dad was five steps ahead. Determined to do whatever it cost to keep me here against my will - while I was struggling uphill against a raging avalanche, slipping backwards…falling.

Every bit of energy left my body.

With Mum's fearful face in my mind, I sank to my knees and stared at my only eye to the outside world, more desperate and hopeless than ever.

Chapter 56

I'm not dead. Or am I? No. I feel the same – blind but aware, just. I can breathe again.

Relief makes me want to weep. I may as well be a ghost, but I'm not one yet.

I begin to wonder what happened. Maybe he decided to kill me then changed his mind at the last minute. Maybe he did it on purpose to make me suffer. To punish me. No. If it's him, he wouldn't do that, which makes me think it's someone else. The more I think about it, the more I think it has to be. There's no way he could do this to me. Suddenly, the idea seems insane. Absurd. He hates me for what I did, but he wouldn't take matters into his own hands like this. At least, I don't think he would. It's hard to say. I don't think I ever knew him at all. The way he exploded…I was terrified. And the way he looked at me, like I was something he wanted to rip apart.

Maybe it is him.

No. He loved you once.

I loved him too. Now I don't know what to think.

Is there anyone else who might do this to me?

I think of my friends, people I know. There's no one I can think of who hates me this much.

Or is it even a case of hatred? Couldn't it be madness?

I've met my share of crazy people, but this crazy? No. Then again, you never know what's going on inside someone's head. Everyone has secrets, things they're too ashamed to tell anyone. Everybody wears a disguise. A mask. There's a sort of inner duality to people. A cave-man instinct crushed day in day out by modern social norms. For some, there must be a constant battle: to conform or to rebel. I think about 'The Strange Case of Doctor Jekyll and Mr Hyde'. Picasso's distorted faces. Van Gogh cutting off his ear. Everyone has a beast inside them. Most people keep it locked up for ever. A few don't.

All that's needed is a trigger.

Maybe it is him. Maybe he's deeply disturbed and he's been hiding it for years. What I did drew out the beast that had been hibernating all this time. It's my fault he's doing this, my fault he's snapped.

A door's opening. There's a smell. It's sweet. Sweeter than normal.

There's a voice.

Chapter 57

Dad brought breakfast to my room and set the tray on my dressing table whistling a jaunty tune I recognized but couldn't place. He seemed happier this morning, which annoyed the hell out of me. Was it because he and Rose had christened their relationship in my mum's bed? The thought made me feel like smashing my fists into his face. Accusations whizzed around my brain like fireworks, fizzling out once they reached their climax; I had a plan now and I needed to stick to it. Riling him would be a bad idea. While stoking the flames was tempting, this man held Mum's – and possibly Eddie's – life in his hands. If I went too far, he might explode and turn his wrath on them instead of me.

Still, when he spoke, my words came out acrid and cutting.

'Sleep OK?' he said, leaning casually against the wall.

'I've been dying for a wee all night, so no.'

'You could've woken me up.'

'By screaming my lungs out?'

He held my eye for a few moments. A muscle in his cheek twitched.

I longed to drive a spade into his mind and dig out the secrets buried there. If only I was telepathic…

'Well, you can go now,' he said, standing aside to let me pass.

I took my clothes with me and locked the bathroom door. I went to the toilet and brushed my teeth, then unlocked the door and peeked out. Dad's broad back was all I saw. He was guarding the exit in case I made a run for it.

Shaking my head bitterly, I showered and dressed then took Knightley out for a play in the garden. Dad stood in the kitchen watching us. Forever watching, making sure I was being a good girl.

Rose was nowhere to be seen. Her Figaro was parked by the side of the house next to Dad's Mercedes. A match made in Heaven. Or Hell. Or Purgatory. The seventh terrace: lust. We'd learned about that in English. I wondered if she was still upstairs asleep in Mum's bed on Mum's sheets. I wondered if they'd slept together and felt sick.

Knightley did his business then headed for the cliff. I followed, gaze trained on the patchwork hills that stretched into the distance. I stopped inches from the edge. I could feel eyes on me but didn't care. Looking down, I imagined falling and the freedom of weightlessly dropping through thin air with nothing to hold me down or pull me back, before the sudden crash of soft skin against jagged rocks and the inevitable shattering of bone and brain matter ended everything. There would be a strange sort of release in that. And not much pain. It would be over quickly.

I looked up. My cheeks were wet with tears. Morning sun pushed through the clouds and warmed my face. I turned my back on the cliff edge, throat thick with emotion. Would Mum ever see another morning sun? Would Eddie?

The thought that they wouldn't was unthinkable. I steeled my heart and picked up Knightley. Whispering my plan in his ear, I strode back up the garden towards the glass house.

*

My muscles tied themselves in knots. It was two in the afternoon. Sunny and smouldering outside. The rain

257

clouds had wept themselves dry and the sun had begun to suck moisture from the earth once more. But there was smog on the horizon; any second now, Rose would arrive for our 'session'.

The room was tidy, bed made, charcoal away, clothes hung up or folded in drawers. I was dressed in shorts, a T-shirt and trainers, my hair smoothed into a ponytail at the nape of my neck. No makeup because there was no point. The hairs on my arms were alert, my ears trained on the slightest sound. I wanted to hear her coming.

Dad was supposedly taking Knightley for a check-up. I'd not bothered asking if I could go too. There was no way they were letting me out of here until Rose had bent my mind to her will and turned me into a puppet who would question nothing and agree with everything.

My nerve endings were electric. I couldn't stop getting up from the bed and putting my ear to the door. I looked at the time. It was five minutes past two. The waiting was torture. When was she going to come?

I tried to busy myself by rearranging my books into colour order, from darkest to lightest. My fingers hovered above the Harry Potter collection. I remembered reading them aloud to Mum – or was it the other way around? My memory was so distorted, it was hard to say. All I knew for certain was that our love of the series was another thing we shared.

My chest ached with longing as I looked out of the window at the back garden, at Mum's studio. I thought about the strange sketches she'd drawn of Eddie and me, how they'd grown darker and darker. What had been tormenting her? Dad's affair? Or more – was it the realisation that he wasn't the person he'd always made himself out to be? I wondered what had set Dad off. Perhaps Mum had confronted him about the affair and he'd seen red and acted without thinking. Maybe he'd attacked her and hurt her so badly he'd taken measures to hide the damage, keep her out of sight until he could come up with a plan to dispose of her. That made some sort of sense. It explained why he didn't seem to want to get rid of me too. Perhaps, somewhere deep down in his twisted mind, he still cared about me and wanted us to move on together and pretend nothing bad had ever happened.

It all sounded so unreal, but this was my reality. If only the journal entry hadn't been destroyed...

But there was no point crying over spilled milk. Dad could be spilling more of Mum's blood this very second; that was worth crying about. No. More than that. That was worth risking everything for.

The thud of footsteps drew my ears. I moved away from the door and perched on the bed. My heart rate soared, and my palms sweated as I waited. Rose's steps grew louder and closer. A phone sang, and she stopped walking and answered.

'How is she? ... But I thought ... Really? ... Oh. I see. Yeah ... OK ... Yeah. I'm just about to go in ... I will ... OK, see you soon. Bye. Oh, and Alec, I'm sorry about last night...Are you sure...Phew. Great. Because I was worried that...oh, oh, OK, yes. Bye.'

Was that about Mum?

Yes. It had to be.

I exhaled. If they were talking about Mum like that, it meant she was alive.

The bolt screeched. My body stiffened and my hands clenched on my lap.

Rose opened the door and smiled down at me. Falseness radiated off her in a syrupy swell of perfume and pretence. Today, she resembled a 1950s housewife. Bright red lipstick stained her lips and, I was pleased to see, her teeth. As always, her feet were bare. Another sign she was making herself at home in my house.

Anger frothed my blood. My adrenaline fired up.

She stood in the doorway for a few moments. 'I see

you've tidied up. Looks lovely. Alec will be pleased.'

I faked a smile. 'Thanks.'

'You're so good for agreeing to this. We're both so relieved.'

I bet you are.

She entered the room and sat on my desk chair. After crossing her legs and arranging her dress, she said, 'Ready?'

I braced myself, then said, 'Are you in love with my dad?'

She rolled her eyes to the ceiling and laughed. 'Really? This again?'

'I'm serious. I want to know.'

She ran her tongue around her gums as if considering what to say, and then, to my astonishment, she said, 'We're very fond of one another.'

I stared at her open-mouthed.

'There's no need to look so horrified about it.'

'You're admitting it - you and Dad are together. You've both done something to Mum.'

She rolled her eyes again and snorted. 'Don't be so ridiculous. That's absurd. Alec wouldn't hurt a fly, and anyway it's impossible. It's all in your head. That's why I'm trying to help you. Look, you've been through a terrible experience that's made you repress certain memories. As I've told you before, with hypnotherapy I can help to bring those memories to the surface safely. That's all we're trying to do here.'

'And the affair? How can you so casually admit that to me? And isn't that a, a -'

'Breach of professional conduct? Well, yes, but when you find the man of your dreams what are you supposed to do?'

'You're disgusting.'

'I'm sorry, but sometimes you must be cruel to be kind. Often the truth is a bitter pill to swallow but it's best you know, don't you think? I really don't know why Alec insists on keeping it a big secret.' She looked genuinely confused, hurt even.

'Maybe he's using you. Have you ever considered the fact that he might be keeping a secret from you? A secret about Mum? How can you be so sure he hasn't done anything to her? I read his journal. He admitted he's done something unforgivable to her. How well do you really know him anyway?'

She laughed weakly. 'He'll be referring to me of course, nothing else.' A sliver of doubt darkened her eyes. 'I'd do anything to protect him. Anything at all. He wouldn't hide anything from me. He loves me. We love each other.'

'How can you be so sure? Has he told you he loves you?'

She rubbed her throat. 'Not yet. But I know he does. It's obvious. He's moved me in for God's sake! And he's entrusted your care to me. He doesn't really know what to do with you. I've been guiding him, offering him daily advice, doing everything I can to support him. I've been helping you too. You ought to be thanking me not challenging me. I've been extremely patient up until now, but this resistance needs to stop. You're upsetting Alec and that won't do.' She exhaled heavily and flapped her hand next to her cheek as if she was suddenly too hot. 'Right. Enough talk. Onto business, yes?'

'No. I don't think so. Not now, not ever.'

I swallowed a crash of fear, stood up and raced to the door. To my surprise, she was quick, faster than I thought possible. She darted after me and grabbed my arm. I spun around and slashed at her with the nail scissors. She gasped and jerked away, letting go of me and darting backwards, her hand cupping her cheek, blood seeping through her fingers.

I whirled, ran out of the room, slammed the door behind me and slid the bolt through the lock. Fear rammed its knuckles into my stomach as I tossed the scissors aside and ran across the landing, trying to ignore Rose's crazed screams at me to stop. Blood pounded in my ears as I tore down the stairs, turned and sprinted through the house.

From here, I had no clear plan. All I knew was that I had to get out and as far away from the house as possible before Dad came back. His car was gone but Rose's wasn't. Her keys had to be somewhere.

I checked the hooks next to the front door, but no new keys hung there.

I ran to the kitchen and scanned the surfaces – there, on the kitchen island - a set of keys. I ran over, picked them up and headed for the back door. It wasn't locked, so I dashed out and around the side of the house, unlocked the Figaro and slid in behind the wheel. It was automatic like the Merc. I put the car in Drive and sped the Figaro up the pathway. I imagined Rose's frustration and Dad's outrage. A hysterical laugh burst out of my mouth and I looked ahead, horrified to see the Merc hurtling down the gravel towards me.

I hesitated then slammed the car into reverse. Dad kept coming. Pebbles clattered and smacked against the windows as I drove too fast on the uneven ground, desperate to get away.

If I could spin the car around and drive through the fence, I could escape through the fields then re-join the road at a later point, and surely Dad wouldn't come after me if he thought I'd done something to Rose. He'd go inside to check she was OK first, especially if he loved her as much as she said he did.

I reached the back garden and swerved to the left, bringing the bonnet around to face the fence. Tensing every muscle, I gripped the steering wheel hard and slammed my foot down on the accelerator. Behind me, Dad stopped the Merc, got out of the car and waved his hands at me to stop.

There was no way I was stopping.

The Figaro smashed into the fence, but instead of breaking through it, the bonnet crumpled and the car refused to go any further. Bizarrely the words *reinforced with concrete* jittered across my brain as the airbag blew up in my face. Vicious arrows of pain shot down my neck. With a groan, I reached over and opened the door; and Dad yanked me out of the car. His hands were all over me, face blurry, coming and going in waves of black and grey. I tried to fight him off, but I was weak and so, so dizzy. Pain thwacked against my skull and I staggered to the right and fell over. He picked me up and threw me over his shoulder. I battered my fists against his back to no effect.

He carried me back into the house in silence and I began to fear the worst. His rage was in the jerkiness of his strides and the tightness with which he held me. I stopped hitting him and told him I was sorry, that I'd been stupid, but he said nothing.

Upstairs, Rose continued to scream for help. Dad pounded along the landing and slid back the bolt on my bedroom door. Rose stared wide-eyed at me. Blood dripped out of a two-inch slash on her cheek.

'I told you she couldn't be trusted. She's out of control. Get the stuff,' he barked.

Rose nodded and rushed out of the room.

'Put me down. I'm sorry,' I said again.

'You've left us no choice,' he murmured, pinching the space between his eyes.

Still hanging upside down over his shoulder, I watched Rose rush towards me with her hand raised, something gripped between her fingers. When she got closer, I realized what she was holding and began to struggle with all my might. 'No - please – I won't do it again!'

But Dad threw me onto the bed and pinned me down. He looked at Rose. 'Do it.'

I shook my head and bucked my hips, but he was too strong. Rose lowered the needle to my arm and stabbed.

Chapter 58

I weave in and out. One second I'm listening intently to the voice, the next I'm plunging into darkness. It's as if my brain wants to function, but is too tired to work. Smudges of shadows dance in front of my eyes too, like the skin is beginning to thin. This could be momentous. It might mean the poison he's feeding me isn't working any more.

The voice — but I must concentrate on the voice. Before, I heard grumbles, the odd word. I remember I heard 'and' and 'she' once. Another time 'fault'. That was all. These words told me nothing, except that my abuser is a man. The growly depth in his tone is undeniable. But this voice is totally different. Oceans upon oceans apart. This voice is higher, faster, lighter. It plucks at my ears like a toothpick, making me jump at unexpected moments. Like now — 'remember' she says.

Excitement grips me. It's a woman. I know that now. I know it better than I know the terrible look on Eddie's face the last time I saw him. His expression is emblazoned on my brain like nothing else. Even his fury…that's nothing, it pales in comparison to the terror in Eddie's innocent eyes.

But I'm fading again, losing focus. I must listen, work it out. I could know her. Maybe she's here to help me.

'I'm so sorry.'

I jump, but of course my body does nothing to show my surprise. The voice was clear. Like the crystal chandelier in the living space in our house. A house I don't think I could ever return to even if I did get away.

So — yes — the voice — her voice. She speaks again and I'm acutely aware — more than I've ever been since being taken — of every nuance, inflection, rise and fall, the pace, the breath, the tone that accompanies these words.

'Dear me. This is wrong. I wish there was something I could do.'

She's soft-spoken, lilting, slow, sad yet bitter. And there's something there. A feeling inside. A stirring in the depths of my brain. I know this voice. I know it well. But I can't pinpoint her. Her face won't come. Her name stays hidden.

Speak again, I beg, please, God, please.

And she does.

'... suffering.'

It's just one word and it's not enough. I scrabble blindly for a name, a face, a laugh, a smile, a frown and get nothing.

The door opens and she leaves, and I am left screaming inside.

Chapter 59

Blinded by light, I tried to orient myself. I was sitting not lying, my mouth tasted gross and my head felt fuzzy. An engine growled. The road was bumpy.

I was in a car. I'd been injected with something. What was happening?

I dropped my chin to my chest. Sunlight as bright as fire flashed between the trees. The seat was cream leather, the car wide. I was in the Merc.

Two people sat up front. Black hair and broad shoulders, auburn curls and sugary perfume. Dad and Rose. Of course. They'd injected something into my veins against my will and now they were driving me somewhere. Viscous fear bubbled up like lava in my throat. I pressed a hand to my chest, despising the grogginess in my brain that was making my processing ability so slug-like. In the blacks of my eyes, I saw the sun, felt the heat through the window on my skin. Where were they taking me? What were they planning to do to me?

I wasn't tied up. My hands and ankles were free. I wasn't gagged either. They must have thought the drug would keep me unconscious for longer. Either that or they thought I'd be a good girl and behave.

I stayed stock still.

They drove in silence. Dad tapped a random beat on the steering wheel. Was that a sign of nerves or impatience?

There was no radio. No exchange between them. No smiles or conspiratorial glances. Tension thickened the air. Their bodies were rigid. Dad focused on the road ahead. Their mirrors were pulled down. The sun was blinding them too. Rose's face was turned to the passenger window. A bandage covered her cheek. I remembered how I'd slashed her with the nail scissors. It had clearly been the final straw for them. They knew I wasn't going to accept their lies. There was nothing they could say or do to make me forget Mum, and they'd finally accepted that. Now they'd have to erase me too.

Houses appeared. Pavement. Front gardens. Picket fences. A rope swing. Tulips. A sharp pain fractured my temple. I winced, fought the memory. It was like poison in my veins, but it fired me up, brought me back to life. Mum needed my help. I couldn't give up. And I was out of the house in a public place. It would be harder for them to catch me with people around.

But the car was moving at a pace. Thirty or so miles an hour. Too fast to jump out.

I turned my face ever-so-slightly and stared at the row of terraced houses on the right. People were in their front gardens mowing, playing with their children, gardening. Could I bang on the window and scream for help? Would anyone hear me? Would they even notice? The Merc would be there then gone in a flash. Too little time for someone to register me properly, let alone my distress. There had to be another way.

I turned my focus to Dad's head. Imagined wrapping my arms around his face to blind him. The scene played out in my mind. Dad would let go of the steering wheel with one hand to try to pry me off, and Rose would attack me too. Two against one wouldn't work. And it would risk other lives as well as my own. If we crashed, innocent people could be hurt because of me. I envisaged a little boy Eddie's age flying through the windscreen of the car in front. Searing pain split my skull in two and I tasted blood. I winced, shocked by such a visceral reaction, but knew what it meant. Mum wouldn't want me to endanger others' lives, even if it meant saving her own.

What to do? What to do?

The Merc slowed for a roundabout. I tensed. Looked at the door handle. Maybe I could jump out – but the car was on the move again. I'd waited too long. I sighed. Rose's head whipped around. I closed my eyes, heart thumping. Had she noticed I was awake? I waited, but she said nothing.

Silence reigned. Even Dad's drumming on the steering wheel had stopped.

I waited a little while longer, then opened my eyes a sliver. My gaze landed on my arm where they'd stabbed the syringe into me. An ugly bruise darkened the skin. Blood pounded in my ears and my head roared. I glanced at the door handle again. The next time the car slowed, I would do it. I had to.

Rose cleared her throat then said, 'This is good.'

Keeping the rest of my body still, I inched my fingers towards the door.

The road seemed to stretch on endlessly, and I began to wonder if it would ever stop. We rushed past trees and hedgerows and houses. Pedestrians walking their dogs, headphones in, chatting to invisible friends. My fingertips trembled. I kept my eyes open, praying Rose wouldn't look around and see the way my hand hovered next to the door.

Finally, the Merc slowed for traffic lights. Twenty-five, twenty, fifteen, ten, five.

Rose glanced around again. I closed my eyes, but her sharp gasp told me she'd seen what I was about to do.

I didn't have time to think. Impulse drove me on every level.

I seized the door handle as Rose reached out one manicured hand, her mouth open in a silent scream.

Moving through a chemical sludge, I scrambled out of the car and staggered across the road. A horn beeped and I jumped and stared like a deer in headlights as a car screeched to a halt a foot away from me. Dad's voice boomed. Rose's enraged shriek followed. The driver who'd almost hit me waved his fist.

I stumbled onto the pavement and didn't look back.

I ran on jelly knees with my heart pulsing savagely in my ears. Up ahead, there was a close. I turned right and ran along the pavement in front of a row of terraces. Bushes. Fences. Flowers. Stone ornaments. A black cat. My trainers drummed concrete. My limbs felt loose and floppy. Sweat licked my temples. The sun was a toxic mass burrowing into my skull. No one was around; the pavement and roads were free of cars or people. I had no idea what time it was. I'd lost track. It could have been late morning, noon or after. The need to find somewhere to hide was all there was; all that mattered.

Dad's voice rode the hot air, distant but not distant enough. He was keeping pace; if I didn't hide soon, he'd catch up and find me.

I stopped, glanced around. Dad hadn't reached the close yet. Any second he would.

I ran across a car-free drive and tried a gate attached to the side of the house. It wasn't locked. I yanked it open and ran down a paved pathway into a small garden. A washing line hung with clothes. Pretty flowerbeds. And at the back, mostly concealed by an apple tree: a black wheelie bin. I sprinted across the neatly mown lawn, ducked under the branches and crouched down behind the bin. The ripe smell of old food mauled my nose. I held my breath and listened. Dad's voice rang out. I couldn't tell where he was and didn't dare check to see if he'd seen me run into the garden. He shouted again. His voice was louder this time. I heard the squeal of the gate. Had he seen me or was it blind luck?

Again, he shouted. His voice was raw with rage. Closer. Getting hotter. The memory of playing that game with Mum when I was little panged in my breast. *Warmer. Warmer. Hot. So hot!*

I tried to make myself smaller, shrinking inwards, sucking my belly button into my tummy as if that would help to make me invisible.

Another voice pierced the air. A woman. Needle-sharp. 'What the fuck are you doing in my back garden?'

Dad tried to speak. She cut him off. 'I'm calling the police.'

He spluttered something incoherent then cried out as if in pain.

'Get off my property!'

Dad muttered an apology. The gate squealed.

Was he gone?

In the shadows, I remained curled up. Behind me, bushes rattled. I had three options. One: stay here for ages. Two: leave now and hope Dad had gone for good. Three: ask the woman who'd scared him off for help. I immediately eliminated the third option. The houseowner didn't sound like the understanding type. But the first and second options battled, and indecision trapped me in its jaws.

Dad might have left the garden, but he could be hovering outside the house waiting for me to make my move; however, the longer I stayed here, the longer Mum remained in danger. Eddie might be in danger too. I couldn't hide here forever. The risk was too great. If Dad gave up the chase, he might decide to kill Mum and get rid of her body, because he thought I had evidence to show the police. I'd told him and Rose about the journal entries I'd found but hadn't given away the fact that they'd been destroyed by the rain. Although he'd tried to twist the police against me, if I turned up with evidence, they'd have to follow through. I had no evidence, not anymore, but I had an idea. I knew where Maggie lived. 1 Peacock Lane in Kilton village not that far from our house. If I could make it to her house and tell her everything, she'd believe me and the police would believe her. She was a responsible citizen with an unblemished record. They'd have to trust her over Dad. It was my only option. If I went straight to the police, they'd ring Dad and he'd come and collect me and spew his lies again. I shuddered to think where he and Rose had been taking me. What they had been planning to do.

I had no way to get to Maggie's, no money, no phone and no idea where I was, but that wasn't going to stop me. The question was how long to wait. I guessed I'd been hiding behind the bin for about ten minutes. Would that be long enough or should I give it more time? How long would it take Dad and Rose to reach Mum?

Not long enough.

With a grunt at the pain in my knees, I pushed myself up and peeked over the bin. The garden was empty. There was no sign of the owner and, more importantly, no sign of Dad.

Drawing a deep breath through my nose, I hurried across the grass.

Chapter 60

Lightning speed was what I needed, but I was sapped, legs heavy as sandbags. I moved as fast as I could, which wasn't fast enough. My mouth tasted like a maggot-infested apple and my tongue was a strip of sandpaper. The sun wouldn't let up. Neither would Dad. The fury in his voice reverberated around and around my brain reminding me that he was a strong, unrelenting enemy; not someone to give up easily.

The close remained empty of human life. I jogged past house after house, brain fizzing with a whirlwind of emotion and one target: convince Maggie so that she would convince the police.

I exited the close and looked left and right. Unable to ascertain where I was, I turned left and headed up a slight incline along a road called Marrow Street. Two boys cycled down the hill on the other side with reckless speed. One performed a wheelie and I watched, fearful he'd fall, but the front wheel slammed tarmac and he continued smoothly.

Eddie hasn't even learned to ride a bike yet.

The realisation that I had no idea how much time had passed since Rose had injected me barrelled into my gut. What day was it? How long had they kept me drugged for? Was I already too late to save Mum?

But there was no time to dwell. Aware I was exposed, I headed for the shadow offered by a row of fir trees. The relative cool was welcome on my hot skin, and I hovered there for too long trying to work out how to get to Maggie's. A red Peugeot drove past and I stared at it, words stuck in my throat, wanting to scream after the driver and signal for help. Maybe a stranger would believe me and help me. Dad and Rose were awful people, but the world wasn't filled with savages. Mum was a good person. So was I. Isla was too. There were plenty of good human beings around. Not everyone lied.

A huge, human-shaped shadow fell on the grass. I squinted into the sun. Dad stood staring down at me, chest heaving. He moved to the side and blocked the sun. My stomach lurched. His nostrils flared and his tongue flicked out and licked his upper lip. 'Come with me. Now.'

His muscles were coiled tight, veins pulsing. He stood incredibly still. Waited for me to react, do the sensible thing.

Everything around us blurred into insignificance. I couldn't look away from him. My ribs squeezed with fear and failure. I'd not stayed hidden for long enough. I was an idiot.

I expected him to lunge for me, but he didn't move. He didn't want to make a scene. Someone might see.

'We need to show you something important. Something that will help you gain perspective,' he said.

I opened my mouth to speak, but the words curled back down my throat. Panic snaked upwards, spotting my sight. I blinked, noticed a figure moving towards us. Training my peripheral vision, I made out a couple with a child. The child was giggling. Her parents were swinging her between them.

Dad glanced around at the family. He turned back to me and subtly shook his head. Reaching out a hand, he murmured, 'Don't.'

Slowly, he moved his hand into his pocket and withdrew a syringe just enough for me to see. He slipped it back in quickly and smiled. 'Come on, Darling. Time to go home.'

The family were almost level with Dad. I saw the woman register me. I was crouched on the ground, body tense. She must realize something was wrong. Her eyes narrowed. She glanced at Dad, then back at me. I waited, hoping and praying she would intervene, ask me if I was OK, but she averted her gaze and carried on walking. I wanted to yell at her to come back, help me, but feared what Dad would do. There was a child with them. It was impossible to predict how far he'd go to keep me quiet.

'Come *on*,' Dad growled.

I stood up. The drug hadn't worn off. I felt like I'd been padded with cotton wool. My senses were slow, thick.

'Where's Mum?' I said.

He ignored me and breached the distance between us in two strides. 'Please, don't make a scene. Rose will be here any second.'

'Why are you doing this?' I croaked. 'What's happened to you?'

But he wasn't focused on me any longer. He was looking at something behind me. I twisted around. The man who'd been swinging his child stood a short distance away. He was short, but muscular. Bald with a tattoo on his neck.

'Can I help you?' Dad said.

'My wife says you're the one who needs help,' he said, looking at me.

I hesitated, nodded. 'Yes. He abducted me. I just got away, but he found me.'

Dad's jaw clenched. 'She's confused. Stay out of it, mate.'

'I ain't no mate of yours,' the man said. He squared up to Dad. Glanced at me. 'Go. I'll deal with him.'

Dad's hand shot out and clamped down on my wrist. 'No. This isn't what it looks like.'

The man took a step closer. 'Let her go.'

Dad shook his head. 'I don't think so. Leave now if you know what's good for you.'

The man didn't move.

I sank my teeth into Dad's upper arm, twisted out of his grip and staggered away.

Darting a glance behind me, I saw Dad holding his arm where I'd bitten him and trying to talk to the man, who was blocking his path.

I sprinted out of the close and emerged onto a bigger street lined with houses, knowing I'd made a lucky escape, adrenaline rocketing, eyes darting everywhere. I had to be quick. Get as far away from Dad as possible. A car drove down the hill. It was a white van. Van man stories rattled around my head, but I pushed them away. There was no time.

The van was moving slowly. The sun prevented me from seeing the driver, but I didn't care. I moved out of the shadows and held up my thumb. I tried to imagine what the driver would see: a scruffy teenager with wild, haunted eyes. A young lady who shouldn't be hitching a ride from a stranger. Part of me hoped the driver would ignore me. I heard Mum's voice warning me never to talk to strangers. At school, we'd been taught to shout 'Stranger danger!' if someone we didn't know approached us when we were on our own. I was taking a risk. A small one. I was 17, almost an adult. So far, I'd outwitted Rose and Dad. I could protect myself. And I didn't have a choice. If Dad got past that man, he wouldn't be far behind.

Still, as the van slowed, my stomach quivered and unease wormed across my back.

The window whirred down and I took a step closer to the vehicle. Up close, I noticed how grimy and dented the van was. A stale, fusty smell oozed out of the open window. From the mirror hung two fluffy white and black dice, swinging like pendulums. Seeing that, I relaxed and forced a smile. Anyone who owned fluffy dice had to be decent. I could hardly imagine a Jack the Ripper type choosing those for his car.

'Thanks for stopping,' I panted.

A grubby hand held the top of the window. I peered into the van at the driver who tipped a straw hat at me. He had a Beatles haircut, but instead of being black, his hair was the colour of a dried apricot. Hair dusted his sun-pinked arms and freckles sprinkled his face like rain. He wore faded jeans and a red T-shirt with a funny monkey to man evolution print across the front. His age was hard to judge. I guessed 40. More than double mine.

'Need a ride?' he said in a strong South-West accent. 'Everything all right, love? I'm Rich, and my friends call me, well, Rich!' He slapped his thigh. 'I'm madder than a wet hen! You hopping in?'

I nodded and opened the rust-flecked door.

There was no air-conditioning and damp-smelling air blew into my face. I clicked on my seatbelt and shut the door. The floor was a mess of crisp packets and soiled tissues. I looked back the way I'd come. There was no sign of Dad. I wanted to scream at Rich to drive, but couldn't let him know there was anything wrong.

'Sorry about that,' he said, jerking a thumb at the air vent, 'Hot as a pot of neck bones out there and little better in here. Van's not what she used to be. Hopper's pretty busted these days.' He slung an arm over the back of my seat. 'What's your name, love?'

I cleared my throat. 'Arrietty.'

'What a pretty name! Me and the Mrs are about to have a little kicker. My Mrs'll like that. Where'd your folks come up with it?'

'*The Borrowers*. It's a children's book.'

I glanced at his ring finger. There wasn't a wedding band. Was he lying?

No. He's a nice guy. Just a bit weird. Stop being paranoid. Not everyone's like Dad.

'Nice. Got a destination in mind, Arrietty? I, myself,

276

am ready and raring to go,' he said, eyes keen, sharper than before.

The engine grumbled like an old man as he threw it into life. The furry dice quivered.

'1 Peacock Lane, Kilton. Do you know Kilton?' I said quickly, looking around again. No Dad.

'Nope, can't say I do. How far is it?'

'I'm not sure.'

Rich raised an eyebrow. 'Come again?'

I plumped for a half-lie, desperate to get on the road. 'I'm going to visit my great aunt, Maggie, but ran out of money for the rest of the taxi ride. I don't have my card and I lost my phone, so...'

He scratched beneath his hat and chuckled. 'Bless your heart. Luckily, I have got my mobile. Let me do a search.'

I sweated and waited, fearing Kilton was miles away and any chance of hitching a ride was non-existent.

'Geronimo! OK – it's not far off my patch as luck would have it.'

I exhaled with relief and managed a smile. Rich patted my hand and I flinched. For a second, a frown creased his brow, but he smoothed it quickly and rapped his knuckles on the dashboard. 'All right, love. Let's hit the road.'

I bit my lip and hoped I was doing the right thing. There was no going back now.

Chapter 61

The mystery woman's voice teases me, dripping incessantly like a broken tap, taunting, just out of reach. However much I strain, her identity remains hidden. I try to think of every woman I know and my brain won't work. Nobody will come. It's like someone has erased that part of my memory. It's bizarre and frustrating. I know him and only him. My captor and tormentor. No – wait - I think I know another man. A teacher. A good man. I can picture his face: kind, apple-green eyes, strong jaw. He nurtured my love of art. He had a barking laugh. But where? When? What was his name?

Why am I wasting time thinking about this? Switch on. Focus.

The room is silent – or my ears are off again. Sometimes it's hard to tell. My eyes are blackout curtains, trapping me in darkness. But – hold on – there's something…a smell. It's harsh, acrid.

I sniff. Catch a stronger scent that even the other one can't mask.

My lungs constrict. This smell is meaty, ripe, dirty. My tummy turns. Recognition quivers like violin strings deep down in my stomach. The first odour is bleach. A cleaning agent. The strongest type of chemical detergent. People use it in their homes to clean the filthiest of stains. Killers use it to cover their tracks. To get rid of the blood. The DNA.

The second stench is body odour.

Oh God, oh God, oh God. No.

His stink invades my nose, stronger than before, closer, hotter, so hot. I conjure his face. See his dark, piercing eyes in the blacks of my eyelids. Sense the rage emanating off his body. The air is electric with energy – I can feel it. I can feel him staring down at me.

He's here and he's come to kill me.

I've done a terrible thing, but it was an accident. I don't deserve this. I can't die. I won't. No matter what he does, somehow, some way, I'm going to fight to stay alive.

Chapter 62

According to the Sat Nav, Kilton wasn't too far away, but I felt sick to my stomach. I knotted and unknotted my fingers, trying and failing to still my legs. Rich didn't seem to notice my distress; he was too busy talking a mile-a-minute. At first, I wished he would put the radio on and be quiet, but he was doing me a huge favour and the more he spoke, the nicer he seemed. In an attempt to make the journey seem quicker, I tried to make conversation, which energised him all the more.

'Have you lived in the south-west your whole life?' I said.

'Yep. Met the Mrs – Penny's her name – at a craft fair in Salisbury town hall. Oh, Arrietty, you'd love Salisbury. Most beautiful cathedral you've ever seen. Gothic style. Incredible feat of man. You been?'

'Yes. It's stunning,' I said, wondering if I was telling the truth. A vague memory chafed my senses then drifted away like tumbleweed.

'Nice. Anyway, so I had my stall – carpentry by trade – I fix up chairs, tables, dressers, desks, bureaus, the whole shebang – and this pretty little lady with girt big green eyes came up to me and you know what she said?'

I raised my eyebrows. 'What?'

He laughed and wiggled his straw hat. '"What's a handsome cowboy like you doing in a place like this?" And I tell you now, she had me at that. I asked her out on the spot and blow me down she said yes and two decades later, here we are. Mind you, it hasn't all been smooth sailing.'

'Oh. Why?'

He sighed. 'We've been trying for a family for – God

– how long now? Must be twelve, thirteen years. No luck. Pen's had five miscarriages. Never gone past the first trimester until this one. She's five months in now. Can you believe it?'

'That's great,' I said, surprised to see him wiping his eyes with the back of his hand.

'I won't let Pen do a thing. Wait on her hand and foot. Can't have her risking any heavy lifting, you know?'

I nodded and thought about Mum. She'd suffered a miscarriage before she had me. It had been one of the hardest experiences in her life. I couldn't imagine what it would be like for someone to go through that five times. I thought about Dad, how he would have behaved during that time and my insides went cold. My airway constricted and suddenly I couldn't get any air into my lungs. I clasped at my throat and rasped, 'I – can't – breathe. Help – me.'

Rich swore, swerved the van to the curb, jumped down from behind the wheel and ran around to my side of the vehicle. 'Do you think getting out will help?'

Through a blur of tears and panic, I managed to nod. I watched him undo my seatbelt, lift me off the seat and sit me down on the grass verge. Air was what I needed, but it wouldn't come. I looked at him, confused and desperate, as he crouched in front of me, took my hands in his and said calmly, 'You're fine. Most likely this is a panic attack. My mum, God rest her soul, got them from time to time, but they're not dangerous, just shit-scary. It'll pass. Trust me on that. Now, look in my eyes. Come on. That's right. Focus on my voice. Breathe in for one, two, three, and out, one, two, three. Come on. You can do it. That's right. In, one, two, three and out, one, two, three. Concentrate on your breathing. Good job. That's great.'

He repeated the counting over and over again, never releasing my hands. Panic resurfaced multiple times, but I managed to find the rhythm in his voice, latched on and forced myself to try to do what he was telling me to.

Finally, the pressure in my chest lifted. Gorgeous, glorious air was breathable again. I gorged on it, head between my knees, Rich's hand on my back. 'Good girl. You did great. Real great.'

We sat for a while on the grass, Rich rubbing my back, which helped me find a calm I hadn't for ages. He talked nonstop, commenting on passing cars, the weather and his excitement for the birth of his baby.

Hot from the sun, and knowing time was short, I let him help me to my feet and stuttered an apology. I felt embarrassed that a stranger had needed to tend to me in such a way, that I was so helpless and dependent on someone I'd only just met, but Rich brushed away my words with a wave of his hat and, ever-the-gentlemen, gave me a hand up into the van.

We drove in silence for a whole minute before Rich spoke, his voice soft and careful, 'You had one of those before?'

'No,' I said, 'At least, I don't think so.'

He raised an eyebrow. 'Don't think so?'

I swallowed drily and rushed out my words, 'There's something wrong with my memory. For a while now, I haven't been able to remember...stuff.'

'But there's more going on than that, isn't there?' he said, glancing at me from under the brim of his hat. The concern in his voice touched me and his astuteness stunned me speechless.

'If you want to tell me, Arrietty, I'm all ears. I'm wiser than I look. If you don't want to say, that's fine by me, but I always think a problem shared is a problem halved.'

I sniffed, unable to control the urge to cry. A tissue, grubby and crumpled, appeared in my hand.

'You poor thing. Come now, tell old pastor Rich.'

I snorted out a laugh and looked at him, thinking how wonderful it would be to tell someone everything that had been going on.

'Pastor Rich is listening,' he said with a wink.

I sighed and rubbed my forehead. Was there any harm in telling him? No. I didn't think so, and I needed this hideous beast off my chest before it crushed my lungs again.

Staring out at the whizzing cars, I said, 'My dad has done something terrible to my mum.'

I glanced at him.

His eyebrows rose. He went very still and looked at me askance. 'Go on.'

'I tried to tell the police, but they didn't believe me.'

'What? Why?'

I sighed. 'Dad cottoned on to the fact that I know what he's done, so I had to use his car to get away. The police caught me speeding. I told them all about him, but they were having a hard time believing me. Then he turned up at the station claiming I'm unstable.'

'*Unstable?* But why did the police believe him over you?'

'I don't know for sure. I think it might be because he's having an affair with my therapist and got her to feign a document classing me as mentally ill.'

Rich's jaw dropped. 'So, what happened?'

'I had no choice but to go back to the house with him. The police wouldn't let me leave on my own. I pretended to be sorry, but in the back of my mind I thought there was a chance I could hunt through the house again and find out where he's keeping her.'

'Christ.'

'Yeah. And it's not just my mum. My brother is missing too. I don't know where he is or what's been done to him.'

'And you can't tell the police, because they think you're ill?'

I said nothing. A sea of emotion welled in my breast.

For the first time, Rich was lost for words.

After about a minute, he pulled over into a layby, took off his hat and stared wide-eyed at me. 'Well, no wonder you look like you've seen a ghost. Christ. What're we going to do?'

I shook my head and looked dead in his eyes. 'Not we. Me. You can't get involved in this.'

'You really think he's hurt your mum?'

'All I know for certain is that he's keeping her locked up. Either he keeps her prisoner forever or he kills her.'

'I take it this Maggie person we're driving to isn't your great aunt?'

I shook my head. 'Sorry I lied to you. She's our cleaner. Worked for us for years. She knows me and Mum. I'm hoping she'll speak up for me. Go to the police, convince them to investigate Mum's and my brother's disappearances. It's the only shot I've got.'

'OK. Right. What in hellfire am I doing hanging around here?'

Rich accelerated away from the verge. I found myself watching the clock, hoping and praying my panic attack hadn't wasted too much time. Images too real and painful to name circled my mind like piranhas. I glanced at Rich, at his hands gripping the wheel, chest pushed forward, and thanked the stars for this one piece of luck. I hadn't found a pervert in a white van who was going to try something and waste my time. I'd found a carpenter with the heart of a hero. If anyone was going to get me to Maggie's in time, it was Rich.

Chapter 63

'Hey – I've had an idea,' Rich said.

'Oh yeah? What?' I said flatly.

'I can call the police, tell them everything you just told me. How's that?'

I shook my head. 'It won't work. You don't know Dad. Only someone like Maggie, who's known us for years, will stand a chance of persuading them to take what I'm saying seriously. Plus, Maggie came over a couple of weeks ago and Dad sent her away. She's not stupid. She must know something's up. Maggie can tell the police what he said to her and that'll add substance to my story.'

Rich sighed long and loud. 'I guess you're right. Christ.'

Nervous energy pulsed in the air between us. Rich seemed deep in thought, so I watched the countryside out of the window and tried to imagine Maggie's reaction to my story. She had to believe me. If she didn't or refused to help, I couldn't think of a plan B. There was no one else…unless…Isla's mum, Cora, was a recently retired doctor. She'd had to retire early due to health problems. It was Sunday, which meant there was a high chance she would be at home. If Isla was too, that would be amazing – she'd help convince her mum to do the right thing. But it was likely that Isla would be out on a sunny afternoon like this in the field behind their house riding her horse, BoJack.

I loved BoJack, but found myself wishing he was sick so Isla couldn't ride him. I instantly felt guilty. Then I recalled how Isla had abandoned me. It stung when I thought about how my best friend hadn't bothered to write me a letter these last few weeks, but maybe she'd been told not to. Maybe her mum had said that telling me about all the cool stuff she was doing would only make things harder for me. Apparently, I had chronic fatigue. Dad would have made sure everyone at school knew why I was off, even if it was a lie. The more I thought about it, the less I believed it was true. He'd probably forged a doctor's note and given it to the school. In fact, I couldn't even remember seeing a doctor, let alone being told by one that I was suffering from anything. Dad must have lied about that, just like he'd lied about posting my letters.

Isla and Cora lived in Shepton. Cora was a quiet, stern woman, not very warm or friendly, but if I explained everything properly, I felt sure she'd believe me and decide to help. She and Mum weren't close by any means, but when they crossed paths, they got on pretty well. They'd known each other for six years now, ever since Isla and I became friends when I joined secondary school. And Cora was genius-bright; she'd listen and realize I was telling the truth and would know exactly what to do.

I looked at Rich, wondering if I should ask him to drive me to Isla's house instead, but the sign for Kilton appeared, and I realized I had to stay on this path now. Surely Maggie would believe me, and she was bound to be at home. I remembered her telling Mum how she went to church every Sunday morning without fail then cooked herself a roast dinner and slobbed out on the sofa feasting on crappy TV.

I shook my head; it was a wonder I could remember trivial things like that yet fail to recall the important stuff.

'Nearly there,' Rich said. He sounded nervous.

I gave him a grim smile. 'Let's hope she believes me.'

Rich turned right onto Peacock Lane and we bumped along a pocked road lined with cottages. He stopped the van outside number one, which perched on the edge of some woods. I'd never been to Maggie's house, but it was exactly as I'd imagined: quaint, cosy and full of character. A front garden bursting with flowers created a delightful frontage to the white cottage, and a low fence neatly enclosed the small space.

'This is it,' I breathed.

Rich laid a hand on my shoulder and squeezed. 'Shall I join you?'

'No, I'll be fine. Thank you so much, Rich. I'll never forget how much you've helped me. I hope everything goes smoothly with your baby.'

Rich removed his hat. 'Thank you, Arrietty. Now, off you go and good luck to you too. Let's hope this bastard goes down for what he's done to you and yours.'

I turned to go, then swivelled back and threw my arms around his sweaty neck. 'Thank you.'

Leaving him blushing, I climbed down from the van and waved bye, but he leaned over and called, 'I'm not leaving until I know she's there.'

I nodded my thanks then stepped over the fence onto a steppingstone path that led to Maggie's front door. This was excellent. I'd got here safely. All I had to do now was explain everything really well, as quickly as I could.

With the van's engine humming at my back, I knocked on the door and waited.

Maggie answered the door looking flustered, yellow Marigolds dripping water onto the doormat. A light sheen of sweat covered her face and dampened her grey curls.

'Oh, my dear, good day to you! Is everything all right?'

'Is Shane here?' I wanted to make sure he wasn't involved in Dad and Rose's plan.

'Oh no, no – Shane's gone off travelling with James Broughton's drug-addict sister. Poor James – he's tried so hard to help that girl over the years.'

'Is that why Shane stopped working for us so suddenly?' *Drug-addict sister – what?*

Maggie frowned. 'You don't know?'

'No – I – well, I can't remember much lately. I've been having memory problems.'

'Alec gave him the boot, thought he was up to no good, with, well, um…' she cleared her throat. 'He wasn't of course,' she added hastily, clutching my forearms, 'I know that now.'

I bit my lip and shook my head. So Dad had told me the truth about firing Shane. Tears bubbled up in my throat. Everything felt too much – there was so much I didn't know, so much I'd forgotten, 'I'm sorry -'

Concern furrowed her forehead, and she drew me into a hug and led me into the cottage, which smelt warm and clean.

'There, there, now. Tell me all about it. You sit there and I'll fetch us a nice cup of tea.'

She turned to leave the small living room and I said, 'No. Don't. I mean. Sorry. There's no time. I have to tell you now.'

'Goodness gracious. Of course.' She sat down beside me and patted my knee. 'Go on, go on.'

I tried to order my thoughts, but my brain swirled like a twister, and a wave of dizziness made the patterned sofas, black beams and cat ornaments slant and spin. It was happening again. My chest tightened, yanked taut by an invisible hand. I gulped air and inwardly repeated Rich's words. *Just breathe. In, one, two, three. Out, one, two, three.*

'What is it? Asthma? I've got an inhaler somewhere – you wait there,' Maggie darted out of the room, leaving me alone.

I focused on breathing, cleared my thoughts of the terrifying feeling that this was going to kill me, that I was having a heart attack. Maggie rushed back into the room and banged her knee against the coffee table.

She snatched off the lid, shook the puffer and thrust it into my hand, but my breathing was starting to slow. I gave her a tremulous smile, 'I'm OK.' I sucked air into my body and the panic receded as quickly as it had come. 'It's not asthma.'

'No?'

'I think it's a panic attack. I'm OK now.'

'You sure? Maybe I should phone an ambulance?'

I shook my head and gripped her gloved hands in mine. 'I have to tell you something. You're the only one who can help me. It's going to sound crazy, but I promise you, it's the truth.'

Maggie nodded, eyes wide as saucers, curls quivering. 'Go on, dear. I'm all ears. You know me. Anything I can do to help, I will.'

I told her everything, unable to stop glancing at the gold clock on the mantlepiece, wishing I could tell the story faster. After ten minutes, I shut up and watched Maggie for her reaction. Throughout she'd been silent. At times I thought I'd seen a flicker of confusion. Other times I feared I'd seen disbelief, but when I'd finished, she nodded urgently and pushed herself up from the sofa. Glancing worriedly behind her, she said, 'Right. I'm going to make the call. Stay here and try to relax. You did the right thing by coming to me, dear. You really did.'

Her reaction was just as I'd hoped. She believed me. She was going to help. There was no doubt in her expression, only unflinching certainty about what she had to do next.

She hurried towards the door.

In a shaky voice, I said, 'Maggie, you can't know how much this means to me.'

She looked back, nodded once and darted out of the room.

I collapsed against the slouchy sofa. Now that help was on its way, my adrenaline seemed to have died a sudden and awful death. Exhaustion flooded my blood, melting my energy, and I sighed. Maggie would convince the police I was telling the truth. The authorities would interrogate

Dad and get answers out of him. Mum and Eddie would be found. We'd be reunited and work together to put all of this behind us. It would be hard, but in time, we'd be happy again. I'd get better and go back to school. Mum and I would cook together and discuss books we'd read and films we'd watched. We'd create art together and Mum would help me improve my sketches. Eddie would start school and discover a whole new world filled with fun, friends and learning. I'd teach him to ride his bike, and we'd make Mum a special cake to put a smile on her face. Things would go back to a new kind of normal. Dad would no longer haunt our lives. We'd be free.

Tears leaked out of my eyes, but they were tears of relief.

It would be OK now that the police knew the truth.

Chapter 64

I had fallen asleep. *Damn.*

I sat up and scanned the lounge. How long had I been asleep? Where was Maggie? The cottage felt too quiet.

I stood up and ventured into the centre of the small room. 'Maggie?'

There was no answer. I wondered if she was in the bathroom. I was desperate for a wee, so I crossed the carpet and opened the door. It led to a small, narrow kitchen that looked like it had been decorated in the seventies. A fluffy white cat stared at me from on top of the microwave.

'Where's your mummy?' I said, thinking about Knightley, hoping he was OK.

The cat stared at me unblinkingly, its pale green eyes intense and hard. I walked to the next door, which led to a utility room. There was another door. I opened it to discover a tiny bathroom with a one-tap sink and a toilet. I went as quickly as I could, desperate to talk to Maggie and find out what the police had said.

Shutting the bathroom door, I glanced into the back garden. It was a pretty blend of rockery and flowerbeds. There was a sweet little pond too. Maggie took pride in her garden. She was such a lovely person. So kind and gentle.

I walked back into the lounge and stood at the bottom of the stairs. 'Maggie? You up there?'

I thought I heard a door close above me and looked up at the low ceiling. Maybe Maggie was hard of hearing. She'd never mentioned she was, but it could be a recent problem.

I stepped onto the stairs and halted in my tracks. The

hairs on my neck prickled. I could hear voices coming from outside. Men's voices. Angry-sounding. Heated. Tearing at the air like thunder.

Recognition clogged my airway. *No. It can't be. Maggie wouldn't.*

I didn't want to look, but I had to know.

I ran to the window and ripped back the net curtains.

Dad was in the front garden with Rich. They were shouting at each other. Both red-faced, rigid with tension. Rich was just as angry, but Dad was bigger. Bullish in comparison. A head taller. Wider and stronger.

Dad shouted, 'I warned you,' and ran at Rich.

I felt a presence behind me and turned around. Maggie stood at the bottom of the stairs twisting her hands. In a thick voice, she said, 'I'm sorry. The police are looking for you. I didn't have a choice.'

I stared, slack-jawed, too horrified to speak. She was as bad as Dad. A dark, traitorous version of the person I used to know. I wanted to knock her to the ground, scream at her that she'd just signed Mum's death warrant, but there was no time.

I ran to the front door, yanked it open and raced across the garden. Dad locked his arm around Rich's neck, forced him to the ground and straddled him, raised his fist and shouted incoherently into Rich's face.

'Stop!' I screamed.

Both men's heads jerked towards me. Dad squinted against the sun. Sweat coated every inch of his face and body and vitriol reddened his cheeks. He was panting. Livid.

'Get in the car,' he barked at me, pushing himself to his feet.

Rich remained on his back, watching Dad.

I wondered if he was hurt and guilt cut a new pain in my heart.

'Leave her alone,' Rich grunted, rolling onto his side.

'Stay out of it,' Dad shouted over his shoulder.

I glanced towards the van. The engine wasn't running any more. The Merc blocked it in from behind. I wanted to tell Rich to leave, but how could he when Dad's car was there? And besides, a glance at his face told me he wasn't going anywhere. Grit was in his eye and determination set his mouth in a hard line.

I licked my lips and said, 'I'm not coming with you, so you might as well go.'

Dad snarled and took a step closer. 'You know you hurt Rose? Did you tell your new friend that? She's in hospital having stitches.'

I said nothing. My heart was about to rip through my ribcage.

'The police are looking for you. I've told them you're ill. They won't stop until they find you. You need to come with me now.' He tried to soften his voice, but his eyes glinted with malice.

I glanced to my right. Another cottage garden lay that way, followed by another and another. There was nowhere to hide. To the left lay the woods. Better, but not perfect. Dad was fast, faster than me. If I ran, he'd catch me.

Rich caught my eye. There was a silent message in his gaze. I tried to read him, work out what he was telling me to do, but I didn't want to involve him any more, so I told him to go. He shook his head a fraction.

Dad glanced over his shoulder and growled, 'She's right. You need to leave. You've no business getting involved. This doesn't concern you.'

'You're wrong,' Rich said, reaching for his hat. He stood and planted his feet wide. From his back pocket he withdrew something metallic that caught the sun. He flicked it with his thumb and a blade shot out.

I stared at the penknife. Hope leapt up and down in my chest as I looked from Dad to my friend.

Dad turned and called out, 'Maggie, call the police.'

I turned to see Maggie scurry inside the cottage. *Shit.*

'Go back to your car and drive away before I turn ungentlemanly on you,' Rich said, taking a step towards Dad.

Dad didn't back up. I stared at the back of his head wishing he would listen. If Rich got in trouble for hurting him, I'd never forgive myself.

'You haven't got it in you,' Dad said.

Rich raised an eyebrow and took another step.

Dad was distracted, his back to me. The police would be here any minute. I had to go. Maggie wasn't going to vouch for me. No one was.

I edged away. Dad whipped around and ran at me. I jerked back and stumbled over a flowerpot. I hit the ground hard and flinched as he tried to grab me, but he was dragged backwards and thrown to the ground.

Rich shouted at me to leave.

I didn't wait to be told twice; I jumped the fence and ran. A scream shattered the air and I glanced around to see Dad lunging at Rich. I hesitated as the two men struggled. Dad was bigger and wider, stronger, but Rich was faster. Mum's agonised face appeared in my mind, and I turned away and ran on, praying Rich would be OK. There was nothing I could do to help him. I had to help Mum now. I had to find her and Eddie. Make sure they were safe.

'STOP!'

I entered the trees and looked back. Dad was coming. With a terrified sob, I lurched forward.

Chapter 65

I didn't know how long I'd slept at Maggie's or how long it had taken Dad to reach her house, but new clouds had formed in the sky and smothered the sun turning the woods a green-blue tinge that reminded me of frost-hardened bodies pulled from freezing water. The trees were tightly packed, the woodland floor alternating between moss, earth, leaves and fallen branches. Thorny bushes snared my leggings and tore at my ankles. Trees towered high into the dimming sky like mythical giants. I'd never set foot in here before and I didn't know where I was going. I'd gone off the beaten path into denser ground in an effort to stay hidden, but the crack of sticks and sway of branches as I crashed through them were too loud and I feared any moment I'd feel a hand clamp down on my shoulder or a hard shove in my back. He'd stopped shouting, but that didn't mean he'd gone. I had to keep going until I found a way out of the woodland. From there, I'd try to get to Isla's house. How, I didn't know. With no vehicle and no money, I was screwed. Maybe I could hitch again.

Adrenaline was my fiercest friend. I ran until I thought I was going to throw up, then crouched behind a holly bush for a short rest. Birds tweeted and chirped from the darkening canopy above like nothing was wrong. Nothing sounded from below - nothing, that was, except for my laboured breathing and chaotic heartbeat. I listened, straining my ears for the tiniest sound. Chills ran down my arms and my hairs stood on end as his voice reverberated through the trees.

'STOP! COME BACK HERE!'

I glanced around and tried to work out where he was. He called again, a vicious bark that rushed towards me sounding closer than before. Knowing I had to move, I shook out my already stiffening joints. Pins and needles attacked my right foot and I straightened cautiously and peered over the bush. A holly leaf caught my cheek and I pulled away ripping skin. His voice rang again and it was a lot louder. Other sounds accompanied his cry: snaps and thuds.

I never should have stopped. How was he tracking me?

I looked down and noticed a tear in my leggings halfway up my shin. Blood oozed from a wound that was clearly deep. Pain shot into my leg, and I winced and squinted at the ground, tracing the route I'd taken. A haphazard pattern of blood painted the leaves. The tulip painting flashed up like a red-eyed demon. I saw a mobile phone hitting the wall. The image was gone in less than a second. I let it go, knowing I needed to deal with the blood.

Swearing, I bent over and tugged up my leggings so that the material bunched over the cut. I hoped it would ebb the flow but wasn't convinced it would work.

Dad's voice came again – a vicious boom that penetrated the shadows like thunder - followed by utter silence. I froze, fear rendering me immobile, certain he'd seen me. He sounded like he was only metres away.

I fixed my attention on my goal: reach Cora Hamilton. With an almighty effort, I blocked out the fear and sprinted away from his voice, out of my hiding place into the blackening trees. Rustles and thuds followed in my wake. I risked a backward glance and saw Dad, purple-faced, huge and worryingly agile raging through the trees after me.

'WAIT! YOU HAVE TO -'

His voice cut off, morphing into an anguished cry. I

heard him hit the ground and didn't look back.

This was my chance.

I ran on aching legs, every muscle burning, lungs tight with fear. The instinct to turn around and see if he was still following me almost won, but I resisted and pushed on, leaping over roots, twisting my face away from spiky branches at the last second, terrified, desperate, bursting for breath. With every step, he could be gaining, or I could be losing him; I couldn't know without stopping and scanning the woods and there was no way I was stopping now.

Blood drummed in my ears making it impossible to focus on any sound coming from behind me. He could be close now and I wouldn't hear him. The thought was terrifying.

I ran as quickly as I could. Adrenaline thrust my limbs forward, but my leg was hurting, and my energy was draining.

It didn't take long for my lack of fitness to defeat my need for speed. Try as I might, my legs grew heavier and slower. Every stride was a struggle, like wading through cement. My lungs screamed for a break. Shaking with the urge to be sick, I slowed to a walk, hands on my hips pinching the stitches needling my muscles. I could taste blood on the back of my tongue. I thought I heard a noise and whipped around, but there was no sign of Dad – not yet. I scanned the silvery spaces between every tree and saw nothing. The trees lay silent. Eerily, but wonderfully so. I'd lost him. The relief was like an ice-cold drink in the Sahara. But I couldn't relax yet.

I needed to get out of here before darkness swallowed and blinded me. In a sense, I was already walking blind because I hadn't a clue how vast these woods were or how to get out of them. Panic had stolen every sense of time I possessed, but the need to hurry was greater than ever. With darkness coming, the risk increased; night-time would be the ideal moment for Dad to dispose of a body.

I walked faster. My thighs blazed in protest and lactic acid flooded my system. The desire to sit down and stop was so strong I almost gave in. I spotted a fallen branch that suddenly looked like the comfiest seat in the world and found my legs carrying me towards it. There was a carpet of squidgy moss atop the bark; a soft cushion for my weary body...

No.

The voice came out of nowhere. It was Mum's voice not mine; strong, powerful, confident. I clung to it and fought a savage need to scream at myself for my weakness. Mum could be fighting for her life at this very moment and I was giving in to a little bit of pain. Shaking my head angrily, I clambered over the trunk, palms scraping against rough bark, and broke into a jog.

If I'd thought my limbs were heavy before, that was nothing compared to now. Oxygen might have reinvigorated my lungs, but it seemed to have done little for my muscles. My thighs felt like they were on fire.

Still, I pushed on.

And on.

The sun sank lower and lower, the woods grew darker and darker, and I became more afraid with every passing step that I was going to be lost in these ghostly trees for ever. Eventually the police would find my body, half-eaten by vermin, writhing and squirming with maggots. The image was so appalling that I retched. Nothing but stringy saliva came up. I suppressed a sob and carried on, looking back every few seconds, just in case Dad was still on my trail – even though the gloom rendered me as blind as a bat. Though I'd heard nothing bar the odd flutter of wings or caw of a bird, he could still be preying on me, waiting for the perfect moment to attack. In fact, the sense of being watched seemed to grow, enveloping me in its quivering arms like the craggy branches around me. I felt as if I was watching someone else stumbling through the wilderness, another person with long, black hair and frantic eyes, someone horribly vulnerable, lost and alone riding solely on a wing and a prayer. A wild, helpless girl struggling to survive against the odds, pinning her hopes on some ridiculous idea that she was doing the right thing, going the right way. I watched this poor young women and pity consumed me - and then I was back inside myself and Eddie was running alongside me, his face milk-white in the fading light - and a bolt of horror hit me. But instead of blinding me, its light illuminated a long-buried fact: Eddie wasn't here now. He wasn't here *then*. He couldn't have been, because…because…

I stopped moving and blinked into the trees where he'd just been. A ghost beside me. But he was gone. He always had been.

My gorge rose and I retched over and over again, spraying the ground with bile as pain like no other tore out my soul and the past attacked my consciousness with merciless force.

With a scream of agony, I bent double and gripped my head in my hands. My brain was on overload. Skin, hair, blood – random images flashed, faster and faster and faster, darting up then zooming back down into blackness, too fast to catch, too dark to see. Sparks of grass, metal, concrete, blood, bone. All of it racing up to seize my throat. And then a hair-raising scream. Horror – grief – blame. Guilt ramming a screwdriver into my spleen, over and over and over and over again.

The walls fell, crumbling around me like a child's sandcastle.

The truth flooded my senses, painful as acid.

I gasped and clutched my throat with both hands.

Suddenly, I knew the truth.

And my world imploded.

Part 4

Chapter 66

TWO YEARS AGO

Mum, Dad, Eddie and I arrived at Shepton Park. It was a gorgeous, sunny day, the last Saturday in June. A dozen or so children ranging in age from two to seven scrambled around the wooden play equipment giggling and squealing. Parents and grandparents sat at picnic benches, half of them looking at their phones. I hadn't wanted to go, but Dad had told me I had to. I was feeling down, because I'd only received a B in my Macbeth essay. It was part of my GCSE coursework and English was my best subject. I was used to getting A or A*, so B felt rubbish in comparison. Mum tried to bolster my mood by saying she'd cook my favourite meal, but nothing could lift me out of my slump, not even the joy on Eddie's face when a strawberry-blonde girl in a Peppa Pig dress started to chase him around the roundabout.

Dad snapped at me to stop sulking. I turned my back on him and got my mobile out of my pocket.

'This is supposed to be a lovely family outing,' he said.

'Leave her alone,' Mum said, 'She needs to work through it in her own time.'

'B is good,' Dad persisted.

'Not when you want to do English Lit for A Level it isn't,' I said.

'Take this as a lesson. Learn from your mistakes and do better next time,' he said.

I snorted.

'Maybe if you didn't spend so much time on that contraption,' he said, prodding my phone, 'you'd get an A.'

I glared at him, unable to believe he'd just said that. Anger burst in my veins, and I said, 'Fuck off.' It was the first time I'd ever sworn in front of my parents, let alone at one of them.

Dad stood abruptly and towered over me, face flushed. 'Please tell me you didn't just say what I think you did, Arrietty?'

Mum darted in front of him and placed her hands on his shoulders. She spoke to him quietly. He sighed, scowled, then stormed away to play with Eddie.

Mum wrapped her arm around my shoulder and hugged me close. 'He's only trying to help.'

'He's doing a crap job.'

'You know what he's like. He sees things in black and white, but he just wants what's best for you.'

My blood was still boiling, but deep down I knew she was right. Still, that didn't mean I was ready to forgive him.

An ice cream van tinkled along the road and parked on the other side where there was enough room. Eddie sprinted over to us, Dad in pursuit. 'Daddy says I can have an ice cream! Arri, can you take me to get one, pleeeeease?'

I looked up from my phone at my brother's sweet little face. 'All right.' Mum handed me a five-pound note and helped my red-faced brother out of his stripy hoodie. Dad smiled at me. I ignored him and took hold of Eddie's hand. 'Come on then.'

Eddie squealed and skipped along beside me. I slipped my phone into my shorts and sighed heavily. I'd give anything to be hanging out with Isla right now. Mum knew it. Dad did too. But they insisted on me joining them on outings like this. It drove me crazy. Mum had tried to persuade him that I should be able to do what I wanted at the weekends now that I was fifteen, but he'd put his foot down, saying that family time was important. Soon I'd be off to university and we'd never get moments like this again. Even if I argued until I was blue in the face, he wouldn't change his mind. He hated it when I got my phone out during days like this too, so I did it more to spite him.

I glanced around. They were both watching us.

With a smile, I got my phone out of my pocket and went on Instagram. Eddie yanked on my hand, yelling at me to hurry up. We stepped onto the pavement. My focus was on my phone. In my peripheral vision, I registered that the curb was lined with cars, that we'd need to walk between a white and a blue car to get to the other side of the road where the ice cream van waited. Eddie was shout-singing Baby Shark and tugging at my hand to make me go faster. I glanced up from my phone and stepped between the bonnet of the white car and the rear of the blue car. To block out my brother's tuneless singing, I slipped in my earphones and concentrated on my screen again. We stepped out from between the cars. Eddie grinned back at me. I barely noticed. Music was thumping in my ears and I only had eyes for Insta. He pulled his hand out of mine and ran towards the ice cream van. I looked up to check he was OK and a bus appeared out of nowhere. Eddie's body flew into the air like a rag doll. He made no sound. The bus screeched to a stop. Eddie lay on the middle of the road on his side, his neck at a strange angle. He was wearing his dinosaur trainers.

A blood-curdling scream came from behind me. I knew it was Mum.

Chapter 67

I didn't know how long I walked for or how I kept going. All I could see was the accident. All I could hear were two dreadful words: *Eddie's dead.*

Eddie's dead. Eddie's dead. Eddie's dead.

I told myself it wasn't real. The memory wasn't a memory; it was a figment of my imagination or, more likely, a lie planted there by Rose on Dad's command to make me seem more unstable. It was a stupid mental blip. There was no truth to any of it. Eddie was alive. Of course he was. I'd been with him at the house. I'd taken care of him, washed him, read to him. There was no way I could have imagined all of that. No. My mind was playing a vicious trick on me. Rose had screwed with my subconscious and done this to me.

My eyes brightened - Dad had talked to Eddie too! Back at the house. In the car. If that wasn't proof that my brother was alive, I didn't know what was.

I nodded sharply, massaged my chest with the heel of my hand, and forced the fake memory aside. Mum needed my help. So did Eddie. Rose had implanted a brutal fictional story in my head and it had just emerged. That was all that had happened here. It had to be.

Licking my trembling lips, I walked on focused on my goal, the false 'memory' locked up in the darkest corner of my brain, never to be released again.

*

At last, a glimmer of moon winked and the trees thinned.

I stumbled forward, arms wide to guard against encroaching obstacles, and saw something I never thought I'd be happy to see: a barbed wire fence. This was it. Finally, at long, long last, I'd reached the end of these godforsaken woods.

Words couldn't describe my relief in that moment. I didn't even care when a barb ripped a fresh cut in my thigh. All I cared about was the fact that I was out in the open, in a flat field under the gleaming moon.

Triumph renewed my energy like an injection of caffeine and I ran across the dusk-grey field towards a few houses.

Lights glowed from behind people's curtains. High wooden fences barred entry into back gardens. I reached the end of the field and climbed over a fence onto pavement. Turning, I stared at the closest house and wondered what my next move should be. I seemed to be on a country road dotted with only a handful of buildings. There were no streetlights and everyone's downstairs curtains were drawn against the encroaching darkness. Judging by the moon and the dusky light, I guessed it was about eight-thirty, but I could have been way out. I thought about knocking on someone's door and asking to use their phone. I could call a taxi. But I had no money or card to pay for one, so I hesitated. Maybe, just maybe, the person who opened their door would be awesome like Rich and offer to give me a ride to Shepton.

Tears sprung up and I squeezed them back, battling a vivid replay of Dad and Rich fighting.

Please let Rich be OK. Please.

Dad could have got hold of the penknife and stabbed him with it. Rich might be dead.

The idea was too much. I locked it away in the furthest, blackest corner of my mind. I was wasting time. I needed to be quick. So much time had passed. I could already be too late.

I looked at the car parked on the curb outside the first house. It was a white Mini Cooper. A woman's car maybe?

I tucked my hair behind my ears and strode to the front door. A porch light came on and I thought about the state I was in and how the person inside would react when they saw me. I must have looked mad. I was dirty and bleeding and probably as white as milk.

Still, I had no choice.

I rang the bell, which chimed a merry tune that laughed at my situation. A large shadow appeared in the frosted glass pane and a very tall man with a bushy beard opened the door. He frowned and looked me up and down and I reciprocated, dismayed to see he wore a police uniform. For a couple of seconds, his body was relaxed, and then, like Jekyll and Hyde, he transformed. Recognition pierced his eyes and his back straightened bringing him a head and a half taller than me. Looking at the ground, I muttered, 'Wrong house,' and turned quickly, heart stuttering, but his hand shot out and clamped my arm in an iron grip.

Chapter 68

I'd failed. My only chance now was to try to convince this man that I was telling the truth, that Alec Black-Hawkins was a liar, a sociopath who'd manipulated the police into believing I was deranged. But, looking up into the officer's ruddy face, the feeling my words would be in vain seemed magnified by a thousand. There was no compassion, no patience, no willingness to stop and listen; only a greedy kind of victory. He'd found the fugitive and was bringing her in. He was probably imagining a promotion, his next summer holiday, somewhere pricier than the last place he went, somewhere he could brag about to his colleagues when he returned to work.

'Please -' I began, but a voice from behind me made me stop.

'Dad? What's happening?'

I glanced around. A tall, lean girl a year or two younger than me stood in the garden holding the handlebars of a violet bike.

'Hazel, go around the back. Now,' her dad barked.

She frowned and glanced at my leg. 'She's bleeding.'

'NOW!' he shouted, making us both jump.

'But -'

'Hazel, so help me. Do what I'm asking. She's dangerous.'

'She doesn't look dangerous,' Hazel said, angling her head and staring at me like I was an interesting book.

Swearing under his breath, the man let go of my arm, strode past me and bore down on his daughter. He looked over his shoulder at me and said, 'Don't move.'

He pulled the bike out of Hazel's grip, laid it on the

ground and dragged his daughter across the garden towards the side of the house. 'Why do you always have to argue?' he snapped.

The girl was silent, but didn't fight. ''Cos I'm fifteen,' she mumbled.

Her dad muttered something in response and started to open the side gate. Adrenaline spiked in my blood as I ran for the bike, heaved it upright and swung my leg over it. The movement caught his eye and he shouted at me to stop, face contorted with a mixture of anger and disbelief. I leaned low over the handlebars and pedalled as fast as my knackered legs would allow, expecting any moment to hear a car zooming after me along the descending road. But a kind of unearthly silence settled over the fields and I had the uncanny feeling apocalypse was imminent with me one of a few surviving humans. I looked back; no one followed. The officer and his daughter were already invisible, swallowed up by the distance and darkness.

On either side, the road was empty of civilisation. No houses, no animals, no cars. I rode for a couple of minutes then entered Kilton proper: a Georgian village full of narrow alleyways and quirky cottages lit by old-fashioned streetlamps. Still pedalling like a maniac, I rode past The White Hart. A warm glow and chorus of laughter followed my path, reminding me of normal times. I'd been to that pub before with Eddie. I knew it instantly. With Mum too. I couldn't remember if Dad had joined us. Maybe my brain had banished the memory because I despised him so much.

But this was good news. I was on a bike and the police were looking for me, but if I kept my wits about me, senses peeled for any sign of a police car, I could ride off the road and hide in one of the numerous narrow alleys. If I kept going and wasn't caught, it wouldn't take me too long to reach Cora's. My legs seemed to have found a new purpose and cycling was a lot easier on my injured leg than stumbling over uneven ground. All I had to do was remain incognito and focus. The slightest sound of a car and I'd hide. Streetlights helped me identify paths to concealment as I rode. I kept my eyes and ears open. Hope dared to float upwards, but the fear that the police could appear at any moment popped it and brought me back down to reality. The police officer might have decided not to pursue me straight away – for what reason I couldn't fathom – but he'd have called it in. He'd seen the direction I'd taken so in that sense the police had a slight advantage, but what they didn't know was that while I wasn't mega fast on a bike, I knew back roads and short cuts in Shepton that would take me to my destination quickly while offering extra anonymity. I just had to get there without being seen, which seemed possible right now because the village was sleepy and still. No cars broke the quiet. A dog walker raised their hand as I rode past. I nodded, kept my head low and pedalled harder, leg throbbing. The road was still sloping south. Any moment it would begin to climb, not steeply, but enough to slow me down. Kilton would melt into another village called Marsh before Marsh became Shepton. I still had some distance to travel and the police were on my case. I could almost hear them communicating over their radios, voices urgent, fingers itching to snap cuffs onto my wrists.

Approaching the edge of Kilton, I encountered a sharp bend and saw the glow of headlights. There was no siren, no flashing blue light, but I had to be safe. I turned left up a narrow side street, sped along the bumpy road then pulled close to the wall, switched off the bike light and pressed myself into the shadows. A car roared past. The driver drove on. I breathed out, in, out again, trying to calm my nerves, then rode back onto the main road feeling twitchier than before.

The road began its ascent subtly and I changed gears, the movement natural like I'd done it recently. In the summer Mum occasionally went cycling, but I hadn't ridden since I was about ten. Or at least, I didn't think I had. But I supposed the skill of riding a bike was like that. Unforgettable. Wired into your body and brain like breathing or walking. Once you mastered the art, you never looked back. A bit like your first experience of pain or fear. Touch a hot iron once and you avoided it for ever after.

My body was fatiguing again. I rode as fast as I could through Marsh. A car approached and I looked up, clocking it, fearful it was a police car. The lights blinded me and I whipped the bike off the road and hid inside someone's front garden, scrambling off the saddle and crouching behind a wall. A light came on bathing me in light and an old woman in a dressing gown appeared and shrieked at me to get off her property. I hurried away and continued up the gentle slope, legs heavier than before, wishing Shepton was Marsh.

But Marsh was a small village with a direct route through and I reached Shepton after a few short minutes. Here, three cars whizzed towards me in quick succession. I turned right and took the short cut I knew would take me to Isla's house. Hidden by houses and riding through cuts, I relaxed, thinking it unlikely a police car would be driving around closes like this. They would, I hoped, stick to the bigger roads.

Luck, it seemed, was on my side for once.

I leaned the bike against the wrought iron fence that enclosed Isla's front garden, opened the gate, limped up the path and hammered on the door. My leg was oozing warm liquid and throbbing like nothing I'd ever known, the pain startlingly raw.

Isla answered. It took her a moment to recover from the shock of seeing me. She tucked a strand of corn-blonde hair behind her ear and raised her eyebrows.

'Hi,' I said, 'can I speak to your mum?'

'Hi, uh, yeah, sure. You OK?' She sounded like she barely knew me, and didn't look pleased to see me at all.

'Yeah. But I need to speak to Cora, now.'

Isla nodded hastily and beckoned me inside the bright hallway. I smelled their family scent: fresh and lemony, familiar but not overly so. How long was it since I'd been here? I couldn't remember.

'Don't worry about your shoes,' Isla said.

I looked down. My trainers were still filthy from the woods.

My best friend jogged up the hallway. 'Mum! Mum, come quick!'

Cora Hamilton appeared a moment later, her bald head gleaming like a pearl beneath the hallway light. She'd lost weight since I'd last seen her and brown bags circled her sharp eyes. In spite of the warmth, she wore a grey cardigan over a baggy shirt and jeans. Isla hovered behind her mum as if she didn't know whether to stay or go. Cora took one look at me then ordered Isla to leave. My friend gave me a sympathetic smile and hurried back into the living room, closing the door softly behind her.

'Alec called,' Cora said, staring intently at me, 'he's worried about you. We all are.'

'It's not me you need to be worried about. You can't trust him. He's done something awful.'

'Awful?' Cora said. 'To whom?'

'To Mum, maybe to Eddie too, and I need your help. You can tell the police what he's done. They won't believe me, but they'll believe you.'

Cora frowned. 'I don't understand. What do you think he's done?'

'I'll tell you everything, then you can call the police. They need to question him, find out where he's keeping her and Eddie, before it's too late. It might already be too late, but I can't let myself think like that.'

My chin started to tremble. I fixed her with a begging

gaze. 'Please.'

'Alright. Let me just get my phone. Wait here.' She turned and walked into the living room. I followed and watched over her shoulder as she picked up her mobile and began to search her contacts.

Isla sat on the cream sofa. She looked up warily at me then at her mum.

'What are you doing?' I said sharply.

Cora whipped around. 'Look. I'm sorry, but I need to call Alec and let him know you're here. He's terrified something's happened to you.'

My heart pounded in my throat. I shook my head. 'You can't do that. If you tell him I'm here, it's over.'

'I'm sorry, but I don't have a choice.' She pressed dial and put the phone to her ear.

Isla left the room without looking at me and ran upstairs. I heard her bedroom door slam and music pulsing through the ceiling. She was a coward. Too scared to stand up to her mum and help me.

I jerked Cora around and snatched the phone away from her ear. She cried out and tried to grab it back, but I threw it as hard as I could at the TV, which shattered, sending glass all over the navy carpet.

Cora's nostrils flared and she folded her arms across her flat chest. 'OK. Fine. Tell me everything and I'll see what I can do.'

Chapter 69

Cora told me to sit down. I did as I was told. The fact that she was willing to listen gave me much-needed hope.

'Before you start,' she said, moving to sit beside me, 'I need to take a look at your leg.'

'OK, but we need to be quick.'

She gave me a look. 'Turn and lie down.'

With difficulty, I lifted my leg onto the sofa.

'I'm going to wash my hands. I'll be back in a moment.'

I jerked up onto my elbows, worried there was a house phone in the kitchen that she was going to use to call Dad, but she returned quickly, handed me a pint of water and knelt next to the sofa to inspect the wound. 'Drink all of it. It looks like you've lost quite a lot of blood.'

Using a pair of scissors, she cut through my leggings to reveal the injury. I watched her work. Her movements were quick and precise. She had small hands with clipped nails. There was a slight tremble in her. I wondered if it was because of me or her illness. The cut was still bleeding and my leg was a mess of blood and dirt. She cleaned and dressed the wound, apologising when I winced. With a curt nod at her handiwork, she leaned back on her heels and turned her intelligent eyes on me. 'How did it happen?'

'In the woods, when I was running away from Dad.'

Shock pulled at her features, but she only said, 'I'll get rid of all this and fetch you another glass of water, then you can tell me what you think I need to know.'

She sounded business-like and matter-of-fact, but there was a cynical edge to her tone that I didn't like.

I scanned the room for a phone. There wasn't one.

The four-bedroomed semi-detached house was rather

like our old house in Shepton: modern and spacious with high ceilings. Cora was clearly a fan of blue, because flashes of every shade appeared in the form of large velvet cushions, lampshades, curtains and hand-painted coffee tables. Blue-framed photographs of snowy landscapes adorned the walls. Cora and Isla were huge skiing fans. They'd gone to the Alps every year since Isla turned seven. I'd never been skiing. Mum wasn't keen because of the risk involved.

I recognized Isla's smell in this house; a light, fresh scent a bit like citrus shampoo. I'd been here so many times and yet the living room felt new, as though I'd only seen it once or twice. I wondered if it had been redecorated since my last visit. Again, I tried to remember when I'd come here, and the information eluded me. No surprise there.

Guilt skittered across my chest as I looked at the smashed TV and glass-strewn carpet. Cora's phone lay on the floor, the screen cracked like a shell on the beach. The hairs on the back of my neck tingled and a memory exploded with such vividness I felt like I was back on the landing outside my bedroom where the tulip painting now hung.

Dad's screaming – we're both screaming back at him. There's so much anger, a world of hatred. The landing is bright, but it's dark outside. I'm sobbing uncontrollably, begging him to calm down, to stop saying such hurtful things – be quiet before he goes too far - and then he's grabbing one of our phones – I can't see which - and he smashes it against the wall over and over again. I'm overwhelmed. I bury my face in my hands, but she screams at Dad again – something ridiculous and awful - and then she turns and runs - and he runs after her, but I don't. I'm too upset to go after them. I know I should, but I can't, and then…and then…

The flashback vanished like smoke leaving a crushing sensation of dread: something even worse had happened after that awful incident, something so hideous my mind had constructed a wall to block it out. But there were cracks in the wall and a ghastly truth was seeping through and tickling my senses. Whatever had happened after Dad smashed the phone into the wall outside my bedroom was, I felt certain, the key to everything. If I could remember that, I would know what he'd done to Mum. Maybe, even, where he was keeping her. Now that I was no longer under Rose's mind control, it seemed as if my mind was softening and opening up. Little by little, yes, but it was better than nothing. Maybe, soon, I would remember it all. But it hadn't happened yet, and Mum was in danger. Cora was my only hope.

She returned to the living room frowning heavily. For a horrid second, I thought she was going to change her mind and refuse to help without even hearing what I needed to say, but she sat down on the opposite sofa and said, 'Tell me everything.'

Feeling like a stuck record, I repeated the whole story to her just as I'd done to Maggie. Throughout, she spoke little and her face remained impassive, her emotions guarded. Her body was stiff and cold, but her eyes never left mine and I felt reassured by the fact that she seemed to be listening closely to every word I said.

When I finished, I waited, chest tight. She glanced behind me and I spun around, afraid I'd see Dad in the doorway, but it was just Isla, her mouth an 'o' of shock. She must have heard everything I'd said. She looked from me to Cora and back again.

'Sorry, I -' she started.

'Be quiet,' Cora said, cutting her off. She stared at me. 'All right. I've listened to everything you've said and I'm not going to ring Alec. Neither do I intend to ring the police -'

'But -' I said.

She held up a hand. 'Wait. I haven't finished yet. I'm not going to call the police until I've driven you to Shepton

Hospital and we've sorted out your leg. Then, and only then, will I phone the police on your behalf.'

Isla gasped. I turned to see her gawping at her mum like she thought she'd gone crazy.

'That'll take too long,' I said.

'I used to work there, remember. I can get you seen straight away.'

'It'll still waste time. Please,' I said, leaning forward, 'my mum's life is at stake. What would you do if it was the other way around and Isla had been taken? You'd stop at nothing to get her back and you'd do it as quickly as possible. Please. Ring now. She could be dying. Another wasted minute and I could lose her. *Please.*' Tears spilled down my cheeks. I told myself Cora was a human being. Only a monster would refuse to call the police now.

But she shook her head. 'No. Hospital first. Police second. It's that or nothing. Your choice.'

'Please, Cora. This is my mum and little brother. Please.'

She ignored me and stood up. 'I need to speak to Isla for a second then we'll go.'

I stared after her, insides burning. I knew she was a cold person, but this was beyond anything I could've imagined. The problem was that I had no choice and I couldn't afford to waste any more time arguing.

Wincing at the pain in my leg, I stood up and limped to the doorway. Isla and her mum parted quickly, and my friend ran upstairs without a backward glance or a word. I scowled at her retreating back then followed Cora to her car.

Chapter 70

During the drive to the hospital, I was tormented by the memory I'd relived in Isla's house. Over and over again it played, crashing through my mind like a cyclone, but always ending at the same inconclusive moment, the finale obscure. Unreachable. So close I could taste it.

The taste was poison; the not-knowing torture.

In the passenger window, my ghostly reflection looked altered: a thin, broken face stared back at me. I didn't look like me any longer. I looked like a grief-stricken phantom, a non-person whose essence had drained away like water down a plughole. I'd lost my dad to madness and my brother and mum to him. Isla seemed to hate me now. Maggie had betrayed me. Even Rose, a supposedly trustworthy professional, had lied and tried to manipulate me. The police were convinced I was unstable, and they were probably right – who would be stable after going through all of this? The only way I was going to survive was if I got Mum and Eddie back.

The streets were dark, the night stuffy, but I was chilled to the bone. I wrapped my arms around myself and closed my eyes against the occasional glimpse of inside someone's house – a child being swung around in her dad's arms, a mother bringing in a birthday cake, two people kissing. Why were people leaving their curtains open? Didn't they know it was night-time?

Longing ploughed into my body, and I folded in on myself, distancing from Cora, who drove in silence, throwing the odd glance my way. There was nothing more I needed to say to her. If she betrayed me when we got to the hospital, so be it. I'd find another way…but I was lying to myself. There was no-one else to go to now. She really was my final hope. There was mum's friend Patricia, but I didn't know where she lived. Mum had an address book in the house somewhere – she was old-fashioned like that.

I bit my lip. Hopefully, it would never come to that. I looked at Cora and wondered what she was thinking. Would she do the right thing?

'How's your leg feeling?' she said.

'Painful.'

She nodded. 'It's going to need several stitches.'

Cora indicated and turned off the roundabout onto New Street. The feeling I'd been here recently crept into my mind, tickling and prickling my flesh like an army of ants.

My palms started to sweat and my pulse accelerated.

I stared at the sign for Shepton Hospital, and the realisation struck like a lightning bolt. Sudden and spinetingling. I'd been here. Not long ago.

The knowledge was like a slap in the face. Worse though, was the tightening sensation in my lungs. Not again. I pressed my forehead to the quivering window and curled inwards, feeling déjà vu wash over me, a cold, crawling dread pervading every impulse and thought. I'd come here, but when? Why? Was it to visit someone or to be treated myself? Answers hovered just out of reach. But it was important. Essential that I grasp them.

'I've been here recently,' I murmured, more to myself than to Cora.

'Yes, I know.'

I stared at her. 'Why was I here? I can't remember.'

Cora nibbled her thumbnail. She seemed worried, her calm façade fading. 'I'm…sorry. I shouldn't have said that.'

I frowned and grabbed her arm. 'What do you mean?'

She pulled into the car park and stopped the car. Avoiding my eyes, she said, 'Nothing. I didn't mean

317

anything.'

'But -'

She got out of the car and hurried away.

The hospital loomed large and intimidating, a vast brown structure that had seen better days. Night had fallen now, rendering the building a hulking mass that shrieked of death and grief. Every impulse screamed at me to run in the opposite direction, but I needed to obey Cora.

Shrinking inside, I followed her into the main entrance. She spoke to someone at the reception desk then gestured for me to follow. The lights were too bright, the receptionist a ventriloquist dummy with lips like blood.

Cora carried on walking and I limped after her across the stained laminate floor, desperate to ask more, but unable to catch up. She stopped at a pair of metal doors and stabbed a button. The doors screeched apart and we entered a lift. I spied a mirror on the back wall and saw a blurry echo of myself. Me but not me. Colours with no distinction. An impression of a person. I opened my mouth to speak and my breath caught as déjà vu suckered me into its uncanny grasp. I surrendered to it with a strange willingness; I'd walked through this very lift door feeling just like this: terrified, stricken with longing, agonised. Consumed by dread and guilt.

Was this memory real or an electrical blip in my brain?

No. I felt it in my gut. This was real. Horribly, brutally real. Same place. Same spiralling fear. Same gut-watering anxiety.

Stabbing pains erupted in my stomach.

'Tell me,' I said, seizing her arm. 'Why did I come here? What happened? I need to know.'

She unpeeled my fingers and said, 'You're wasting time.'

She exited the lift and I followed, limping down the corridor, shaking with flashbacks; that peeling door, that healthy eating poster, that sign – wonky – it needed straightening. That broken strip light, that scent of bleach. Surreal. An outer body experience. Someone else was noticing these physical details from a great distance. Me, but a different me. A parallel me who knew too much. A me who had been here before and locked it all away.

Terror bloomed - unflinching, all-encompassing. I was broken, my life at an end. I knew it now as I had known it before, but I didn't know why. Something had devastated me. An incident so terrible I had imprisoned it in the darkest recesses of myself - but I was a shell that could break at any moment. I could feel the shield I'd constructed quivering, the barrier bending to some greater need.

My knees buckled. Cora looked back. She hooked an arm around me, pulled me along.

Abruptly, I was overcome by a loss so great it cleaved apart my heart. Set it on fire. There was a blistering void inside me where my heart used to be. Someone or something had cut out everything that mattered. Hollowed me out like an egg.

I should have been there. Not her. Me. I should have defended her. Protected her. Reassured her.

What? Where did that come from?

Why had I been here? When?

Dread suffused my veins. I couldn't speak or form a coherent thought.

Cora knocked on a door. The sound hit my ears like a whip.

Shaking uncontrollably, I followed her inside a small, bright room. She introduced me to a doctor, but I couldn't focus on anything he was saying.

Cora guided me towards a bed and panic splintered all thought. I wanted to turn and run, but she pushed me down. The doctor loomed over me, spectacles glinting. He smiled revealing sharp yellow teeth. I didn't recognize him, but I knew the smell of this place intimately. I knew these

319

walls, this bed, this room.

The doctor stitched my leg and I tried to be present, but fear sucked me into a whirlpool of fear and confusion. Loss shrivelled my throat. I croaked, 'Water.'

The memory I'd had in the woods unwound in my mind again, scene by scene, line by line.

Cora handed me a cup of water, but it fell through my fingers and clattered to the floor.

Rose hadn't implanted the memory about Eddie.

It was real.

Chapter 71

I blinked. A high-pitched keening sound was coming from my throat. Cora held me. The doctor watched from afar, looking alarmed.

'Please God, no, no, no, no, no, no. Not Eddie. Not my Eddie.'

I jerked back and grabbed Cora's shoulders, shook my head violently. Though I looked at her, I didn't see her. Images rampaged through my mind – Eddie running into the road – the bus – the ice cream van – the blood – the road – 'No, it can't be. It's not real. Please tell me it's not real.' My voice sounded alien, whiny and shrill, like it was coming from another person.

Tears lined Cora's lashes. One dribbled onto her cheek and snaked down her greyish skin. I watched it fall. Saw it through a veil of tears so thick I was almost blind.

'I'm sorry,' she murmured, 'I'm so sorry. Eddie was such a lovely little boy.'

'But -' I pulled away from her and shook my head. 'No, he's alive. I was with him a few days ago. He was fine. We were baking cakes, playing in the garden…'

Cora shook her head.

I pushed her away, twisted around, strode to the window and looked out at the black sky, my body quivering uncontrollably, head on fire. 'He's fine. He's just gone away. Dad's sent him somewhere. He's OK. Someone's looking after him. Keeping him safe.'

I turned back, waiting for Cora to confirm what I said, to tell me I was right, but her eyes were red and wet, her shoulders rounded, her expression the epitome of pity.

'Please, tell me he's OK?'' I whispered. Even as I said

the words, I collapsed to my knees. 'Please?'

The memory replayed in my mind – phone – cars – road – van – bus – blood – neck - and my heart shattered. I fell to my side on the cold, hard floor, unable to battle the truth any longer, too agonised to breathe.

*

'Eddie's dead,' I said.

I looked into Cora's eyes. She nodded. 'Yes. He died two years ago.'

'I kill – ed – him,' I sobbed.

'No.'

'Yes. It - was - me. I was - on - my phone. I le - let - him go.'

Cora shook her head and squeezed my arms. 'No. It was an accident.'

But her words meant nothing. I knew now why Dad hated me so much. Why he barely talked to me, why he thought I was unstable.

'I saw Eddie, in the house. I thought…I thought,' I swallowed, 'I thought he was still alive. I thought he was real.'

'Trauma like you've experienced can make people see things that aren't there,' she said softly.

I thought about the days before Eddie disappeared. They'd been so vivid, so real. How could I have possibly imagined it all? He'd been gone for two years not a few days. Two whole years.

I felt like smacking my head into the wall, hurting myself, numbing my mind so that I could forget all over again that he was dead. I covered my mouth in horror. Mum. Her little boy. All that grief and suffering. Had Dad blamed her for letting me use my phone? Was that why he'd shut her away somewhere? Was that my fault too?

Mum.

I swiped viciously at my tears and stared into Cora's eyes. 'Mum still needs our help. Dad's got her. Eddie might have been in my head, but not Mum.'

Cora glanced at the doctor. He nodded and left the room.

'Where's he going?' I snapped, 'What's happening? You need to do what you promised. You need to call the police.'

She moved away, pulled a packet of tissues from her bag and handed me one.

I took it and fought to focus on the present, but my mind slipped back to the day Eddie died.

*

Mum got to Eddie first. His eyes were wide open, glazed with shock. She put her fingers to his neck, but there was nothing. No pulse, no movement. She put her ear to his mouth. No breath. She put her ear to his chest. Nothing.

She lay down on the road beside him and pulled him into her arms. Wild, tortured moans exploded out of her as she rocked Eddie's lifeless body back and forth, lips pressed to his bleeding head.

Dad joined her; he wrapped his arms around both of them. They cried together, and I stood apart from them unable to move, silent tears streaming down my cheeks.

Strangers gathered around us forming a circle. I wanted to shriek at them to get away. Nobody should witness this; this was our Eddie, not theirs.

Mum looked up at me. In her eyes, I already saw forgiveness.

Dad looked up too, but he didn't see me; he only saw what I'd done.

*

'I can't do this,' I said.

'You can. You have to. You still have Alec. He needs you. He loves you.' Cora's words penetrated my grief and alarm ricocheted around my body.

'What? I told you he's hurt Mum. Have you phoned the police yet?' I jerked away from her.

Cora's eyes moved past me. I turned and followed her gaze. PC Roberts stood in the doorway, staring at me with the same patronising look as before.

I glared at Cora. 'What have you done?'

She tried to grab my shoulder and I shook her off. 'Because of you, the police won't do anything to find her now, and she's going to die. I'm going to lose her too.'

'I'm sorry. I asked Isla to call Alec before we left.'

'But - why?'

'I'm only doing what I think's best for you. And for your family.'

PC Roberts stepped forward. He nodded at Cora. 'Thank you, Ma'am. I'll take it from here.'

She hesitated. 'Would you like me to come with you?'

'No,' I hissed, 'fuck off.'

She nodded. After a moment, she walked past me and left me alone with PC Roberts.

'Mr Black-Hawkins and Ms Weatherby are waiting for us,' he said gently.

'I told you before, he's dangerous. I'm not going anywhere with him – or her. She's in on it all. They're having an affair. He told you I'm unstable because I was seeing my dead brother and thought he was still alive, but I know the truth now, and I'm not wrong about my mum. He's done something to her. He's keeping her locked up somewhere and I think he's going to kill her before I can convince you I'm telling the truth. Please. You have to believe me. I'm not unstable, not when it comes to this.'

As if I hadn't spoken, he said, 'Mr Black-Hawkins has some wonderful news to tell you.'

I frowned. 'Did you listen to anything I just said? He's a fucking liar! He's manipulating you, just like he tried to manipulate me. He's clever. But I found evidence. I found his confession in his journal.'

'And where is that confession now?' he said, tilting his head.

'That's the problem. I got it wet and the ink ran. But I saw it. He also had her mobile taped to the bottom of his desk and he never posted her my letters. Please listen to me. She could be dying this very second,' I choked on my words, 'I can't lose her too. I can't.'

'You won't need to,' he said.

'What?'

'You won't need to, because she's here,' he pressed his hand to his chest.

I stared at him, too disgusted by his ignorance to speak.

He closed the distance between us in two strides. 'Come now. It's time.'

I glared at him until I saw black, and he began to dissolve. The room disappeared and Eddie's face sucked me back in time.

*

Everything was a blur until the funeral.

Dad organised it while Mum and I lay on our beds, sometimes together, sometimes apart, crying or staring, too deadened by loss to do anything more. There was no stage of denial for any of us. We had all seen him die first-hand. We had watched our lovely little boy hit the ground.

I didn't know which was worse: to see Eddie die or to imagine him dying. He may have died instantly, but there was no consolation in that. There was no consolation in anything. He had been four years old. His whole life had lain ahead of him. That bus had stolen him from our lives.

In less than a heartbeat, our lively, loveable, happy little boy had been snatched from us. He would never speak again. Never laugh, never smile, never hold my hand or kiss my cheek, never sit on my lap for his bedtime story. Never pull funny faces or blow raspberries or beg to play hide and seek. Eddie would never learn to read or write. Never grow up and experience his first girlfriend or boyfriend, never have his first kiss, never fall in love. He was gone, eradicated from our family in an instant. Alive then dead. Just like that. The devil had clicked his fingers and taken him from us in less than a single second of time. That was all it took to destroy a life and eradicate four years of existence, growth and happiness. Less than one second.

My world had ended. I couldn't eat or sleep. In the back of my mind, I knew I still had people I loved, family to keep me going, but at that time, the loss was a cancer and it was killing me.

The funeral was the second-worst day of my life.

The service was held in Shepton Church. I had been there only twice, once for a wedding and once for a funeral. The grey stone building was cold inside and out. Clouds veiled the sky like a pall. Not many people came. Dad had only wanted people who knew us really well and Mum hadn't argued. Everyone wore black, which felt wrong. Eddie loved colours.

Once the small group was seated on the hard pews, Dad and one other man carried in the emerald-green coffin. Green because it was Eddie's favourite colour. At least Dad had got that detail right. The coffin was too small, unbearably tiny. I couldn't breathe. Mum and I held hands so tightly it hurt. Dad stood and faced us. His face was ashen but his cheeks were dry. He raised a piece of crumpled paper and began to read.

'Eddie Black-Hawkins was born with Harry Potter hair and one spectacular dimple. He wasn't planned, but he brought an unexpected wealth of joy to our lives. Eddie was the life and soul of every party. A smiler, laugher, teaser, jester, helper, and a giver. A brave, bold little person who embraced every new experience with confidence and curiosity. A wonderful brother and an incredible son. When he grew up, he wanted to be a police dog – and why not?'

A chuckle whispered around the pews.

Dad looked up from the paper. 'Eddie would…' his voice cracked, 'I'm sorry…Eddie would have made a fine man. Whatever he put his mind to, he would have done it. He was special. So very special,' he paused, his chin trembled, 'He is – *was* – my son. Sofia and I will never forget him. We will cherish him for ever and we will miss him every day for the rest of our lives. He was everything. Our world. I…sorry.' He stumbled back to his seat. Mum slipped her hand into his and they put their heads together.

I stared unseeingly at my hands, wanting to die.

*

After the funeral, guilt mounted hour by hour, day by day, week by week until it absorbed my every thought, drawing me down into a black tunnel from which there was no escape. And, like a dying rose, I withdrew from the world and everyone around me. Dad couldn't look at me. We barely spoke. Though he didn't say it, I knew he blamed me for Eddie's death. And I knew he was right to.

As the weeks grew to months, he turned to alcohol to numb the pain and shut himself in his office for increasingly long periods, closing Mum and me out. Mum suggested therapy, but he refused. She insisted I see a school counsellor, and I did for a while before deciding it wasn't helping and forging a note saying I didn't need to continue with the meetings. When Mum and Dad found out, Mum tried to coax me into giving the sessions another go, but Dad went ballistic. I told him he was being a hypocrite and he stormed out of the house and stood at the cliff edge, so close Mum and I were terrified he was going to slip and fall.

After a while, he came back in, grabbed a bottle of whisky from the shelf and shut himself in his office.

Mum was at a loss. Her attention focused on her own grief and Dad, and I slid further and further away from everyone and everything. My only connection to the world was virtual. I lived on my phone and joined suicide chats. At school, I truanted. When I was expelled for graffitiing Edgar Allen Poe quotes about death and madness all over the walls of the girl's bathroom, I returned home and pretended to study.

I drifted about the house like a phantom, jumping when one of Mum and Dad's rows broke the quiet. Insomnia became my constant enemy. Mum knew I was struggling, but with Dad to contend with, I faded into the background. My one pastime was drawing: I drew and drew and drew, sketch after sketch after sketch of Eddie. I couldn't bear the idea of forgetting his face. Dad had taken all of his photos down. This was all I had left. I stopped texting Isla and told myself I was doing the right thing – she wouldn't want to be friends with a depressed loser like me. I wouldn't want to be friends with me. No one would.

I avoided Dad at all costs. On the rare occasion our paths crossed, if he was blind drunk, he'd have this wild, haunted look about him that scared me. One night he entered my room. I looked up from my phone, unable to read him, unable to work out what he was looking at. Alcohol wafted off him in thick, sour waves. He lost his balance. Leaned a hand against the wall. He stared and stared until I felt sure he was going to do something awful, then he turned and left without a word.

It was only when he left that I realized he'd been staring at my phone.

Guilt gnawed and champed and ripped, driving agony into my veins.

I wanted to go to Mum. I stood up and Dad's voice fractured the silence. Mum's shrieked back. They were screaming at each other right outside my room. I opened the door and -

*

PC Roberts was staring at me. 'Come. We need to go now.' The man's patience was thinning. He took my elbow and steered me towards the door.

I searched for the rest of the memory, but it had receded like the calm after a storm, flattening out and lying motionless as the dead. No currents stirred. Faint wisps of that night permeated my thoughts, however, and I felt for the first time that I was on the precipice. One small push, and I would remember; I would find out what had happened. It was paramount that I did that before I got back in Dad's hands again. If I could recall that night, I felt certain I'd know what he'd done to Mum, so I allowed myself to be guided, but dragged my feet, stopping every other second and complaining that I had terrible head pain.

Roberts bent over me with a frown. His skin was pungent with spicy aftershave that itched my nose. He couldn't tell whether I was lying or not.

I moaned and held my hand to my head. 'I think it's a migraine.'

'Oh dear,' was his response.

I groaned, but his hand found my elbow and he tugged me across the yellowy laminate. I walked as slowly as possible, eyes on every wall, surface and doctor who crossed our path, feet heavy with grief. The hospital had triggered memories. There was a chance something inside this building would do so again. I pushed the horror of

Eddie to the back of my mind and thought about Mum. I needed to help her. I couldn't give in to the overwhelming urge to curl up into a ball and give up. Mum had lost Eddie too and she needed me now more than ever. I couldn't fail her. I couldn't lose her as well.

Every corridor looked almost identical. The pale yellow walls reminded me of nothing. The squeaky floor was hard underfoot, the lighting harsh. A fiery-haired nurse wheeled an old man past. The wheels of the chair whirred setting my teeth on edge, but nothing sprang to mind. I focused on the smell; the sterile, chemical, clinical odour that clung to these walls like a second skin. I brought Mum to mind. Tried to spirit myself back to that night.

Focus. Concentrate. There was screaming and…and…

Nothing. Nada. Zilch. It was as though my brain hated me. Like it was punishing me. Withholding what I needed most to deepen my pain.

I dug in again, bent double and groaned. 'My head.'

'Not far now. Mr Black-Hawkins can take you home and get you some painkillers.'

I shivered at the idea and remained slumped over. 'I need a minute.'

Roberts made a clucking noise in the back of his throat and shifted from foot to foot, checking his watch.

I stayed bent over for a couple of minutes, scared I was wasting too much time. Mum needed me. I could already be too late.

He took my elbow and pulled me towards a set of double doors. A woman and a man in casual clothes walked through holding hands. The woman's eyes met mine then flicked away. She was holding a red phone. Something twitched in my brain. An undercurrent that was so powerful that I stopped. Roberts sighed and tugged my arm. I ignored him and stayed where I was. The memory was so close I could taste it.

'Come,' Roberts snapped.

'No – wait – I just need a moment,' I said.

I wasn't in the hospital anymore. I was at home, standing on the landing.

I became insane, with long intervals of horrible sanity

DARKNESS THERE,
AND NOTHING MORE

DEEP IN EARTH
MY LOVE IS LYING
AND I MUST WEEP ALONE

Chapter 72

One Year Ago

It was as if I was watching myself. Like I was viewing everything through a ghost's perspective. I could only see myself and Dad. I couldn't see Mum. She had disappeared. It was as if I was having an outer body experience. Something felt wrong, but I couldn't place it. I watched myself slam my bedroom door. Watched Dad swing around clumsily.

I was holding my phone. Dad glared down at it and turned his ferocity on me. Before, he'd been shouting at Mum, but my appearance switched his attention. He stabbed a finger at me and snarled, 'If you know what's good for you, you'll go back in your room.'

His voice was slurred, eyes bloodshot. A network of veins crisscrossed his cheeks and nose. He swayed and righted himself.

Other me stared back at him. My mouth opened and closed like a fish. Fear, pain, guilt and a million other emotions blitzed through my face, landing on an ugly, twisted expression that made me look psychotic. I raised my mobile and waved it in front of his face. 'Just say it, Dad. I know you want to.'

He went completely still.

I lowered my phone, terrified of the look that had darkened his eyes.

'Give it to me.' He held out his hand. It was shaking with anger.

I hesitated. Lifted my chin. 'No.'

He closed the space between us and loomed over me.

I stared up at him, too scared to move or speak.

'Now,' he said. He cracked his knuckles, making me jump.

'No.'

'Fine.' He ripped my mobile out of my hand, strode away and smashed it into the wall five times. With a manic smile, he turned on me and said, 'This is what I should have done years ago, before you killed your brother.'

Regret entered his face almost as soon as the words left his mouth. He reached out to me, aghast and white, but I turned and fled. I ran along the landing and sprinted down the stairs.

I watched myself go, black hair flying behind me like a torn scarf, face stricken with grief. I reached out to myself, tried to grab an arm and skimmed hair. Dad flew past me and ran after other me. I heard him screaming that he was sorry, begging other me to come back.

I followed, down the stairs, through the long, black tunnel of the house. I saw Dad run out of the back door into the garden. The door stayed open and I dashed through the opening out into the black night air. Dad was half-running, half-stumbling up the garden. His voice was raw with desperation as he called my name over and over and over again. I tried to see myself but I must have been blocked by his body.

I ran after him, screaming my own name too, cold with dread, because I knew what I was going to do, and I knew I was going to be too late to stop myself.

*

'Madam?' Roberts's face was inches from mine. His breath was hot with garlic. Exasperation pinched his voice.

'What? Oh.' I was sitting on the hospital floor hugging my knees. Tears glued my lashes together. I blinked them out and my vision cleared.

Roberts extended a hand and helped me up. 'You collapsed. Are you OK?'

I almost laughed at the question. Instead, I mumbled an apology and allowed him to guide me along the corridor, trying to bring back the memory, but it slipped away like a fox in the night.

What had happened next? I tried to see past that moment and drew a blank. My brain had been set on pause. If I could press play and set it rolling again, maybe I would finally know what Dad had done to Mum.

But there was no time left.

Roberts, brighter now, said, 'One more right and we'll be there. You'll see. Everything will be better for you now.'

Dread choked my lungs. I imagined Dad wrapping his arms around my body in mock-relief, Rose smirking from behind him, the two of them walking either side of me like prison guards as they took me back to the car then drove me somewhere unknown. A pre-dug grave? The hovel they'd been keeping Mum in? An asylum? That would be the perfect answer to their problems. No killing necessary, but a way to shut me up for ever and make sure nobody ever took me seriously.

I couldn't let that happen. If Mum was still alive, I couldn't give up. I had to find a way to save her.

I dragged my heels again. My thoughts tried to veer towards Eddie and I steered them away. If I focused on what had happened to him, grief would consume me, and I couldn't let that happen. Not now. Not when Mum was still in danger.

Up ahead in the middle of the corridor a cleaner with a silver wash bucket on wheels mopped the floor. She was old and wiry with a rounded back. I watched her push and pull the mop back and forth across the floor. A scene unfolded in my head. I knew what to do.

My heart lurched to my throat as we neared her. Not for the first time, I was glad PC Roberts couldn't hear what was going on inside my head. I stole a glance up at him. He was looking straight ahead, glazed with boredom. A wart on his chin sprouted long, brown hairs. He stood to my right, his fingers brushing my elbow with the lightest contact. Behind the cleaner stood another set of double doors. Before those doors it was possible to take a right; the route Roberts intended us to take. Due to the maze-like nature of the hospital, I'd lost track of where I was. I had no clue how to get back to the main entrance, but I had to try.

We neared the cleaner. I shifted direction, heading for the left side of the woman. As I'd expected, Roberts shifted course with me. We passed the wet floor sign and drew level with her. She glanced up, brow sweaty, and gave me a nod, and I shoved her backwards into Roberts. He cried out and stumbled over. The cleaner fell too. I ran for the double doors, took a left and sprinted up the corridor.

I was running from a policeman, and I didn't care. What I cared about was getting out of the hospital without being stopped. From there, I would find a way to help Mum or I would die trying.

I passed a middle-aged man in a suit who gave me a raised eyebrow as I ran past. I followed the corridor around to the right and carried on running. The walls were blurs either side of me, the floor loud with the slaps of my trainers. My leg protested in a series of needle-sharp pains that slowed me down. I glanced back, relieved to see no sign of Roberts. The overhead speaker's voice boomed into the air, 'If you see a slim, black-haired woman on her own in the hospital do not approach her. She may be dangerous. Please alert reception immediately.'

Dangerous? Me?

Fear uncoiled as I locked eyes with an elderly woman on crutches. She lowered her head when I passed her. I looked back and she hadn't turned around to stare at me. I hoped she was hard of hearing or had decided to ignore the announcement. If she was an excellent actor, she could have just fooled me. I glanced back again and saw Roberts standing at the end of the corridor.

'Stop! Ms Black-Hawkins, stop!'

I did the opposite. Footsteps thundered after me. I ploughed through a set of double doors, dodged a random wheelchair and ran on. The corridor ended in a T-junction. I took a right.

Doors lined the walls. Roberts's footsteps were loud, but he hadn't reached the junction yet.

I yanked open the third door on the left and slipped inside. To my relief, the room was empty. I ran to the window and lifted the blinds. We were three floors up. There was no way I could climb out and escape through the window. Another door was inside the room. I opened it to see a toilet and sink. There was a lock on the door. I hesitated, unsure what to do. There was no sound of Roberts outside. He could have taken the other turning. Then again, he could be in this corridor checking inside every room. Stay or go? What would Mum do?

My nerves were about to snap. If I made the wrong decision now, it could be over. I had to think clearly, think like Roberts – what would he be doing? He might not even be looking for me anymore. He might have decided to recruit more officers. The hospital was huge. Maybe he'd returned to the main entrance to wait for me there. He knew I'd have to get down to the ground floor in order to escape, so that made the most sense. But maybe there was a fire escape I could use...

I grabbed paper off the roll and dried my face. Drawn like a magnet to the mirror, I froze, paralysed as light pierced the darkness.

Chapter 73

One Year Ago

Drizzle fell from the black sky making the grass slippery underfoot as I ran towards the cliff edge. Ten feet away, I stopped and wrapped my arms around myself. Other me was standing facing away from Dad. She was about three feet from the precipice. Dad's voice travelled, a broken, tortured cry, 'I didn't mean it. Please forgive me, Arrietty. I'm sorry.'

Other me would not turn around to face him. Her shoulders shook. Words tore from her throat. 'You're right. It's my fault he's dead.'

'No, no, that's not true.'

I wanted to go to them, put my arms around her, but something held me back. I knew they needed to have this out. I opened my mouth to say let's go back inside, but other me said, 'It is true. You hate me. I should be dead not him.'

'No. I've handled it badly. Am I angry? Yes. But I'm angry at myself. I knew you were upset. I never should have let you take him when you weren't on the ball. It's my fault, not yours.'

I wanted to tell them it wasn't anyone's fault. But the words wouldn't come.

She spun around then. Her teeth flashed white in the darkness. 'Then why did you say it?'

Dad dropped his head. Huge, desperate sobs heaved out of him. He sank to his knees and held out his arms. 'Please, sweetheart, I didn't mean it. I'm drunk and upset. People say things they don't mean all the time, especially when they're a wreck like me.'

Other me shook her head wildly. When she looked at Dad, she gazed through him. Her voice was distant, unrecognisable, old and tired beyond its years. 'I can't do this any more.'

'What?' Dad struggled to his feet.

*

Horror winded me. I clawed at the mirror, desperate to unsee the truth. I scratched at my cheeks and ripped out my hair. Turned my face to the ceiling and screamed. Screamed and screamed and screamed until my screams disintegrated into guttural moans and I lay down on the bathroom floor and curled into a ball. I wept until my top was soaked and my eyes were swollen shut. I rocked back and forth, unable to stop seeing the hateful truth.

No, no, no, no, no.

A monstrous groan left my lips. I grabbed frantically at my clothes, inspected my skin, my fingers, my hands. This couldn't be happening.

I began to moan low in my throat as the truth of the last year unravelled, too real, too acute, too hideous. Things I had forgotten pierced my brain like serrated blades, stabbing, gouging, slashing through an invisible barricade I'd not known existed until now.

I saw it again with a vision as clear as spring water: Eddie pulled away, ran into the road. A bus hit him. He flew through the sky like a ragdoll. There was no scream. Nothing. Only his limp body in the air. And then gravity worked its evil, and he smacked the ground. His skull cracked. He was dead before any of us could compute what had happened.

My hands found my mouth. Eddie was gone. He would never come back. He was only four years old when he was taken from us.

These were the facts, but they failed to communicate the impact. Words could never express what I lost that day. What *we* lost.

On my knees, I wept, but my mind worked, ploughing through the horror with unstoppable urgency. Now, with the pathway clear, a dreadful story played out, but it wasn't a play. It was the truth, the dark, detestable truth; a tragedy I'd rewritten, a reality dammed up, and now the dam was broken and heinous event after heinous event flooded my brain like molten rock. No longer was my mind caved in by opaque walls; now it was all glass, exposed and un-tempered.

For a year, I existed in a state of utter depression, moving through the motions like the living dead. I had nothing to live for anymore. I wanted to die. I refused to take antidepressants, spent most of the day in bed, barely ate and never slept. I blamed myself. Life was torture. And I deserved it. Suicidal thoughts were a daily occurrence. On three separate occasions, I took a knife to my wrist and pressed down hard enough to break the skin, but something stopped me. I'd lost Eddie, but the others remained, each suffering in their own distinct ways. I knew I had to be strong for them, and I tried, but each time grief stole my strength and I failed.

Yet I clung on. Somewhere inside me, a voice urged me to keep going; promised that time would help. It was a platitude I despised, but part of me began to listen, and an infinitesimal speck of light shone in the darkness. We were still a family. A unit of three. My family loved me and I loved them. Together, in time, we would find a way to live.

Then, one year after Eddie's death, that night happened.

I dug my teeth into my wrist to stop myself from screaming as the awful truth came again, but properly, through the eyes of the right person. This time, I wasn't blinded by a self-imposed barrier. This time, my perspective wasn't skewed. This time, I wasn't displaced. This time, my mind was clear. Because this time, I saw that night how I had originally seen it. I saw it as *me*, not as Arrietty. I saw it as a mother and a wife. As Sofia.

Chapter 74

One Year Ago

Alec sat in his armchair slugging whisky from the bottle. He was already halfway through the contents. That night, he was in one of his blacker alcohol moods, but as I stared at the back of his head, I couldn't suppress the anger seething inside me. In truth, it was a relief to feel anything other than misery. The rage made me feel strong, but it also made me impulsive.

I walked around the chair and looked down at him. His eyes were hazy and bloodshot. They found me and I saw the absence of the man I knew, a person expunged by alcohol, and I couldn't bear it any longer. He needed to snap out of this; stop drinking; make an effort to pull himself together for me and Arrietty. I'd tried to speak to him before and he'd cast off my words with an empty promise that he'd stop, but he hadn't. If anything, he'd got worse. He was drinking earlier and earlier in the day and confining himself to the house as if afraid to go outside and face the real world.

I was trying to focus on Arrietty now. I felt ashamed for how I'd closed off from both of them over the last year, but that was over. A new me was starting to emerge from the darkness. I knew I had a lot of making up to do, especially with regards to Arrietty. For the last year, I'd shrunk away from her. I'd failed to offer her the support she needed for too long. It was unforgivable of me, because deep down I'd known all along that she blamed herself. In the beginning, I'd offered kisses and cuddles, but then she'd pulled away, shut herself in her room, closed herself off to me. And I'd buried myself in my own grief, too self-focused to help her.

In Alec's worst moments, he confessed his darkest thoughts to me; part of him couldn't stop blaming her. I'd hated him for that, but I hadn't the energy to convince him that he was being irrational and destroying himself by letting his thoughts stray down such a poisonous path. He attempted to conceal this from Arrietty, but she knew, and I'd been so consumed by my own suffering that I'd not broached the topic with her. I'd shied away from it, hoping that Alec would stop drinking and move on from such a destructive, blameful mindset. I should have spoken to my little girl, helped her understand it wasn't her fault. It was a terrible accident. It could have happened to any of us. But I hadn't gone to her. I hadn't summoned the energy and positivity to reassure her that she wasn't to blame for Eddie's death.

That night, as I stared down at my intoxicated husband, I knew I had to put an end to this once and for all. Arrietty needed our love and support. We needed to work through this together, as a family, united in our common goal to move forward.

Deep down, I knew this wasn't the time, but I couldn't stop myself.

'You need to stop,' I said.

'Stop what?' Alec slurred.

'This.' I waved a hand at the bottle, tried to keep my voice even.

He snorted and raised the whisky to his lips.

'Please, Alec. If you don't -'

His eyes flashed. 'If I don't, *what?*'

My heart drummed against my ribs. 'I'll take Arrietty and go. We need to work together to move on. We have to stop pulling away from each other.'

'You'll...go? What - leave? Where exactly will you go?' He laughed and slugged more whisky.

'I mean it. Arrietty's suffering. I know you are too, but this is making things a million times worse.'

'Oh, and you've been a fortress of support, have you?'

Guilt scorched me. I hadn't been there for either of them, but I was going to be from now on. The problem was that I couldn't do it alone. I needed his help.

He barked out a brittle laugh and downed three gulps of the murky liquid, a large portion of which missed his mouth and dribbled down his chin. I could see nothing I said was going to get through to him. I'd picked the wrong moment. He was too drunk. I'd thought an ultimatum would make him see sense, but in this state, every effort I made would serve no purpose other than to further aggravate him.

Still, as I looked down at him, common sense flew out of the window and words flicked from my mouth like poison. 'She knows you blame her.'

He shrugged, and I saw red. He raised the bottle to his lips, and I lunged forward and snatched it out of his hand.

'Hey!' Alec stood up and swayed, regained his balance and towered over me.

'Give it back,' he barked.

'No.'

He lunged for the bottle and I darted out of reach.

We stared at each other, breathing hard.

'That's it. We're leaving. Me and Arrietty. You won't see us again until you've stopped drinking.'

I dropped the bottle and strode away, taking the stairs two at a time, heart thwacking so hard I wondered if I was about to have a heart attack.

Alec's footsteps thundered after me.

I headed for Arrietty's room intent on telling her to pack a bag of essentials. Hopefully, this would be enough to make him realize he needed to stop. Come morning, he'd look back on this with regret and realize he needed to pull himself together before he lost us too.

But outside her room, Alec grabbed my arm and spun me around. 'You're not going,' he said. There was a wildness in him. He was panicking but seething at the same time.

'Let go,' I said, twisting out of his grip.

I tried to walk to Arrietty's bedroom, and he ran around in front of me, blocking the way.

'If you leave, that's it for us. There's no going back from this,' he growled.

'Get out of my way,' I said shakily.

Arrietty's door opened and she frowned at us. She looked awful; pale, hollow-eyed, too thin. She was holding her phone. I saw Alec fix on the device, saw the nasty twist of his lips, and I knew what was going to happen, but felt frozen, powerless to stop it. He turned his fury on her, on my little girl, and I just stood there. I tried to speak, but something stopped me. Maybe they needed to have this out. Maybe –

'If you know what's good for you, you'll go back in your room,' he said.

Arrietty's mouth worked. Tears seeped from her eyes, but a deep frown crushed her forehead. She raised her mobile and waved it in front of his face. 'Just say it, Dad. I know you want to.'

He went stock still. She lowered the phone, took a small step back.

'Give it to me.' He jutted his hand forward.

Arrietty's voice was hard. 'No.'

'Now,' he said, knuckles crunching.

'No.'

'Fine.' He ripped the mobile out of her hand, turned and smashed it into the wall. With a wild grin, he spun around and said, 'This is what I should have done years ago, before you killed your brother.'

Shame and regret flashed in his face almost as soon as he'd said it. The words 'killed your brother' lingered in the

345

air, toxic and terrible. I felt like screaming at him, pummelling my fists into his chest until it turned to a bloody pulp, but I couldn't move. Couldn't speak.

Alec reached out to Arrietty, and she turned and fled along the landing down the stairs.

He ran after her, and I ran after him, through the house, out into the back garden.

Alec screamed her name over and over, begging her to stop. I ran after him, screaming her name too, desperate to wrap my arms around her and tell her she wasn't to blame. It wasn't her fault. I loved her. Alec did too. He was just being a grief-stricken, drunk bastard.

I slipped on the wet grass and nearly fell. Righting myself, I followed them to the end of the garden and stopped. Alarm seized my heart; Arrietty was standing too close to the edge. What was she doing?

Alec said, 'I didn't mean it. Please forgive me, Arrietty. I'm sorry.'

Arrietty faced the drop. Her entire body shook. In a small voice, she said, 'It's my fault he's dead.'

Alec told her it wasn't true. I stepped forward, desperate to hold her, but she said, 'You hate me. I should be dead not him.'

He spluttered an apology, tried to explain himself, and I prayed she'd listen to him, move away from the edge.

She spun around. 'Then why did you say it?'

Alec hung his head and began to cry. He fell to the ground and reached out to her with both arms. 'Please, sweetheart, I didn't mean it. I'm drunk and upset. People say things they don't mean all the time, especially when they're a wreck like me.'

I was certain she would walk into his arms. They would hold each other and say sorry and make up. After tonight, Alec would realize he had to stop drinking, and we would give our one remaining child the support and love she so needed.

My heartbeat began to slow. I waited for her to close the distance between them. A little hope flared inside me; in time, we would get through this. This terrible night was what we all needed; sometimes things were better out than in. Now that feelings – no matter how awful or irrational they were – had been aired, we could fight to move on, as a family.

I smiled at my little girl encouragingly. She didn't respond. Her eyes were glazed over. Empty.

A bolt of panic hit me.

She said, 'I'm sorry, but I can't do this any more.'

Alec struggled to his feet and I ran forward, but she closed her eyes and walked backwards off the edge of the cliff.

Chapter 75

Now

I knew now. I knew everything, and I wished I didn't. Enlightenment was brutal. The truth brought a new torment, another level of misery, and yet I couldn't stop myself from reliving the months that followed, the hateful past uncoiling like a roll of barbed wire in a series of tortuously slow scenes that I was powerless to stop, glimpses of my daughter penetrating my mind, spearing my conscience and devastating all hope – because – somehow, Arrietty survived the fall. She hit her head and lost consciousness, but the ambulance made it in time. I sat by her side and held her limp hand all the way to the hospital. It was like living through Eddie's accident all over again, but the surrealness of the situation was blasted into the background by terror.

Her face was unnaturally white, her body so still. Blood seeped through the bandage around her head. I wondered how so much blood could come out of my little girl. She was so good, so young. Why was this happening to her? To us? What had we done to deserve such a tragic turn of fate? Again.

At the hospital, they wired her up to a machine that kept her heart beating and breathed for her. She was alive, but barely. Just like me. I remembered staring down at her, wishing it was me lying in that bed. I'd have done anything I could to swap places with her. Anything. I turned and watched Alec for a moment. A vicious part of me wanted to blame him, scream at him, hurt him, yet the blame fell on me more than him – I'd failed to support her after

Eddie – I'd failed to put my own suffering behind hers – I'd ignored her silent pleas for help. And as I watched him, the father of my children, the sheer misery in his face made me realize he'd do anything to take back those dreadful words. *Anything* to save our baby girl. He'd swap places with her too, if he could. We would both sacrifice our lives for hers. If she'd needed a new heart, I wouldn't have hesitated, but of course, there was nothing I could do to switch places with her. The helplessness left me a rambling, disjointed mess. I scraped what remained of myself off the floor and fixated on all that remained: the tiny hope that she might pull through.

For months, Alec and I waited and hoped, waited and hoped. We visited. Held her hand. Kissed her and talked to her. Nothing changed. The life support bleeped on, but Arrietty showed no signs of coming back to us.

And then the doctor said he thought we should think about turning off Arrietty's life support, and that was it. I felt an immense crushing pressure in my head, saw black and then…nothing.

I broke. Something inside me snapped. Somehow, I lost myself. Became her.

The truth was achingly simple, the reality torture. I pressed my hands over my face, shook my head. I'd believed Eddie was alive. I'd played with him, read to him, bathed him, and all the while Alec – oh God. The knife twisted deeper. I stopped breathing. He'd lost Eddie, Arrietty, and then me. Son. Daughter. Wife. How he must have suffered. How he must still be suffering.

Sick rose in my throat. Realisation after realisation and memory after memory surfaced, hissing and snapping at me like a pit of snakes.

Rose Weatherby wasn't Alec's lover and co-conspirator – she was his therapist. I remembered now with startling clarity. He'd started seeing her about two years ago because he was worried about his jealousy issues.

For a while, he'd thought I was having an affair with Arrietty's art teacher, James Broughton, and I'd made it worse by hiding the fact that I was mentoring James. I'd kept the mentoring from Alec because I'd feared his envy might cause problems. Alec had kept the fact that he was seeing a therapist secret at first, worried I'd judge him. After several sessions he'd felt better but then, after Eddie and Arrietty, he'd started seeing her again. Alec had blamed himself for Arrietty's suicide attempt. He'd wanted to get better. He'd stopped drinking and made every effort he could to support me. He'd encouraged me to speak to Rose, and I did, over the phone, the day before the doctors rang and said those destructive words.

Good God.

Numbness set in and I blinked at the tiles, unable to stop shaking. It was too much to take in. Too insane to grasp.

*

I struggled to my feet and stared at my reflection. What I saw was real. It was me. Thirty-nine-year-old mother and wife, Sofia Black-Hawkins. Me. I saw the grey streaks in my hair and the lines at my eyes. I saw the dead expression of someone who had suffered horrors no human being should ever have to suffer. I no longer saw myself as my daughter, which was a blessing and a curse, because I would never see her again. I would never hold my baby girl, never get to tell her how sorry I was, how I should have been there for her when she needed me most, how I would give anything – anything at all – to bring her back. How I would happily lie down in front of a train if it meant she would get to live. Because it was too late. She was dead. Alec had turned off her life support and because of me, he'd done it alone. I should have been with him – with her

– instead of disintegrating into a mad woman bent on blaming her husband for some heinous, ludicrous crime.

My throat ached with despair. Grief crawled deeper; a mass of black scorpions scuttling, laying eggs, multiplying and thriving. Blackness swallowed my vision. Fear ravaged every thought, eradicating any possibility of hope, and panic glistened inside my skull, spitting venom. A kind of madness seized me.

I gripped onto the edge of the sink to steady myself, and stared at my harrowed reflection. Was our relationship beyond repair? Was Alec lost to me too? Our lives would be for ever entwined by loss, by a grief so deep and unbearable that death seemed merciful, but that didn't mean we would stay together, not now, after everything I'd done. I didn't know if it was possible for him to forgive me; he'd lost as much as me and I'd drenched his wounds in acid. But he wasn't entirely innocent because he was having an affair with Rose. Could I forgive him for sleeping with another woman? Maybe he sought comfort in her arms because of me, because of what I'd put him through. Did his suffering justify his betrayal? Would I have done the same thing in his position?

With strangely heightened senses, I relived the last few weeks, wincing at each wound I'd inflicted on him, each detail I'd misconstrued and used to turn my husband into a monster. I'd thought him guilty of something atrocious, concocted betrayals of the severest sort – but *everything* he'd done had been to protect me from myself - everything except for sleeping with Rose. My phone had been taped to his desk to prevent me from seeing it and finding out the truth. I recalled Rose's words, which I now knew had been nothing but honest: the truth would have been too much for me to handle. She must have cautioned Alec against divulging my misconceptions in case it made me spiral deeper into a black hole from which I'd never escape. I remembered all too well Rose explaining how memories needed to be retrieved safely and slowly.

I swallowed thickly and put a hand to my lips. The words in Alec's journal must have been about the unforgivable thing he said to Arrietty that night, and how he'd kept her alive on the life support machine for himself – for me too – rather than letting her go and be in peace. That was one of the worst things about my little girl being in a coma: it was impossible to tell what she could hear or sense. Could she take in anything we said to her? Or was she deaf to her surroundings, suffering in eternal torment as nightmare after nightmare attacked her unconscious mind? The doctors had promised she wasn't in any physical pain, but it was impossible to know what went on inside her brain, below the surface. She could have been screaming for our help while we carried on thinking she was dead to the world.

But that was over now. Alec had put her out of her misery. On his own.

I clutched my chest. There were so many things I'd got wrong, so many incidents I'd misread, including Knightley. Alec must have thought a puppy would comfort me, and I'd turned his caring gesture into one of manipulation. I'd even believed he'd asked Rose to hypnotize me into forgetting, when she was only trying to restore my real self in a safe way.

I thought of Maggie; she'd only done what was best for me. When Alec sent her away from the house, he must have informed her of my struggles – my…delusions - so when I'd turned up at her cottage, she'd known immediately what she had to do. Call my husband.

Cora and Isla too. They must have known that I thought I was Arrietty. No wonder Isla seemed so distant and concerned. No wonder Cora had 'betrayed' me. And James too. He'd tried to help Alec and me when he'd found me on the roadside after I took the Merc. And Hugo – Alec must have sent him away because he was worried

Hugo would tell me the truth or let the truth slip out unintentionally. The truth Rose believed I hadn't been ready to face. Then there was the note I'd found in my studio; I remembered now: Hugo had gifted me the book as a thank you present for the work I'd done in his house. There had been nothing sinister about his message at all – it was just Hugo being Hugo.

Rich was the only one who'd believed me, because he'd been in the dark. God – how was he? Had Alec hurt him?

I tore at my cuticles and rested my pounding head against the cool tiles.

I'd put everyone through so much. Alec most of all.

We'd lost our children and each other, but I was me again.

Alec thought he'd lost me too, but I was back.

I had to find him. Tell him I was sorry. Tell him it was OK that he'd turned off the life support. He must have done it alone. I couldn't bear to think of him having to do that on his own. He'd been through so much and I'd made it a thousand times harder. But I was back. Now, I could give him the support he'd tried to give me.

The desire to wrap my arms around him was overwhelming. After everything we'd lost, we still had each other. We needed one another now more than ever. But would he see that? Had I done too much damage? Would he ever be able to find it within himself to forgive me? And would I ever be able to forgive his affair with Rose? Would he even want to be with me anymore? Was he in love with her like she claimed he was? She'd said he hadn't told her he loved her yet – the question was: would I be able to move on knowing he'd been with another woman? I'd never been unfaithful to him and I never would.

I left the bathroom, walked across the room out into the corridor and limped along as quickly as I could. People floated past and I hardly registered. I reached the lift and stabbed the button, and a hand clamped down on my shoulder.

I spun around. Alec stared down at me, forehead crumpled, clothes dishevelled. 'Please, don't run. Listen to what I have to say.'

I looked deep into his eyes. 'It's me, Alec.'

Confusion fluttered across his face. He went still. Silence hovered in the air between us, dragging on for too long. In his stare, distrust smouldered, and fear lanced my heart. I couldn't lose him too. If I did, I'd die.

Tentatively, I put my hand to his face.

He frowned, took a step back.

My heart lurched and I croaked, 'Please forgive me. I'm so sorry for everything I put you through. I -'

His frowned deepened and I went quiet.

I held my breath. Time drew on, each second another cut to my bleeding heart. I was already a crushed shell; one more blow and I would splinter into a million pieces.

He hates me for what I've done to him. He can't forgive me. That's it. I've lost him too.

Tears beaded on his lower lashes and his jaw softened. In a desperately vulnerable voice that broke my heart, he whispered, 'Sofia?'

Chapter 76

We pulled apart after a long time, Alec's T-shirt wet with my tears. He led me to some seating, and we sat as close as we could, gripping each other's hands like lifelines. I looked up at him and wondered how I ever could have become so confused. How I could have believed the man I loved capable of such atrocities.

As if reading my mind, he murmured, 'It's not your fault. Rose said you had a breakdown. Displacing your identity with Arrietty's provided a coping mechanism. A way of protecting you from the trauma you'd experienced.'

'I'm so sorry. After everything, I left you too.'

He cupped my cheek. Shook his head. 'Don't be silly. Your mind did what it had to do to help you survive. Suppressing the horror of Eddie's death and Arrietty's fall kept you alive. As Rose always says, the brain's an irritatingly complex creature. A bastion of existence. It had to do something to help you cope.

'Before Arrietty's fall, you were slipping further and further away, dying inside. When you shifted into Arrietty's persona, you came back to life. You had something to get you out of bed every morning, even if it did mean you believed me guilty of doing something awful to you.' He slipped his hand into mine. 'It's all so confusing, isn't it?'

'Is Rose OK? I hurt her.'

'She's fine. Ten stitches. She understands.'

'I feel so terrible about it. All she was doing was trying to help me remember in a slow, safe way and I thought she was trying to manipulate me, make me forget something heinous I'd seen you do.'

'You mustn't blame yourself. You didn't know any better. I wanted to tell you everything, but when I rang her and told her about your breakdown, she said telling you straight off could do a lot more harm than good, that it could shock your brain into an even more severe coping mechanism that could have irreversible consequences.'

'God. It must have been so hard not to blurt it out, especially when I was being so irrational.'

He managed a weak laugh. 'It was hard. Sometimes, I didn't know if I could carry on. And I hated having to lie to you all the time.'

'Lie? About what?'

'About the condition. You don't have chronic fatigue. It was the only way I could justify keeping your devices away from you.'

"But why did you need to keep them from me?"

'To stop you from stumbling upon information that might set you back. That's why I couldn't have you leaving the house on your own either.'

A lead weight plummeted into my stomach as I realised what he was getting at. 'You couldn't have me finding out about Eddie's accident or Arrietty's...'

He nodded grimly. 'I couldn't see any other way.' He dragged a hand through his hair, 'It was Rose's idea. So many times I nearly gave in, but the thought of you seeing an article about what happened always stopped me at the last moment. Rose said it could destroy you.'

I looked away. Guilt licked at me with a forked tongue. I'd put him through such immense pain. I'd fought him and blamed him. Bitten him. But he'd done wrong too. He'd had an affair. I swallowed a bitter pang of jealousy and said, 'I know about you and Rose.'

He frowned. 'What?'

'She told me.'

'Told you what?' He seemed completely mystified.

'About the affair.'

Alec pulled a funny face. 'What affair? What – me and Rose? She told you that?'

'Yes. Please don't lie to me. I don't know if I can take it after everything else.'

His larynx bobbed and a frown crushed his brow. 'Rose told you that?'

'Yes.'

'That's odd. I've never laid a hand on the woman. Swear on my mother's grave.'

'But she said you were in love. That she loves you. That you love her.'

He ran a hand through his hair and shook his head. 'Well, she did try to kiss me goodnight the night before last – only on the cheek, mind. I didn't think anything of it at the time, but she apologised the next day as if it was a big deal.'

'Maybe it was. To her.'

Alec snorted. 'I don't think so. And this thing about being in love with each other? That's new to me. I've been friendly and grateful for all of her help, but an affair?' He grimaced. 'Rose? *No way.*'

'Then why would she say that?'

'I don't know. Maybe she's got a thing for me. I am rather dashing, aren't I?'

I managed a small smile. Relief swelled in my chest. He was telling the truth, and now that I thought about it properly, Rose was the opposite of what he found attractive in a woman. I also couldn't imagine them together, and suddenly found the idea as absurd as Rose's lie.

'You believe me, don't you?' he said.

'Yes. It's just, she was so convincing.'

Alec frowned, clearly concerned. 'I'll talk to her. Find out what's up. I'm sure it's just a misunderstanding.'

'Good. I think it's important. Oh, and where were you two taking me earlier?'

'Before you legged it and made me chase you around the whole country?'

'Yeah.'

He sighed. 'Horrible to think about it now, but we felt like we had no option left than to have you sectioned. After you lashed out at Rose...well, you were getting increasingly difficult to control. Rose was worried you were becoming a threat to others and to yourself. She knew it was the last thing I wanted and tried her hardest to help you remember everything safely, but it didn't appear to be working. She'd sent your case file to the hospital in case we had to resort to that, and they phoned this morning to say we could bring you in.'

I nodded, my mind already on who else I'd hurt. *Oh God.* 'Rich – is he OK?'

'Yes. A few bruises, like me,' Alec raised his T-shirt to reveal a red swelling above his hip, 'but he'll be fine. He's such a nice guy. Just wanted to help you. When I couldn't find you in the woods, I went back to Maggie's and she'd explained everything to him. He was really apologetic, told me to let him know how you are and he'd come visit you as soon as you're feeling better.'

I let out a whoosh of air, too relieved for a moment to speak.

Alec brushed his lips against my hair. 'I love you so much. I'm so sorry for everything. If it wasn't for what I said, Arrietty -'

I put my fingers against his lips. 'Don't you dare. She was struggling more than either of us knew.' I tried to focus on the fact that Alec was alive and well. We had each other.

He said nothing. I could feel his heart beating against mine, his chest strong and hard.

'I love you,' I said, stroking the nape of his neck, 'more than you know. If we support each other rather than pulling away, maybe we'll find some sort of peace.' Even as I said the words, my airway constricted. I would never get over this loss. Neither would he. What I was saying was a lie. Eddie's face commingled with Arrietty's and my heart broke all over again. I saw the bus – the cliff – I buried my face in Alec's chest, unable to breathe. The pain was too deep. Too much to bear.

Alec stroked my back, murmuring soothing words that I clung on to and tried to believe. I looked up at him and fought to envisage a future where we would one day regain some semblance of happiness, but an infinite black tunnel stretched ahead; a long, austere existence where every day dragged us deeper and deeper into a well of despair. This grief would never leave us. It would linger in our bodies and minds for ever. We would be slaves to it for the rest of our lives. It had already infected our souls and the infection would spread and worsen until we gave up and died. No one could live like that.

Hopelessness blackened my heart and mind. Death, when at last it came, would be a relief. I looked at Alec wondering if he felt the same rotten certainty, but he seemed strangely calm.

He wiped my tears with his thumb. 'Come with me.'

He put his arm around my shoulders and guided me away from the lift along the corridor.

'I'm so sorry you had to,' I paused, waited for the flood of pain to ebb, 'turn off the life support alone.' I couldn't say her name.

He paused beside a door, looked at me and smiled, 'I didn't.'

Chapter 77

'What?' I said.

He opened the door and gestured for me to go inside. Bewildered, I limped into the room. My heart skipped. I looked back at Alec, who nodded, eyes wet and gleaming.

I turned to face the girl lying on the bed. Her eyes were closed. No mask covered her face. No tubes entered her body. No life support machine beeped.

I took a tentative step forward and stared down at my daughter.

There was colour in her cheeks. Her chest rose and fell deeply.

I wondered if I'd had another breakdown. If I was imagining what I was seeing. But then I reached out and stroked the soft skin on her cheek and I knew she was real. My baby girl was alive.

From behind me, my husband's voice came, and it was the most wonderful music in the world, 'I went in to turn off the life support and the monitor showed improved brain activity, so the doctors told me to hold off. And then late last night they turned everything off and she breathed on her own.'

He reached out and pulled me around to face him. His voice shook but happy tears glistened on his cheeks. 'The doctors say it's a miracle. She's not woken up yet, but they say it's only a matter of time, and she's going to make a full recovery. Apart from an ugly scar on the back of her head, our girl's going to be OK.'

'This is where you've been coming every day?' I whispered.

He nodded. 'Go to her.'

I perched on the bed, unable to speak, heart too full.

Alec moved to stand behind me. 'I'm just going to text Rose and let her know you're you again, and that everything's Ok.'

I gazed down at my beautiful, sleeping daughter, unable to believe she was still alive.

There were so many things that needed to be said. The road to recovery would be long and hard. We'd been shattered by loss. My little boy would never come back and nothing would fill the void he left, but my little girl was with us. We had a second chance. Together, with support, compassion and time, we would heal.

Looking at my daughter, I made a promise to my son.

This time, my sweet, special boy, I'll make sure that losing you brings us closer rather than tearing us apart.

I leaned over, moved Arrietty's silky hair away from her ear and whispered, 'Don't worry, sweetie, Mummy's back.'

To my surprise, her eyelids fluttered. I held my breath, not daring to hope. The movement stopped and I sagged, terrified she was slipping into another coma, but then the most magical thing happened. My little girl opened her eyes.

She focused on me. Her voice was small and cracked. 'Mum?'

I gasped. 'I'm here, sweetie. Don't worry. Everything's OK now. You're going to be fine.'

I wrapped my arms around my beautiful girl and held her for a long time. She collapsed into me murmuring how much she had missed me. How she'd thought she was going to die and never see me again. I told her she was safe now. Dad and I were here. The doctors said she'd make a full recovery. As I spoke, I stroked her hair and inhaled her gorgeous smell. My baby was alive. She was back. I'd thought she was dead, but here she was, warm and perfect and lovely as ever and safe in my arms. Words could never express how I felt in that sacred moment. I wanted it to go on for ever, but at last, she pulled back.

I handed her a cup of water. She took three tiny sips then gave it back to me.

In a raspy voice, she murmured, 'I dreamt that -' she stopped and stared up at Alec, 'Dad? Oh God, I thought you'd...' She buried her face in her hands. Sobs shook her shoulders.

I enfolded her in my arms. My little girl. 'It's OK.'

'I'm so, so sorry, I thought Dad had locked me in this room because he blamed me for,' she shuddered, tried to say his name.

'I don't blame you, sweetheart,' Alec said, stroking her face, 'I love you so much. I'll never forgive myself for making you feel so guilty, but I was hurting deeply. I lost myself, my way.'

Arrietty looked from me to him. The faintest of smiles twitched her dry lips. Her face fell. 'I thought I was about to die. And there was a woman. I thought she was going to save me, then she said something about not been able to stop it. It was all so weird. So confusing.'

'It could have been Maggie,' Alec said, 'She came to visit you a few times. I know she had misgivings about the doctor advising me to switch off your life support and thank God it never came to that.'

Alec smiled at me then at Arrietty. 'Your brain activity started improving a couple of days ago. I couldn't believe it. They took you off the life support and you breathed on your own. A few hours ago, they called me to say you'd woken up and that you asked for Mum. Do you remember that?'

She shook her head. 'No, but I remember everything else now. From before.' Her chin quivered as she looked at us, 'I remember the cliff. I, I can't believe I did that. I'm sorry. I'm so, so sorry.'

I shushed her and pulled her teary face into my chest.

362

'It's over now. And we both understand. You blamed yourself and we weren't there to tell you that it wasn't your fault. We pulled away to cope alone instead of supporting each other. We love you, sweetie. So much.'

I kissed her forehead, then moved away so that Alec could sit down.

Watching my daughter and husband, a tinge of happiness warmed my heart. In time, maybe this feeling would grow. Perhaps, one day, in the not-so-distant future, light would overtake the darkness. We had all suffered so much, but if we could learn to cherish the years we had with Eddie, be kind to each other and live in the moment, there was hope. There had to be.

Chapter 78

We stayed with Arrietty until she fell asleep. The nurse had made an exception and allowed us to stay beyond visiting hours, but we were told we'd have to go home for the evening and come back the next day at 10am.

I didn't want to leave. Every impulse screamed DON'T LEAVE HER. STAY. IF YOU GO, SOMETHING BAD WILL HAPPEN, but Alec was with me, and Arrietty was asleep, so there was little support we could offer. The nurse reassured us that the best thing we could do was to go home and get some rest. Everyone told me leaving was the right thing to do. It felt like the worst course imaginable, but I didn't have a choice.

I pressed my trembling lips against Arrietty's forehead and closed my eyes, waiting for the panic of leaving her to subside. It didn't. Eventually, Alec tugged me away, his arm around my waist, and we walked together through the hospital out into the car park.

Rain drizzled on our heads from a dark, starless sky, the air no less humid than before, the earth continuing its relentless cycle, nature unmoved by our experience, unrelenting and ever persistent in its circular narrative. I looked up, wondering bitterly at how the physical world could remain so unchanged when my entire universe had been rewritten. *Eddie's dead. Arrietty's alive.* Two polar opposites existed on the same plain: one devastating, one sublime. It was a mind-churning paradox; the bleak, heavy weight of grief eased a fraction by the knowledge of a second chance for my little girl. Nothing could eradicate the terrible truth, but hope glimmered in the future like a liquid mirage in the desert, and it was this hope that I clung to, this hope that lit a candle in the darkest corner of my mind and gave me the strength to put one foot in front of the other and keep breathing.

Alec opened the car door for me and helped me in, handling me as if I was made of feathers and might flutter apart at any second. I was dosed up on pain killers, but my adrenaline had dwindled long ago, and exhaustion hit me like a truck the second I touched the passenger seat.

'Asleep already?' he said softly.

'Almost.' I closed my eyes, intending to rest them for a moment, too tired to speak.

The next thing I knew the Merc was crunching along our pebble driveway. Alec's hand found my thigh and squeezed gently. 'We're home. Do you want a bath?'

A bath sounded good. I said as much, and he switched off the engine.

In the ambient glow of porchlight, the back garden stretched into blackness, a blackness that ended at the cliff. We sat in silence for a while, each staring out at the darkness, thinking our own private thoughts which were probably much the same, our feelings tangled and murky, a mixture of sadness and relief, hope, and a profound sensation of loss coupled with the devastating knowledge that this loss would be ingrained in our hearts and minds for ever.

'Knightley will be pleased to see you,' Alec murmured.

I yawned. 'God, poor little thing. He's been alone all this time.'

'He'll be fine. He's a tough little guy.'

Alec got out of the car, walked around to my side and helped me out. With an arm hooked around my waist, he half-carried me to the back door.

'I can walk, you know,' I said.

He kissed my head. 'I know. I just want to be your knight in shining armour again.'

I managed a smile.

As he unlocked the back door scrabbling sounds made me wince – poor Knightley.

I hurried into the house and scooped Knightley up in my arms. He quivered with excitement and licked my neck frantically. Loving the affection, I let him, the feeling of his small, warm body against my collar bone good. Better than good. Wonderful.

'Told you he'd be happy to see you,' Alec said, giving him a pat on the head.

'Oops.' I gestured towards a small puddle of wee.

'Hardly surprising. I'll get the mop in a minute. Let me get you settled on the sofa first and start running your bath.'

He flicked on the lights as we bypassed the kitchen and walked through the central walkway to the living space, the house quiet, its homely smells comforting and familiar in a way that brought tears to my eyes.

When we drew level with the fireplace, exhaustion attacked again, and my knees buckled. Alex scooped me up like a baby and laid me on the leather sofa. 'Stay there. I'll get the bath started. Don't move.'

I cuddled Knightley close to my chest and yawned again. 'Thanks.'

He smiled and climbed the stairs two at a time. I wondered at his energy and thought it must be the last dregs of adrenaline coursing through his veins. He probably still felt elated at having me back and talking to Arrietty had been a dream come true for both of us, a miracle. According to the doctor, she'd be able to come home in a few days' time, which seemed astonishing given what she'd been through. Of course, I wasn't going to argue with that. The sooner I had my baby girl home, the better.

Knightley nuzzled my ear, and I stroked his soft curls and allowed him to bury his nose in my hair. Arrietty was going to adore him. She'd always wanted a dog.

Drowsiness descended, but my eyes latched onto the glass wall that looked out towards the cliff, and I stiffened. I winced and turned my back on the night-black view, pressing my nose into the rich leather and trying not to think about the reason I couldn't bear to look in the direction of the cliff. Maybe moving house would be a good idea? Living somewhere less remote in a seaside town near the beach where the crash of waves against the rocks would hypnotise me into a thoughtless state and I could, just for one second, forget everything...but changing homes would involve leaving Eddie behind all over again, closing another door on the past and opening one up to a new present. I couldn't do that. Not yet. Perhaps not ever.

I brushed tears away and exhaled shakily. Eddie was still in the house. I could feel him, smell him. I couldn't leave him, and no one could make me.

I flinched as Alec's weight crushed the sofa at my back.

'Ready for your bath?' he said, stroking my arm.

I nodded.

He lifted Knightley off me and put him on the floor. Knightley immediately jumped up at my ankles, begging to be picked up again.

'I'll bring him up with me,' I said, reaching to pick him up.

'Don't. It'll be more relaxing without him, and I need to take him outside before bed anyway in case, you know...'

'Yeah. OK.'

Alec helped me stand and we ascended the stairs carefully, Knightley scrambling after us. At the bathroom door, he picked him up, kissed my cheek and smiled. 'Camomile tea in bed before lights out?'

I didn't know if I could stay up for a drink but nodded anyway.

After letting me give Knightley another stroke, he

closed the door, and I drifted into the steamy room, surprised to see that he'd lit tea lights and placed one on each corner of the tub.

My husband's so kind. How could I have believed him otherwise?

With a groan of pain, I removed my stained clothes and placed them on top of the toilet. I looked at the mirror, shocked to see how thin and pale I was, not to mention grimy. Dirt smeared my cheeks and forehead, and scratches criss-crossed my chin.

Feeling shaky, I climbed into the bath and submerged my body and face in the water. It felt wrong to enjoy something, but the feeling of hot liquid on my aching muscles was incredible. I allowed my arms to float to the surface and inhaled the rose-scented bubble bath. Shadows skulked beneath my eyelids, but I pushed them away and focused on Arrietty, on bringing her home and looking after her, on how Knightley would, I hoped, bring a smile to her lovely face. Then Rose appeared in my mind's eye and my thoughts turned to the psychological help Arrietty would need to aid her recovery. She'd suffered a great loss, blamed herself for Eddie's death and tried to take her own life; even though she might have recovered physically, she was injured internally. Nothing but time and special care would help to mend her wounded mind. Would Rose be the right person for the job? She'd certainly helped me to regain my memory, but the fact that she'd told – no, *suggested* – that she and Alec were having an affair troubled me more than I wanted to admit. A voice rose, hissing that Alec was lying. How could Rose be so convinced they were in love unless Alec had given her the impression that he loved her?

NO. Alec's innocent. He's telling the truth. Don't do this. Stop blaming him. That's exactly what you did before and you were wrong. Stop being paranoid. It's Rose - she clearly misread the situation, read more into his behaviour than she should have.

I realised I was biting the skin around my nails and stopped. We'd find someone new to help us with our grief. Rose would understand that I was me again and that I needed to start afresh with a new therapist. Alec would clear up any misunderstanding on her part and everything would be fine. Arrietty could see someone different, and life would move on, for everyone. Rose would get over her little crush on Alec and one day he and I would be able to laugh about the fact that he'd unwittingly seduced my counsellor.

The water had cooled, and tiredness was dragging me down into its woolly embrace, so I clambered out of the bath, wrapped myself in a towel and limped out of the room. It felt strange to head towards the master rather than Arrietty's bedroom. My feet carried me there nonetheless and I got dressed in a pink bed shirt then perched on the bed waiting for Alec to bring up my cup of tea.

After a couple of minutes, my pillow proved irresistible, and I pulled back the duvet and lay down. It was a struggle to stay awake. My eyelids felt as though they were weighed down with pennies and my limbs sank into the mattress like butter into warm bread.

'Alec?' I called, throat hurting from the effort.

He seemed to have been gone a long time.

Sleep caressed my brain with soft, lullaby fingers, but I fought it, wanting to say goodnight to him before I fell asleep. This was the first time we'd slept in the same bed together for ages. I wanted to feel his arms around me one more time before morning; hear him say Arrietty's name and reassure me that everything was going to be OK now that I was back to my normal self. I needed to tell him again how sorry I was for everything I'd put him through; to reassure him that I loved him, wrap my arms around him and just feel him there, with me, holding me.

I called again, louder, throat grating, but he didn't

answer. If he was in the kitchen, he probably wouldn't be able to hear me, so I didn't try again.

Silence invaded the room, building until it was almost deafening in its intensity. Where was he? Why wasn't he up here yet? Was he still sorting out Knightley? Had my puppy had another accident? Yes, that had to be it.

Certain that Knightley explained Alec's absence, I relaxed a little, felt my muscles ooze into the bed softener, my lungs deflate like a hot air balloon. Despite myself, my eyelids drooped, and sleep enveloped my brain, swaddling all thought in a thick, black blanket of nothingness.

Sometime later, the sound of the bedroom door made me twitch, flinch, jerk awake. I opened my lips to welcome my husband, but my mouth froze and I jerked upright, heart clanging against my ribs.

Chapter 79

Rose stood in the doorway. 'Sorry I startled you.'

'Oh, Rose. Hi.' I forced a smile to hide my displeasure at her being here. The last thing I needed was to have to explain everything that had gone on at the hospital or discuss my feelings, but guilt sloshed in my abdomen and dark flashes of me slashing her with the nail scissors skittered around my mind's eye like cockroaches. I'd hurt her. At the very least I needed to apologise. If I did so quickly, maybe she'd leave.

'I'm so sorry,' I said, 'for everything. Alec's told you I've remembered, hasn't he? And about Arrietty? How's your face?'

Her fingers fluttered up to the injury. Stitches criss-crossed her cheek, sewing the skin together with a train track of black kisses reminiscent of Frankenstein's monster. Her face was abnormally pale and lipstick was smudged across her teeth. She shook her head. 'No need to apologise for that. You weren't in your right mind. It's wonderful news about Arrietty. And you, of course.'

'Still, I feel terrible about it, and I want to thank you for all you've done for me. For both of us. If it wasn't for you -'

She smiled and waved her hand. 'Don't mention it. It worked better than I expected. To tell you the truth I didn't expect you to remember. I'm still surprised you did. But that's good, of course. And now it means you can move on. And so can Alec.'

'Well, thank you so much for coming over to check on us.'

'It's my pleasure. I needed to see Alec. There are things

to be discussed and it has to be tonight.'

I almost asked what she was referring to, then realised that it might be something to do with payment. Not wanting to make her feel awkward, I didn't ask. I stood and headed for the bedroom door. 'I think your things are still in the spare room. I'll help you pack if you like.'

'Pack?' she said.

I turned, surprised at the confusion in her tone.

She blinked, smiled. 'Oh, yes.'

Her earlier words floated back to me; *we're fond of each other. He loves me.* Alec had said there was nothing between them, that she'd misinterpreted their relationship, but she was a rational, intelligent woman. How could a person like that misconstrue something to such an extent? Doubt stirred and the green-eyed monster reared its head. Was there something between them? Had Alec lied to me? I watched her for a moment. She rubbed her eyes and yawned. I picked up her yawn and berated myself for questioning Alec. I couldn't let paranoia creep in and curdle my thoughts. I was myself again. I needed to think rationally and fight this inclination towards pessimism that seemed to have buried into my psyche like a parasite.

Desperate for Rose to be gone so I could crawl back into bed, I stood aside quickly so she could enter the spare room.

She walked straight over to the double bed and, to my horror, grabbed a black lace thong and stuffed it inside her holdall. *A lace thong. What? Why?* Sirens belted an alarm in my head. I swallowed, tried to quell surfacing fear. Watched as she flew around the room stuffing more garments into the bag. Her movements were fast, rushed, as if she suddenly couldn't wait to be packed up and gone. Either that, or she didn't want me to see any more sexy lingerie. Any more *evidence*.

Trying not to fixate on the thong, I looked around the room and saw her make up bag on the dressing table. I moved to pick it up, and she spun around and snatched it out of my grasp, but not before I'd seen what was inside: the small photograph of Alec I'd found in her bedside table. She'd brought it with her, put it in her make up bag.

I cleared my throat. Questions stung my tongue. I swallowed them down and pretended I hadn't seen the photograph, choosing to ignore the elephant in the room. I had to trust my husband. If he said she'd got the wrong end of the stick, she had, and it wasn't my place to interfere. I didn't have the mental or physical energy for a peaceful interaction let alone one that could be highly charged with emotion. If Rose still thought there was something between them, she could ask Alec and he'd clear things up.

She stuffed her make up bag inside the holdall and heaved the strap over her shoulder.

'It was so kind of you to move in to help me,' I said quietly. I walked out of the room and she followed me.

'Alec needed me, and I was more than happy to oblige,' she murmured.

'Did he ask you to move in?' I said, unable to stop myself.

'Not in so many words, but I knew what he needed. I suggested it and he said yes. I know he was relieved to have me here, especially when you...' She looked away. Her fingers brushed her cheek.

'I'm so sorry, Rose. All you were trying to do was help me,' I said, pausing at the top of the stairs.

'Like I said before, there's no need to apologise. The important thing is that you can get on with your life now, with nothing to hold you back, as can Alec.'

I nodded, reassured by her words.

I led her downstairs and we walked in tandem along the walkway. The conversation seemed exhausted, and I was relieved. The quicker she left the better. Even walking was a challenge; every step an uphill battle as my wounded leg and weary limbs strove to keep working.

In the kitchen, Knightley ran at me and I picked him up.

Alec smiled at us from the other end of the room. Three cups of tea sat on the kitchen island.

'Everything all right?' he said, looking from me to Rose.

Rose let the holdall thud to the floor. She beamed, ran her fingers over her lips, strode towards the kitchen island and sat down. 'Yes, super.'

I put down Knightley and joined them at the table, wishing it was just me and Alec.

Alec sat down and nursed his cup in his hands. He looked at me. 'Rose just came over to see how we're doing.'

'Yes, I know. I've apologised for...everything.' I glanced at Rose and managed a pained smile, yawned and tried to catch Alec's eye. I wanted her to go. I needed sleep. Alec was good at tactfully getting rid of guests when needed. He caught my eye and registered my need with a nod.

He smiled at Rose and said, 'Thanks again for coming round. I see you've got your things. I bet you'll be pleased to get home and sleep in your own bed tonight. You must be just as shattered as us.' He yawned as if to punctuate the message.

Rose coughed delicately, picked up her tea cup and said, 'Are you sure you're ready, Alec?'

'Ready for what?'

She dipped her head to the side. 'Ready for me to go?'

'Oh. Yes. I think we'll be fine. Now that Sofia's feeling a lot better, I think we'll be OK. We just need to get some rest, don't we, Sofi?'

'Yes. In fact, I'm sorry to be rude, but I think I'll go back up to bed now. Alec, how long do you think you'll be?' I was giving him the out and Rose a clear sign that it was time to go.

Alec looked at Rose. She peered down into her tea, took a tiny sip.

He smiled at me and said, 'I'll be up in a moment.'

Now was the time for her to leave, the natural break in conversation where the guest picked up the social cue and understood you wanted them to go, but Rose took another sip of her tea and sighed. 'This is nice.'

I hovered at the kitchen island. 'Thank you again, Rose, so much. Night. Alec, I'll see you upstairs in a minute.'

I turned to go. Out of the corner of my eye, I saw Rose lean across the island.

In a stage whisper, she said, 'Alec, I think it's time to tell her.'

My spine tingled. I stayed where I was. Glanced over my shoulder.

Alec frowned. His eyes flicked to mine then back to hers. 'Tell her what?'

She paused, glanced back at me before reaching out a hand and placing it on top of his. 'About us.'

Alec's eyebrows shot up and he moved his hand out from under hers and placed his cup down. I turned around. Rose picked up her cup and cradled it in her palms. Her back was to me, so I didn't know whether she was smiling or frowning, angry or happy, but the air felt strained, irrevocably altered.

'Rose,' Alec said softly, 'what do you mean?'

Her head dipped to the other side. Beneath the kitchen light, her copper curls glinted metallically. 'She needs to know. I know she's remembered who she is, but that doesn't matter because we love each other so much. All I want is to be with you. I know that's all you want too. You just have to tell her it's over and make her leave, then we can be together properly, at long last.' She glanced around at me. 'I'm sorry, Sofia, but we love each other. Even you

375

must be able to see that. And now that Arrietty's on the mend, you'll have her. Alec and I will have her at the weekends, but all of that can be arranged later, can't it, darling?' She looked back at him.

A shudder rippled across the back of my neck.

Alec stood up from the kitchen island and shook his head. 'Rose, listen to me carefully. You've got this all wrong. I'm grateful for your professional help and the compassionate support you've shown me during this time, but that's it. I've never wanted more than that and I've never said as much. You've misread the situation. I'm sorry, but I love Sofia. I'll always be grateful for how much you've helped me, and what you've done for her, but she's my wife.'

He smiled and reached out to her. 'Look, why don't we talk in a few days' time when everything's calmed down?' He sounded relaxed, but his entire body was stiff.

A loud sniff came from Rose. She stood slowly, back rigid.

Alec walked around the bench and said, 'It's late. We're tired. Let me see you to the door.'

But she didn't move. She sniffed again and muttered something I didn't hear then moved so fast it caught Alec off guard, throwing her hot tea in his face. He cursed and stumbled backwards, and she swivelled, grabbed a knife out of the block and ran at me, face contorted with grief and rage.

She swiped the knife at my face, but I ducked and staggered to the left, and she fell against the counter where the blade smacked the surface. With a shriek, she spun and went for me again, but Alec ran in front of me and blocked the knife with his forearm. He cried out as she sliced through his skin. Her eyes widened in horror, and she dropped the knife and ran for the back door. One of her shoes flew off her foot. She kicked off the other one, looked around wildly then bent over, seized Knightley and turned to face us. Tears streamed down her cheeks and ran through her stitches. She smeared her hand across her eyes, smudging her mascara. With one arm, she crushed Knightley against her breasts as if he was a cuddly toy. He yelped and squirmed like mad, but she held him tighter, eyes fixed on mine, gaze unblinking. Her breath rattled and her bulbous eyes glinted as she took a small, unsteady step backwards.

Chapter 80

'Rose?' I said, 'You need to calm down.'

I took a small step towards her.

She snapped, 'Stay where you are.'

The edge in her tone and the way her nails disappeared into Knightley's fur told me to obey. I swallowed, waited for her to say something. Knightley whimpered and pawed futilely at her chest.

Alec held up his hands. 'Rose. Listen to me. You're upset. Come and sit down with me. We'll talk about it.'

She ignored him, stared me up and down, tilted her head at an odd angle. In a strangled voice, she said, 'You remembered everything.'

It wasn't a question, but I nodded. 'Yes. Thank you. You helped me remember. I'm me again. I'm so grateful. We both are.' I hesitated, said, 'Can I hold Knightley please?'

She glanced down at the frantic puppy and frowned as if surprised to see him in her arms. She shook her head slowly and murmured, 'No. He's mine.' Her head jerked up and she glared, daring me to argue. Her arm tightened on Knightley and he whimpered again.

'Please don't hurt him,' I said.

'Rose?' Alec tried.

She frowned and shook her head angrily. Frizzy corkscrews stuck out at random places making her hair look like a wig. Her body quivered like a poised arrow. 'I'd never hurt him. I love him. I've always loved him. And he, he, he loves me. I know he does.'

Alec edged closer.

Knightley was shivering now and whimpering

continuously.

'Alec of course,' she snapped as if I'd asked her a question. She barked out a high-pitched sound, half-laugh, half-cry. 'You weren't supposed to remember. I helped, because he asked me to. He said he wanted you to remember, to be Sofia again, but I knew deep down he was only saying that because it was what society wanted him to say. He didn't really want you back. He wanted you to stay gone. To be sectioned, out of the way so we could be together. But I didn't expect...' She trailed off, eyes narrowing. Knightley yelped as her grip tightened. I imagined his tiny rib cage pressing into her chest bone, being crushed against her body.

She eyeballed me, nostrils flaring. 'You're not supposed to be here. Why are you here?'

It was as if she'd forgotten everything she'd said. As if someone had hit rewind in her head and wiped her memory.

'Rose,' I said, 'I think you're confused. Maybe you hit your head. You might need to see a doctor. Alec's got his phone. He can -'

'Don't be so ridiculous. I'm fine. It's just, this isn't supposed to be...you shouldn't be here. You should be in the hospital, not here, not in this house, in his bed. Our bed. Alec moved me in, told me to sleep in the spare room while you were still here, but I was going to move in there after you were gone. He couldn't wait for it to just be me and him, for you to be out of the picture. All that rubbish about fixing you was just his way to appease his conscience. He's such a good man. Such a kind, generous soul. I knew, as soon as he smiled at me that first time. That twinkle in his eye. And only I can make him smile. After everything he's been through, all I want is to make him happy. To protect him.'

Alec and I exchanged glances. I looked at the cut on his arm and my insides clenched.

'Please, Rose. Come and talk to Alec. He'll put everything right. But first, please can you give Knightley to me? You're scaring him. He's just a puppy.'

'Yes. Let's talk this all through calmly,' Alec said, holding out a hand.

Her frown eased a fraction, and she jolted as if touched with a cattle prod and loosened her grip on Knightley. 'Oh, yes, OK. I suppose you're right. I don't want to scare him. Alec wouldn't want that.' Her eyes brightened and she focused on my husband. 'You wouldn't want that, would you, darling? You want us to be a happy family. You, me, Millie, Bruno and Knightley. That's what you want isn't it?'

To my relief, she smiled, walked towards Alec and changed the way she was holding Knightley so that she could pass him over.

Alec ignored her question and glanced at me, and that was it. Rose's eyes widened and her face went puce.

With a growl, she pulled Knightley back into her chest, spun around, yanked open the back door and sprinted outside.

Alec lurched after her out into the garden.

I followed.

Chapter 81

Rose raced across the grass towards the cliff; Knightley's yelps tracked back through the garden like a baby's cries; Alec pursued her using his good arm to help propel him forward; and in what felt like a terrible sort of déjà vu, I limped after him screaming Rose's name and begging her to stop.

In the seconds it took Rose to reach the cliff edge, the last two years flashed before my eyes. Eddie – Alec – Arrietty – me – not me – me again – Eddie – Arrietty - Alec. Alive, dead, alive, dead. Horror, denial, anger, misery. Confusion. Despair. Enlightenment. Relief. Hope. And now this.

I suddenly felt foggy, tight-chested. Everything was slipping through my fingers, my hold on the present evaporating into fog.

I blinked. Ran. Blinked. Ran. The past blurred into the present and back again. *I'm in the park watching Eddie...at the end of the garden begging Arrietty to come away from the edge...in the hospital cuddling my daughter...on the road cradling my little boy's head.*

I felt myself shifting and drifting away, untethered and split apart like a dashed dandelion, lost to some third person who watched the scene unfold through a pair of fractured lenses. A ghost rendered helpless by dread. An outsider unable to do anything to stop this terrible new madness.

Rose stopped at the precipice and held Knightley out over the drop. Her toes teetered on the edge and she swayed dangerously. Behind her lay the black hills, ominous and silent as giant graves.

'Tell the truth, Alec, or I'll drop him,' she screamed.

Knightley whimpered. His little legs kicked thin air.

'Give him to me, Rose,' Alec panted.

He edged towards her.

Too close. That's too close.

I wanted to tell him to stop, stay where he was, but I couldn't speak, couldn't think. Everything was a blur, a bloody puddle; too much to cope with, too much to grasp.

'I'm sorry if I gave you the impression that I loved you, but I didn't mean to. Please, Rose, this isn't you. You're a kind, gentle person. You wouldn't hurt a fly let alone a dog. I've seen you with Millie and Bruno. You love dogs. Think about what you're doing.'

'Sometimes you have to be cruel to be kind,' she said, her eyes flashing to mine, 'I learnt that a long time ago.'

'No, Rose. That's not true. You know that's not true. If you love me, you'll stop this now,' Alec said. To my horror, he took a step closer.

Rose's chin trembled. Tears fell down her cheeks and dripped off her chin. 'I love you so much, that's why I'm doing this. Don't you see that? Why don't you see that? It's her, isn't it? She's twisted you against me, against us. Oh God, why did I help her? I never should have helped her – but I did it for you, darling, I did it for you, so you'd be happy.'

'If you want to make me happy, give Knightley to me and get away from the edge. We'll sit down, talk this through.'

The blood on Alec's arm looked like tar. I wanted to scream at Rose to put Knightley down and get the hell away from us, but if I spoke, things might go from bad to worse. In her disturbed state of mind, she thought I was her enemy. She wouldn't listen to me. She was barely listening to Alec.

'Tell her to leave, and I'll think about it,' Rose said, shooting me a glare.

'OK, Rose. Sofia, go back to the house.'

'NO!' Rose screamed, shaking Knightley violently, 'Tell her to leave and never come back.'

Knightley squealed in pain.

Alec held up his hands in appeasement. Both arms shook. Blood dribbled down his sleeve. 'OK. Sofia, please leave. Rose and I need to talk this out.'

Alec glanced back and nodded, urging me to go.

I didn't want to. The urge to stay hammered my heels to the ground.

'Go, or I'll do it!' she shrieked. She switched her grasp with clumsy, drunken hands so that she was holding Knightley by the scruff of his neck.

Alec looked around, pleading with me to leave, begging with his eyes.

With sick in my throat, I turned my back on my husband and limped across the garden away from the cliff. I dragged my feet, half-expecting to hear her attack Alec, but a hush fell. Indecipherable whispers teased my ears, but no words formed, leaving me clueless as to their conversation.

I looked back; from this distance it was too dark to see more than two amorphous shapes imprinted on an inky canvas. It was the sort of sketch I might draw; gloomy, gothic, uncanny. But this was real. Horribly, shockingly real, and I was living it, enmeshed in this living, breathing hell, a pawn in a game that was anything but black and white. Rose had held it together for so long, but now she had snapped, and we were the targets of every bad thing that had ever happened to her. Like a flooded dam, the tide was impossible to halt, the currents of her breakdown too strong to stop.

I reached the back porch, hurried around the side of the house and crouched down out of sight behind the Merc.

Little by little I felt myself return; this was my reality. I was me again. Sofia Black-Hawkins. Mummy and wife. Artist and fully fleshed human being. For the sake of my family, I had to hold it together. I had to think.

I scanned the driveway. There was no sign of Rose's car. She must have had a taxi drop her off and waited here for us to come home. The thought made my tummy cramp. I considered creeping back inside the house, grabbing the knife and racing up the garden. Maybe if I could throw it to Alec, he could threaten her and she'd let Knightley go.

In my head a nightmarish result played out: Rose somehow got hold of the knife and plunged it into my husband's stomach, slit his throat then came after me. When she was finished, she went back for Knightley; found him cowering behind my studio and threw him off the cliff. When the police finally came to the house and discovered our bodies, they visited the hospital to tell Arrietty what had happened and she wanted to die all over again.

It was all just too much. My thoughts spun in a million different directions, all ending with the same fate. If I didn't do something, Alec wasn't going to make it. I was going to lose him too. I just knew it. Life looked kindly on some people, but I wasn't one of them.

I raised my head and peered over the bonnet at the back of the house. If I hunched over and moved quickly, she might not see me. She was probably so focused on Alec that she'd forget to worry about me. I hesitated, unsure. Instinct told me to get a knife, but caution told me that reintroducing a weapon into this situation might incur terrible consequences.

Indecision nailed my feet to the pebbles, panic a slice of raw chilli lodged in my throat.

I tried to think clearly, hoped now that he was lying to her, convincing her she was right, saying anything he could to get her to put down Knightley and stop acting so crazily.

She was clearly having some sort of psychotic episode. She needed help. But first, she needed to be dealt with. Quickly. Before she did something terrible.

I sucked in a sharp breath. Raised voices exploded from the cliffside – his and hers – angry, volatile, heading somewhere bad.

I peered towards the cliff, but all I could make out were two blurred shadows. As far as I could tell neither of them had moved. Rose remained on the edge; Alec a little distance away. I hoped he wouldn't get too close, wouldn't take a stupid risk. I wanted Knightley safe, but Alec couldn't endanger himself. I couldn't lose him. We – me and Arrietty – couldn't lose him.

The moon slid into view; a slice of a face, a broken whole, just like Rose. Just like me. The drizzle evolved to rain and just as abruptly the moon vanished and plump, warm droplets fell like blood from the oil-black sky.

Blood. Please don't let any more blood be spilled tonight.

Porchlight illuminated the back door and patio area and the first half of the garden. If Rose looked up at the wrong moment, she'd see me. There was no way to turn off the automatic light. All I could do was hope she was too fixated on Alec to notice any movement.

It was now or never.

Chapter 82

I pushed wet hair out of my face, bent over and limped out from behind the Merc. Alec needed my help. I wasn't going anywhere. If anything happened to him now after everything we'd been through, and when we'd just got each other back...the thought was unbearable. That Arrietty might lose her dad after losing Eddie...*NO. I can't let that happen.*

I reached the house, yanked open the back door and hurried inside. I scanned the kitchen for Alec's phone, but it wasn't there. Should I search for it before going back outside? Oh God. I didn't know. Had Alec been anywhere except the kitchen since we'd got home? Yes. The living space and the bathroom. I couldn't recall seeing it when I'd had a bath, but I was so tired I might have missed it.

Cursing my injured leg, I spun around and limped back across the room, slipping on my own footprints. It seemed impossible that this was happening. As I hurried down the central walkway, I tried to think of any signs I'd seen before this night that suggested Rose was unstable. Deluded. She'd been very touchy-feely with Alec, and now that I thought about it with a fresh perspective, he'd never reciprocated, not even once. She'd also mentioned him a lot and had seemed to light up whenever he entered the room. And she'd had that passport photograph of him in her bedside table. It had been her suggestion to move into the house. She must have manipulated him into thinking it necessary. Now that I knew her true colours that seemed like the logical answer. Not that any of this was logical. This was another level of madness. She was clearly obsessed with him. The question was could she be reasoned with? How far gone into mental instability was she?

Far enough to attack Alec with a knife and hold Knightley over the cliffside.

Swallowing, I scanned the living room. Nothing.

I turned and limped over to the stairs, used the banister to haul myself upwards faster, ignoring my leg's protests.

Had Alec talked her down? Maybe everything was OK now. Perhaps Knightley was in my husband's arms and Rose was sitting cross-legged on the grass apologising for her psychotic behaviour, happy to leave us in peace.

But that was a fantasy. Her infatuation ran too deep. There had been something strange about her eyes, a wet brightness that spoke of mania, her mind a volcano with its contents gushing out, livid and uncontainable as lava. Nothing Alec or I said or did would reverse this eruption. No amount of coddling or cajoling would sooth her broken mind. Time was needed for that, and we didn't have time. We weren't experts. We had no idea what kind of beast we were dealing with.

Fear lassoed my heart as I reached the landing and propelled myself towards the bathroom. In my head I heard Alec's screams. They were imaginary but felt real. I shuddered. Told myself to get a grip.

Inside the bathroom the steam had gone but the tub remained full; a bad habit of mine. I scanned the sink, the toilet, the floor; no mobile phone. Shit. I'd wasted time.

I turned to go back downstairs for the knife.

Rose stood in the doorway, her sodden head dipped to the side, a broken-necked doll, eyes glinting buttons. Her hair, wet and shiny as coiled eels, dripped onto the white tiles counting down the seconds.

Drip.

Drip.

Drip.

Three.

Two.

One.

The stitches on her cheek had come apart and fresh blood oozed from the cut. The cut I'd given her. For a second, I wished I'd gone deeper. Sawed through skin and bone and brain matter so that she no longer breathed. But I hadn't, and now she was here, ready to reap her revenge.

Chapter 83

'Where's Alec?' I held my ground, met her gaze, tried to convey fearlessness despite the frantic thudding of my heart.

She filled the doorway, sodden from head to toe. A dreamy smile perked one side of her mouth. 'He's fine.'

'Rose, listen to me. If Alec's hurt, we need to -'

'*We?* There's no *we*. Only me and him.' Her eyes narrowed and she closed the space between us, stabbing a finger at me. 'You shouldn't be here. I don't understand why he brought you back. He should have had you sectioned, like we planned. I'm not angry at him. I'm just upset. He's promised me it's over between you, but him bringing you here...I don't understand it. It's wrong. You shouldn't be here. You never should have come back.'

She was bigger than me. I tried to think of a way to get round her, but she blocked the only exit. I scanned the room looking for something – anything – to use against her. There was nothing, only a bath full of dirty water.

'Rose. Please listen to me. You're not well. You need to see someone, talk all of this out with them. You helped me so much. Talking to you was so good for me. You saved me. Alec's so grateful. But this is wrong. He's my husband and he still loves me. He loves you too, but as a friend. If you really want to do what's best for him, you'll leave now. He'll get in touch and you can talk all of this through when everyone's calmed down.'

She shook her head and laughed scornfully. 'He doesn't love you. He loves me. He's kind so he's taken pity on you. That's why he's brought you back.'

I was right. Logic, reason and truth weren't going to

work. I back-pedalled, gave her what she wanted. 'Then why don't you take pity on me too? Let me stay here for a little while. Just for tonight. I'll leave tomorrow, I promise. I won't come back. You and he can be together.'

'No. No, that won't do. You need to go now. Right now.'

'OK. I will. I'll go straight away. I'll call a taxi. If you give me your phone, I can call one right now and be out of your hair in no time.'

Her nostrils flared. She took a step closer, so close I could smell alcohol on her breath. 'But you won't do that, will you?'

I considered shoving her. My heart slammed. 'Do what?'

'You won't call a taxi. You'll call the police.'

'I won't. I promise. I can see now that you love each other. Alec wants me gone too, so I'll leave. Just give me your phone – or, I know, you can call a taxi.'

Outside, the rain picked up, battering the window like Zeus's fists.

She frowned, as if considering my suggestion. A second later, laughter barked out, bitter and false. 'You'll just call the police from the taxi driver's phone. You're lying. You still think he loves you. You'll phone the police and tell them I hurt Alec.'

'No. I promise I won't.'

'You will. But I didn't mean to hurt him. I really didn't. It was an accident. I'd never hurt him on purpose.'

'I know. It was a mistake. It's fine. Is he OK now? You said he's having a nap?'

'I just gave him something to help him sleep, that's all.'

'A sedative? Like you gave me?'

She nodded. Scratched her bleeding cheek. 'He needed to calm down. You got inside his head, but once you're gone, he'll be fine and things will go back to the way they're supposed to be. Millie and Bruno will move in too.

They'll love Knightley -'

'Knightley's OK?'

'Yes, of course. He's outside with his daddy playing in the rain.'

I swallowed. Relief spread through me like honey, but it didn't last long. She could have been lying. Maybe she'd knocked out Alec and was now lying to herself, telling herself that she'd sedated him. Maybe he was dead. Every word that came out of her mouth was tainted by the sickness in her brain.

'Are you going to call a taxi now?' I urged.

A slow smile spread across her face. Her eyes brightened. 'Yes. I think I will.' She pulled her phone out of the pocket of her skirt.

I smiled back, relieved beyond words, but instead of unlocking her mobile she tossed it into the bath. I watched it sink, heart plummeting, and screamed as fingers dug into my head and my face was thrust down into the water.

'You'll never let him go. You'll destroy him in the end. You won't mean to, but you will, and I won't have that. You have to go. This is a mercy, a kindness. You're obsessed with him but he can't give you want you want because he loves me. I'm doing this to protect him. That's all...that's all. I'm doing this for him.'

Oh God Oh God Oh God Oh God.

I struggled, pushed back, gripped the edge of the bath, tried to fight. My ribs pressed into the side of the tub so hard it felt as though they were going to crack. She dug her knees into my shoulder blades, using her whole weight to pin me against the panel, her grip fierce, breath hot in my hair, panting, grunting as she held me under.

Panic flared like fire inside my skull and my lungs began to burn and tear at the seams. Tears streamed from my eyes into the lukewarm liquid and my insides screamed. The seconds turned to hours, weeks, months. Pressure built inside my head, my chest – tighter and tighter and tighter – so tight – so dreadfully tight, my body a pressure cooker left on for too long, my internal organs fireworks set to explode.

Horror kicked in: agonising and all-consuming.

I'm going to drown. I'm going to die. She's going to kill me.

Arrietty's face popped into my mind like a splash of colour on a black canvas.

Die, Arrietty said, and I realised with a jolt what I had to do.

I unpeeled my mind from my body and let everything go limp. Let myself droop like a wilted flower. Lay face down in the water; an abandoned doll in a lake.

Despite my floppiness, Rose continued to hold me under.

An all-consuming mantra shrieked inside my head: *Please, please, think I'm dead. Please, please think I'm dead.*

My ears roared.

She held firm, claws digging into my skull like screws.

I began to die for real. There was no more time.

Arrietty's face flickered and faded, and I closed my eyes, felt my mind drift away from my body.

Her fingers loosened. She sniffed. Her dress brushed against the back of my legs. The door opened. Her feet carried her away.

The relief was like oxygen, but I waited one more second, two more - then yanked my head out of the water and sucked in huge gulps of sacred, delicious air. Nothing had ever tasted so sweet.

For a few moments, I listened, terrified she'd heard, certain she was coming back, but her feet padded across the landing and down the stairs, moving away, blissfully away.

I swallowed a sob and pushed myself to my feet. The room swayed and danced like a forest in a gale. I blinked to clear my vision and tried to work out what to do.

What will Rose do next?

Alec. Alec was what she wanted. If she'd left him outside in the pouring rain, she'd want to move him inside the house, which meant she was going to find my husband.

Chapter 84

I crept out onto the landing. It was empty. I hesitated then limped into the master bedroom and quietly opened the wardrobe. In the bottom right compartment was our sport equipment. I grabbed my tennis racket, pursed my lips and hurried out of the room, pausing at the top of the stairs to check she wasn't in the vicinity. The coast was clear, so I descended lightly and peered up the walkway. The long mile. If Rose peered around the kitchen wall or walked across to the front door, she'd see me. I was vulnerable now, totally exposed, Alice in No Man's land.

Holding my breath, I limped as fast as I could up the path, eyes pinned on the far wall, praying she wouldn't appear.

I reached the turning and lingered, listening hard. There were no sounds coming from the kitchen which suggested she was outside. Outside looking in? I hoped not.

I exhaled. Inhaled. Dashed towards the back door, which stood ajar, rainwater puddling inside the doorway, pelting the house with strange ferocity.

Shaking, I clenched the tennis racket tighter, inched open the door and peered outside. Rose was almost halfway up the garden, a ghostly figure illuminated by porchlight, dragging Alec's limp body towards the cliff. What was she doing? Why wasn't she moving him back inside the house? Knightley jumped up at her ankles, oblivious to the danger, whining, begging for attention.

I stepped into the deluge and ran towards her as fast as my leg would allow, slipping and sliding, leg screaming. *Limp. Run. Limp. Run. Go. Go. Faster. Go.*

Ten metres.

Five.

Four.

Three.

Water thundered down on my head, drenched my skin, my body, my hair.

Two.

One.

I raised the racket, and she glanced around, saw me, and hurtled away, hauling Alec by his ankles with unbelievable power, hair dripping across her face, clothes soaked.

I limped after her, lunged and skidded, swiping with the tennis racket, the rim skimming her face.

'Rose - stop - don't!' My voice was devoured by the downpour.

Blood oozed down my leg and my knee buckled and hit the ground. I forced myself to my feet and gritted my teeth, narrowed in on my target. One need rang louder and fiercer than any other, but it couldn't be formed into words; it was a primal need to protect my husband, a need that ran deeper than anything else, even my own survival. A need that gave me untold strength.

I moved. Rose moved faster, possessed by monstrous speed, dragging Alec along faster and faster, closer and closer and closer to the cliff. We were both possessed now; she by a false utopia, me by real love.

Rain drenched us both, slowing me down, bolting blackly from the dark sky like a flood of tears.

I hobbled as fast as possible, but my leg was a deadweight and I moved at a snail's pace across the slippery grass, too slow to catch up, my body succumbing to its injury.

She was only a metre or so from the edge now; and she glanced over her shoulder and grinned, eyes glinting madly, teeth bright in the dark, the Joker's smile. Would she rather kill Alec than let us be together? Was she that far gone?

No. Please God no.

Rose yanked Alec's body around so that he lay parallel to the edge.

She was going to do it.

'Get back! I'm warning you!' she shrieked.

She stepped to the side, swayed, righted herself. Her entire body shook. She looked about wildly as if searching for someone or something to come to her aid, as if I was the one who posed a threat.

As I opened my mouth to plead with her to stop, she stepped back and slipped on the wet grass. I threw myself forward and smashed the racket into her side. She hissed and staggered closer to Alec, then screamed and turned on me. Hands raised, fingers curled, eyes savage, she lunged, but I raised the racket again and hit her full force in her injured cheek. It connected with a thudding pop. Shock and pain bulged out her eyes and she stumbled to the right but managed to stay standing. With a witch-like shriek, she whirled and lunged for Alec. I pulled back the racket and smashed it into her nose.

This time there was no scream. Rose's eyes rolled back in her head and her lips parted in a silent 'o' of shock.

As the rain stopped, she thudded to the ground.

Chapter 85

My nerves were acute, taut as fiddle strings, my heart a drum. But there was no music. No madness. No thoughts. No feelings. Not now. Not anymore.

Abruptly, my head was as quiet as the world around me. Almost too quiet, as if someone had cut all sound. Above, blackness stretched on as endless and unknown as time itself, but the moon made herself known again, a white clock face on black parchment, yet to be written. The stars appeared, flickering on one by one like fairy lights on a timer and the scent of spent rain drifted through the damp air, sulphury and familiar. All was calm. Still. Close, even, to peaceful.

I inhaled deeply and my senses stirred. A blackbird landed beside my studio and pecked at the earth. Wet grass tickled my ankles. Blood ran from Rose's nose, and I could smell it. Her chest lifted and lowered. My leg throbbed and my eyes stung. My entire body thrummed like a hummingbird's wings. Alec lay perilously close to the precipice, dead or alive, I didn't know.

In that tiny capsule of time, I stared at Rose's bleeding face and felt nothing.

Little wet paws pulled my gaze. Knightley's eyes shone up through the darkness. He wanted me to pick him up, but I couldn't. Not yet. It was time to see if Rose had told the truth about Alec still being alive.

I looked up and made a silent wish, then knelt in the wet grass and put my ear to his mouth to see if he was breathing.

Epilogue

It is a sad irony when a psychiatrist who has helped many people and worked long and hard to be able to make a difference to the lives of those who have suffered, becomes unable to function with 'normal' mental capacity. This is what happened to Rose Weatherby.

About a year after the incident, Rose wrote a letter of apology to us detailing the neglect and emotional abuse she had suffered at the hands of her father. In her letter, she also disclosed that she was diagnosed with Attachment Disorder, from which arose Obsessive Love Disorder, and that she is slowly but surely coming to terms with her diagnosis. She wrote that psychological treatment is making steady inroads, and even suggested that one day in the not-too-distant future we might be able to meet up for a coffee. Alec's reaction was visceral and immediate: I think his words were something along the lines of *no way are we ever seeing that woman again*; but my reaction was not quite so black and white.

They say that what doesn't kill you makes you stronger, but I prefer to say what doesn't kill you makes you kinder. Kinder emotionally. Kinder in the way only a deep understanding of a complex issue can engender. I think I've learned that trauma begets trauma, and that anyone who has ever suffered such immense emotional pain - be it at the hands of another person or at the terrible hand of fate - needs compassion, empathy and help.

Will I meet with Rose one day and tell her all about the wonderful progress Arrietty has made and that, somehow, we're regaining a fragile sense of happiness amid our grief? Perhaps.

At the end of the day, without Rose, I might still believe myself to be someone else, an imposter in my own body and mind, a doomed force bent on my own destruction. Without her intervention, misguided or not, I could still be drowning in a sea of mental illness, and Alec and Arrietty would have lost me too.

Acknowledgements

In 2012, I wrote a gothic psychological thriller called *Blackened Cottage*.

Due to Dad's hard work and determination, *Blackened Cottage* acquired 72 reviews, most of which made me feel great about my writing. Most importantly though, I felt overjoyed that I was able to create something people found moving and immersive. Bizarre as it sounds, it was the first time since I'd started writing that anyone except for my parents had read the whole manuscript of one of my stories. Having only received rejections from literary agents, I was blown away to discover that people liked my work. So thank you SO MUCH to those readers who took a chance on an indie author and took the time to write a review – you'll never know how much your words meant to me and how much they motivated (and still motivate) me to keep writing.

Over the last 21 years my dad has read and re-read – and re-read – every novel I have ever written. His unending support means the world to me. He is a legend. And my mum…well, she read and re-read – and re-read – every piece of homework I ever did, including the incredibly boring 10-page kidnap story I wrote when I was 7. Poor mum – but what a legend! She reads my first drafts too, and her eye for inconsistencies and melodrama is invaluable.

Special thanks must go to my long-suffering husband, Tommy, for his unending support, fantastic ideas and wise words, and to my little girl, Heidi, for understanding that Mummy needs to lock herself away to write sometimes rather than go bug hunting.

I'd also like to thank my awesome beta readers Derryn, Sarah and Cathryn, whose insightful, honest feedback helped me make *Arrietty* a whole lot better for my readers.

Huge thanks too to Alex Lake, Tina Baker, Carolyn

Kirby, Sarah Linley, Paula Johnston and Alice Hunter for being kind enough to take the time to read and review my book.

A big thank you to Olly at More Visual Ltd for designing such an awesome cover. Thank you to Anne Cater for a smashing cover reveal and blog tour, and to everyone who helped with the launch. A huge thanks to Sally Swift, my awesomely talented audiobook narrator. Many thanks to Dr Stephen Henning for his wonderful artwork. Stephen started his art career illustrating the wildlife books and scientific papers that he authored over the years as a zoology lecturer, taxonomic lepidopterist, and conservationist. He is especially well known for his accurate portraits of people and pets.

And lastly, a tremendous thank you to all of you lovely bookworms out there for reading, posting, talking and blogging about my books. I love hearing from you, so please get in touch and keep reading!

ABOUT THE AUTHOR

Abby Davies was born in Macclesfield in 1984. She grew up in Bedfordshire in a seventeenth-century cottage near Flitton Moor and started writing thrillers when she was 7 years old.

After reading English Literature at Sheffield University and training to be an English teacher, she wrote novels in her free time and attained an MA in Creative Writing.

She was shortlisted for the Mslexia Novel Competition in 2018 and longlisted for the Blue Pencil Agency First Novel Award in 2019. Her debut *Mother Loves Me* was published by HarperCollins in 2020. *The Cult* came out in 2021. *Arrietty* is her third novel.

She lives in Wiltshire with her husband, daughter and two crazy cocker spaniels.

Find out more about Abby and her books online at

www.abbydavies.com

Twitter: @Abby13Richards

Instagram: @abbydaviesauthor

Please Review

I hope you enjoyed *Arrietty*! I would love to know your thoughts, so if you can find the time, please post a review on Amazon and other social platforms to share your views and help spread the word to other thriller lovers.

Thank you so much.

Made in United States
Orlando, FL
03 August 2023

35727097R00245